MEKONG DELTA BLUES

For information about James Ballard's other work,
including his multi-award-winning novel, Poisoned
Jungle, visit the author's website at:

james-ballard.net

James may be contacted at: jamesballardnovels@gmail.com

POISONED JUNGLE

ISBN: 978-1-64663-114-8

**2020 Benjamin Franklin Silver Award Winner
For Best New Voice in Fiction**

1969, MEKONG DELTA

MEKONG DELTA BLUES

JAMES BALLARD

MEKONG DELTA BLUES

Cover photo from iStock

Published by Analect Press, Edmonton, Canada
Stories that illuminate

ISBN:
Paperback 978-1-77354-458-8
Hardcover 978-1-77354-460-1
    ebook 978-1-77354-459-5

Publication assistance by

PAGEMASTER
PUBLISHING
PageMaster.ca

DEDICATION

For every medic on both sides of the Vietnam War. The task on our shoulders—treating and healing the gruesome wounds of war—seemed endless. We couldn't put everybody back together, but we tried.

Contents

AUTHOR'S NOTE

Mekong Delta Blues is the first novel of my *Mekong River Trilogy*. Set during the Vietnam War, each book stands on its own, but there is some overlap of characters. If the reader wishes to read them in sequence, *Poisoned Jungle* and *Endless River* are the second and third novels. Throughout the three works, themes and threads from my war experiences are explored through the eyes of third platoon's medics, each doing a one-year tour. In literature, it is the lives of the characters which should speak to the reader, not a didactic narrative. My protagonists are medics, and while their individual stories and backgrounds differ, their experiences in the war zone shaped their lives and left long-lasting impacts.

When I arrived at Ft. Sam Houston, Texas, to begin training as an army medic, I'd had no previous medical experience. Nineteen-years old, and not far removed from high school, the ten week training course is all that stood between me and treating wounded soldiers in Vietnam. Types of wounds I could not have imagined before going to war. Or, as some veterans express it, "the things you cannot unsee."

Rumors of fifty percent casualty rates among medics were rampant as I arrived to begin my training. Hundreds of young men were assigned to the training companies, and we all knew Vietnam is where we were headed.

Sometimes, the reality exceeded the rumors, as I learned from other medics during and after the war. As one medic told me as we waited for our flight home from Vietnam: "You know, I arrived in-country with twenty-two medics. Only five of us completed our tours without being killed or medevaced out of country with serious wounds."

In fact, for every twenty-six Americans killed in Vietnam, one was an army medic or navy corpsman serving with the Marine Corps.

I owe much to the medics I served with. Sharing information with each other saved lives. With only ten weeks of training, it was crucial we learned quickly on the job. For those of us with infantry platoons, no matter how serious the wound, it was only a medic with an aid bag initially providing care. None of us wanted to screw up and lose someone from not knowing something. The best medics performed remarkably, under fire, and under enormous pressure to get the bleeding stopped and keep casualties alive until a medevac arrived. Some wounds were fatal, which left invisible scars on surviving soldiers.

There is a triad of psychological consequences from war trauma—PTSD, survivor's guilt, and moral injury. It is no surprise that survivor's guilt haunted many medics. Personally, it had a tenacious hold on my psyche far beyond my tour in the war zone. Initially, PTSD was rejected by the psychiatric community, even though different terms were used in previous wars. I am convinced that the negative reception many of us received on our return increased our isolation and exacerbated our mental health. A reception veterans of other wars did not have to contend with. When the psychological concept of moral injury arrived in the 1990s, it was like a light bulb went on in my mind, explaining many of my emotions and inner turmoil that PTSD never did.

This triad of psychological factors overlap. Generally speaking, PTSD is fear based. Survivor's guilt is what the term implies. And moral injury, in my view, occurs when our human core is violated by what it knows is wrong—participating in the killing of other human beings. No amount of patriotic fervor or nationalistic sloganeering can trick the innermost reaches of ourselves into feeling otherwise. Being human gives us the capacity for empathy, and even killing a hated enemy does damage to our own psyche.

Of course, we also have the capacity, as individuals and as countries, to cover up, suppress, and deny what we know is wrong because we are self-centered enough to have a deep capacity for justifying our actions. I am suggesting that the trauma embedded deep within our psyches from participating in war needs to be addressed by veterans of combat if we are to reassume healthy roles in society. Even in self-defense, and even if we sincerely believe our side is justified in fighting others, killing goes against what it is to be a moral human being. Psychological wreckage occurs, relative to an individual's proximity to the killing and the validity of the cause.

Concerning the latter, I have met troubled WWII veterans and it has been helpful sorting out what we do and don't have in common. It's complicated. Whole cities were incinerated by our side in the Second World War. None of the vets from that war that I knew ever expressed guilt about tactics. Perhaps it was because both sides waged extensive bombing campaigns on civilians. And our WWII vets didn't have doubts about the necessity of going to war. What portion of my moral injury is due to my country waging a questionable war in Vietnam, and what is due to being close to the carnage perpetrated on innocents? I found it heartbreaking treating wounded children in the war. They were not my enemy. And if my country's cause was not justified, how responsible was I? These are some of the moral themes explored in my writing, and some of the questions I have asked myself ever since arriving in Vietnam over fifty years ago.

The terms PTSD, survivor's guilt, and moral injury will not appear in any of the novels of the trilogy, but the characters live with their shadows. All of these years later, I am struck by how little un-derstanding of the psychological consequences of war the general population "gets," and how little of the true costs are factored into the overall impacts of going to war. From the human to the fiscal, they are enormous.

In *Mekong Delta Blues*, four medics receive orders for Vietnam upon completion of their training. In the trilogy, the novels explore what happens to individuals in war, and in its aftermath. Not just to soldiers, but to a society in turmoil over its collective mores and divided views on Vietnam. To a society that drafted some young men, sent three million to war, yet allowed others legal avenues to avoid it.

In a paradox of war, positive transformation is also possible. I became a more empathetic person because I'd witnessed at close-hand the suffering of others. Termed post-traumatic growth, positive and negative repercussions are not mutually exclusive. They can coexist. As human beings, we have tremendous range for good and evil. Philosophers, psychologists, and religious thinkers have debated for centuries the interplay between what we choose and what is determined by our environment.

While fictional, the characters in the *Mekong River Trilogy* are drawn from my wartime experiences as a medic. I have attempted to portray the Vietnam War as it was experienced by those who were there. The characters speak to the complexity of going to war and living with the psychological and societal impacts.

The history of the times, and events in Vietnam, are presented as accurately as I can write them, including how the protagonist in *Mekong Delta Blues*, Johnny Ornowoski, wound up in Vietnam. It is not intended as an endorsement of marijuana use. It is indicative of the town and place he came from, and where I spent part of my youth. In the trilogy, I have taken minor liberties with the Ninth Infantry's timelines during the war. The Division began exiting the Mekong Delta late in August of 1969. A glossary has been provided for both military jargon and slang common to American soldiers.

I am still learning about the Vietnam War and the impact it has had on my life. I hope that my writing contributes to the understanding of that war and the times and culture it sprang from.

PROLOGUE

Cam Ranh Bay, Vietnam
1967

The Boeing 707 banked slightly and approached the runway in a steep descent. They were finally here. The flight had been a daylong journey toward an unknown destiny yet to be played out in the lives of Johnny Ornowoski and fellow medic Daniel Holt. Along with the one hundred and eighty troops on board they were about to begin their year-long tours in Vietnam.

The flight exhausted them. With the nervous tension palpable on their young faces, it reflected the inner stresses of not knowing what a combat tour in Vietnam would be like. There was no turning back. They were all captive in a war that would be their reality for the next year, if they were lucky, and didn't go home early in a body bag.

The first thing Johnny noticed was the hot wind in his face. Rather than refreshing, it burned like a furnace turned too high blasting heat all around him. Sergeants in jungle fatigues shouted instructions to form up and prepare for more processing. In the near-dark Johnny could see a long line of men moving towards a Quonset-shaped building with lights emanating from the structure.

Inside, an army clerk, indifferent and bored, callously handed out orders that stated which units to report to.

"Name?" he questioned. "Welcome to the Nam," he said matter-of-fact-ly, but with an edge to his tone. He handed Johnny the set of papers that told him where he would spend the next year in the war zone.

"Barracks are over there," the clerk motioned with his head. "You can bed down for the night and proceed to your unit in the morning."

Danny Holt, Johnny's friend and companion through medics' training, waited for him and strained to read his set of orders in the poor light.

"Says I'm to report to the 29th Evacuation Hospital in Binh Thuy. Never heard of it. How 'bout you?"

Johnny could barely make out the print, had trouble finding his name, but there it was telling him to report to the Ninth Infantry Division in Dong Tam. Neither had a clue about their destinations--or how to get there. They would have to sort it out in the morning. Johnny had been awake for the better part of three days with nervous tension. He needed to sleep.

They found the barracks crowded with metal-framed bunks and soldiers. Johnny hated that aspect of the army, the lack of privacy, thrown together with other young men, each with a story but facing their ordeal alone.

As Johnny laid down on a cot, he closed his eyes and thought how complicated his life had become, in the army and beginning a tour in Vietnam. Many events had brought him to this point. A flood of memories washed through his mind as he drifted off to sleep…

PART ONE
CROSSING OVER

CHAPTER ONE

Santa Cruz, California
1966

Spring burst forth in vibrant renewal, the year Johnny met CC. Their newfound love added potency to the life emerging all around them. He'd always liked the way the daffodils pushed through the warmed soil in March, their dark green shoots appearing overnight, topped by a perfect yellow flower.

The sandstone cliffs were beautiful that time of year, shrouded in morning mists along the ocean, the wildflowers in bloom by afternoon. Green and yellow were Johnny's favorite colors, vivid against the deep blue of the sky.

After finding one another, they had a perfect life for a while. Looking back, he knew their lives were folly, could not go on forever creating their own special world of being young and in love, ignoring the intrusions sure to come.

Cecelia brought most of her clothes over and stayed with Johnny. At twenty, he was a year older and lived in a small flat two blocks from the ocean in an old coastal mansion converted into apartments.

They were a handsome couple. Johnny's last name of Ornowoski gave his Polish background away; he also inherited the dark good looks of his Italian mother. Cecelia got her beauty from her Mexican mother and Irish father. The combination was striking, enhanced by the girl's sex appeal.

Her friends called her CC. She was the type of girl that men noticed, and women knew their men noticed. With her dark hair worn long and falling below her shoulders, it accentuated her slender body and the lovely olive hue of her skin. The whole package captivated Johnny. He got lost looking into her green eyes and had fallen for her in a big way.

Johnny had a nickname, too. Friends called him O. With his dark hair combed straight back and parted slightly on one side, it contrasted nicely with the handsome angularity of his face. His lean frame moved with ease and suggested a sensuality that girls were drawn to.

The early days of their love coincided with the new rock and roll filling the airwaves with the music from the British rock bands and their influence on American pop culture. Johnny and CC liked listening to it on an old record player in his flat while they sipped wine snuggled against one another.

Sometimes Cecelia would dance for Johnny. She had a comical, yet sensual, way of pleasing him, putting on her oversize sunglasses while keeping beat to the music in a pair of cut-off jeans, her hair tied in a ponytail bobbing all around her. The rhythm and blues hit "Slow Down" by Larry Williams spoke to the speed at which they'd fallen in love.

The song could have served as a warning given the times that brought the counterculture so quickly to Santa Cruz but slowing down was not the way of their romance. They were in their own lover's world, participating in the changing times, not analyzing them.

Johnny had been on his own since dropping out of high school at seventeen. He'd moved in with a couple older friends and supported himself by working odd jobs around town, cleaning swimming pools and doing yard work in affluent neighborhoods. Steady jobs were hard to come by, and he was always short of cash.

His roommates liked to party on the weekends and smoke weed. They often sent Johnny to buy it from an old beatnik turned hippie named Ralph Barnes, who sold enough to keep himself supplied and rent a place in a rundown area near the boardwalk. The old hippie liked Johnny and enjoyed visiting with the personable kid when he came to buy marijuana for his friends.

Barnes grew his hair long. It looked odd on Ralph with his bald spot on top and greying strands of thin hair growing to his shoulders. Usually in an old t-shirt and unshaven, he enjoyed talking philosophy inspired by the poetry of Allen Ginsberg, Lawrence Ferlinghetti, and the beat poets of the era. The sedentary Barnes enthusiastically introduced Johnny to Jack Kerouac's *On the Road.* They'd smoke a joint while Ralph talked, the young poet-songwriter, Bob Dylan, playing in the background. The lyrics influenced those drawn to the music of changing times and a new age of personal freedoms.

Johnny started dealing on a small scale when short on cash for his rent. Ralph sold him what he needed to tide him over until he could find work. Selling marijuana was easy. Ralph approached him one evening.

"I been thinkin'," he began. "I'm havin' trouble gettin' enough local supply of weed to keep my customers happy. All of the hippie kids are smokin' a lot more dope. Either I tap into a larger supply or get out of the business and find some lousy job somewhere. But if I was to bring in a partner, someone to make the buying runs, I have a contact in southern Cal bringin' grass in from Mexico. Interested?"

"Kinda," Johnny said. "Your contact, is he violent?"

"No need to be when we pay up front and in cash. It's the guy's business. If you go down and make the buy, I'd cover expenses and cut you in on ten percent of the product. It'll fit in the trunk of a car."

It sounded easy enough. A lot of kids already pestered Johnny to bring them more weed.

"What kind of volume are we talkin' about, Ralph?"

"Your share," the old hippie mused, "be around two thou."

Johnny shifted in his seat. Bob Dylan's voice sang "Blowin' in the Wind" in the background. "Okay," he said, "I'll do it, but just a couple of times, enough to get ahead, save some money."

Ralph smiled and rolled another joint. "It's a deal then. Just be careful Johnny. We always gotta be careful."

✳ ✳ ✳

That's how Johnny got started. From his share of the first shipment, he found his own place to rent, the cozy suite in the old mansion. The beach provided good locations for business. He blended in with the youthful crowds on the boardwalk, good for transactions. He wasn't sure about the hippie lifestyle, but Ralph was right about them smoking a lot of dope. Johnny kept a low profile except for two things. He took fifteen hundred dollars from his profits and bought a used blue and white Thunderbird convertible. Then, he met Cecelia Jones.

A customer invited him to a party. The pungent odour of marijuana filled the room while long-haired boys and girls danced to the sounds of the Beatles. It's what he expected, and Johnny always made friends easily.

Cecelia noticed him when he arrived. Wearing a leather jacket that fit well, the handsome boy mingled as he chatted amiably with the partygoers. Johnny sipped on the wine he brought and offered some to Cecelia when he saw her, the prettiest girl at the party. Johnny sensed a shyness in the way she carried her beauty. Something drew him to the girl beyond her looks.

They chatted for the evening before strolling along the beach. Cecelia put her arm through his and walked close against him. When she started to shiver, Johnny put his coat around her. She felt warm and protected, engulfed by the presence of this young man so different from the other boys she'd known.

"Is there someplace warm we can go?" she asked.

"My place is not far," he said, putting his arm around her. Cecelia leaned her head against his shoulder as they walked to his place.

Johnny checked for wine while Cecelia warmed herself still wrapped in his coat. Finding none in the fridge, Johnny had nothing to offer his pretty guest. Before he could explain, Cecelia stepped out of his jacket and kissed him.

Their romance blossomed quickly. With long hair falling below CC's shoulders, she appeared no different from many pretty girls hanging around with the surfers or hippies. The differences were in her background, the cause of an inner vulnerability underneath the captivating exterior.

She never knew her father. Her mother, Benita, Mexican by birth, retained an accent and worked low-paying jobs hairdressing and cleaning. CC helped by babysitting and waitressing. Meeting the self-reliant young man mature beyond his years was the first boyfriend she'd felt so deeply about.

While CC never knew her father, Johnny was raised by his. His dad never remarried and showed no interest in women. Gregor put a roof over their heads and kept food on the table, drinking quietly in the evenings or tinkering with vehicles in the garage.

The son of Polish immigrants, Gregor, firstborn in the new country, arrived at school not fluent in English. His parents never learned the language. Gregor felt caught between two worlds, belonging to neither.

Gregor didn't know how to be a father. He provided the basics and let Johnny grow up fending for himself earlier than most boys his age. Johnny's situation didn't seem all that different from a lot of kids. Parents worked, and children found things to do. *Who could afford not to work?* Johnny's boyhood pals fished and played ball, caught turtles and eels in the creek. Many dads didn't show their kids how to bait a hook or catch crabs.

In many ways Johnny and CC were good for each other. He had the time and money to be attentive and dote on his girl. The bond between them filled voids in their backgrounds, reaching beneath the surface of the attractive couple.

A typical day would include sleeping until midmorning, sipping coffee after rising, then eating a late breakfast or early lunch at the Santa Cruz Café. Afterwards, they'd cruise along West Cliff Drive with the top down on his convertible, picking up a six-pack of beer along the way. CC squeezed in beside Johnny as he drove, looking pretty in her sunglasses and whatever headband or hat she wore to keep her hair in place.

If Johnny had business, he'd leave Cecelia at her mother's while meeting with customers. He adhered to a simple set of rules. Everything was on a cash basis. He never did a transaction from his flat or convertible, and he didn't involve Cecelia. He sold marijuana to the hippie crowd and stashed the profits.

Johnny made friends with his customers, including members of a band called Big Rock. They attracted a large following locally and played the Cocoanut Grove on the boardwalk and the Catalyst Café on Pacific Avenue.

Their lead guitarist, Cliff Morris, played well and studied the music. Fronted by a singer who went by the stage name of Suzi Q., the band opened with a raunchy version of the song. Strutting on stage, her auburn hair, thick and with a natural wave, fell on shapely shoulders above an exposed mid-drift in a tank top not designed to contain her ample breasts. Suzi completed her stage presence with a pair of tight leather pants, her potent sexuality expressed in voice and appearance.

Cliff and Suzi were lovers, living for the new rock and roll which a generation of youth embraced as a statement of lifestyle and defiance. The local crowds grew with each performance.

Cliff Morris fascinated Johnny. The brains behind the band looked like Keith Richards and tried to play like him. Nominally enrolled at Cabrillo College to avoid the draft, which took more young men each month for the ramped-up war in Vietnam, Cliff had no intention of going. Johnny knew nothing about Vietnam, yet Cliff could list a dozen reasons why the US shouldn't be there.

Johnny liked hanging out in his friend's apartment. Full of music, books and magazines, Cliff exposed Johnny to more than the beatnik stuff that interested Ralph Barnes. The names of Kant, Kierkegaard, and Sartre, philosophers Johnny had never heard of, came up in conversations with Cliff, who looked at life in ways new to Johnny.

And their girlfriends got along. Suzi often took CC with her while she looked for the latest rock and roll albums or searched for unique clothes in secondhand shops. They laughed at the combinations they bought and modelled them for their men. It was a good time to be young and in love and dripping with excitement before listening to the newest Beatles' or Rolling Stones' album.

Cliff worried about maintaining his student deferment while working hard to land a recording contract for Big Rock. Attending school prevented focusing all his efforts on the band. He wanted a more permanent solution. While Johnny tinkered with a speaker for Big Rock's sound system, Cliff thumbed through an article in *Time Magazine* recounting the week's casualties in the Vietnam War.

"I've got it," he exclaimed, "and this will work for you, too, Johnny. I have a friend in the rock group Magnitude out of San Jose who's classified 4-F by the draft board, totally unfit for military service. He's so shortsighted he needs glasses with lenses in them as thick as the bottoms of coke bottles. And that's not the worst of it. He had polio as a boy and is partially crippled. I know he would take my physical for me. He hates the system. He's lost a cousin in Vietnam and is bitter about it."

"Isn't that kind of risky?" asked Johnny. "What if they find out?"

"Not likely, the way they're processing young men for this war. Hundreds are being put through their physicals daily."

Johnny finished tightening a connection on the speaker and looked at Cliff. "How do you get called in for your physical?"

"Are you kidding? All I'd need to do is let my student deferment lapse and they'd be all over me. Or I could volunteer for the draft and flunk my physical big time. Get the uncertainty over with once and for all."

Johnny looked troubled. "I've got another problem. I'm not registered for the draft. Maybe the war will end sooner than you think."

"Holy shit, man," Cliff exclaimed. "They're gonna call you up if they find out. And this war ain't ending anytime soon. The French were there a hundred years before calling it quits after their defeat at Dien Binh Phu."

"A hundred years?"

"You better read some history, man."

Cliff liked Johnny, the high school dropout who absorbed intellectual concepts like a sponge. His innate intelligence and easygoing manner appealed to the lead guitar player intent on making it big. Johnny didn't play an instrument but liked tinkering with Big Rock's sound equipment, essential to the group's live performances. He even invested some of his own money into the most sophisticated electronics available. Johnny knew he couldn't sell dope forever without attracting the attention of the police. He believed the band would make it big, and it might be his way out of dealing.

Cliff Morris pursued his rock and roll dreams with passion and intelligence. He studied the music and how to play the guitar. He always had one in his hands and practiced riffs constantly. The band's repertoire included songs by the Rolling Stones and Animals, the Yardbirds and Jefferson

Airplane. Suzi Q. covered brilliantly what Janice Joplin sang with Big Brother and the Holding Company.

Big Rock opened with a bluesy instrumental Cliff wrote, then broke into their version of "Susie Q" while their own Suzi Q. strutted on stage in her tight leather pants and brief top to the delight of the crowd. They were booked solid every weekend. Fans followed the band wherever they played.

Cliff wrote songs for Big Rock. He studied the blues roots of rock and roll and knew the history of Robert Johnson and the playing of Leadbelly and Howlin' Wolf. Familiar with the folk music of Woody Guthrie and Pete Seeger, he would keep writing songs until the band hit the big time.

Bob Dylan released "Rainy Day Women #12 and #35" that April. It rose on the charts and the lyric's meaning were a hot topic of discussion. Not just by the kids getting high on marijuana but by a society trying to figure out the cultural changes transforming the nation. The poet-songwriter, prophetic with his multi-layered lyrics, could have penned the words for CC and Johnny. Foretelling a warning as they held on to each other listening to Dylan's song, the whole world was getting stoned in some way or other.

Johnny and CC were carried along by the current of the times, the excitement of their friendship with the members of Big Rock, the new rock and roll, and their love for each other.

CHAPTER TWO

January 1967

A few miles outside of Santa Cruz, Johnny pictured CC at their place waiting for him. She usually fixed a simple meal before they cuddled underneath a blanket sipping wine and listening to music. The buying run had been routine.

Johnny's thoughts of CC were interrupted when a patrol car came into view behind him. Nothing too worrisome. He never drank or smoked any dope on these trips and followed speed limits and traffic regulations. The persistence of the tail concerned him when he arrived at the city limits. Near the Morrisey Boulevard exit, the cruiser flashed its lights and forced Johnny to take the off-ramp. Two police cars waited and forced him to pull over.

CC paced in the apartment. Johnny usually made it back by eleven. After one o'clock, she feared the worst. She tried to stay busy but couldn't concentrate. She phoned Ralph.

"I'll get back to you as soon as I know something," he told her, but he already had his own worries.

Ralph's telephone rang again. "They've got Johnny."

"And the dope?"

"All of it," the voice said, a contact in his distribution loop. "The police leaned on one of the underage hippie kids they busted. Read him the riot act in front of his parents and he fessed up, told them about Johnny."

Ralph phoned CC back. "It looks bad, dear. Johnny's been arrested. Lay low for now until we figure things out. Someone will be in touch."

"Is Johnny okay? What will they do to him?" CC's voice quavered as she sat down, her hand shaking while holding the receiver.

"Someone will be in touch," Ralph repeated, not wanting to say more over the phone.

Johnny sat in his cell and thought about what had happened. The police tried to get him to talk in the first hours after his arrest. He'd already thought this scenario through. He'd asked for a lawyer. The police weren't happy, but Johnny knew not to say anything without counsel. He opted for a public defender. Using his money, stashed throughout the city, would only help the prosecution make their case.

Midafternoon the next day, his lawyer arrived and introduced himself. Freddy Dempster, late thirties, pudgy, with glasses and brownish-blonde hair that hung just below his collar, got right to the point.

"My understanding is that you haven't said anything to the police. That's good. Continue to communicate through me or anyone else you choose to represent you." Dempster took a breath and thought before speaking.

"I have to be honest with you. They've caught you red-handed with marijuana worth about twenty-five thousand dollars on the street. No way we can argue simple possession. There aren't a lot of options available, but I'm here to help you plan a defense. Feel free to discuss anything with me that may help your case."

Johnny already knew everything Freddy Dempster had said. Blaming himself for not getting out soon enough, he'd miscalculated, always thinking about one last run. He worried about CC.

"Can you get a message to my girlfriend? She's not involved in any way. I was careful about that. Can you make sure she knows what to expect? The police are going to question her."

Freddy paused a moment. The criminals he represented usually tried to implicate others to deflect blame, spread it around. This young man worried about his girlfriend.

"I'll get in touch with her immediately," he told Johnny.

"When will she be able to visit?"

"Soon."

"So, what happens next?" Johnny asked.

"We mostly wait. Bail will probably be set high. Any way of raising it?"

Johnny shook his head.

"A lot will depend on the judge assigned to your case. We'll plan a strategy when we know who that is. I'll be back when the date of your preliminary hearing is set."

Johnny looked around his cell. Concrete and metal, a single bed with a simple frame, a toilet bowl and sink. Something like this could be home for a long time.

✳ ✳ ✳

CC arrived the next day. They talked in subdued voices while a guard looked on, bored and disinterested.

"What happened Johnny? I've been so worried." CC pressed against the bars and their fingers touched.

Johnny tried to remain calm in front of CC. "I got caught with the entire load," he levelled with her. "It's not good."

"I'm scared they're going to send you to prison, Johnny."

"It looks that way," he said. "My lawyer says we'll know more at the preliminary hearing. There's not much we can do until then."

CC began to cry. She felt the steel rods of the cell as she leaned against them, the barrier between her and Johnny impenetrable. He touched her face through the bars, and she wept harder. An emptiness settled over them as they realized their lives would never be the same.

✳ ✳ ✳

The hearing went as Dempster predicted. With bail set high, Johnny sat in his cell and waited for the trial date. CC visited every day, and Cliff brought a stack of books to read.

He couldn't concentrate enough to understand most of what Cliff provided. Johnny did read *Huckleberry Finn* and fantasized about floating down a river. He wouldn't be in jail forever. More realistic, but just as unattainable, he spent hours reading *Walden* by Henry David Thoreau and felt an affinity with the author leading a simple life in the woods. Too late for that now.

Freddy arrived at the jail a week before his trial.

"I have more information about the presiding judge, Mortimer Stone. He's old school straight-arrow and proud of it. You want the good or the bad news first?"

Johnny liked his lawyer's habit of getting right to the point. "Is it complicated?" he asked by way of answering.

Dempster paused and looked at Johnny after the guard opened the cell door. "May I?" he said, gesturing at the cot for a place to sit. Johnny smiled at the polite request given the circumstances. He nodded an okay.

"Judge Stone has a reputation of coming down hard on drug cases but believes in second chances. I see a way forward. You were caught with the goods. No sense trying any convoluted arguments that would only piss the judge off. I would also not advise a trial by jury. The prosecution will easily find twelve housewives, businessmen or carpenters who will be threatened by what you represent to them—someone who is trying to sell dope to their kids. For that, they would like to put you away for a long time." Dempster let the information sink in.

"I think we should elect a trial by judge only. Plead guilty, apologize to society and try and convince Judge Stone you're through with dealing drugs. Think you can do that?"

"I am done with selling drugs," Johnny said. "Convincing the judge of that is another thing, but I'll follow your advice."

"Good," said the lawyer. "You're on the level about wanting to quit the drug business?"

Surprised by the direct question, Johnny answered truthfully. "In here, I've had nothing but time to think," he began. "I've got myself in lots of trouble thinking I could just do one more run before getting out. Now others are making choices for me. I'll be facing the consequences for a long time."

Not many of my clients are that reflective, Dempster thought. "I'll do everything I can to get you a lighter sentence."

"It's a deal, then," Johnny said.

Dempster smiled slightly and shook his head. *If only most of his clients were that likable.*

In April, Mortimer Stone looked down sternly from his perch on the bench. He reminded Johnny of a teacher he'd had in sixth grade determined to use his authority to get things done. The judge got right to the issue.

"It is my understanding you wish to plead guilty, Mr. Ornowoski, and accept responsibility for your actions. Is that correct?"

"Yes, Your Honor."

"I'm fully aware of the details of this case and the fact you were apprehended with enough marijuana to poison a great many minds. You comprehend the seriousness of the charges?"

"I do, Your Honor."

"Son, how old are you?"

"I've just turned twenty-one, Sir."

Stone shuffled papers on the bench and looked at one before speaking again. "This is your first arrest, I see."

"Yes," Johnny said. He glanced at Freddy beside him who acknowledged the look with an encouraging nod. Johnny's stomach tightened as he waited for the judge to proceed.

"Judging by your attitude, I'm presuming you don't wish to live a life of crime. I'm going to give you a choice, young man, something I don't often do in these kinds of cases."

The judge paused, looked at Johnny, and removed his glasses before continuing. "Our nation is at war and needing the services of men your age in our armed forces. I'm giving you the option of serving your country by volunteering for the draft in lieu of two years in prison. If you choose the military and are honorably discharged, your criminal record will be wiped clean. You have two days to decide. I trust you will use this opportunity to serve our nation and turn your life around. Do you have any questions?"

Johnny tried to grasp what the judge had just said. Freddy hadn't mentioned this possibility. Cliff's tactic of failing the draft's physical popped into his mind. Could that work for him now to avoid prison and the army?

"Your Honor, what if it's found I am unfit for military service?"

"Then I'm sure San Quentin won't have such stringent entrance requirements. Choose wisely, Mr. Ornowoski. The court will see you in two days with your decision." The judge banged his gavel and retreated into his chambers.

Johnny turned to Freddy. "What just happened?"

"I'm as surprised as you. The judge has given you two days to get your affairs in order. He's giving you a second chance by serving in the army."

"Have you ever been in the army, Freddy?"

"No, I'm afraid I can't help you there. Your choice would be a lot easier if there wasn't a war going on. I will say this. If you are serious about getting out of the drug business, the fact you won't have a criminal record is huge."

Johnny had expected to go back to his cell after court. Instead, he hurried back to his place to find CC.

"They let you go?" she said, wrapping herself around him.

"Not exactly. It's complicated, CC, not the outcome any of us expected. I've been given the choice to do two years in prison or the army."

"Then let's run away somewhere, Johnny. Don't go to prison and don't go and get yourself killed in Vietnam. That's where they'll send you if you go into the army."

"They probably will, but not everybody is getting killed over there. I'll have some leave time if I choose the army. If we ran away, we'd be on the run forever. If I did get caught, I'd end up in prison for a long time."

"Don't go, Johnny, please don't go away and leave me."

"I'm not leaving you, CC, just going away for a while. Will you wait for me? I have enough money stashed to take care of you while I'm gone. I'll show you where it is, and we can be together when I come home on leave."

"I'm afraid, Johnny, afraid of what will happen to you, of us, of me."

Johnny had already decided he wanted out of the drug business. He needed more information before deciding to volunteer for the draft. He found Cliff at a band rehearsal in a community hall the band rented.

"Hi, Johnny, I heard what happened. They didn't give you much choice, did they?"

"I don't have much time, Cliff. I was expecting to go to prison. You are the smartest person I know. What can you really tell me about Vietnam because I'll probably end up there if I choose the draft?"

Cliff motioned for Johnny to have a seat on the edge of the stage. He lit a cigarette before speaking. He really did resemble Keith Richards, especially when he smoked.

"I can't make that decision for you," he began, "but look at it this way. Right now, the US has five hundred thousand troops in Vietnam. Combat deaths are in the hundreds every week, the numbers of wounded even higher. If you do the math, you will have about a one in twenty chance of being killed or wounded, maybe higher if you are in the infantry. But war is not about math, Johnny. War resistors who choose civil disobedience over the draft are getting similar prison sentences to yours. This war is mindlessly stupid but remember this--you did not start this war. You may not have a choice, but maybe you could be in the medical corps. At least you wouldn't be killing anybody. They need a lot of medics over there."

Johnny shifted his weight back and forth. Cliff hadn't been in the army either. Not comprehending everything his friend had told him, he hopped off the stage. "Thanks, Cliff," he said, "I've gotta go."

Cliff hesitated saying goodbye. He searched for the right words before speaking. "One more thing, Johnny. I hate this war with a passion, but right now I'm feeling guilty about the choice you have to make. My music career is going great, I have 4-F status because I evaded the draft, and you are probably going to end up in Vietnam. Take care of yourself, Johnny O."

Johnny looked at his friend. It wasn't in him to blame Cliff for his predicament or to envy him. "I guess I won't be seeing you for a while. You'll be rich and famous by then." Johnny smiled.

They shook hands, then Cliff grabbed Johnny in an embrace. Before turning and heading towards the door, Johnny looked into his friend's eyes. Saying goodbye was more emotional than he'd anticipated.

✳✳✳

Johnny drove to the north side of town to see his father. The older Ornowoski had been in the Second World War but never said much about it. With the possibility of Vietnam in his future, Johnny wanted to hear about his dad's experiences.

He found Gregor working on an old car in the garage. He tinkered with vehicles like some fathers watched sports to relax after their jobs. Johnny suspected it gave him a sense of satisfaction, but Gregor never showed his emotions.

"Hi Dad," he said. "I need to talk to you. I've been given a choice to volunteer for the draft or go to prison for two years."

Gregor nodded.

"I'm leaning toward the army but want to know why you never talked about your war?"

Gregor looked at his son and wiped his hands on an old rag to get the grease off. "Let's go inside."

The older Ornowoski motioned his son to sit at the kitchen table and took two beers from the fridge. He looked at Johnny before speaking. "I guess I never talked about it because I didn't know how. We Ornowoskis were always workers and not much for talk. I was the first to really know English. I was the only child, and my parents were older. They didn't speak much English."

"Can you talk about it now?" Johnny asked. I need to figure some things out."

"I can try," Gregor said.

"Just tell me your story, Dad. What happened in the war, and what happened between you and my mother, why I've never known her?"

Gregor shifted in his chair, visibly uncomfortable with the subject. He stared at his hands for a moment but began to speak. "I was still a boy and in high school when the war broke out. A lot of us worried it would be over before we'd be old enough to go and fight the Germans or the Japs. Ma and Pa were from the old country and were dead set against me joining the fight. They knew of the devastation in Poland. They came to America to start a new life and didn't want their only child to return to fight the old battles of Europe. I signed up anyway as soon as I finished high school."

Gregor hesitated again. "I've never told anyone about some of this stuff, never talked about it at all."

"Go on Dad, I need to know," Johnny prodded.

"I wanted to be a part of the US Army. It made me feel I belonged in the country in a way I'd never felt before. I was glad when they assigned me to the infantry. I shipped out as soon as I finished my training. I arrived as a replacement with the 45th Division just before the battle of Nuremberg. We captured the city after five days of heavy combat. The Germans, fierce in their desperation, were outnumbered. The fighting destroyed the city. It was the only action I saw, but what followed was worse."

Johnny looked at his father but Gregor's gaze, internal and unfocused outwardly, had changed his demeanor. He struggled to put thoughts into words but continued.

"The battle for Nuremberg ended on April 20, in 1945. After that, our unit marched toward Munich. Before we got there, we were ordered to move out to one of the concentration camps on the outskirts of the city. As we approached, there was the most horrendous stench imaginable. We followed the railroad tracks toward the camp and entered a new reality. We came upon dozens of boxcars full of corpses in varying degrees of decomposition. Most of us were vomiting from the stench. Hardened combat veterans who'd been with the 45th all through Italy and at Anzio had tears streaming down their faces. Our commanders were on their radios trying to reach their commanders for instructions. A call came down asking if there were any Polish speakers in the ranks. I was ordered into the camp where there were thousands of prisoners clinging to life, nothing more than living skeletons. There were Polish among them, and I was assigned as an interpreter. They were so weakened by hunger and disease that dozens were dying every day even after our arrival. The camp was Dachau."

Gregor's eyes looked at Johnny, but his thoughts were somewhere far away.

"Our guys were angry at the madness and cruelty of the camp. Prior to Dachau, there was even some talk as to why we were fighting the Germans. Now we knew. German civilians were forced to come and help bury the dead. I spent the next weeks speaking for Poles who had lost their entire families to the camps. Poles forced to watch loved ones executed in front of them and then work without food or proper clothing. I listened and translated their stories. We had liberated Dachau, but even witnessing such depths of human suffering had tainted our own survival.

"Rotting corpses were everywhere. A camp guard dressed in a formal uniform came out and surrendered. He presented his pistol in a ritualistic manner he expected everyone to understand. Our guys were disgusted. It was like the very stench of the dead went unacknowledged before our arrival in the camp. A member of the 45th who'd been in all the battles of Europe with the unit, one of the few still left from the beginning of their deployment, walked up to the man, took his pistol and shot him in the head.

"I was only in Europe a few months but came back a different man. Your mother and I were sweethearts in school. She came from a similar background as mine, except Italian. Her family spoke no English in the house and were staunch Catholics. We married too soon after the war. I couldn't be a proper husband to your mother. Images of the corpses intruded every time I tried to make love to her. You were conceived one of the few times we managed. She didn't believe in divorce, or her family didn't. After you were born, she plotted her escape—from me, her family, the Catholic Church."

Johnny sat transfixed, his decision made. "I have to go into the army, Dad. I don't want to be a convict, and I don't want a life of crime. If I end up in Vietnam, I will have to face it like thousands of other young men. I don't want to live separately, not anymore."

CHAPTER THREE

Johnny laid on his back, his arm around CC. Due at the courthouse at ten o'clock, Freddy told him to pack a few clothes, mostly underwear. After appearing before Judge Stone, he would go directly to Oakland for his physical. From there he would be inducted into the army and report for basic training.

"I'll wait for you, Johnny."

"Of course you will," he said, but his heart sank. A pretty girl, alone for long periods, would have many boys vying for her attentions. He stroked her cheek gently and wiped at her tears.

Johnny attempted a philosophical outlook about his departure. He knew CC loved him but wasn't sure she'd wait two years. They'd lived in an unrealistic bubble where their needs were met without having to work. He knew it couldn't last; he hoped CC would.

"I should have my first leave in about six months," he told her. "I'll write often, phone when I can. Be sure and write back, let me know how the band is doing, check in on Ralph once in a while."

He'd not implicated his partner. It would have been dangerous for them both. He'd grown fond of the older man and didn't blame him for what happened.

"I love you, Johnny," CC cried as she clung to him. He had to pry her arms from around his neck. He wanted to look at her face, but she buried it in his chest. "I'll be back in six months," he said, kissing her a final time.

✳✳✳

The physical in Oakland took place in a large building with a maze of hallways and substations for taking blood and urine samples and assessing the physical dimensions of mostly healthy young men. Dozens of inductees moved through the process in their undershorts. After the medical procedures, achievement tests were given in a large room filled with school desks.

An army sergeant in starched fatigues creased at the seams instructed them. "This will help us decide what MOS to assign you. That's military occupational specialty for you civilians. I would advise you to take them seriously lest you do poorly and wind up in the infantry."

Johnny found the examinations simple. How pertinent were the number of pool balls in a rack, or the proper way to pour beer into a glass? After the tests, he sat for a one-on-one with a sergeant. "How did I do?" he asked.

"Confidential," said the stern-faced examiner, Johnny's attempt at levity going unnoticed. "What would you be most interested in doing for the army, son, not that we're giving you a choice. Sometimes openings fit with a draftee's skills."

Johnny remembered his conversation with Cliff. "I think I'd like to train as a medic."

"No guarantees, son, the infantry is taking most of you, but I'll put you down as a 91B20."

"What's that?"

"Combat medic."

"I thought that medics patched guys up after they were shot, somewhere away from the frontlines."

"There are no frontlines in Vietnam, son, and besides, the grunts need medics out there with them when they do get shot. I think you'll do fine. Next."

After the physical, Johnny stood with a group of young men and was sworn into the United States Army. A bus took them to a barracks nearby. Surrounded by dozens of newly inducted draftees, Johnny felt the ache of loneliness. He talked to no one.

In the morning, the same group was instructed to board a bus. Once seated, a short and stocky red-haired kid began talking. "Looks like we're headed to Ft. Lewis for basic, where my brother trained before he shipped out for the Nam," he confided. "Been over there three months now, in the thick of it with the Big Red One. That's the First Infantry Division. Probably heard of it from the Second World War. That's the division I'd like to be with. Course, they don't like putting brothers in the same unit in case they both get killed. It's too hard on the families."

A group of apprehensive inductees crowded around him. He was holding court now.

"So, what's your brother say it's like over there?"

"Says it's a real shithole. None of the people give a damn, can't tell who the enemy is by looking at them. We're over there tryin' to help these people. Some of them are workin' on our bases during the day and fighting with the Viet Cong at night. Said one of the dead VC they shot in a firefight was actually workin' in the base mess hall. Fuckin' crazy if you ask me."

"So, what's boot camp like?"

"Boot camp ain't nothin' compared to the Nam, just a bunch o' drill sergeants yellin' at ya all the time. Pay attention and stay out of trouble and you'll do fine. If you're assigned to the infantry, you'll probably stay at Ft. Lewis for AIT, that's advanced infantry training. If you do, you'll probably be headed for the Nam after they give you a thirty-day leave. Myself, I wouldn't mind going because I could use the extra money they give you for bein' in combat."

"How much is that?" someone asked.

"Works out to about sixty-five dollars a month."

Sitting close enough to hear the conversation, the guy next to Johnny said: "The kid wants to risk his life for sixty-five bucks a month he can take my place."

The new soldier was right about Ft. Lewis. The bus dropped them at the airport, and they were escorted to a commercial flight. More busses picked them up in Seattle and transported them to the base, a sprawling military complex near Tacoma. On the post, it took another twenty minutes to arrive at a warehouse where a sergeant boarded and began yelling instructions.

"You will disembark in an orderly fashion and form up into some semblance of a military formation. Is that clear?" When no one responded, he shouted it louder.

"I asked you sorry-looking assholes a question. I expect an answer. You will address me as Drill Sergeant. Is that clear?"

Some in the group responded: "Yes, Drill Sergeant."

"I cannot hear you," he screamed at the top of his voice.

"Yes, Drill Sergeant," the group responded louder.

"You will disembark from this bus and line up single-file."

He had the group's attention. "I am Drill Sergeant Noble," he enunciated clearly and louder than necessary. Noble stood ramrod straight and scowled at them. "To my left is Drill Sergeant Willis."

A tall, lean Black sergeant stepped forward and nodded at Noble.

"We have been given the undesirable and almost impossible task of turning this hopeless group of civilians into fighting men of the United States Army." Noble glared at the recruits. Without hesitating, he lunged at the man two spots from Johnny and backhanded him across the mouth.

"Are you smirking at me boy? Now let's get one thing straight." The recruit, bleeding from the blow and with his eyes watering, stood erect without looking at Noble. "You will pay attention to Sergeant Willis and myself or we will make your world one with a lot of hurt in it. Is that understood?"

"Yes, Drill Sergeant." The group began to comprehend.

Next were the haircuts. Barbers set up in the warehouse shaved everyone to their scalp. Afterwards, helmets and boots, olive green ponchos and sets of fatigues, M-14 rifles and packs were issued. Noble shouted for them to form up.

No busses waited. It was time to run to the next destination with their gear. Fifty-five strong, the training platoon set out. Soon, Johnny breathed heavily and wondered when they could rest. They kept going. A chubby kid dropped out gasping. Drill Sergeant Noble, not carrying any gear and not at all out of breath, was all over him.

"Get your fat tubby ass off the ground and keep moving. You need to lose some of that lard, soldier. I ain't gonna coddle your fat ass while Charlie's waiting to fuck with you in the jungles of Vee-et-nam. When I get back over there I ain't about to have the likes of you getting me greased because you're a fat tub of lard and out of shape. Get up and keep moving before I fuck with you myself."

"Yes, Drill Sergeant," the kid sputtered.

They ran until they reached dozens of two-story rectangular buildings.

"It's the barracks," someone shouted. The platoon weaved through a whole suburb of box-shaped quarters, running through a maze of identical structures. Their ordeal ended outside one of them.

Inside, rows of bunks lined both walls, a drab-green footlocker at the base of each. More instruction in military protocol—how each item of their issued gear was to be folded and placed inside. How the linoleum floor must be maintained with a high-gloss shine after mopping and buffing. Rules existed for how to tuck the corners of the covers on a bunk, where to place a toothbrush, when to eat, sleep and use the latrine.

They ran or marched everywhere—to the rifle range, the obstacle course, in the rain, sun and in the dark. Sergeant Noble yelled at them through it all.

"Don't call this a gun." He held an M-14 in the air with his left hand.

"Repeat after me:
This is my rifle
This is my gun (holding his crotch)
This is for fighting
This is for fun (still holding his crotch)."

Johnny found the training physically demanding but none of the instruction difficult. Smart enough not to take the constant yelling personally, he followed regulations without bringing attention to himself. Some of it he found amusing.

At the chlorine sheds, they were taught how to clear their gas masks. Before going inside to test their ability with the real thing, Noble gathered them beside a white cross in the ground near the entrance.

"Now this dumb shit didn't pay attention while the rest of his platoon learned how to clear their masks. Didn't make it out of the chlorine chamber alive. Had to bury the dumb fucker here. Course, that's better than doing something stupid in the Nam and getting a bunch of other people killed besides yourself because you're not paying attention. Have I made myself clear?"

"Yes, Drill Sergeant."

Noble and Willis were big on cadences while they ran and marched. Echoes of the rhythmic chants reverberated in the distance where the combined voices of other platoons filled the air. Not to be outdone, their drill sergeants would begin with "a left, a left, give me a left, right, left" in sync with the slap of boots on the ground in unison. "All right let's hear it," Willis would holler. "Repeat after me.

> *If I die in a combat zone*
> *Box me up and ship me home.*
> *Pin my medals on my chest*
> *Tell my mama I've done my best.*
> *Lay my body six feet down*
> *Till you hear it hit the ground."*

Johnny found barracks life difficult, fifty-five guys crammed into one building with no privacy. Even the toilets in the latrine had no stalls and were open for everyone to see. When they did have a few minutes break from training the banter started. Guys bragged about their girlfriends and their sexual prowess, told stupid jokes, and got on Johnny's nerves.

Noble and Willis told them all about Jody, the mythic figure who looked after their women while they were training. "Keep your mind on your business, here," Noble told them, "and Jody will look after your girl." Both drill sergeants worked him into chants.

> *Your baby was lonely as could be*
> *Till Jody provided the company.*
> *Ain't it great to have a pal*
> *Who works so hard to keep up morale.*
> *Sound off...1,2*
> *Sound off...3,4*
> *Sound off...1,2...3,4...*

"Fuck that Jody shit," said Marvin from South Dakota. "If Jody be messin' with my girl then I be messin' with Jody soon as I get my leave."

"Aw, they're just messin' with your mind, Marvin, his pal from Georgia assured him. "Ain't none of them know nothin' about your girl."

Johnny worried about CC but knew Willis and Noble weren't reliable sources for advice about women. Could the depraved Noble even have a girlfriend?

✶ ✶ ✶

Two weeks into basic, exhausted, and still getting into shape, five platoon members sat on a bunk near Johnny's and shared photographs of their girls. "This girl be waitin' on me back home," said Formis, a big Swede from the coast of Oregon.

"I'm sure," said Randolph, a light-skinned Black from Oakland. He had an edge to him that made Johnny wary. "How 'bout you, Orno, how you say your name? A handsome guy like you ain't got a photograph of a girl back home?"

The group looked at Johnny. Reluctantly, he showed them a picture of CC.

Randolph made a fuss. "Now that be a fine-lookin' woman," he said. I wouldn't be leavin' her behind for the army."

"I didn't have much choice," Johnny said, an edge in his own voice.

"What's that girl's name?" asked Formis.

"Cecelia Jones," Johnny said.

"That's too bad," said Randolph.

"And why would that be?" Johnny said, glaring at him.

"Well," he responded, "if the girl be Betty or Belinda then her nickname would be BJ, represent all the blow jobs she be given' to Jody back home."

Johnny had reached his limit. He lunged at Randolph and delivered the first punch. He'd had enough of the endless stupidity of the banter, the juvenile obsession with Jody the drill sergeants had instilled in the platoon.

The two rolled around on the floor exchanging blows. It didn't last long. Hearing the commotion, Willis flew out of his office and intervened. He grabbed Johnny in a powerful grip and pinned him against the wall. Fury in his eyes, he glared at the trainee while an artery pulsed violently in the sergeant's neck. Barely able to control his rage, he let go of Johnny but continued his menacing stare.

"I'll see you in my office—now," he shouted. "And you next, Randolph."

Behind the closed door he let loose, screaming at Johnny. "You know what I detest, Orno, whatever-the-fuck your name is? You know what I hate more than anything?"

"No, Drill Sergeant."

"Well I'll tell you what that is, Orno," pretending to be calmer. "It's White boy pussies," he yelled, on the verge of erupting again. "You White boys come into my platoon actin' like you is tough or somethin'. I'll tell you this. That little yellow man in the jungles of Vee-et-nam is the tough one and he gonna have some fun fuckin' with you in his jungle along with all the other White boy pussy we send him. Is that what you gonna be, Orno, White boy pussy? Or maybe you a little bit queer, enjoy Charlie fuckin' you up the butt. He be smilin' while he doin' it. So, you better save some of that weak-assed fight you think is tough for someone who truly wants a fight with you. You think you got that, Orno? Now get out of my sight before I get angry."

"Yes, Drill Sergeant."

Willis wasn't through. After shouting at Randolph in his office, he ordered the platoon to form up and stand at attention outside the barracks. He paced in front of them while they waited for him to speak.

"Here's the deal. If any of you feel the need to fight before you get to Vietnam, before we can actually train your sorry asses for a fight with Charlie, then you come to me, we'll have a little tango. So, who will it be? Randolph, Orno, you wanna go some more?"

"No, Drill Sergeant."

"Anyone else? You get the urge to fight, I wanna know about it and you'll be goin' through me. Got that!"

"Yes, Drill Sergeant."

CHAPTER FOUR

Half of the basic training platoon were eighteen-year-old kids who joined the army out of high school. The rest were draftees like Johnny. Everybody assumed they would end up in Vietnam. Noble and Willis thought so and used it like a blunt-force club to motivate them.

They all had questions about the war. Noble and Willis had been there but only spoke about "Charlie," the mythical little yellow man who would be pissed off to see you showing up in his jungle. It took Johnny several days to figure out who Charlie was. He remained mysterious, skinny but tough, underfed but wily and willing to fight to the death to get you out of his jungle.

The unit patches on the right shoulders of the drill sergeants told which divisions they'd served with in Vietnam. They got no specifics beyond that. Willis' bright yellow insignia with a black horse's head designating the Air Cav stood out as he yelled about the prowess of Charlie.

"You might want to laugh at the little yellow man in sandals, but he'll be glad to slit your throat if you ain't payin' attention. Just because he ain't big don't mean he can't fight. He might be skinny, but he's tough. Not carrying a ton of lard around like some of you fatsos."

Noble's bitterness and vulgarity came through in his obsession with Jody, representing the lover of the platoon's girlfriends in their absence. Johnny wondered if he'd lost a wife that way? His smaller combat insignia, a bolt of yellow lightning against a red background, meant he'd been with the 25th Infantry Division. His eyes burned with hatred.

Charlie's nickname originated with the military's phonetic system used for clarity during field operations. A word represented each letter of the alphabet so a "B" would never be confused with a "D." The tough little yellow men Willis screamed about were the Viet Cong, the VC. "Victor" stood for

"V" and "Charles" for "C" in the phonetic system. The nickname "Charlie" the result.

Jody's origins were more obscure, but everyone with a girl feared the infidelity he represented. While Willis focused on the prowess of Charlie, Noble always came back to Jody and continued working him into the cadenced chants.

> *When I finally make it back*
> *Jody be driving my Cadillac.*
> *Maybe I'll buy a Chevrolet*
> *With my extra combat pay.*
> *Jody he is such a pal*
> *Looking after my sweet gal.*

Five weeks in, Johnny got a chance to speak with a medic. The platoon marched to a medical clinic and formed up outside its doors. Sergeant Noble got to the point.

"The army needs a lot more blood in Vietnam; our platoon is going to provide it. Step forward if you are willing to donate a pint for the guys needing it in Vietnam."

Half of the platoon stepped forward.

"I sure as hell hope those of you not volunteering never need any blood over there. You certainly don't deserve any if you're not willing to provide some while you're just training."

Half of those left stepped forward.

"I see that we are not yet at a one hundred percent ratio of the platoon, Sergeant Willis. What does that say to you?"

"It says we're not training hard enough, Sergeant Noble, not preparing for Vietnam. If anyone in this platoon is too chickenshit to even provide a little blood for our fellow soldiers in need, it means we do not have them ready to face Charlie. I shit you not, Sergeant Noble."

Six more came forward. Only five remained while the rest of the platoon filed inside the clinic. Johnny noticed a unit insignia on the right shoulder of one of the medics drawing blood. "You been over there?" he asked.

"Depends what you mean by *over there*?" he said. He puffed on a cigarette while inserting needles into veins and collecting bags of blood, which didn't seem to bother him in the least.

"In the Nam," Johnny said.

"That's Vietnam to you, shithead, and yeah, I been there."

The sleeves of his fatigues were rolled up and exposed an ugly scar on his forearm. He noticed Johnny staring at it. "Napalm," he said.

"What was it like as a medic?" Johnny asked. "The army might be sending me to medic's school."

"You better hope they don't. What does that tell you?"

"I don't know, just asking."

"You'll find out soon enough. I arrived in country with twenty-two medics assigned to the 101st Airborne. Five of us were left after a twelve-month tour. You better think about that, shithead. Maybe rethink your MOS. Stay away from those crazy fuckers who jump out of airplanes. Spent my whole tour with them up north fighting North Vietnamese Regulars pouring across the DMZ. Those gooks were always looking for a fight."

Marvin, distraught, paced back and forth holding the letter in his hand. The first *Dear John* had arrived. Not taking it well, he kept reading it, trying to comprehend the bitterness behind the words.

> *Dear Marvin,*
> *Fuck this shit.*
> *Julie*
> *P.S. Fuck You*

"It'll be alright, Marvin, things will get better," his friend from Georgia tried to console him.

"Where? In Vietnam? Because that's where we're all going."

Sitting on his bunk, Johnny read the only letter he'd received from CC. He wasn't sure it made him feel better. The emptiness of barrack's life depressed him. Fifty-five men plucked out of their lives training for a war none of them knew anything about. It didn't prevent the constant banter.

Nothing more than bullshit, really, guys just trying to console themselves while facing the uncertainties in their lives. Johnny wanted CC to be there for him more than ever. He had written twice. There wasn't much to say. What was he going to write about, the obstacle course, the rifle range, rolling around on the rain-soaked ground, listening to Willis rant about Charlie, Noble obsess about Jody? He just tried to be upbeat, said he missed her and thought about her all the time.

For her part, CC also tried to keep it light. She had never written letters and had no idea what to say, so she didn't say much:

> Dear Johnny,
> I wish you were here. I sure do miss you.
> Went up to the Fillmore with the band last weekend.
> They sure are sounding good. Cliff says to say hello.
> Well, not much going on in my life. Hope you are OK.
> Much love and kisses,
>
> CC

Johnny went outside to smoke and saw Ben Marconi, probably the oldest guy in the platoon at twenty-three. He suspected he was in the army for similar reasons. Or maybe the draft had simply caught up to him. Marconi never got excited about anything, just minded his business and stayed out of trouble by not attracting attention.

"My old lady do somethin' like that, that's it. Half the world is female. There's lots more women out there. Stupid kid. They are such fucking babies. If she can't be faithful for the eight weeks it takes to get through basic training, she sure as hell won't be for his tour in Vietnam. He doesn't know it, but the kid is better off without her."

Johnny nodded. "The kid has a point about Vietnam, though."

Marconi grunted an assent. "Woman has a mean streak, don't she, ending it like that? Maybe Willis could put her onto the VC."

"Oh, she's mean enough," said Johnny. "When do you think we'll hear about where we're going? When we were at the clinic giving blood, I asked the medic with the combat patch what it was like in Vietnam. He practically bit my head off."

"They have to tell us by next week. It's the end of basic. Don't expect anything but the infantry if you were drafted."

"I told them I wanted to be a medic."

"Shouldn't tell them anything. Stupid fuckers who started this war should be in the infantry."

The platoon lined up in formation and readied to practice their graduation ceremonies. Sergeants Noble and Willis had trained them, but it was the snarky second lieutenant, Lufton, who addressed them before receiving orders for their MOS training.

Johnny remembered an incident with the lieutenant. He'd been assigned to the orderly room watch and instructed to wake Lufton at 0530. He did so. The asshole got angry with Johnny for disturbing him and went back to sleep. At 0630, he ripped into Johnny for not getting him up. Now he stood before them, his ninety-day ribbon on his chest, and addressed the platoon.

"You have completed the first stage of your life in the United States Army. As you know, our nation is at war in Vietnam. Many of you will be serving in Vietnam in the future. I hope to serve there myself. Congratulations on your completion of basic training. Work hard at learning your occupational specialties, and good luck in your military service."

The lieutenant called out each platoon member in alphabetical order; the recruit saluted, received his orders, and returned to the formation. There were not a lot of surprises. Everybody hoped for a miracle to spare them from the infantry, but that is where three quarters of the platoon were headed. A handful of guys who'd signed up for three years received an MOS to train driving heavy equipment with the engineers. One trainee's orders assigned him to cook's school, another to the quartermasters. Johnny's instructed him to report to Ft. Sam Houston, Texas, where every medic in the US Army trained.

CHAPTER FIVE

Johnny sat with Ben Marconi in an Italian restaurant. His friend wanted a decent plate of spaghetti. Johnny had the weekend to get to Ft. Sam Houston in Texas, while Marconi wasn't going anywhere. He would report for Advanced Infantry Training on Monday morning.

"It's funny how life goes," Marconi began. "I'm a pretty good mechanic, so the army puts me in the infantry so I can walk everywhere. I don't have any papers, but I can fix anything. Told that to the guy at the induction center, but who listens to anyone in the army? They have their own way of doing things."

Marconi had charmed the older waitress, saying only his mother's spaghetti tasted better. She responded by mothering them, bringing a variety of Italian desserts, and making sure they had bottles of beer to drink.

"You know my friend here," he said, pointing to Johnny, "is half Italian. You wouldn't know it by his last name, just his good looks." When she left to wait on another customer, he asked Johnny: "So what did you do to deserve the army?"

Johnny told no one his full story. He shrugged. "Wasn't paying attention to the fact there was a war going on and I got drafted. How about you?"

"My old lady turned me in."

"What?"

"I had a big fight with my girl, and she told the draft board I hadn't registered. Simple as that. We broke up, she was still mad, end of story. My Mom keeps sayin' to me, 'you not stupid, why you do stupid things? Why not be big shot lawyer, big shot doctor instead of greasy hands all the time in old cars?'"

"Well?" asked Johnny.

Marconi shrugged. "A little late for that now. Look at us, on the verge of

Vietnam. I wonder what it's really like? Can you believe Willis? The man has a Charlie fixation. Him and Noble probably can't wait to get back over there. They never talked about it much. Two angry motherfuckers, though."

"We'll find out soon enough," Johnny said.

"Can't say I'll miss boot camp," said Marconi.

"Can't say I'll miss Willis and Noble," replied Johnny.

"Now that we're fed, let's go do some serious drinking," Ben said. "Try and forget we're in the army for one night."

A military bus took Johnny and a dozen soldiers from the San Antonio Airport to nearby Ft. Sam Houston. Dropped outside the door of a company orderly room, flower beds ringed with stones painted white contrasted nicely with the neatly trimmed grass. Other new arrivals milled about. Johnny didn't recognize anyone.

A sergeant appeared in neatly pressed fatigues and addressed them. "All right, people, listen up. My name is First Sergeant McGill. Your commanding officer, Captain Wren, wishes me to welcome you to Ft. Sam. Your training will commence at 0700. There will be a formation for roll call, with chow right after. Fatigues with army-issue ball caps are to be worn. You will be given a chance to ask questions at that time."

That was it, a simple set of instructions. Absent were the shouting and threats so prevalent during basic. Johnny easily found the assigned barracks and laid his duffel bag on an unoccupied bed. He overheard a man with a southern drawl talking to a boyish-looking kid with glasses two bunks away. The speaker, his gear already in his locker, and dressed in civilian clothes, must have arrived earlier in the day.

"Could be just a rumour. Fifty percent casualty rates seem high. One of my friends from high school got back from the war just before I left for basic. Said there was nothing more valuable to an infantry platoon than their medic. Called him "Doc." Told me they really looked after him. Didn't want him doin' anything stupid to get himself killed. Wanted him around to look after them if they were hit."

"So where was your friend stationed over there?" asked the kid in glasses.

"Pleiku, I think, but I don't know where in Vietnam that is. Didn't know I'd be training as a medic."

"What else your friend say about Vietnam?"

"Not much, just that he couldn't wait to get out of the army. Was pretty sure he'd be out before he had to do another tour."

"Drafted?"

"Yeah, too much partying at the University of Mississippi. Didn't keep my grades up. Lost my student deferment. You?"

"Wasn't ready for college after high school. Didn't want to wait around and be drafted, so I signed up to be a medic. Thought it would be better to treat the wounded rather than kill anyone."

"Amen," said the southerner.

Johnny wandered over.

"John Ornowoski," he said, putting out his hand. "Some of my friends at home just call me O."

"Don Palino," said the man with a drawl. "Pleased to meet you. Just got in from Ft. Benning, Georgia, where I did my basic."

"Danny Holt," said the kid with glasses. "Did basic at Ft. Lewis."

"Me too," said Johnny. "Can't say I'll miss it, but I guess we're all a little closer to Vietnam."

At 0700 they gathered outside the company orderly room. After roll call, the company marched to the mess hall for breakfast. They ate better food in a more relaxed atmosphere than in basic training, and without any shouting or bullying.

Afterwards, they assembled in a large conference room for orientation. A short and portly sergeant, who didn't look like he'd seen any combat, addressed them.

"Welcome to Ft. Sam," he began. I'm Sergeant Hurtz and will oversee your training for the ten weeks you'll be with us. You are a select group. The army doesn't take dummies and try and make medics out of them. You have all scored highly on your achievement tests and should be proud you have been chosen to become medical specialists. The troops in the field need you."

Hurtz took a moment to survey the two hundred trainees seated in the room. "Most of you will serve in Vietnam at some point during your military commitment. Many of you will be with the infantry in the jungles and rice paddies of Vietnam. You will need the training we are about to give you, so pay close attention and do your best. Lives are depending on it."

Johnny glanced at the room full of young men. He'd had breakfast with Don Palino and Danny Holt, who now sat on either side of him. He returned his attention to Sergeant Hurtz, who spoke with an intelligence not indicated by his pudgy physique.

"You will be trained in the basics of saving lives. Your first priority is to make sure a casualty is breathing. Sometimes this will require clearing an air passage. In more extreme cases, you may need to use CPR to resuscitate, give a shot of adrenaline into the heart, or perform a tracheotomy. You will be trained in these procedures, but your ability to act decisively and with confidence is crucial. The infantrymen in your care deserve your best.

"How about the bleeding?" he continued. "Once you've established your casualty is breathing, you must stop any hemorrhaging. Sometimes a simple pressure bandage will suffice. But what if an arm or a leg is blown off, a major artery severed? You may need to tie off that pulsing artery, apply a tourniquet above where a limb is missing. We will train you for this."

The sergeant stopped for a moment and looked at the young men assembled before him. "So, what next?" he asked. "Your casualty is breathing, and you've got the bleeding stopped." He paused again. "You must prevent shock. It is a killer. Trauma will cause shock, pain will cause shock, loss of blood will cause shock. You will learn when to administer morphine and how to start an IV in the field. You will be the most critical factor in whether a seriously wounded casualty lives or dies. Lives will depend on what you are taught in the ten weeks we have you.

"Much of your training will be hands-on, drawing blood and starting IVs on each other. To begin, we have a film to show you the proud history of the Army Medical Corps, a tradition you join as you train and are assigned to your units as medics."

***

Johnny walked out of the orientation into the bright sun of a Texas morning, one man among two hundred future medics in his training company. He did a quick calculation. Ten weeks at Ft. Sam and a thirty-day leave would put him in Vietnam three and a half months from now. He'd gambled with his life in the choices he'd made.

Much of the first week concerned basic hygiene and the application of standard field dressings. Indoor classes were primarily conducted in platoon-sized groups of Johnny's barracks mates. Outdoors, they were introduced to the medevac system used in Vietnam. They carried each other on stretchers to simulated landing zones and were shown how to improvise slings for transporting the wounded.

The first needles appeared at the beginning of week two. The entire company assembled in a room with syringes, vials of saline, cotton swabs and isopropyl alcohol. The portly sergeant who had conducted the orientation opened the session by calling on a volunteer.

"I know some of you probably think it's not wise to ever volunteer. In this instance I recommend it. I will administer a shot less painfully than the man sitting beside you who's never given one."

A recruit stepped forward and took off his fatigue shirt. "The rest of you may do the same," he said. After the men had their shirts off, he took a cotton ball and placed it over an opened bottle of isopropyl alcohol and tipped it so the swab absorbed some of the contents. In one motion, he wiped the man's shoulder and injected him with the syringe. Instructors fanned out through the room to assist with the procedure, ensuring each trainee gave and received an injection.

By the end of the week, they'd given and received several shots. Weekend passes were promised after an afternoon triage class.

A tall and slender instructor briskly entered the hall where they'd assembled. Johnny noticed the same unit insignia on his right shoulder that Drill Sergeant Willis wore, a large yellow background with a black horse's head in the right upper corner. He strode to the front of the group with purpose, stopped, and surveyed them for a moment before speaking.

"Good afternoon, gentleman. My name is Specialist Ron Vittner, and I'm here to introduce you to triage medicine. Listen carefully. I'm one of the few instructors at Ft. Sam who's been to Vietnam." He paused for a moment to let his remark sink in.

"Remarkable, isn't it? In my opinion, all your instructors should be veterans of Vietnam. That's where all of you are going. It's not a big secret." The room had quieted completely. He had the attention of two hundred men.

"How many of you have met a veteran of this war?" Half of the trainees raised their hands, Johnny included. "How many of you learned a lot about the war from your encounters with that vet?" Only a few hands remained in the air.

"I'm here to teach you what I can about what it's like to be a medic in Vietnam. So, listen up and try learning something. The army has a curriculum for this course. My curriculum begins and ends with Vietnam. The army only has to put up with me for a few more weeks. In the vernacular, I'm short, and ain't about to re-up or do another tour in Vietnam." Vittner paced a few steps before speaking again.

"This is a shitty war," he began. "Your enemy is crafty, and he hates you. Charlie is the Viet Cong. The further south you go the more prevalent he is. He will use any means possible to kill or hurt you. He lives and operates in and among the rural population. The Vietnamese peasants hate you. You show up in their village it only means trouble for them. They are getting it from both sides. Forget all the crap about winning the hearts and minds of the Vietnamese. We've already lost that battle. Fifty percent of the casualties I treated in the south were from booby traps when Charlie wasn't even around. Your enemy will use anything to make them, from tin cans and stolen grenades to pits dug in the ground. Put twenty sharpened bamboo stakes in that hole, smear them with feces for good measure, and cover it up. What can be simpler? The villagers never fall in.

"Go further north and it gets no better. There you will find the North Vietnamese Regulars who are well-trained and willing to die for their cause. They are tough and disciplined. And they hate you. They are much more willing to engage you directly in a fight. They are willing to take unbelievably high casualty rates to defeat you. Do I have your attention?"

The class remained riveted to every word.

"So, what kinds of wounds are you going to encounter? You are spending lots of hours during your training tying neat square knots on field dressings. What are you going to do when you have multiple shrapnel wounds? You are dug in for the night, Charlie knows you're there, and he starts walking in mortars on your position. Some of your platoon members are hit. Now that Charlie knows exactly where you are an intense firefight erupts. It's dark. You can't see. Are you going to use a flashlight? That will get you and your casualty killed quicker than anything. Charlie can zero in on that kind of light.

"No, you're going to have to find and treat your wounded in the dark. But you must know where the wounds are before you can treat them. Even in the light of day, it's easy to miss a serious wound. I know that must sound incredible to you, but it's often muddy and difficult to see a small entry point. It's important not to miss anything.

"If your casualty is conscious and coherent, he can help you. If not, you must feel for his wounds. Rip or cut the clothes off him. You don't have much time. You probably have other casualties you need to get to. Your platoon members will help you out there, let you know who's hit. But you will have to move fast and make quick assessments. Maybe one of your guys has lost a lot of blood. Have you ever tried to start an IV in the dark, under fire? Good luck.

"A neat square knot on a pressure bandage might be nice, but get some pressure on those dressings. Carry tape and wrap them if possible. I liked to carry extra elastic bandages in my aid bag. They applied a nice even pressure and I could adjust them to the type of wound. You will have to think fast and get creative. Oh, and you have to keep yourself alive. A dead or badly wounded medic isn't good to anyone, is he?"

Vittner paused and looked at his audience, lips pursed. Before speaking, he turned and took three paces to his left. Facing the trainees again, he thought for a moment and continued.

"Your enemy likes to take out key elements in your platoon, your LT, radio operators, M-60 machine gunners—and the medics. If you are any good, it demoralizes a platoon to lose you. Forget that image of the medic wearing a big red cross while treating casualties on the battlefield. In Vietnam, it's a nice target for Charlie. I never saw a medic wearing one during my tours.

"Time is also your enemy. It's important to stabilize your wounded and get them out of there. It is your platoon commander's responsibility to call for a medevac, a dust-off. Let him know the condition of the wounded. The sooner you get your casualties to an evacuation hospital the better their chances are."

Vittner gazed at the room full of medics who would soon be in the situations he described. Nobody moved. Johnny, like everyone else in the room, sensed the importance of the information Vittner related. Here was a veteran telling them about the war, giving them advice that might actually help them, and their future casualties survive.

"Your worst-case scenario?" he continued. "You have several wounded, the weather is fogged in, you have a hot LZ, or no LZ, and you need to get your guys out of there. It's up to you to keep them alive.

"A triage situation is all about common sense. I have no list I can give you. It makes no sense spending time on a head wound you can't do anything about while a casualty loses blood from something treatable. Make sure you get the worst of your wounded on a medevac if there isn't room for everyone.

"There you have it, gentlemen. The war as Ron Vittner sees it. I wish I could just impart what I know into your heads, but I can't. I hope that I have at least given you a better context to proceed with your training and about the war you will face in Vietnam. Good day and good luck."

Vittner exited the room through a staff door. The kids who were training looked younger with each group. They had noticed the unit insignia on his right shoulder. At one time he'd been proud to wear the designation of the First Air Cavalry as they were known in Vietnam. He had deployed with them in 1965 in a battalion that had been in the Battle of the Little Big Horn a century ago under George Custer's command. There was a perverse pride in serving with the Air Cav.

It had not been Vittner's first tour. The son of a career NCO, he had joined the army in 1961. He spent most of 1963 as an adviser in Vietnam before US combat troops were deployed. He felt good about his role in training Vietnamese medics and conducting clinics in the rural villages. He enjoyed the friendship of Nhan, his Vietnamese counterpart. From a rice-farming village, Nhan, a patriot, wanted to see his country advance.

He hoped to become a doctor and establish hygienic standards for all of Vietnam.

Nhan knew more English than Vittner's limited Vietnamese. To the villagers, Vittner was Nhan's assistant. It contributed to his friend's prestige. They worked well together. He saw only sporadic combat during his first tour and left Vietnam committed to US involvement. Vittner re-enlisted when his three-year hitch ended.

When he deployed with the Air Cav in 1965, he was glad to be going back, this time in a combat role. In November, his battalion helicoptered into the Ia Drang Valley and were surrounded by a division of experienced North Vietnamese troops.

They suffered heavy casualties and had no secure LZ to get the wounded out, or supplies in. Vittner knew all about the difficulties of triage firsthand. He lost men who would have survived if he could have gotten them to an evacuation hospital. A young medic from a sister platoon was killed early in the fighting. Vittner had mentored him. He felt the guilt of not doing more to help him and the others who'd died in the week-long battle.

By the end of his second tour, the war had gotten uglier. He experienced so many firefights that he'd lost any sense of purpose beyond surviving and helping his platoon members do the same. The body count had become the measurement of success in the war. Civilian casualties were common. He put friends on medevacs and never learned if they'd survived, lost arms, legs, or even the will to live. The war had become his reality, and the killing pervasive. Before returning, he realized he no longer wanted a career in the military.

He came home with an impressive set of decorations. They no longer meant much. He dwelled on the men he failed to help. When the army asked him where he'd like to be posted and what he would like to do, he thought of the young medic killed in the Ia Drang. It seemed like a lifetime ago. He told them: "I'd like to train other medics."

CHAPTER SIX

Spellbound by Vittner's presentation, the class remained seated after he left. A combat medic who'd been there telling them about the war, the real one they'd be facing. The quiet turned to murmurs throughout the room as men softly verbalized their feelings to those seated next to them.

Near Johnny, Palino spoke first. "I guess that gives us some perspective. What have we gotten ourselves into?" Johnny liked his fellow trainee from Mississippi. Bright and funny, suave in manner, his drawl sounded urbane in his cultured voice.

Danny Holt, still reflecting on the talk, nodded. Johnny found the kid from Colorado sincere and likable. With his oversized spectacles and smooth complexion, he looked sixteen. They'd been pairing up in courses where they inserted needles into each other. A fourth trainee from their barracks, Richie Cordero, joined them.

"It doesn't sound good, does it?"

Danny Holt nodded again. He stared straight ahead, not looking at anyone.

"Vittner survived," Johnny said.

"And here we are," Palino said, "our whole tours ahead of us."

Johnny remembered how naïve he'd been to think the war might end before the draft caught up to him. He thought of Cliff Morris and Big Rock, worlds away from his reality now. He wondered about CC. It wasn't just the time apart, he realized, but how different their lives were.

"I say we go into San Antonio and eat a big pizza and drink beer," Richie Cordero said, referring to their first weekend passes.

"Might as well," Palino said, "enjoy what little of life we have left."

"Don't be so pessimistic," Richie said. "You never know. You going, Johnny?"

"Sure," he said.

Danny Holt adjusted his glasses and forced a smile. "No sense staying on the base and being depressed when we don't have to."

After eating their fill in a cheap pizza joint, the four friends found a tavern and ordered pitchers of beer. Palino filled a glass and drained most of it before setting it on the table. "I miss that," he said, "having the freedom to have a drink. Mostly, though, I miss women."

"I thought you were gonna say *your mother*," Richie teased him.

The two exchanged lighthearted barbs in between swallows of beer.

Johnny interrupted them. "I think that's Vittner sitting over there." He pointed to a lone figure at a corner table.

"You sure?" Richie said.

"Should we bother him?" asked Danny.

"He don't look busy," said an inebriated Palino.

"Just because he ain't busy doesn't mean he wants to be disturbed," said Richie.

"Oh, for fuck's sake," said Palino. "What's he gonna do, send us to Vietnam? And if that's where we're going, we might as well get some more information."

"Go and see if we can join him," Richie said to Johnny.

"Me…you think he wants to talk about Vietnam on the weekend?"

"He talked about it during the week. What's the big deal?" Richie continued.

"Then you go," said Johnny.

"Okay, okay, I'll go," said Palino. "I'm not that drunk."

He sauntered towards the corner table where Vittner nursed a beer. In civilian clothes, the Vietnam vet looked up just as Palino said, "good evening, Sir."

"What's with the *Sir* crap. I'm off duty, and besides, I'm not an officer. Do your friends address you as *Private*?" Vittner taught hundreds of trainees every week. Even he was surprised by how many medics the army prepared for the war. He didn't recognize the man with the southern drawl but knew from his appearance he'd been in one of his classes.

Palino recovered his smooth manners after the clumsy start. "My apologies," he began. "My friends and I were in your triage class. We wondered if we could ask you a few questions. If the war's as bad as you say, we could use all of the help we can get."

"Good answer, Private. Send your friends over."

Palino waved an arm in the air to indicate they should join him and Vittner.

Johnny spoke first. "Thanks for your class on triage. In basic, I asked a medic who'd been with the 101st Airborne about the war. He got angry and didn't say much. Told me to change my MOS."

Vittner thought for a moment before replying. It must be in the thousands now, medics back from the war, living with the pain of friends lost, unable to stop the bleeding or get a medevac in soon enough. Was there anything he could say to help them?

"We've all lost people over there we cared about," he began. "Sometimes we blame ourselves and lash out from thinking that."

"You don't seem angry," Palino said.

"I'm more hurt than angry. I spent two tours in Vietnam, and they were different. I think any medic who's been there will have regrets he couldn't save everybody and will have to live with it. So, what can I tell you, gentlemen?"

"We don't even know what the right questions are," said Richie Cordero.

"I'm not sure myself anymore," replied Vittner. "I used to believe in the war. After my first tour I left feeling good about what we were doing. Then it all deteriorated into body counts and killing more of them than they could kill of us. I won't do another tour. That's why I'm getting out."

"You think the war's gonna last a lot longer?" Johnny asked.

"Definitely," Vittner nodded. "It didn't seem to matter how many we killed. There were always more. And now the Vietnamese hate us."

"What went wrong?" asked a sobering Palino.

"It all went to shit," said Vittner. "We were the great power that was going to save Vietnam from the communists. Trouble is, to most Vietnamese, we're just the most recent meddlers in their affairs. Most people in the villages want to be left alone to farm their land and have enough to eat for their families. During my first tour I went into hamlets with a Vietnamese counterpart and set up medical clinics. By my second, we harassed them looking for Charlie. So much for winning their hearts and minds. I had a sergeant who used to boast, 'grab 'em by the balls and their hearts and minds will follow.'"

"Sounds like a mess," said Danny Holt.

"Remember this," said Vittner. "When you get there, try and learn as much as you can from any medic who's been in the shit. Be a pest if you have to and glean everything you can from him. It may not be possible, but go on patrols with him, and don't be afraid to ask questions. Over there, most of the medics will share what they know. It will be invaluable. I wish I could help you more." With that final bit of advice, Vittner excused himself and left the bar.

On the same weekend, Johnny found a pay phone and tried to reach CC. No answer. Same story with Cliff, who would probably be booked and playing somewhere on the way to the big time. He phoned his father.

"Hi Dad, Johnny phoning to check on things."

"How's medic's training?"

"Intense, but I'm learning lots. The war doesn't sound good. Everyone here figures we'll get orders for Vietnam after we finish at Ft. Sam. What's the news on your end?"

"Not much. I ran into Cecelia's mother at the grocery store. She said your girl is lost without you."

"I'm a little worried. Can you check on CC, tell her I phoned and that I miss her."

"Sure."

"If I do get orders for Vietnam, I'll be home on leave in eight weeks."

"Don't worry about things here, Son. Concentrate on what you need to learn."

"I know. Thanks, Dad. Better go."

✶ ✶ ✶

Week three, and they were starting IVs on each other. A circle of empty seats surrounded a kid named Foster, the class fuck-up. Nobody wanted to pair up with him. He was trying not to be embarrassed. The sergeant in charge intervened.

"All right, tighten it up in the middle there. Everybody in this class will leave knowing how to start an intravenous. We don't need any of you fumbling around when a casualty actually needs one, so get paired up ASAP. If you like, I'll do it for you."

Johnny and his friends developed a routine. They participated within the foursome, but alternated partners. Palino inserted a needle into Johnny's arm during the class, and then reciprocated. Besides learning the technique, it got them used to needles and the sight of blood, which they also drew from each other.

Johnny had never been to the doctor much in his life; now he trained to treat traumatic wounds. Some of the classes were difficult to simulate. Applying a tourniquet, a simple procedure on an undamaged leg, would be different when blood gushed from an actual wound. Johnny paid attention. The war loomed over them as they trained.

During the fourth week, a clerk arrived in the barracks with mail. He called out the names on the addressed envelopes.

"Donald Palino," he shouted.

"Must be from his mother," Richie Cordero said. "Who else would be calling him Donald?"

Palino retrieved the letter. "Actually, it's from Miss Clarissa Montgomery, the prettiest girl in Mississippi. She always calls me Donald. Smell this," he said. He inhaled deeply before passing around the perfumed letter.

"Get real," Richie protested. The prettiest girl in Mississippi wouldn't be your girl."

"Oh, she's not my girlfriend," a smug Palino replied. "If she was my gal, I could have found a way to avoid the army. Her daddy is so rich he owns half the town she hails from. All those pretty girls from the University of Mississippi have such rich daddies. My downfall," he sighed, smelling the envelope again. "My girl is good-looking and wild to boot. I call her Stormy Beth. What does that tell you?"

There was much to Palino's story he didn't confide. He'd been taken with the girls at university. His goal was straightforward—get a law degree and marry one of them. Beth McTeer was pretty and her daddy rich. She loved the handsome man with the suave manners and quick wit. Her daddy didn't. Wealthy and well-connected, a call to the local draft board regarding the young man's status rectified the situation.

"Johnny Ornowoski," the clerk continued. *It must be from CC*, Johnny thought. He took the letter to his bunk and opened it.

> *Dear Johnny,*
> *Your Dad said you were worried about me.*
> *Please come home soon. I miss you*
> *and don't see why we have to go through this.*
> *There is talk of young men going*
> *to Canada to avoid the draft.*
> *Can we talk about it? I love you and miss you.*
>
> *CC*

Glad to hear from his girl, the letter also unsettled him. Two years would be a long time to be separated. He reminded himself of the alternative. The army had only been a way to avoid San Quentin. And going to Canada? He knew their authorities would never allow him into the country with a criminal record, which would not be sealed until he'd completed his draft commitment. *Talk was always so easy.* He looked at the other men reading their letters. They were from all parts of the country. There was even a Canadian from Quebec who spoke English with an accent he'd not heard before. How ironic CC wanted him to flee to Canada to avoid the war. Here was a Canadian training with him to go to Vietnam. Johnny wondered about his story.

The four friends headed into San Antonio again on Saturday night. His heart not in it, Johnny went along to get off the base for a few hours. Rumours about the war ran rampant through the training company. Johnny tried to ignore them. Sometimes he felt like a doomed man.

Their training continued unabated. Ten weeks did not seem long enough to teach them what they'd need to know in the war Vittner described. Having the talk with him helped.

The company assembled in a formation near the orderly room. The captain, rarely seen during their ten weeks at Ft. Sam, issued orders for their end-of-training duty assignments. To Johnny's relief, he gave no lengthy pep talk. The new medics wanted to know one thing—were they going to Vietnam?

Many were convinced it would be a death sentence. In fact, many men in the courtyard that morning would die in Vietnam. The captain greeted them and proceeded in alphabetical order.

"Richard Cordero, Republic of Vietnam."

"Daniel Holt, Republic of Vietnam."

"John Ornowoski, Republic of Vietnam."

"Donald Palino, Republic of Vietnam."

A thirty-day leave was all that separated the four friends from Vietnam. Like eighty percent of the company, their next duty would be in the war zone. They gathered near their bunks and talked while they packed their bags.

"Well, now we know," said a resigned Palino. "Here we come Vietnam. But it will be thirty days of wine and women in Mississippi before I go."

They compared orders. They were identical, so they agreed to meet in Ft. Lewis, Washington, before deploying.

Johnny noticed Danny Holt sitting by himself on the edge of his bunk. "You packed already?"

Danny nodded. "You think we'll survive?"

Johnny had no idea. "Go home and try and forget about it for a few days. We'll meet up at Ft. Lewis before we go. That's all we can do."

Danny nodded again. "I'll see you in thirty days," he said.

CHAPTER SEVEN

CC missed Johnny and the life they'd had together. He'd been gone four and a half months in the army and was in jail before that. She wanted them to run away and start new somewhere. Now, as he finished medic's training and would probably end up in Vietnam, she worried he would be killed.

She tried sticking to a budget and schedule but was lonely and frightened about the future. She got depressed and couldn't focus on even the mundane tasks of tidying the apartment. Dishes piled up in the sink; heaps of clothes were scattered and unwashed. The T-bird wouldn't start. Instead of getting it repaired, she stayed high and used too much of the money Johnny had left her. CC hatched a plan to replace it.

Ralph Barnes, back in business, had established an elaborate delivery system utilizing fake identities and a legitimate shipping company. CC bought dope from him and resold some of it. The old hippie cautioned her not to get into the drug trade.

"I can help you out with some of the rent money," he offered. "It's been expensive setting up again, but I can do that while Johnny's away. I don't think you should be dealin' any drugs, Dear. It's too dangerous, even worse than before."

"It's mostly for the band members," she argued. "If you won't sell me any, I'll just have to go somewhere else. I'm careful, Ralph. Please?"

The girl had a point. He genuinely cared about Johnny and knew getting her supply from him would be safer. He shook his head. Events hurtled forward beyond his ability to keep pace. The news reported the war, the US more enmeshed each week. The hippies avoided it while they continued smoking a lot of dope. "Just be careful, Dear. It could go badly for you if you're caught." He remembered saying similar words to Johnny.

✳✳✳

Johnny's flight put him in San Francisco at ten o'clock at night. He found a restroom and changed into civilian clothes, then took a city bus to the Greyhound Depot. Another would leave for Santa Cruz at six in the morning. His worries included more than Vietnam.

Johnny would be home in a few hours. He didn't know what to expect from CC. They had not communicated much during his absence. Would it be the same between them? Vietnam dominated his thoughts in between his worries about his girl. Two possibilities remained. He would die in the war or make it out in good enough shape to get on with the rest of his life.

Johnny checked into a cheap hotel and looked for a bar close by. He entered the Blue Note Club and Grill. Crowded with everyday people, Johnny noticed them enjoying their lives. A young couple sat near the entrance with tall drinks he didn't recognize. They talked and laughed and kissed between sipping on them. The man had longish brown hair over his ears. The woman's dark hair hung below her shoulders in a hippie style.

Johnny sat on a stool at the bar.

"What'll it be, young man? You look like you're in the service."

"How can you tell?" asked Johnny.

"Hey, I'm a bartender," he smiled. "I get to know people. What branch are you in?"

"Army."

"You been overseas yet? My guess is, no."

"Why do you say that?"

"You look like you have the weight of the world on your shoulders, only healthy. A younger brother of mine was career Marines. He even looked different when he came back from his first tour. He didn't survive his second. Said they kept killing gooks but there were always more. Couldn't stand the Vietnamese. Said they'd go into a village looking for the VC and all the villagers would be shouting 'no VC, no VC, no VC, you GI *di di mau.*' It means 'go away' in gook talk. Right outside the village they'd run into an ambush and get chewed to pieces. Happened all the time."

"I'm sorry about your brother," Johnny said.

"You know, he couldn't wait to get back over there and even the score.

He lost too many friends on his first tour. Now he's dead, too. Where you headed, son?"

"Home, to Santa Cruz. I just finished medic's training. Got thirty days before I go over."

"Would it piss you off if I gave you some advice?"

"Of course not," said Johnny.

"Do your time over there and get out. The war got into my brother's head, and it changed him. It's not for me to say whether it's a good war or not. I suppose none of them are. Just watch yourself."

"Thanks. What do I owe you?"

"It's on the house." He looked into Johnny's eyes. "And kid."

"Yeah?"

"Good luck."

The Greyhound pulled into the Santa Cruz depot at nine in the morning. Johnny grabbed his duffel bag and decided to walk the few blocks to his apartment. Nervous about his reunion with CC, he collected his thoughts as he ambled along the sidewalk. As he got closer, he heard the faint crash of waves against the shore and smelled the salty mist that blew in off the ocean. The ever-present gulls circled overhead, and birds chirped in the shrubbery. He'd missed that about Santa Cruz.

Half a block from the apartment, he noticed his blue and white T-bird parked on the street, a relic from his previous life. He loved that car and the few months he and CC had together before it all disintegrated into their current reality.

Johnny climbed the stairs to their second-floor suite and unlocked the door. Everything looked familiar. He smiled when he saw the stack of clothes near the bed and dresser and looked at CC sleeping. He wanted to get undressed and get into bed beside her but didn't want to startle her. Despite his uncertainty, a tenderness came over him. Johnny placed his hand on her cheek.

"Johnny, is that you?" She opened her eyes and rolled towards him. "Get undressed and come and hold me," she said.

When she put her arms around him, she squeezed him and whispered: "I have missed you." Without looking at him she asked: "Does your being home mean you are going to Vietnam?"

"Let's not talk about that right now," he said. "I just want to lay here beside you for a while."

Johnny fell asleep in CC's arms. When he awoke, she was naked and wrapped around him. Nothing had seemed to change between them. CC got out of bed to make coffee.

"We can stay in all day if you like. I have everything we need. Your father told me if you were going to Vietnam, they would give you a thirty-day leave."

Johnny sat on the edge of the bed and watched CC make coffee.

"Most of the new medics got orders for Vietnam. They gathered us together at the end of our training and read out our duty assignments. It's no surprise."

"We can still go away, can't we? There's talk of guys going to Canada to avoid the war."

"You know, it's surprising how little I learned about Vietnam during my training. Most of the guys who'd been there didn't have much to say about it. Some of them got angry when I'd ask. I don't want to go. I could get killed, but I'm going to have to take that risk."

Johnny stood and moved towards CC.

"I've never considered myself a criminal for selling a little weed to hippies who just wanted to get high. Going to prison would have meant becoming a felon. Going on the run would not lead to our freedom. Canada would see me as a convicted offender, not some scared young man trying to avoid the war."

"Cliff says it's a stupid war and that the country is drafting more and more young men to feed the war machine."

Johnny nodded. "And I'm one of them, CC. But I need to know if you will be waiting for me when I get back?"

CC walked over to Johnny, wrapped her arms around him and held him tight. "I'm your girl, Johnny. Nothing's going to change that." She took his hand and led him to their bed.

Johnny slept again after they'd made love. When he woke, CC was still beside him. Restless, he wanted a part of his life back.

"Let's go for a drive," he said. He hadn't really thought about the specific things they'd do on his leave. At that moment, he wanted to be riding around in his T-bird with his girl snuggled beside him, reliving some of their former life together.

"Johnny," she said, "I want you inside of me again, so deep that I can feel you there for the whole time you're gone. I want you there forever."

Immediately hard and holding her, they were making love again. If he had any doubts about CC, they were being washed away in the flood of passion he felt. Her lovely body groped for him, not just wanting him, but needing him. Her pretty face was his to kiss. She groaned as he did.

"Just like that, Johnny. I never want you out of me." She grasped him tightly, gently, like she would never let him go.

Afterwards, Johnny felt a contentment he hadn't known for months. At home now, holding his girl, thinking they could survive anything the world threw at them, he basked in their love. They lay holding each other for a long while. Johnny no longer felt the need to get up and go anywhere. He was exactly where he wanted to be.

They created their own reality the first week of Johnny's leave. They slept when they wanted to sleep, got up and went for drives in the T-bird, sipped wine in bed and made love often. This was their time together, and CC was happy. They purposely avoided friends and family.

By the second week it was time to go and see people. Johnny found Cliff in his apartment working on a song.

"Haven't hit the big time yet, my friend, but if I keep at it, I figure something original will pop into my head. The record companies are interested but haven't offered us a contract yet."

"CC is saying you guys are sounding better than a lot of bands with hit records."

"There are a lot of good bands out there, but how are you doing? Does your being home mean they're sending you to Vietnam?"

"It does."

"How are you feeling about it?" asked Cliff, with a genuine look of concern.

"Sort of resigned to the fact, I guess, and trying not to let it intrude too much on my thirty-day leave. The war has been looming over me for a while. Maybe it's just time to go and get it over with."

"They trained you as a medic?"

"Yeah. Now I'm worried I'll forget some of my training before going. Being a medic isn't as safe as I thought it would be, but I don't know what to expect. All through training the army emphasized how bloody the war is, but nobody gave many details, just kept saying how bad it was."

"I'm sorry you have to go, man. The war is tearing this country apart. I can only imagine what it's doing to Vietnam. So many of the old guard, the country-right-or-wrong types can't conceive that the US might have made a mistake. They're not about to learn anything from what the French experienced. 'Anything the French can do, we can do better.'"

"I wish I knew more."

"You would not have learned it in school, Johnny. The pledge of allegiance, yes, but not any history that wasn't about making you a compliant citizen. But I have an advantage. My father's a history professor at the new university in Santa Cruz. He knew a lot about the country before most Americans had even heard of Vietnam, back when it was known as Indochina. He's appalled at the stupidity of our policy there. There's no way we can win this war."

Cliff paused and looked away for a moment. "Forgive me, I don't mean to sound preachy. I feel guilty men like you must go, and others don't, another little ugly aspect of the war. My father thinks there shouldn't be any student deferments. It's creating a privileged class that's getting an education while the poor are off doing the nation's dirty business. It leads to some interesting discussions with his students."

"A lot of guys I trained with got caught in a web not entirely of their making," said Johnny. "I sold marijuana and broke the law. A friend from basic had an angry girlfriend turn him into the draft board for not registering. Does that justify a possible death sentence?"

"Of course not, but the types manning the draft boards think it's good for young men to serve in the military. I haven't got a clue how they justify the hundreds of soldiers killed and wounded each week? Is that a good experience for them?"

Johnny nodded. Nothing Cliff said would help him now.

"I have to see my father," he said, ending the conversation. They stood and looked at one another for a moment. "I'll see you again before I go," Johnny said.

"You take good care over there, Johnny O."

Johnny drove around Santa Cruz and reflected on his situation. Ten days into his leave, thoughts about Vietnam surfaced constantly. Not prone to feel sorry for himself, he still noticed how Santa Cruz looked and felt as it had before the war. People were busy with their lives. Young men his age wore their hair long and went about their regular business. Cliff told him half a million American soldiers were in Vietnam. Where had they come from? Johnny only knew a few guys he'd gone to school with who were in the military. None of his friends had joined or been drafted.

He pulled into his father's drive and sat for a minute. Gregor Ornowoski would be home from work. Until recently, he'd never wondered why his father had not remarried or shown an interest in women. The simple bungalow on the north end of town, built after the Second World War, and made affordable by the low-interest loans available to veterans, looked the same as other houses in the neighborhood.

He found Gregor in a pensive mood. "I've been thinking," his father said, "about all of the time that passes while we work and go through life without really noticing. The Ornowoskis are workers, not a reflective people. Being first generation only put me between two worlds, not fully into the life of the new one. I wanted to belong, be called Greg, not Gregor. When I went to my war, it was all about fitting in and not wanting to be left out of this great event my generation faced.

"Of course, no man can know about war before he gets there. I was no different. But now, in Vietnam, it's not making any sense. You were such a good kid, never caused me much concern, got along with everyone while you fended for yourself. I was absorbed too much in my troubles, didn't notice my failures as a father.

"My war was supposed to make the world a better place where there would be no more wars. Now your generation faces its own. It's more difficult sending my son than going myself."

Johnny didn't know how to respond. Not knowing his mother, he never missed her. It never occurred to him to feel bitter. Gregor wasn't harsh, only inattentive. Johnny hadn't understood how difficult it is to shape your life when you don't know the factors controlling it. Cliff knew all about Vietnam and avoided it. Johnny had never heard of the place before his country got involved in the war. Now he'd have to fight there.

"You know, Dad, I never felt deprived. I don't want to go to Vietnam, and don't know why we're there. I'm afraid of losing my girl. There's a chance I may die or be badly wounded. If I get through my tour, I want to return and become something more than what I've been, someone who ambled through life without a plan. My friend, Cliff, says we've all been let down by poor leadership, that we've grown fat and arrogant, aligning ourselves with corrupt dictatorships instead of leaders interested in the well-being of their people. That may sound naïve until I look at who I'm going to Vietnam with. If the war's so important, why are only some of us fighting it? Those who are smart enough, connected enough, and rich enough to attend university, don't have to go. The war's not so important those men have to fight. I don't have that choice."

Gregor looked at his son. "Now I understand how my parents felt when I went overseas. 'Let someone else's kid go fight in the war,' they said. Somehow, this is a smaller war, but my kid has no way out of it. I see young men around the town, at work, living normal, able to avoid it. It makes no sense."

"Were you nervous before your deployment to Europe?"

"Yes, of course, there was some fear, but I would have felt shame and disappointment if I hadn't gone. This war is different. So many opinions about it. People don't agree if it's a good thing or bad thing. Some think it's good but only if someone else's kid goes to fight. Now, everyone wants to be a special case. You go to school, okay, we don't send that son. He can get educated and become a big shot while my son goes to Vietnam."

Johnny smiled at his father. "Have you seen the list of deferments?"

"Who gets to decide?"

"The local draft board, I guess, prominent citizens. There are lists of things you can be exempted for. None of the guys I trained with met the criteria."

Johnny fidgeted with his hands. "I have a favor to ask," he said. "Will you watch over CC while I'm gone, make sure she's okay? Talk to her once in a while? A year is a long time. I won't be able to phone. Letters are the only way to communicate, and she doesn't write many of them. I need to know how she's doing."

"We talked while you were in training. I'll look in on her. You concentrate on coming back to us."

"Speaking of CC, I have to go and pick her up at her mother's. We'll stop in this weekend and maybe bring her mom."

CC visited with Benita while she waited for Johnny. Before seeing her mother, she'd run errands and notified her customers there would be a limited supply of grass for the month. She'd managed to make enough money so Johnny didn't notice anything amiss. She hated hiding her dealing from him and would have to sort everything out while he was gone.

CC had never been in love before. As an adorable child, the boys had flocked to her. It continued as she grew older. Loving Johnny changed her outlook.

At first, she'd been angry with him for going into the army. His absence depressed her. She felt vulnerable. She missed him and started smoking a lot of grass to take the edge off her anxiety. Her loneliness trapped and confused her. She needed Johnny to help her sort it out, but he was gone. In three weeks, he would be gone again, maybe forever. It terrified her.

In turning to Ralph, the old hippie, she'd been desperate.

"I don't think it's a good idea," he told her. "A beautiful girl in this business is risky. You'll be noticed and attract too much attention. Please reconsider."

"It's only until Johnny gets back."

Ralph wanted to see Johnny before he went to Vietnam, wish him well. He knew it would be best if they had no contact. Eyes were always looking for connections. He still felt guilty about Johnny taking the fall for their dealing. It was part of the risk.

What a strange world it had become, Ralph surmised. Johnny, going to Vietnam, where he might be killed, for selling marijuana to a bunch of music-loving hippies who bothered nobody except the crazy sons of bitches who started wars like Vietnam.

CHAPTER EIGHT

A constant pang of anxiety accompanied Johnny as his thirty-day leave wound down. He felt like a condemned man unable to enjoy the simplest pleasures. Food had no appeal. A restful sleep eluded him; making love to CC lacked the passion earlier in his leave.

During the night he would sometimes walk to the ocean while CC slept. The sound of waves along the shore soothed him as he sipped on a can of beer. His thoughts calmed in the dark with the steady presence of the ocean. The moon emitted enough light to accentuate the white foam created from the turbulence of the tides.

After an hour he'd feel the need to return to the apartment, get undressed and return to bed with CC. They slept naked. Her body next to him was his greatest comfort.

Two days before his departure, he went and said goodbye to his father.

"I've asked Cliff Morris to drive me to the airport in San Francisco. I have to fly in uniform, and I don't want you and CC's last image of me saying a strained farewell in an airport lobby in my army greens. My friend from Colorado, Danny Holt, is meeting me, and we'll travel together to the staging area at Ft. Lewis."

Gregor nodded. "This is the most difficult thing for a father, sending his son to war. I have no parting words of advice that would mean anything right now. Please be careful and come home safe. I love you."

"I love you, too, Dad. I'll write as soon as I get to my unit."

✶✶✶

Johnny had decided not to run and hide anymore. Facing a year in Vietnam was the hardest part of the bargain he'd made with himself. Aching with anguish on the morning of his departure, a gloom overtook him. He watched CC weeping quietly, unable to hide her despair.

"You know, I dropped out of high school," he told her. "I never meant to keep dealing drugs for a living. I'm done with that part of my life. We'll make a new start when I get back. Are we together in that?"

"I'm with you, Johnny," she assured him, "but am so afraid of losing you in Vietnam. I'm having trouble imagining you gone for a year."

"It will pass quicker than you think," he said, but his words sounded hollow and unconvincing "Will you do something for me?"

"Anything, sweetheart. What is it?"

"Write to me more often. It helps to hear from you."

"I'll try, Johnny, but I'm not good at writing."

"Just let me know that you love and miss me. That's all I need to make it back to you."

CC buried her head in Johnny's chest and sobbed. Afraid of what he faced, and ashamed of keeping secrets, she silently vowed to do better.

"I'll do everything in my power to return to you," he said, before turning away and taking his first steps into an unknown void as alone as he'd ever felt in his life.

Johnny found Danny Holt waiting for him in the departure area. He looked so young in his khaki uniform that he could be mistaken for a boy playing dress-up in his father's army clothes. He looked tired and like he hadn't slept much.

"How was Colorado?" Johnny asked.

"Did you have a good leave?" Danny asked by way of response.

"I did, for sure I did," Johnny said without elaborating. It was good to meet at the airport and have a friend to travel with. He was feeling overwhelmed by the strain of the day, and it took the edge off the loneliness he felt in the pit of his stomach.

"Let's get some coffee," Johnny suggested, or a beer. Our last day of freedom for a while."

The four medics had agreed to meet at a motel called the Dreamland

Inn, a dumpy place in a rundown part of Tacoma. It was cheap and had a bar, the most important things for the night they would spend before reporting. Johnny and Danny found Don Palino and Richie Cordero having drinks.

"Right on schedule," said Palino. "I tried to drink myself to death in Mississippi, figured it would be a more pleasurable way to die than facing the Viet Cong. Alas, Winston and me survived. What a party."

"Who's Winston?" Danny asked.

"That's his dick," Cordero said, disgustedly. Nobody seemed amused, but Palino, already drunk, continued.

"My Stormy Beth nearly killed us for sure. Of course, her daddy was ready to by the time my leave was over. Asked me, 'haven't you got a war to go to, son?' Fuck that shit. I had thirty days leave coming, and I spent every one of them with his daughter. I'm going to miss that girl. Said she would wait for me, not have sex while I'm gone. Said if I thought the sex was good before going to the war, just wait until after I returned, her having a year's worth of passion stored up."

"Are we going to have to listen to this shit all the way to Vietnam?" asked Richie.

Johnny sipped at his beer. He was not in the mood for banter, so he didn't say much. He didn't feel like drinking, wondering what the next year held in store for them.

To save money, they had rented just one room. They took a bottle of whiskey to sip on. Palino was so drunk he crashed early. Richie tried to stay awake but soon faded as well.

"You know," said Danny, "walking out the front door to leave for the airport was the hardest thing to do. My mother was distraught at my leaving for Vietnam. She tried to hold it in but broke into tears right before I left."

"My girl was crying, too," said Johnny.

"Give me another sip of that," said Danny. "My dad drove me to catch my flight, and I thought he was going to cry." Danny took a swig from the bottle as his eyes misted.

"Your dad in World War Two?" Johnny asked.

"In the Army Air Corps, but never posted overseas. Your dad?"

"Yeah, he was in Germany for a short while right before the war ended. Saw some combat. Wouldn't talk about it for the longest time."

"Think we'll be okay?" asked Danny.

"We're about to find out."

The four friends had identical orders to report to the large staging area at Ft. Lewis by nine o'clock in the morning. They arrived and found the grounds packed with soldiers waiting to deploy to Vietnam. Huge buildings acted as temporary barracks. Long lines formed for everything from getting fed to receiving details about flights and times. Richie Cordero and Don Palino were scheduled to fly out early the next morning. Johnny and Danny would be on a plane that would follow six hours later.

They sat together in the mess hall before Richie and Palino had to catch a bus to the airport.

"Can't say I'm all that hungry," Richie said.

Palino looked recovered from his drinking binge two nights earlier, but only picked at his food.

"Can anyone tell me how army cooks can ruin eggs like this?" Palino put down his fork after taking a bite. "Do they actually teach them how to cook them like this? These don't even resemble eggs."

"Maybe they aren't real eggs," said Richie. "Who gives a shit right now anyway?"

"I do. I'd like a decent breakfast before shipping out," said Palino.

Johnny wasn't hungry, so he just had a cup of coffee. It wasn't much good either. He wanted to say something meaningful to his friends before they left, but everyone was on edge, bored and nervous at the same time.

"Any chance of us being together in Vietnam?" Danny asked.

"Naw," said Palino. "There's only one medic per platoon. We won't know where we're going until we get there."

"Good luck, you guys," is all Johnny could say. "Try and stay in touch if you can." Danny had everybody's home address and said he would obtain their Vietnam unit postings and let them know where they were located in-country. They shook hands, and then Palino and Cordero were on their way to catch their plane.

"Let's try and find a good cup of coffee somewhere," Johnny said.

Later that day Johnny Ornowoski and Danny Holt boarded a bus to catch their flight, joining 180 troops on a Boeing 707. It was a grueling ride, nearly halfway around the world. It took twenty-two hours to get to

Vietnam. The friends were able to sit next to each other on the plane. The mood was subdued, tense and somber. Nobody had much to say.

PART TWO
VIETNAM

CHAPTER NINE

Cam Ranh Bay, Vietnam
October 1967

The flight had been a daylong journey hurtling them toward a certainty of destination—Vietnam—but an uncertain destiny. It was half a world away from anything Johnny Ornowoski had ever known.

After landing, heat blasted them from an incessant wind, persistent and grating on the nerves. Lines formed with anxious young men proceeding slowly and resignedly into their tours.

"Let's get some sleep," Johnny said to Danny as they entered the barracks. Hot and stuffy, and smelling of perspiration, the murmur of quiet conversations could be heard along with snoring. Some guys could always sleep. They found two bunks not far apart and plopped down.

Before dawn, Johnny woke to the sound of automatic weapons fire in the distance. He wondered who would be on the firing range at that time of night, then realized a firefight was taking place beyond the perimeter. Unable to get back to sleep, he wandered outside to have a smoke and get some fresh air. The night had cooled only slightly. He found a bench near a runway and sat for a while before lying down and trying to get more sleep.

Johnny woke before dawn and was chilled. Feeling refreshed to be a little cold, he walked back into the barracks and sat down on his cot.

"Where you been?" asked Danny.

"Out for a smoke and to get cooled. Feel like a cup of coffee?"

They found the mess hall nearly empty at five in the morning. A sergeant and a private entered and sat nearby looking at a duty list. They eyed Johnny and Danny having coffee.

"FNGs?" the sergeant asked.

Johnny didn't understand.

"Fucking new guys," he explained. "You two must be looking for something to do if you're up so early."

Johnny took the opportunity to get some information.

"Can you tell us something about Dong Tam and Binh Thuy? We have our orders but don't know how to get to either place."

The sergeant, older, lean and fit, took a deep puff on his cigarette before replying.

"Dong Tam is division headquarters for the Ninth Infantry way down in the Delta. Couldn't tell you where Binh Thuy is. Tell you what, grab some breakfast with this REMF, go and empty the shitters with him and we'll look at a map in the orderly room. If I were you, I wouldn't be in a big hurry to leave Cam Ranh."

The private glared at Johnny and Danny, then protested. "Why can't these two go and burn shit without supervision?"

"Go and show them how it's done and stop complaining before I decide to send you out to the boonies where the real shit happens."

When they arrived at the latrines, Johnny wished he hadn't eaten breakfast. Fifty-gallon drums had been cut with a torch to a height of two feet, filled with diesel fuel, then slid underneath the outhouse toilets. Two holes at the top were drilled across from one another so a stout metal bar could be placed through them. The drums were carried to a burning site where they were lit. Some containers didn't light easily and had to be stirred and ignited by dousing the surface with gasoline. The stench was horrendous. Danny gagged uncontrollably.

After the drum's contents were burned, the charred remains were dumped in a pile of dried feces. Johnny and Danny carried the empties back to the latrines and filled them with diesel through the holes in the toilet seats. Johnny's eyes stung from the thick smoke. His nostrils retained the stench of the burning waste.

"Let's get out of here," he said, "and see if we can't get a shower somewhere."

The private, still glaring at the newcomers, was no help. "What the fuck you think this is, assholes, a resort?"

Cam Ranh, a huge staging facility, was a resort for some of the field troops allowed on the beaches for an in-country R and R. If there was a place to get clean, the hostile private was not about to tell the new guys.

"Let's just go and find the sergeant," Danny suggested, "then get cleaned up. I'd really like to know where Binh Thuy is."

At the orderly room, the sergeant leaned back in his chair behind a metal desk and sipped on a coffee. Johnny noticed the combat infantry-man's badge, in camouflage, above his shirt pocket. In the hierarchy of the war zone, he didn't want to be confused with the REMFs he was now with. He'd earned his assignment in the rear.

"You 11Bs, infantry?" he asked.

"No," said Johnny, "we're medics."

"That explains it," the sergeant said, looking at Johnny. "You, son, will have to get all the way to the Mekong Delta to find Dong Tam, headquarters for the Ninth Infantry Division. Binh Thuy is also in the Delta, not far from Can Tho. Ever hitchhiked at home? In Vietnam it's easy catching rides on aircraft. You'll have no problem getting to Can Tho. There's an army airfield there. It was overrun not that long ago but is up and functioning again. The 29th Evac is only a few miles farther. Good luck to the both of you."

They thanked the sergeant and asked where they could find a shower. He directed them to a gravity-fed line attached to a metal tank mounted on a deuce and a half flatbed truck. The cold water refreshed them. They changed fatigues and set off to find the airfield on the sprawling base.

The tarmac stretched farther than the eyes could see and was lined with hangars and supply depots. Johnny saw two C-130 cargo planes being loaded and asked a supply sergeant where they were headed.

"These two are going north to Danang, but hang around for a while, there'll be something scheduled for Long Binh or Tan Son Nhut near Saigon. From there you should be able to catch a ride to the Can Tho Airfield, which puts you both close to your units. You might want to avoid staying overnight at the airfield. It was hit pretty bad a couple of weeks ago."

They found a shaded spot near the door of a supply depot and sat down on their duffel bags. The day was already hot, and even after their cold showers, perspiration oozed grime from the latrine detail. The concrete tarmac absorbed and reflected heat from the late-morning sun. Despite their exhaustion, they were too hot to sleep. They watched as another C-130 landed, and a crew began unloading pallets. Heading to Long Binh next, Johnny got the okay from the pilot to hop aboard. Within ten minutes the plane gained speed on the runway and was airborne.

The cargo bay, without windows, prevented a view of the terrain below. It was so noisy they couldn't talk. Two hours later they ambled off the ramp at the rear of the plane. It looked the same as where they had come from, lots of supply warehouses and tarmac.

Heeding the sergeant's advice, they decided to spend the night in Long Binh but needed to find a PX where they could get something to eat. An army jeep pulled over to give them a ride and dropped them in front of a post exchange.

"You should be able to find something to snack on in there," the driver said, "and some bottled water."

"Thanks," Johnny said.

"Where you two headed?" the driver asked. It was difficult to tell his age. His jungle fatigues were faded and dusty, his manner brusque but friendly. A scar on his exposed forearm suggested he'd been wounded.

"Dong Tam," Johnny spoke.

"Ninth infantry?"

Johnny nodded. "My friend is trying to get to the 29th Evac Hospital in Binh Thuy."

"No shit. I been there, too, recuperating. Motherfuckers wanted to send me back to the field. I told them to fuck that shit. They finally agreed to send me here where I might actually stay alive for the rest of my tour."

"How long you been in-country?" Danny asked.

"Nine months. You want to survive your tour, don't trust nobody. Charlie will be looking you right in the eye while he cuts your nuts off."

Inside the PX they found some crackers and canned fruit, bottled water and a package of cookies. Outside, they discussed where to spend the night. Miles of perimeter surrounded the largest American base in Vietnam. Finding a stuffy barracks to sleep for the night overcrowded with men didn't appeal to Johnny.

"Let's just sleep outside," he told Danny. "Should be able to make it to our units tomorrow." They walked towards the airfield, found a grassy area near a cluster of buildings and set their duffel bags down. It was beginning to get dark when they heard voices near one of the structures. A small group of men gathered around a makeshift barbecue made from a fifty-gallon drum cut in half and mounted on spindly metal legs. The men sipped on cans of beer and cooked hamburgers.

"That's making me very hungry," said Danny, munching on a dry cookie. Overhearing parts of the conversation, they realized it was a short-timer's party for one of the soldiers completing his tour.

"Here we are, our second day in-country and having to listen to that," Danny continued.

"That will be us someday," Johnny said. "We have to believe it will."

Awake before dawn, Johnny waited until first light to disturb his friend. This would be their last day together. They shared a can of peaches before walking towards the airfield, where crews were already busy loading cargo onto planes. All of the C-130s were headed to larger airstrips. A member of the ground crew pointed to a smaller plane that he thought was going to Can Tho. Johnny hurried over to check.

"Hop in," the pilot said. "We'll be in the air in five minutes."

Crates of ammunition filled the small cargo bay along with a pallet of C-rations and cartons of cigarettes. The plane felt heavy as it lumbered down the runway gaining speed for takeoff. When it lifted into the air, Johnny felt the plane tugging against gravity while struggling to ascend. Once airborne, the plane shook and shuddered worse than it had on the runway. The turbulence worsened when they flew through a heavy rainstorm. Looking forward from the cargo hold, Johnny could see the rain pelting the windows in the cockpit. The pilot, unconcerned, made radio contact with Can Tho Army Airfield. He joked about the shape of the runway after the VC sapper attack everybody seemed to know about. After landing, Johnny was glad to be on firm soil again.

The airfield was noticeably different from the bases they'd just come from. The largest structure, a small terminal building, had a control tower that incongruently stuck out of the main building and tilted slightly. The base appeared to have been built on a filled-in swamp. The runway, constructed from perforated steel matting, was cramped. Two damaged gunships, piles of rubble now from the sapper attack, were visible as Johnny and Danny walked towards the terminal. Undamaged Cobra gunships were beside the tarmac partially protected by walls of sandbags surrounding them.

This must be the real Vietnam, Johnny thought. The friends were exhausted, but the day was just getting started. Inside, they approached a soldier at a desk, the only piece of furniture.

"You trying to get to the 29th Evac?" he said, repeating Danny's question. He waved an arm in the direction of a road just beyond the airfield. "Walk out there and stick your thumb out, head that way, a truck will pick you up. The 29th's only a few miles from here. The road's safe during the day."

Danny hesitated. They would have to part now. It had been a comfort to travel with a friend this far. Both would be expected at their units, and it was best not to wander around Vietnam any longer than necessary.

"I better be going," is all Danny managed to say. "I have your father's address and will write him a quick note with my mailing address at the 29th. You take care in Dong Tam."

"I will," said Johnny. "Stay in touch."

Johnny felt depressed watching Danny's lone figure walking toward the road, where he disappeared into the distance. His third day in-country, and he was dirty, lonely and exhausted. The morning was warming and inside the terminal, if you could call it that, had nowhere to sit or get clean. He drank the last of his water and inquired how to get to Dong Tam from the same soldier that had given Danny directions.

"Dong Tam? There'll be something that'll get you there. See that kid over there?" He pointed to a soldier lying against his duffel bag. "He's looking to get to Dong Tam, too. If there's room, I'll try and get you both on the same flight."

Johnny walked toward the soldier, and the kid made eye contact. "I hear you're heading to Dong Tam," Johnny said.

"Ninth Infantry," the kid said.

"Me too," said Johnny. "Perhaps we can let each other know when a flight's available?"

"Sounds reasonable," the kid responded. "Delbert Kincaid," he said as he rose to shake hands. "Only been in-country two days. You infantry?"

"Medic," Johnny said. The kid looked even younger than Danny Holt but didn't seem the least bit perturbed about being in Vietnam. When he stood, Johnny saw he was only about five foot eight, and his jungle fatigues hung loosely because his slender frame didn't fill them. His blondish hair was cropped close to his head.

"Where you from?" the kid asked.

"Santa Cruz, California."

"I'm from Oakland," Kincaid responded. "Never been to Santa Cruz. Hear it's pretty nice. Your folks got money or something?"

"No, just me and my dad. Been on my own for a while."

"Just my mom and I in Oakland. Never knew my real dad. Ran off before I was born. My mom won't even tell me who he is."

The kid was starting to get on Johnny's nerves. Feeling gloomy after Danny's departure, Kincaid wanted to glom onto Johnny and exchange life stories.

"Wanted to join up at seventeen, but my mom wouldn't sign the papers. I told the recruiter to have them ready when I turned eighteen and didn't need no one's permission to join. Signed them on my eighteenth birthday. Hell, my whole neighborhood's a war zone, figure I'd join the army and have someone to fight alongside, not against me."

Johnny didn't know how to respond, so he didn't. He wasn't sure he wanted to travel with the kid, but said: "Delbert, I'm going to try and catch some sleep. Wake me if anything comes up, okay. I'll be right outside."

"You got it," Kincaid responded cheerfully.

Johnny laid his upper half down on his duffel bag in the partial shade of a small palm tree outside the terminal entrance. He took an undershirt and wiped his face, then placed it over his eyes to block out the light. Napping didn't come easily, but he was so tired he finally dozed. It only lasted a few minutes before Kincaid was shaking him awake. "Our ride to Dong Tam's arrived, better hurry."

A helicopter had touched down to drop a pilot off and would return to Dong Tam with some light cargo. There was plenty of room. A door gunner looked past the new guys as they nodded a greeting while boarding.

"Hang on," is all he said. When he noticed their new jungle fatigues, he added: "Welcome to the Nam. Charlie's expecting you." He let out a crazy laugh and looked back toward the ground as the chopper lifted off.

As they approached Dong Tam, Johnny could see the flat terrain surrounding the base. Built on the north side of the My Tho River, the waterway was so full it looked like it might overflow its banks. Excess silt from the river had been used to fill a square mile of rice paddy. The Ninth Infantry's base camp, built on top, made a statement to Charlie that their control of the VC-infested Mekong Delta would be challenged.

The helicopter touched down on the airfield, and Johnny inquired where to report. "Headquarters is in that direction," a crew member gestured. "Just keep walking until you see the Ninth's insignia on one of the buildings." Kincaid tagged along.

Before arriving, a jeep stopped and gave them a lift, dropping the two in front of a nondescript building. Inside, a clerk looked them over. Like the sergeant in Cam Ranh Bay, he wore the combat infantryman's badge in black above his shirt pocket.

"We're here to report to the Ninth Infantry," Johnny said. "Are we in the right place?"

"Oh, you're in the right place," he said. "Eleven bravos?"

"I am," Kincaid said. "My partner here is a medic."

"No shit," said the clerk. "I have good news and bad," he said, looking at Johnny. "Bravo company has a witch doctor who just might rotate home without going back in a box or on a medevac. Third platoon's clamoring for a replacement before their Doc's tour is up. The bad news is that you'll be replacing Doc Bernie, a fucking legend around here. The platoon commander wants the new medic to spend a couple of weeks with him to have some of his super qualities rub off on you." The clerk eyed Johnny, pausing. "If that's possible." He threw a sheaf of papers he held onto his desk. "Third platoon's a little spooked about him leaving." The clerk turned his gaze to Kincaid. "You might as well tag along. Everybody is shorthanded."

They followed the clerk's directions to the company's orderly room. As they approached, they heard shouting from inside.

"God damn it, Jim, what am I supposed to write that boy's mother, that he went for a stroll in the jungle while on a combat patrol?"

"Sniper, Sir, one shot. Doc Bernie got to him right away, but it was a gunshot to the head. He died instantly. Doc found the letter near the body. It's a 'Dear John' from his girl."

"Any chance it was self-inflicted?"

"No, Sir."

"God damn it, Jim, you're doing a fine job out there under difficult circumstances, but we can't have your platoon members wandering off in the jungle by themselves."

"We were on a break, Captain. Nobody saw Jameson amble off. The guys say he was distraught about his girl breaking it off with him."

"Why can't we get these kids to realize that they'll have their whole lives to meet women, marry them, fuck them, or whatever order it occurs these days, but we have to get them through their tours first."

"The whole platoon feels bad, Sir. He was a likable kid."

"They're all likable kids, nearly all. Doing a hell of a job out there. Let's make sure we get as many of them home as we can."

"Yes, Sir."

"Your platoon is back out on night ambush tomorrow at 1600 hours."

"Any word on the new medic, Sir?"

"No, Lieutenant, I'll check with headquarters again."

As the conversation ended, Johnny entered the orderly room.

"John Ornowoski, reporting for duty, Sir." He saluted the young-looking captain who'd been questioning one of his platoon commanders, a lieutenant who stood casually and looked at the replacements.

"Delbert Kincaid, Sir, also reporting for duty."

"Welcome to Bravo Company," the captain said. "One of you the new medic?"

"Yes, Sir," said Johnny.

"You have mighty big shoes to fill, son. Lieutenant Sanders, you want to get them squared away?"

"Yes, Sir."

CHAPTER TEN

Outside of the orderly room, Lieutenant Sanders looked at the new arrivals and consciously suppressed any visible signs of concern. Still hurting from the loss of Jameson, his responsibilities prevented him from showing it. The death of the well-liked soldier had the platoon demoralized. Sanders wanted to bring every member of the unit home--an impossibility. *Kincaid looks sixteen,* he thought, *too young to be a grunt in Vietnam. My platoon is shorthanded, and the army sends boys to the war.*

"Let's find Doc Bernie and get you situated," the lieutenant said to Johnny. He had pestered the captain to the point of annoyance about getting a replacement before the current medic rotated home. Doc Bernie was exceptional, and Sanders wanted his replacement to spend at least two weeks with him before he left.

Sanders' interests were in engineering, not medicine, but growing up the son of a medical doctor gave him a keen understanding of Doc Bernie's value to the platoon. The lieutenant had left his mechanical engineering program at the University of Washington because the country was at war. He would not make a career in the army and planned to return to academia after his three-year enlistment. His priority remained getting as many of the men under his command through their tours as possible. To a man, the platoon was spooked about Doc Bernie's impending departure and anxious about his replacement.

Bernie had impressed Sanders on his first patrol as the unit's commander. They'd come under fire from a tree line while wading through a rice paddy. Before everyone found cover behind the mud dikes surrounding the field, a soldier took a round ripping his abdomen open, his intestines spilling into the filthy water as he fell. Doc Bernie reached the young man and pulled him onto the top of a mud bank. Positioning his body between the casualty and the direction of fire, the medic gathered the man's entrails while dousing them with a saline solution, placing them back in the soldier's exposed cavity. While treating the wound, Bernie assured him. "I've got you now. The worst is over. All you have to do is hang on for a while longer. The medevac will have you at the hospital in no time."

Bernie finished by improvising dressings and a sling to hold the intestines in place. The dust-off arrived and flew the grunt to an evac hospital fifteen minutes away. Sanders inquired about the casualty's status when they returned to Dong Tam. He'd been operated on within minutes of arriving at the 29th Evac and was expected to recover.

Afterwards, Doc Bernie was surprised that the platoon thought he'd done anything special. What happened a month later was even more remarkable.

A piece of shrapnel sliced the neck of a rifleman named Melvin Rollins, severing his carotid artery. With the rapid loss of blood, and flow to the brain restricted, death was imminent. No amount of pressure to the wound would save Rollins. Quick thinking and a brilliant improvisation by Doc Bernie did.

The surgeon at the evac hospital had a hard time believing what he saw. With the carotid artery severed, blood flow to the brain had been maintained by the field medic inserting a hollow tube from a syringe into both ends of the vessel. Suture thread had been used to secure it. A miracle of factors saved Melvin Rollins.

The dust-off arrived quickly. Only nine minutes from the hospital, Doc Bernie's improvisation held long enough to get the young man into surgery. The medic's instinctive feel for medicine seemed to heal everything his hands touched.

A conscious and recovering Melvin Rollins told the surgeon about Doc Bernie. The doctor wanted to meet the medic who had performed so brilliantly. The surgeon phoned the company commander in Dong Tam who gave his contact information to Sanders.

"I just want the young man's commanders to know how exceptional this medic is. I'm just a drafted surgeon who has no idea what medals are appropriate for such a feat on the battlefield. I'm not sure I could have accomplished what this young man did to save Melvin Rollins."

"What exactly did you find?" asked Sanders.

"Your medic used a tube from a small syringe to join the ends of a severed carotid artery. It held until we got Melvin Rollins into surgery. The fact he survived is a fucking miracle."

Sanders wrote to his father about the incident. The doctor wouldn't have believed the events if anyone else had related them. In thirty years of practicing medicine, Sanders' father never heard of anything similar.

The lieutenant stopped in front of a barracks, a two-story wooden structure. Sandbags ringed the building, and the windows were screened. Dong Tam came under frequent rocket and mortar attacks, and glass was not installed, becoming deadly projectiles when shattered.

"Let's see if Doc Bernie's inside. The platoon's just back from a ten-day patrol and is standing down for a day." Sanders looked at Johnny. "Your job is to learn as much as possible before he rotates home."

Johnny nodded and followed the lieutenant into the barracks. They found Bernie in his hooch, his personal area segmented and defined by a metal locker on one side and a small portable closet on the other. A colorful Vietnamese blanket covered the bed in place of the drab army-green blankets issued. A poster of *Mad Magazine's* Alfred E. Neuman was taped to the side of the locker with the caption: *What, me worry?* Bernie, busy writing a letter, lay diagonally on his cot.

"Doc, your replacement has arrived," Sanders said, introducing Johnny.

"Welcome to third platoon," Bernie said amiably.

"We're beyond the perimeter tomorrow on night ambush," Sanders added. "Can you see that John has everything he needs to go with us?"

"No problem, Sir," he said. "When did you arrive in-country?" he asked Johnny.

"Three days ago," he said.

"You're probably exhausted. I'll show you where to get cleaned up. Then, get some sleep. We'll get you fixed up first thing in the morning, get your own aid bag and go over some things."

Delbert Kinkaid followed the lieutenant out of the barracks. After getting the new medic situated, Sanders turned his attention to the kid.

"How old are you, son?"

"Eighteen, Sir. Am I going on patrol?"

"You are a member of third platoon now," Sanders said, "and everybody needs to pull their weight. No exceptions." It pained Sanders, but it was best for everyone, including Kincaid, not to coddle the new guys.

"Good," said Kincaid.

"You want to go on patrol?"

"Just want to hold up my end, Sir."

"You'll be given every opportunity to do so," said Sanders.

"Way I figure, Sir, my neighborhood's a war zone. Might as well do my fighting in Vietnam."

"I expect you'll find Ninth Infantry's war zone considerably different," offered the lieutenant. "I'm putting you in Sergeant Morales' squad. Listen to what he tells you and you'll be fine."

"Yes, Sir."

⋆ ⋆ ⋆

Johnny spent the morning of his fourth day in-country with Doc Bernie. They put together his M-3 aid bag in preparation for the night ambush scheduled to begin at 1600 hours. The canvas bag had three compartments and weighed thirty pounds when stocked. Contents included several sizes of field dressings, elastic bandages, tourniquet kits, two bottles of IV fluids, morphine, antibacterial and fungal creams and everything from band aids to water purification tablets.

"Memorize what's in your aid bag and where to find what you need," Doc Bernie instructed. "Nothing worse than fumbling around in the dark trying to find something. You'll get the hang of it," he encouraged. "Stick with me and I'll guide you through your first patrols."

Relieved at Doc Bernie's helpful manner, Johnny absorbed everything the medic told him. "I think you're ready," Bernie observed, making a last check of Johnny's medical supplies. "Try and get some rest, and I'll see you when we assemble at the wire this afternoon."

The platoon gathered at 1600 hours and prepared to go beyond the perimeter. Besides intercepting enemy activity in the vicinity of Dong Tam, the platoon looked to disrupt mortar and rocket teams the Viet Cong sent out during the night. The 82mm version, common and lightweight, operated within a 3,000-meter range. The mortar crews packed the 123-pound weapon disassembled and could set up quickly. Each round weighed seven and a half pounds. Four men packing eighty pounds each would have twenty-five rounds to fire at Dong Tam.

Delbert Kincaid nodded at Johnny and said hello. The kid carried an M-16 and had several twenty-round magazines in a bandolier across his chest. Grenades dangled from his web gear. A belt of M-60 cartridges added to his personal arsenal. Everybody packed extra ammunition for the platoon's machine guns. The mood, serious and tense, turned even more somber as they filed through one of the gates on Dong Tam's perimeter.

Johnny fell in behind Doc Bernie near the rear of the platoon. "Just stick with me," Bernie instructed, "but not too close. It'll get pitch dark out there tonight with the cloud cover. Stay alert and you'll be fine."

They utilized the remaining daylight to get close to their position, then went a little farther. As darkness engulfed the platoon, Johnny couldn't see Doc Bernie in front of him. He gauged his distance by the sound of Bernie moving through the jungle. A drizzle began to fall, and the sound of rain dropping on the lush vegetation drowned out any other noise.

"We won't go much farther," Doc Bernie whispered in Johnny's ear, before moving to distance himself again. The experienced medic had his poncho on, so Johnny did the same. He was already wet and uncomfortable, but the adrenaline coursing through his system had him alert. His M-16, which Bernie advised he carry in place of a forty-five-caliber pistol, felt awkward beneath his poncho.

In position an hour after dark, Johnny listened to the sounds of the jungle. Cricket and frog-like chirping and the lone calls of birds rhythmically reverberated through the night. Bernie had warned him. "When it goes totally quiet, it's time to worry. Otherwise, stay alert and listen for anything out of the ordinary. The LT expects sound and light discipline to be strictly adhered to."

Wet and uncomfortable, Johnny focused on the darkness around him. Alternating stretches of boredom interrupted by moments of realization that he was in Vietnam sent waves of anxiety through his body. His stomach tightened at 0100 hours when a firefight erupted east of their position. Too far for third platoon to respond, Johnny listened and pulled his poncho tighter around him as a drizzle returned. Wet, and suddenly cold, he shivered quietly.

An hour later, distant sounds of explosions hitting Dong Tam brought him out of a lull in his concentration. The bombardment originated in another sector far from their position. Nobody said a word or made a sound as they listened. Before dawn, the platoon froze as the jungle quieted slightly. Morales' squad had heard a rustling as an unseen creature moved through the dense flora. Another hour passed, and a faint light gave them the beginnings of visibility. Johnny's first combat patrol passed without incident. The platoon returned to Dong Tam.

Relieved to be back inside the wire, Johnny tried to sleep. He dozed for a couple of hours and woke in a sweat. The barracks were hot. He'd need a fan for sleeping in the day. Johnny peeked into Doc Bernie's hooch to see if he was awake. Not yet. Johnny had questions about their extended patrols. He had much to learn before Bernie rotated home.

The new medic returned to his hooch and heard footsteps approaching through the barracks. "Hey, Doc," a familiar voice spoke, "can you give me something for this?" Delbert Kincaid stood at the entrance to his hooch and waved a hand at him. He became Doc Ornowoski's first patient.

Kincaid had a thorn embedded in his hand which had already become infected. Johnny gave the kid a small injection of local anesthesia and dug out the broken tip in Kincaid's palm while draining the pus forming around it. He smeared an antibacterial ointment over the tiny incision before bandaging the hand.

"That will fix it," Johnny said. "Let me have another look when we get back from tonight's patrol. You get any sleep?" he asked Kincaid.

"Couple of hours. Feel like some lunch? Sergeant Morales said to enjoy the food in Dong Tam as it's C-rats only once we head out to the boonies."

Kincaid referred to the lightweight canned food field troops packed on longer patrols. "Said I can't afford to lose any weight and still carry the gear we need. He's a really good guy. Showed me lots of stuff already."

Johnny felt a pang of affection for the kid. "Sure, let's go get some lunch. Then I want to get a fan from the PX so I can sleep better in the day."

The mess hall was not crowded. Only two members of the platoon were eating. Johnny nodded in their direction and sat down a few seats away at the same table. He didn't want to appear unfriendly, but didn't want to intrude if the two preferred to be alone. He didn't have to worry.

"How did it go last night? Rafe Johnson," one of the men introduced himself as he extended his hand. "This is Calroy," he said, pointing at the other man at the table. Both men were Black, and judging by their accents, from the South.

"I'm the shortest man in the platoon right now," Calroy added. "Makes it kinda hard to see me."

"I think Charlie be seein' your sorry ass jus' fine, brother, so don't be gettin' cocky. He still like to take you out."

Rafe Johnson turned his attention back to Johnny. "My friend keeps remindin' us all how short he is. Jus' in case we forget."

Johnny looked at his tray of food, something resembling meatloaf with canned potatoes and peas covered with an artificial-tasting gravy.

"How many days of night ambush does the platoon normally pull?" asked Johnny.

Rafe Johnson shrugged. "Whatever the man be decidin'. We just the grunts in this war, not the decision makers. I expect we be back in the boonies for a week or two before long."

"I ain't goin' nowhere but home," offered Calroy, *man* or no *man*."

"My friend, here, has a one-track mind," Johnson retorted. "He thinks somebody's gonna forget how short he is and not send him home on time. Me, I got many months to go. Charlie be here forever, long after we all gone. Sick of that motherfucker, for sure, but he ain't goin' nowhere."

Rafe Johnson stood up to go. "A year's a long time in this place. Everybody's jus' tryin' to get home. You the new Doc, now, with big shoes to fill. Pay attention to Doc Bernie and learn somethin' while he still here."

CHAPTER ELEVEN

Third platoon assembled at 1600 hours to go on another night ambush. Mortar attacks on Dong Tam the previous night hit a supply depot, did some damage to the base's runway, and wounded three soldiers when a round landed in their barracks.

Johnny, already tired after only sleeping two hours that morning, had found a fan at the PX. Nervous energy prevented sleep after lunch. Delbert Kincaid had hung around Johnny's hooch after they ate in the mess hall. The kid looked fine as they prepared to go beyond the wire.

Lieutenant Sanders set the platoon in a different direction from the previous evening, not wanting to be predictable. Every night was a battle of wits with Charlie to intercept his mortar teams. The Viet Cong did the same in avoiding detection.

Johnny noticed the mosquitoes were thicker, more persistent, and they distracted him. Their buzzing impeded his hearing. The bug juice doused on his exposed skin didn't repel all of the blood-sucking insects. They took their fill while Johnny alternated between bouts of drowsiness and occasional surges of adrenaline when the platoon sensed any new sound emanating from the jungle.

Brief showers gave temporary relief from the mosquitoes but added the damp discomfort of being wet where raindrops found pathways to Johnny's fatigues. *How is it too hot to sleep during the day yet I'm cold at night,* he wondered? Johnny struggled to maintain his concentration and stay alert as his second night in the jungle passed without incident. More fatigued, and with insect bites accumulating, Johnny trudged back to Dong Tam with the platoon.

At his hooch, Delbert Kincaid had Johnny rebandage his incision.

Johnny found a leech engorged with blood when he took his boots off. He squirted mosquito repellant on it and crushed it when it dropped off his leg.

"I guess we're going back out tonight," Kincaid stated. "Maybe we'll finally run into Charlie. Sergeant Morales says we're due for some contact. He says he can *feel* Charlie's presence before he sees him."

Johnny finished with the new dressing. "It looks a lot better," he said. "I've got to get some sleep," Johnny said. "I'll come by about two this afternoon and we can grab something to eat before tonight's patrol."

"Sounds good to me," Kincaid said.

Johnny slept till noon and woke in a sweat as he had the previous day. So focused on being the platoon's new medic, he had not written to CC or his father. In Vietnam just six days, his former world already took on a dreamlike quality that receded into a realm of fantasy. CC resided there, remote and untouchable from anything his current reality could reach.

He began a letter to CC, then put it down. What on earth could he say? Now it was Johnny who had difficulty writing. He penned a quick note to his father giving him his mailing address and mentioning his location in the Mekong Delta. Rumors in the platoon spoke of a two-week patrol soon. He tried again to write to his girl.

> *Dearest CC,*
>
> *I have arrived in Vietnam and am with my unit at a base named Dong Tam in the Mekong Delta. I'm assigned as a line medic with third platoon and have already been on what is called a night ambush, spending the night trying to intercept the Viet Cong's mortar teams. So far I have not seen the enemy. I think about you while I'm out there. I will write more when I can. Please write when you get this and let me know how you are. I love you and miss our life together.*
>
> *Johnny*

Several platoon members were in the mess hall when Johnny and Delbert Kincaid arrived. Not as friendly as Doc Bernie and Rafe Johnson, most of the men remained aloof. Johnny supposed that would be the case until he and the kid had proven themselves. The only way to do that in an infantry platoon is in combat.

The two new guys sat down a few chairs from where the others were eating, close enough to overhear an ongoing conversation.

"You know it's better not to try and keep a girlfriend back home while you're over here. Keeps your mind from being focused on surviving the Nam. Jamie got wasted because he was off thinkin' about his girl on a combat patrol."

"You mean the unfaithful bitch that *was* his girlfriend?"

"What do you think I'm sayin', motherfucker?"

"Not every girl is going to do that."

"No? You got a girlfriend? Name one member of third platoon who still has a girl back home." The grunt stared at a big red-haired guy with two day's growth of stubble.

"I didn't have a girlfriend before I left for the Nam."

"Big surprise there, Red, such a handsome fucker like you, and with such a big dick to go along with that stunning personality you got."

"Very funny. All I'm sayin' is not every girl is gonna to do that," the red-haired grunt countered.

"And I'm sayin' you gotta stay focused to survive the Nam. Jamie was a good guy, but he let his guard down. Girlfriends back home are a distraction. Besides, everybody in this platoon is too ugly to keep a girl for very long."

"Amen to that," chimed in a third voice.

Johnny stared at his plate, uncomfortable with the conversation. He'd been hungry when he sat down, but now his stomach tightened. He hadn't seen shit yet, and yes, he had a girlfriend at home he wanted to keep. He looked across the table at Kincaid devouring a hot dog, or something resembling one.

Between mouthfuls the kid looked up and asked: "You got a girlfriend, Doc?" Nothing seemed to faze the kid, not judging by his appetite. He was poking around in Johnny's life again. The platoon was discussing Jameson's death on their last operation. Johnny sensed the dead man had been well-liked by his platoon members. Kincaid remained unperturbed by the conversation.

"I don't, you know, have a girl," Kincaid continued, not waiting for Johnny to answer. "Probably best to concentrate on the Nam now that I'm here."

Johnny suppressed a laugh. The kid was so transparent, annoying and likable at the same time. "It's probably best," Johnny told him.

The skies were grey and threatening rain when the platoon gathered for their third night ambush in a row. Sergeant Morales' squad set out in the lead. The red-haired grunt Johnny observed participating in the conversation in the mess hall walked point. So far he'd ignored Johnny and Kincaid, but the new medic learned his nickname, Red Robin. Large and muscular, the platoon seemed to have confidence in his abilities.

Morales usually walked point when his squad took the lead, but he wanted to observe Kincaid closely. Morales wasn't sure what to make of him. Earlier in the day he'd found him in his hooch inserting and removing magazines into his M-16. They were empty, but Kincaid had several lined up on his cot for practice.

"Just practicing up for when the shit hits the fan," the kid had told him. So far, Kincaid had done everything the sergeant had asked of him and appeared eager to fit well into the platoon. But until the kid experienced his first firefight with real bullets whizzing past his ears, Morales would keep a close eye on him.

It was pitch black as the platoon moved through the jungle on the way to their ambush position. The clouds and thick flora obscured any light from the moon. A light rain fell as they continued forward. Water dropped out of the sky with greater intensity until the sound of it hitting the leaves in the jungle was all that could be heard.

Kincaid tugged at Morales ahead of him. Annoyed at the distraction, the sergeant listened to what the kid whispered. Morales worried about Red Robin on point getting separated from the platoon, and Kincaid was breaking his concentration. Concerned the squad was bunching up in the dark, he wanted to make sure they kept proper distance. He wished he'd walked point like he normally did.

Moments later, Morales thought he heard a twig snap where none of the platoon members should be. Not sure because of the sound of the steady drizzle, a muzzle flashed to his right, and the Viet Cong opened fire. The squad dropped to the ground and responded with M-16s and an M-60. Lieutenant Sanders brought the rest of the men forward and spread them out while the entire platoon sent hundreds of rounds toward the enemy. Third platoon's red tracers were visible in the dark while the Viet Cong's green ones answered back. Charlie was not retreating.

Johnny instinctively fell to the ground when he heard the first shots. He and Doc Bernie were just a few men behind the lieutenant. The rest of the platoon moved forward as they fired their weapons and maneuvered into a better position. Johnny heard the rapid-fire of the M-60 machine guns firing rounds at the enemy. Doc Bernie tugged on Johnny's sleeve and told him to follow. Bernie moved quickly in the direction of the initial shots.

A soldier Johnny only knew as Moon had taken a gunshot wound to his shoulder. Doc Bernie motioned for Johnny to help him move the casualty behind a log they'd stumbled over on the way. A burst of rounds from an AK-47 sent Doc Bernie to the ground.

"Shit, I'm hit," Bernie shouted. Johnny got Moon behind the log and was about to retrieve Bernie when the medic dragged himself up and over the fallen tree. Johnny went to treat Bernie, but he waved him off.

"I'm hit in the leg. I can look after it. See to Moon and the platoon will let you know if there are other casualties."

Moon gripped his shoulder with his other arm and writhed on the ground. "You hit anywhere else?" Johnny asked.

"Just my shoulder," Moon replied. "Hurts like a son of a bitch."

"I'll get you something for that, but first I've got to get the bleeding stopped." Johnny's hands were shaking, but he remembered his training. He ripped Moon's fatigue shirt open and felt for his wound, finding only the point of entry. Moon was breathing quickly but without difficulty. The bullet had missed puncturing the lung cavity. Johnny took a pressure bandage and pressed it against the shoulder. Instead of using the cloth straps attached to the dressing's corners, he used an elastic wrap to secure it and taped it so it would hold.

"You're doing fine," he heard Bernie say. The other medic had moved closer and gave him encouragement. Flares illuminated the sky enough to see that Bernie had cut his pant leg above his wound and applied his own pressure bandage.

"Doc, I'm going to have to give myself a shot of morphine for the pain," Bernie said. "I'm not going to be much good to you after that. Make sure Moon gets one as well. Someone else is hit and calling for a medic. The LT will get a medevac in as soon as he can. It's your platoon now. Good luck."

Johnny nodded and took a morphine syrette out of his aid bag and injected half of it into Moon's good arm. He pinned and taped it to the elastic bandage so the medics at the field hospital would know how much of the narcotic had been administered. Johnny's hands were not shaking nearly as bad as he covered the two casualties with their field ponchos.

The firefight ended as abruptly as it had begun, and Charlie disappeared into the jungle. Third platoon had one other casualty. A rifleman called Toad had a minor shrapnel wound in his calf from a grenade that exploded near him during the firefight.

"Let me have a look," Johnny said. "You hit anywhere else?"

Toad smiled and shook his head. "Not quite the million-dollar wound that would get me back home, Doc, but it ought to get me out of the boonies for a bit, wouldn't you say?"

Johnny nodded while he bandaged the wound. "Not so serious," Johnny confirmed.

"Any other casualties?" Toad asked.

"Doc Bernie took a gunshot wound to his thigh and Moon was hit in the shoulder. That's why it took so long to get to you. Need anything for the pain?"

"Naw, it don't hurt that bad. That morphine shit just makes guys goofy. Don't need none of that."

"Let's get you over to where Doc Bernie and Moon are," Johnny said. "Make you a little more comfortable."

The firefight ended, Lieutenant Sanders positioned the platoon and checked on the casualties.

"Anything serious?" he asked Bernie. His Doc smiled at him, the morphine having taken effect.

"Three casualties, Sir," Johnny interjected. "Doc Bernie treated himself and took some morphine. Moon's got a shoulder wound. Toad's not serious."

Sanders nodded.

"Any word on a medevac?" Johnny asked.

"No dust-off's available unless the visibility improves," Sanders said. "They'll risk it if it's life and death. Otherwise, we wait on the weather."

Johnny nodded and checked on his casualties. Their bleeding under control, he made sure they weren't chilled and going into shock from loss of blood or pain. He didn't think any IVs were needed.

"Been in the Nam seven months now," Toad stated. "Sure would be nice to get the fuck out of here."

"You know it will pass, Doc," Bernie said to Johnny. "You will get short looking after these motherfuckers." He smiled, a little high from the morphine but reasonably coherent.

"I thought I was gonna make it out without getting hit. Two weeks is all I had left. Don't know what I'm gonna do, but it won't be the army. Looking forward to that, but you know I'll miss these motherfuckers. Ain't that right, Toad."

"See, what I tell ya, that shit even makes the Doc a little goofy. Get the hell out of here is what I say. Can't see how I'd ever miss the Nam. Certainly not these motherfuckers in third platoon."

By dawn a landing zone was cleared for the medevac. Most of the men had said goodbye to Doc Bernie. His wound wasn't serious, but he wouldn't recover before his twelve-month tour was up. They would not see him before he rotated home.

The firefight had left everybody exhausted and somber as they trudged back to Dong Tam. It would be just like Charlie to hit them again. A couple of gunships were in the air providing protection and looking for the Viet Cong unit that had ambushed the platoon.

Inside the wire, Lieutenant Sanders approached Sergeant Morales. "How did our boy soldier do last night?"

"I was going to talk to you about that, Sir. He did good. Actually, more than good. During the firefight he kept his wits and returned fire. He'll be fine. What I was going to talk to you about happened just before the firefight."

"How so, Sergeant?"

"Well, right before Charlie opened up on us the kid tugged at me and whispered in my ear. Told me the VC were there and pointed in their direction before they'd fired a shot. Nobody else had spotted them."

"A veritable jungle boy."

"That's right, Lieutenant. I think you just gave him his nickname."

CHAPTER TWELVE

Nearing the end of his tour, Sergeant Morales had a decision to make. He wanted a career in the army but wasn't sure he would re-enlist. With experienced NCOs in demand, Morales knew that in a military future he'd be back in the Nam as a platoon sergeant. From his perspective, the war continued unabated and surviving multiple tours would be risky. No matter how many Viet Cong they killed, the enemy resurfaced to fight again.

He didn't want to leave the army. It gave him respect and job security, both difficult to duplicate in civilian life. Morales could negotiate a change in his MOS as a condition of his reenlistment, but doing what? Reading and writing didn't come easily, making training in technical fields difficult. Besides, he liked the infantry. The sergeant had the respect of people who depended on him, like the LT, an educated White guy who appreciated his abilities.

Even the platoon's nickname for Morales implied respect—Steady Eddie. He liked most of the guys in the platoon. Black guys like Calroy and Rafe Johnson were easy to get along with and held up their end in the boonies. Poor White boys like Toad and Red Robin, as uneducated as himself, were no problem. They didn't demand much because they didn't expect much. They were certainly tough enough for the Nam.

The new guy, Kincaid, would be accepted by the platoon now, having done well in his first firefight. The kid was so small nothing fit him properly. Even his helmet was too big for his head, but he packed his gear and ammo without complaint. The entire platoon, aware that Kincaid had spotted the VC before anyone else, was calling him Jungle Boy.

The replacement medic, Ornowoski, had done good, too. Morales, like all of the guys, was sorry to see Doc Bernie go. Too bad he was wounded with only two weeks left in the Nam. He would add a purple heart to his silver and bronze stars. Bernie had assured Morales that Ornowoski would be fine, and that was enough for him.

Johnny was exhausted when third platoon walked inside the perimeter after the night ambush. Relieved to have experienced his first contact with the VC, he'd reacted instinctively when they came under fire. His hands shook while treating Moon, but he hadn't panicked. He'd functioned during the firefight. The guys were already accepting him, calling him Doc Woski. Bernie had told Johnny to trust the platoon. As the medic, they would look after him. At his hooch, he took off his wet boots and jungle fatigues and flopped onto his bunk too exhausted to clean up before sleeping.

Jungle Boy came by his hooch in the afternoon with news. "Two new guys in the platoon," he said, "and we won't be going back out on night ambush."

Johnny already knew that. A grunt called King Tut had stopped by his hooch with a buddy to have him look at an infected lesion on his arm, the festering from the bite of an insect or leech having taken a chunk out of him in the jungle. With Doc Bernie gone, Johnny had the entire platoon to look after.

"There are a thousand things in the swamps and jungle causing rashes, cuts, foot rot and infections," his predecessor told him. "There are hundreds of insects biting and stinging, and leeches in every pool of water." Bernie showed Johnny his array of antibacterial and fungal creams. "A lot of it is trying to keep feet dry and bandages clean, hard to do in the boonies. Be sure and follow up when we're in base camp."

King Tut had an easy manner, especially with his friend, whom he called RC. Johnny assumed the nicknames were derivative of their names printed above the pockets on their fatigues—TUTTLEY and CUNNINGHAM.

Johnny rebandaged King Tut's festering sore after draining the pus out of it. "That should do for now," Johnny told him.

Satisfied, Tut stood to leave. "Thanks, Doc. The platoon's part of a company-sized sweep tomorrow. Pack lots of supplies and ammo."

RC nodded. "Stick with our squad when you can. We look after third platoon's medics," he assured Johnny.

The new Doc double-checked the contents of his aid bag. "Stay organized," Bernie had advised. "There will always be something to look after with these guys." Everything Doc Bernie told him proved valuable. No wonder the platoon liked him. It wasn't just his prowess as a medic. He was just a good guy to be around.

His hooch empty after his visitors, Johnny laid on his cot. Thankfully, there wasn't a night ambush to prepare for. He dozed and woke to a blues riff on a guitar coming from somewhere near one end of the barracks. Johnny listened, impressed by the quality of the playing. He began to make out the lyrics and recognized the song, Robert Johnson's "I'm a Steady Rollin' Man."

Johnny rose and walked towards the music. Calroy and another brother from a sister platoon listened to Rafe Johnson playing.

"That's it, that's it," exclaimed Calroy. "The man sure plays a fine blues," he said when Johnny arrived. Rafe nodded while he continued to play.

"Robert Johnson's 'I'm a Steady Rollin' Man.'" Johnny said quietly.

Rafe Johnson looked up and stared at Johnny. "How you be knowin' that song, Doc? White boy from where?"

"California," Johnny said, "but don't stop playing. I didn't mean to interrupt."

"Just foolin' around, Doc, keepin' my fingers nimble while in the Nam." Rafe Johnson continued looking at Johnny and waited for an answer to his question.

"A friend of mine plays lead guitar in a local band at home. He says Robert Johnson's the best bluesman ever. He has some of his recordings, and his band does a rendition of 'Me and the Devil Blues.'"

"Surprise the hell out o' me, Doc, knowin' that stuff. I'm one of Robert Johnson's grandsons," Rafe said.

Now it was Johnny's turn to be surprised. "My friend won't believe it when I tell him Robert Johnson's grandson is in my platoon."

"It's true," Rafe stated. "Never knew him, of course, because he died so young, maybe twenty-seven or eight."

"How long you been playin' the blues?" Johnny asked.

"Been livin' the blues my whole life, playin' 'em for half of it."

"Play him a couple verses from 'Mekong Delta Blues,'" said Calroy. "Go ahead and sing it for the new Doc. Only thing I'm gonna miss about the Nam is this man playin'. Yes, sir, plays a fine, fine blues."

Johnson broke into a haunting blues riff for a few bars before beginning to sing.

> *Well I left the Mississippi Delta for the one in Vietnam*
> *My Mama she was cryin' and my Daddy he was sad*
> *The day I left my homeland for the fight in Vietnam*
> *My gal she was a looker and she told me she'd be true*
> *Till I got to the Mekong and feelin' mighty blue*
> *She dumped me for her Jody who ain't never gone to war*
> *Just beat a path to my girlfriend's open door*
> *So tell me mister, tell me, when I'm ever gonna lose*
> *Those Mekong Delta blues*

"Man has twenty verses to that song," said Calroy, "ain't that true, Rafe? Play for an hour and not repeat a verse."

Johnny, mesmerized by the song and the melding of Johnson's voice with the brilliance of the guitar work, forgot he was in the Nam for a moment.

"Can't believe what I'm hearing, man. They need to make you a clerk or something, protect those fingers," Johnny said.

"It's just nigger music to the man," said Johnson. "Be in the war till my tour is up or Charlie greases my ass, same as all you other grunts. Now you one of us, Doc, a grunt medic in the man's war."

Johnson set down his guitar and looked at the small group standing in his hooch. "I'm thirsty. Must be some beer someplace in this shithole. Go and fetch that crazy little fucker we're all callin' Jungle Boy and we'll go get us some drinks."

Johnny boarded a Huey at dawn as the company-sized sweep began. Three helicopters transported the twenty-three platoon members to a landing zone at the edge of a village. Flying over rice paddies and swampy terrain, the greens of the Delta landscape presented a profusion of growth in the wet and tropical climate.

Johnny took his cues from Red Robin as the Huey banked to the left, flew just above a tree line at the edge of a rice field, and landed. The rest of the platoon moved quickly toward the edge of the nearby village. Red Robin jumped from the helicopter and took cover at a banana grove. Johnny took a position to Red's right and waited. They'd taken no fire at the LZ and prepared to enter the hamlet.

A single row of thatched dwellings, built along a canal, looked picturesque in the early morning light. The rounded tops of rocks sunk into the ground formed a roughly graveled pathway in front of the houses. Crude planks were anchored to the shore and descended into the muddy canal. Three sampans with rounded bamboo coverings were moored along the waterfront.

Johnny followed Red Robin through the small banana grove, and they emerged into the village. Vietnamese were already gathering in small groups outside their dwellings, silent in their stoicism. Small children clutched the legs of adults, who held the smallest in their arms. Johnny sensed the underlying tension as the search of the village began. The platoon spread out and systematically entered each hut. Lieutenant Sanders walked briskly along the pathway carefully monitoring the two-man teams looking for caches of weapons and abnormal amounts of cooked rice, signs of VC activity.

Nguyen, the platoon's Vietnamese Tiger Scout, paced angrily waiting to interpret language and culture for Lieutenant Sanders. Defected from the Viet Cong, Nguyen's hatred for his former comrades was permanently etched in a scowl as he waited to pounce on any suspicious sign of his new enemy.

Johnny looked at the groups of Vietnamese in front of their huts. Their tattered clothes hung on lean frames bronzed by work in the rice fields. He watched Red Robin check a family for weapons before entering their dwelling. Rifle in hand, ready for a hostile encounter, he rummaged through the simple belongings inside. Finding nothing, he reemerged into the morning sun and glared at the assembled family for good measure.

"You can never tell by their expressions," he said to Johnny. "It's safer to assume they're all VC. Better chance of going home that way."

Johnny simply nodded. He felt like an intruder. He'd been instructed to treat any medical maladies the platoon discovered during the search. When the LT called for him, he found Nguyen interrogating an older man with an infected forearm.

"You VC, papasan?" he shouted at the man. Words were exchanged in Vietnamese, and the farmer looked at the lieutenant. "No VC, no VC," he pleaded.

Nguyen smirked. "This man VC. He say injure arm planting rice, no make war with VC." Nguyen looked at Lieutenant Sanders and said coldly, "This man lie."

The Vietnamese farmer began to shake. "Brave VC," the Tiger Scout mocked him. "Shoot motherfucker VC. No more VC," he laughed sarcastically. "*Fini* Vietnam," Nguyen continued, making a crude joke about equating the man's death with finishing a tour in the Nam.

"See what you can do for him, Doc," Sanders instructed. "That will be all, Nguyen," he ordered.

Johnny tried to maintain a neutral expression, but the incident disturbed him. Sanders moved closer as Johnny looked at the injured forearm.

"Some of these scouts have had family members tortured and executed by the VC. It's a tit for tat brutality we can't sort out. Nguyen came over after learning his sister was raped and killed by a unit of Viet Cong sappers before leaving on a dangerous mission. That's all I know," Sanders said.

"Sergeant Morales," Sanders continued, "have one of your squad stand guard while the Doc treats this man."

"Yes, Sir," Morales said. "Red, make sure the papasan behaves himself."

"Will do." The rifleman aimed his M-16 at the man to convey the order. Red motioned for Johnny to begin after pointing the weapon skyward and positioning himself at an angle with an unobscured vision of the injured farmer.

"It's okay, Red," Johnny said. "I don't think he's in any shape to do something dangerous."

"Sergeant Morales knows what he's doing, Doc. Get him fixed up and let's keep moving."

Johnny got the message. The Vietnamese farmer, still shaking from the encounter with Nguyen and Red Robin, looked past Johnny's shoulder without making eye contact. Dressed in a ragged tan shirt and trousers cut above the knees, he was barefoot. A wispy beard grew from his chin along with several days of sparse stubble on the rest of his face.

Johnny took a vial of lidocaine from his aid bag and injected the pain killer around the swollen area of the forearm. Making an incision with a scalpel, pus oozed out of the wound. Johnny probed for the source of the infection but found nothing. Dousing the area with peroxide, he sutured the incision and bandaged it after applying an antibacterial cream. There would be no follow-up.

"Nice job, Doc," Red commented. "We better get moving, stay with the platoon."

"Sure thing," Johnny said. "Thanks for watching him."

"No problem, Doc."

Johnny was learning about the Nam.

While searching their second village of the day, word came over the radio that a member of a sister platoon had tripped a booby trap nearby and was badly wounded. Rumblings went through third platoon's ranks.

"Ever see the gooks trip any of them?" Red Robin muttered. "See any young men around?" he continued. "All off with VC units. Hate this fucking place. Be easier to blow it to smithereens if you ask me."

Coming out of a hut, Nguyen was having another meltdown. He'd found a large pot of cooked rice. Knocking it over and spilling some of the contents, he'd emerged yelling at a woman.

"Cook for VC," he shouted. The woman spoke rapidly and nervously in Vietnamese. Nguyen translated. "Say family come later today." He smirked and kicked at the ground with disgust. "Much work in rice paddy now, no family come, only VC. This woman lie."

It was the lieutenant's call. Johnny sensed the LT didn't like the platoon's Tiger Scout, but that Nguyen was correct about the rice. Sanders ordered it confiscated and destroyed. Johnny watched as Red Robin and two platoon members rolled it toward the canal and flung the pot in. The rice would be ruined, but the villagers would be able to retrieve the large container. With no refrigeration, the rice would soon spoil. No way the family would eat it in a couple of days; taking it from poor farmers would only harden their hatred of the Americans. The VC would find more. The new medic was glad when the platoon left the village and dug in for the night near a banana grove a klick away.

Johnny attempted to sleep before pulling the 0100 guard during the night. He had his field poncho pulled over him to ward off the mosquitoes that were an incessant presence in the Nam, diminished only when it rained, or a strong wind blew. Jungle Boy slept next to him in the foxhole they shared. The platoon would continue the search for Charlie the next day.

The mortar barrage began shortly after Johnny assumed his night guard position. The platoon had established a perimeter with claymore mines and trip flares to protect against a direct assault. They would need Charlie's bad aim and their foxholes to protect them from the mortars. The VC adjusted their angles after a few rounds, what the experienced grunts referred to as "walking them in." Johnny curled against a temporary wall of sandbags stacked for pulling guard. Filled each night and emptied in the morning for carrying with them, he felt debris from the exploding mortars hitting the barrier. Johnny worried about a direct hit in the next barrage. The explosions were so much louder than he expected. Flares illuminated the air in case a ground attack followed.

"Doc," someone shouted. Johnny used the lull between mortars to reach the wounded man. McDougal kneeled in his foxhole with his face down, trying not to choke on his blood and teeth dislodged by a fragment that broke his jaw.

"Can you hear me?" Johnny shouted. McDougal nodded. "I need to have a look so we can treat your wound." The man nodded again, his coherence a good sign there wasn't a brain injury. When Johnny got him propped against the side of the foxhole, he leaned him forward to make sure he wouldn't choke on any dislodged teeth. When he tried to clear his mouth, McDougal vomited and started to choke. Johnny cleared his mouth again with his fingers. His missing teeth had already been expelled.

"This is going to hurt like hell, but I need to get the bleeding stopped."

The frag had ripped through his cheek, and the wound bled from his gums and face. "I need to insert some gauze in your mouth and apply some pressure. We'll get you a shot of morphine as soon as you're bandaged." Johnny worried McDougal would choke with his face wrapped, but he needed to get the bleeding stopped. He hoped he was doing the right thing but was improvising. He needed Sanders to get him a medevac.

The mortars ended when a gunship arrived, its tracers creating a red streak from the helicopter to the ground. "LT says the dust-off's on the way, fifteen minutes out." McDougal's foxhole mate relayed the information. Johnny stayed with the wounded man to ensure his airway remained open and kept him leaning forward slightly. He didn't know what else to do.

Relieved when he heard the rotors of the medevac chopping at the air, he had McDougal's foxhole buddy help him to the LZ. The dust-off medic got the casualty situated onboard and they lifted off.

Totally drained, Johnny returned to his foxhole and found Jungle Boy sipping on a cup of cocoa made from his C-rations pack. Morales had shown him how to ignite a small wad of C-4 explosive to quick-heat his drink.

"Want some?" Jungle Boy asked.

Johnny looked at him with dismay. "No," he muttered. In a damp hole somewhere in the Mekong Delta after treating another casualty, he finds Jungle Boy drinking cocoa. Johnny calculated the percentages in his head. After two weeks in-country, four wounded. Two were not serious, but at this rate the platoon would be totally depleted in three months. *What had he gotten himself into?*

"I'm going to try and get a couple hours sleep," he told Jungle Boy.

"You got it, Doc," the kid said before taking another slurp of cocoa.

CHAPTER THIRTEEN

By first light, the platoon readied to hump to the next village. Exhausted from pulling guard and the mortar attack, Johnny had only dozed fitfully after getting McDougal on a medevac.

The captain, already on the radio with Sanders, would be with second platoon for the day. Unhappy the company had sustained two casualties without any dead enemy, he wanted third platoon in the next village ASAP to continue with the sweep. Sanders balked at the route the captain expected them to take, a pathway as wide as a country lane with trees on both sides.

It's where I would set up an ambush, thought Sanders. He explained the situation to the captain.

"All right, Lieutenant, I trust your judgement, but battalion is on us to engage the enemy. We know he's out there, so let's find him."

"Roger that, Sir. I'll have my best men on point."

Sanders had already decided on sending two point men through the trees, one on each side. With thick jungle in places, Morales and Red Robin would have to move quickly to stay ahead of the platoon. To keep the pace slow, the lieutenant had Tut and RC out front on the path and peering into the trees as they moved ahead.

Two hundred meters in, Red Robin emerged from the trees holding his hand. "Sorry, Sir," he said, "a snake startled me and I whacked my hand with my machete trying to kill the sucker. Surprised the shit out of me. I need the Doc to bandage it."

Grunts commonly repeated a saying about 100 species of snakes in the Nam-- ninety-nine of them poisonous and the other capable of crushing a man to death. Doc Bernie had told Johnny there were thirty venomous snakes; the Vietnamese suffered thousands of deaths every year. Some were so poisonous that he cautioned against ever sucking the venom out with his mouth.

"Did he bite you?" Johnny asked.

"No fucking way." Sweating profusely from walking point, he looked at his hand. "Not bad enough to get me out of the field is it?"

"Probably not, but someone should take your place on point."

"Fucking Nam," he muttered.

Johnny saw Jungle Boy speaking with the lieutenant.

"I'd like to walk point, Sir."

"You just arrived in-country," Sanders told him.

"Just asking, Sir. I really want to do this."

"Why? It's dangerous."

"Not for me it ain't," he said brashly. Sanders stared at him. The kid continued to surprise him.

"I see real good, LT, and I'm small. I can move through the bush easier."

The kid made sense, thought Sanders. *He'd spotted the VC before anyone else in his first firefight. Calroy was too short to be asked to walk point. Like most of the platoon, Rafe Johnson hated it. He was fortunate to have someone who wanted to.*

"You've talked with Sergeant Morales about the types of booby traps, what to watch out for?"

"Yes, Sir."

"All right, let's get going. And Jungle Boy.

"Yes, Sir?"

"Be careful."

Jungle Boy quickly picked up the trail Red Robin had forged and moved forward. Another two hundred meters ahead, the path curved away from him to the left, a good spot for an ambush. As he got closer, the trees to his right thinned, and the sun shone on a small clearing. Jungle Boy glimpsed movement. He slipped his pack off and continued with his rifle and a bandolier of ammo across his chest. He dropped to the ground and crawled closer for a better look. A young woman sat on a log loading bullets into the rounded magazines used in the AK-47s the Viet Cong carried. The only occupant of a small VC camp, the rest of her unit must be nearby waiting for third platoon. Jungle Boy eased himself back to where he had first noticed the clearing. From there, he continued crawling toward the curve in the path. He spotted a lone VC soldier acting as a rear guard looking in his direction. Jungle Boy froze and angled for a clearer view. Detecting movement behind the guard, he'd gotten close enough to see what looked like a squad-sized unit set up in an ambush. He hoped he had not taken too much time scouting the VC camp and that Sergeant Morales had not gotten ahead of him on the other side of the path. Easing himself backwards again, he returned to retrieve his pack and retraced his route through the trees to where the platoon kept a slow pace on the trail. He emerged unobtrusively and motioned for the lieutenant.

"VC ambush set up and waiting along a curve in the path ahead, Sir."

"Are you certain?"

"I saw them, LT. They also have a small camp in a clearing deeper in the trees. Only one woman guarding it."

Sergeant Morales, sensing Jungle Boy was no longer opposite him on the other side of the trail, had also backtracked seeking clarification of the kid's position. He slipped out of the trees and saw Jungle Boy speaking with Sanders.

"What's up, Sir?"

"VC ambush set up on Jungle Boy's side at the curve. We'll go a little farther and pretend we're on a break. I'll get the coordinates and call for air support. Make sure the platoon doesn't give anything away."

"Yes, Sir." Morales and Jungle Boy rejoined the platoon as they moved forward to where the curve in the path became visible. Sanders motioned for a break and nonchalantly made sure the platoon got the word.

"Air support's on the way. Stay alert but don't give anything away."

Johnny heard the rotors of the first helicopter just before it appeared above the treetops. The Cobra was designed to fly at low altitudes and present a narrow target. The gunner sat below and in front of the pilot. The gunship unleashed its fury at the tree line with a barrage of rockets and its Gatling gun fired several thousand rounds in the first pass. A second ship appeared right behind and unloaded its arsenal from closer range. Shredding the smaller trees that bordered the path, even the larger ones had limbs falling and trunks shattering.

Sanders, in radio contact with the helicopters, confirmed no enemy movement out of the ambush site.

"We'll stick around just in case," one of the pilots assured him, "but I think you're good to proceed and check things out."

"Roger that," Sanders replied, "and thanks. We owe you one."

Johnny moved with the platoon towards the killing zone. "You go with second squad and see to any survivors," Sanders instructed. He caught up to Tut and RC before they arrived at the site. Eleven VC fighters, their bodies as shredded as the trees, lay within yards of each other. Johnny moved quickly to each soldier, but nobody could have survived that kind of firepower. A large tree branch had fallen across two of the bodies, heavy enough to have killed them if their torsos weren't already riddled with bullets and torn open from the rocket blasts. The lieutenant arrived and looked at Tut checking the dead VC for documents.

"No survivors, Sir. We'll keep searching for information." Personal items were also bloodstained and shredded, difficult to find amidst the gore and flora destroyed. Not even the trunks of sturdy trees protected the squad from their fate. Johnny viewed the destruction; his new reality penetrated deeper into his psyche. Numbed by the scene, he mechanically moved from body to body. Realizing if Sanders hadn't resisted the captain's eagerness to find the enemy, it might be several members of third platoon lying dead.

Sanders and Jungle Boy had just saved third platoon from an ambush. Amidst the ravaged terrain, the VC camp was also destroyed. No sign of the woman could be found. Johnny wondered if Jungle Boy would drink another C-4-heated cup of cocoa.

The platoon returned to Dong Tam after three more uneventful days in the field. The captain would have to be satisfied with third platoon's contribution of eleven dead bodies to the count. No further contact with the VC occurred.

Calroy Evans was pleased. He would not be going to one more village, combat patrol, or night ambush. He was so short he would leave the next day. His best friend in the platoon, Rafe Johnson, teased him.

"What you gonna do now, brother? You won't know what to do with all those pretty gals back home after spending a year in this shithole."

"Oh, I think we can figure out somethin', how to go about that one. Never miss this place."

A jovial short-timer's party brewed in Rafe's hooch. Johnny heard the festivities as he sat on his cot and tried to catch up on some letters. A few of the brothers from other platoons dropped by to have a beer and congratulate Calroy on surviving his tour. Johnny overheard Lieutenant Sanders arrive and thank him for being a valuable member of the platoon and wish him well on his return home. Most of the other guys in the unit stopped by too, Sergeant Morales and Red Robin, Tut and RC. Jungle Boy and Johnny would pop by later to say goodbye.

For a moment, the mood quieted, and Calroy looked more serious. "How 'bout playin' somethin' for the guys that didn't make it out, Rafe? A year is a long time to be sloggin' through these rice paddies and swamps lookin' for a fight with Charlie."

"But you survived, brother," said Rafe, in a quieter voice. "Congratulations."

Johnny heard the blues riff Johnson had played the night before the sweep. Transforming the mood in the quieted barracks, evoking the Nam in the haunting blend of blues guitar and Rafe's voice, the tone melding perfectly and reaching deep into the somber part of the listener's soul. Johnny laid on his cot and listened.

I be thinking of my Delila as I lay my body down
Will the dampness of my foxhole become my lonely grave?
My Delila she is pretty, she is tall and quite a queen
But brother let me ask you about a woman so mean?
As cross as a polecat and lethal as a snake
My Delila is at home some other man's delight
While they lay my body down in the ground so deep
You can roll me in the river, roll me through the swamp
Never in the Mekong will I get a restful sleep
Don't mess with me brother, mess with me
Just keep an open mind

But tell me mister, tell me, whenever I'm gonna lose
Those Mekong Delta blues...

✴ ✴ ✴

Rumors ran rampant about a big operation looming near the Seven Mountains.

"Every time we go near those mountains, we start losin' people," exclaimed a concerned Rafe Johnson. "The VC so dug into those piles of rock we can't get close to 'em without a big fight. Ho Chi Minh trail ends somewhere nearby. Charlie's never gonna back down from a fight he's dug in so deep."

"That's just great!" Toad exploded. "Get back from convalescing from the wounds on my last patrol and end up going to the Seven Mountains where Charlie can really fuck with me."

"What's so bad about the Seven Mountains?" asked Jungle Boy.

"You think you seen the real Vietnam yet?" Toad glared at the kid. "Take a tour of the mountains, then you can say you been in the shit, big time. Earn your combat pay there."

"Just askin'," Jungle Boy defended himself.

Bravo company, ordered to play a supporting role in the assault, he-licoptered into the zone within sight of the mountains. Just before dawn, B-52s attempted to pulverize the nearest peak with strike after strike. The 750-pound bombs shook the ground like earthquakes in every direction, only louder. Johnny's stomach tightened as the explosions pounded the earth for an hour after the platoon landed. *Who could survive such a powerful onslaught?* He hoped the bombers would prevent the big fight the experienced grunts feared.

The initial assault, mounted by the Montagnards and their Special Forces advisers, commenced immediately when the air strikes ended. Third platoon, perhaps because of its success on the sweep, would be last into the battle. An hour of that kind of bombardment should have been enough to blow the Viet Cong, and the entire Seven Mountains, to smithereens. Somehow, it didn't.

The strategy had been to hit Charlie so hard with the B-52s that he would not survive the pounding, but if he did, would be too rattled to fight. Dug in deep, he reemerged for battle. From the start, the assault went badly for the Montagnards. Between attempts to take control of the mountains, F-4s dropped napalm on VC positions. Cobra gunships added firepower. Nothing penetrated Charlie's fortified bunkers. Their machine guns, quieted during the air strikes, commenced firing after each onslaught. Montagnard casualties staggered off the mountain, their hatred of the Viet Cong not enough to overcome their positions holding higher ground.

A call for Johnny to move forward came from the captain. All medics were needed at the base of the seventh mountain. He was the only member of third platoon to get near the battle. Special Forces medics were overwhelmed with casualties brought down from where the assault began. Dropped into a mass casualty situation, Johnny arrived and looked at the dead and wounded accumulating in a clearing at the mountain's base. Surrounded by rock on three sides, field ponchos and stretchers were strewn everywhere with mangled and bleeding bodies.

"Got a real clusterfuck going," a Green Beret told Johnny when he arrived. "Do the best you can. If you find somebody too badly wounded to survive, move on to somebody you can help. The dead and ambulatory will have to wait. Too many wounded for ordinary dust-offs, so we're calling for Chinooks."

Johnny estimated over fifty casualties lying in the clearing. As he walked toward the wounded, he watched a Special Force's medic applying a tourniquet to a boy with a hemorrhaging thigh wound. He quickly finished and skipped over a casualty violently convulsing. Johnny felt overwhelmed but didn't allow it to paralyze him into inactivity. He kneeled next to a soldier with a chest wound struggling to breathe, the first sucking chest wound he would treat in the war.

He ripped his fatigue shirt open and found no exit wound. Sealing the entry point with the plastic wrap from a dressing, he placed the bandage over it and tied it in place. Worried it would shift, he took an elastic wrap and wound it around the man's torso.

Next to the chest wound, a boyish-looking soldier had a foot missing. Johnny applied a tourniquet and felt the casualty's pulse. If he hadn't lost too much blood, he would live. With only two bottles of IV fluids in his aid bag, Johnny decided not to use one and moved on.

Another boy had a gunshot wound to his hip. In severe pain, he didn't think the bullet had deflected into his abdomen. Johnny injected him with a partial dose of morphine. Trained to pin the unused portion to the casualty's fatigues so the medics at the evacuation hospital would know how much had been administered, Johnny kept the remaining amount to use on someone else. His medical supplies dwindling quickly, he began ripping strips from fatigue shirts and applying them as pressure bandages.

A Chinook landed to retrieve the first load of casualties. Johnny needed medical supplies; none were on board. A Special Forces medic organized which of the wounded to send. Thirty-five stretchers filled the large helicopter, and it lifted off.

Out of field dressings, IV fluids and morphine, Johnny had to improvise. He continued to cut and rip fatigue shirts into usable strips for applying pressure to wounds and tying them in place. He lost all sense of time.

When a second Chinook landed, it brought medical supplies. After loading the last of the seriously wounded, and a few ambulatory casualties, Johnny paused to swig from a canteen. He noticed a row of corpses beyond where the rest of the wounded huddled. At least thirty bodies were laid in a line along the rock facing at the far end of the clearing. He saw Montagnard soldiers bringing more.

A Special Force's medic approached Johnny after the remaining ambulatory were treated. A third Chinook was on the way to retrieve them.

"Thanks for the help," he told Johnny. He nodded at the Green Beret, a little older and probably career army. "Your company commander is nervous about all his medics being here. A Huey is on the way to fetch you. How long you been in-country?"

"A month," said Johnny.

"Whoa," he exclaimed. "Quite a battle to be near with only that much time in the Nam."

Johnny shrugged, not knowing how to respond. "How about you?" he asked.

"My third tour," he answered. "I won't leave before the war is over, or Charlie greases my ass. I love these people. Been with them since my first tour." He nodded at the Montagnards gathered in small groups in the clearing. Some walked along the line of dead soldiers looking for friends and relatives among the bodies.

"I told headquarters if they try and stick me somewhere else I ain't staying in the army. My commitment to these people is for the duration of the war."

"I'm just trying to get through one tour," Johnny told him.

He smiled. "The Yards are a magnificent people. Loyal and brave. They've been shit on by the Vietnamese for a long time. I'm proud to fight alongside them. The fucking VC are animals. Kidnapped one of our boys and tortured him unmercifully. Sent him back to his village to die, his eyes gouged out and minus his ears. He died in agony. My war with the VC won't be over until the motherfuckers are obliterated."

Johnny heard the rotors of a helicopter in the distance.

"Probably your ride," the Green Beret said.

The sun low in the sky, he had spent the whole day treating casualties. Johnny would be glad to get back to his unit. *Eleven months to go*, he thought.

CHAPTER FOURTEEN

29ᵗʰ Evacuation Hospital
Binh Thuy, Mekong Delta

Danny Holt took extra bottles of IV fluids and began attaching intravenous tubing. The hospital had just received a radio call that a Chinook helicopter had thirty-five seriously wounded Montagnards on board and was a half an hour out. In-country one month, it would be the first mass casualty situation of his tour.

Triage had a capacity for six stretchers, suspended on stands that resembled sawhorses. Overhead, a round metal bar hung from the ceiling and ran the length of the emergency room. Danny hung the bottles on hooks, IV tubing inserted, ready for replacing fluids into the veins of casualties. Blood pressure cuffs and stethoscopes also dangled from the bar, and pneumatic bags for holding pints of blood for rapid infusion. A wall of shelves with emergency room supplies took up one side of the Quonset, where the olive-green stretchers rested on the sawhorse-like stands.

The field hospital, located ten miles northwest of Can Tho, sat in its own compound. Surrounded by a twelve-foot high perimeter fence, three guard towers overlooked a bog of reeds, with an air force base on the other side of the field. The evacuation hospital was constructed of round-shaped Quonset huts placed in two rows of seven. Each building sat twelve feet from its counterpart in the opposite row. The entire complex was joined by a covered hallway to which all units had access via a set of double doors. Most of the Quonsets acted as wards for recovering patients.

Triage, at the east end of the hospital, was across the hallway from the operating rooms and lab, which had their own Quonsets. An asphalt path ran from the outside doors of the emergency room to a helipad fifty yards away. The Chinook, a huge transport helicopter with two rotors, not normally used for medevacs, barely fit on the pad when it landed. Thirty-five wounded Montagnards would overwhelm triage.

Danny's stomach churned as he waited with another medic and two nurses. From triage Danny heard the rotors of the Chinook chopping air as it landed. The doors to the unit burst open. The first casualty entered on a gurney, followed by three others. Danny helped another medic lift the stretchers off the gurneys and set their handles on the sawhorse-like stands. While the gurneys went back to the helipad for more wounded, Danny got to work.

The nurses on duty were already treating two casualties, so Danny went to the third stretcher and began cutting the fatigues off a Montagnard soldier. A field dressing covered one side of his chest and oozed blood as he breathed rapidly in his attempt to get enough oxygen into his collapsed lung. Discarding his fatigues, Danny wiped the blood and mud from the man's body with a saline solution while checking for more wounds. Taking a blood pressure cuff from the bar overhead, he placed it on the man's arm and got a reading. After checking his pulse, he jotted the results on a chart. Next, Danny got an IV started, taking a blood sample for typing in the lab, standard procedure for every casualty. Checking the IV flow into the vein, he taped it securely to the man's arm. A doctor would need to insert a chest tube to drain the accumulated blood in his lungs and reestablish a vacuum in the lung cavity.

Danny adjusted his glasses and moved to the next casualty while gurneys brought more wounded into triage. With the six pairs of stands full, the excess patients were taken into the covered hallway and laid on the floor. Two doctors arrived.

"How many casualties on the medevac?" one asked.

"Thirty-five altogether," a red-haired nurse answered.

The doctor looked puzzled.

"A Chinook brought them," the nurse answered his look.

"We better get everybody in here, then. It's gonna take hours to get all the wounded through surgery. Let's start with these," the doctor said, pointing at two of the Montagnards on stretchers. An OR tech appeared with a gurney and took one of the men. A minute later the other casualty was wheeled away.

More medics and doctors began arriving. Danny moved into the hallway and continued checking wounds and starting IVs. Fatigues cut off the Montagnards accumulated in piles in the hallway. Pools of blood formed beneath the casualties. Danny had to rewrap a thigh wound on a soldier losing too much blood. The most seriously wounded took priority in the operating rooms.

Ambulatory patients came out of the wards to help. Almost healed and ready to go back to their units, they situated the wounded in the hallway, carrying stretchers and holding IV bottles while poles for them were improvised.

"Thanks, man," Danny said to a patient wearing the standard-issue blue pajamas worn on the wards.

"No problem, Doc," he said. "See what I have to look forward to. Nine months left on my tour."

Danny returned to triage and fetched more IV bottles and charts. Blood pooling on the floor made it slippery. Nobody had time to mop or remove the heaps of fatigues that were accumulating. He saw Nurse Tandy, the redhead, kick at a pile before tending to her next patient, a boyish-looking Montagnard with a red bandana wrapped around a head wound.

A call went out through the compound for all doctors to report to triage with a request for off-duty medics to donate blood. The operating room was running short.

A doctor shouted at Danny to give him a hand putting in a chest tube. He wheeled the stand into place while the surgeon put on sterilized gloves. The contraption, designed to drain excess fluids out of the collapsed lung, and restore the vacuum necessary for breathing, had a large glass jug connected to rubber tubes powered by a small motor. The doctor made an incision through the ribs and cut deep between them. Poking his finger through to ensure the depth and placement of the incision, he shook his head.

"Never did things this way at home," he uttered to no one in particular. Sweat accumulated on his brow as he inserted a tube into the incision and sutured the skin around it. The whole procedure only took a couple of minutes.

"I'll never do as many of these in my whole career as I've already done in the Nam." Overwhelmed, he kept shaking his head. "There won't be any room in surgery for a while. Make him as comfortable as possible, and monitor his vital signs, would you?" he looked at Danny, who nodded. "The two on the end can be moved into the hallway."

Danny haled one of the ambulatory patients to help move the soldiers. All the gurneys were in use, so they carried them on their stretchers. One of the Montagnards gazed at Danny as they moved him. He couldn't have weighed much over a hundred pounds. Not a whimper as he clutched his abdomen where a bullet had ripped through his intestines. Danny rechecked his pulse and blood pressure, jotting the time and results on the patient's chart.

As he looked for wounded soldiers still needing IVs, the triage radio crackled with static before a voice broke through. "Two-nine, this is Chinook four-four loaded and headed your way with twenty serious wounded and fifteen ambulatory. Do you copy?"

"Another Chinook?" Nurse Tandy asked the radio operator.

"Yes, Ma'am," he answered, "twenty more on stretchers."

Half the Montagnards were still in the hallway waiting for surgery from the first Chinook. Six more rested on stretchers in triage hooked up to IVs. The nurse looked at Danny, arms full of bloody discarded fatigues, rushing to clear the floor. He hurried out the door into the hallway and dumped them where they'd be out of the way. Right now, they needed space. He hoped he had time to mop blood off the floor before the next medevac arrived.

Tandy checked the charts of the casualties in triage to see when their vital signs were last recorded. A patient shivered. She adjusted his IV, took his blood pressure and covered him with a blanket. "They're all CIDG," she said, looking at his chart.

Danny had not heard the term before. "CIDG?" he asked as he mopped.

"Civilian irregular defense group," she said. "They work for us."

"Some of them look pretty young."

"Yeah, they are," she said. "Our Special Forces train them. Two warrior cultures that understand one another." Danny wasn't quite sure what she meant but had no time to ask. "You'll have to stay and help the night shift. Big battle going on in the Seven Mountains."

Danny nodded. He didn't expect to leave with so many casualties waiting for surgery. Thirty-five more were on the way.

The second Chinook landed an hour before the shift change at seven. The scene in triage repeated itself, except fifteen of the wounded were able to walk off the helicopter when it landed. Chairs were found for the ambulatory, who sat in the hallway while their more seriously wounded compatriots were treated.

A Special Forces sergeant came in with the second Chinook. "Anything I can do to help?" he asked Danny.

"You wounded? Danny asked.

"Only slightly." Danny noticed him limping and saw a field dressing applied to his leg. "You look after the Yards first," the sergeant said.

Danny nodded. "They might need some help out in the hallway." He pointed toward the door. "There should be some chairs to sit on while you wait. It'll be a while before we can get to you."

Unperturbed, the sergeant nodded and walked into the hallway. Danny saw him later, the ambulatory Montagnards gathered around him. Some of the casualties were no more than fifteen-years-old, Danny surmised. *Eleven more months of this*, he thought. *No time for that now*, he told himself.

At 0200 Nurse Tandy approached. They'd both been on shift for nineteen hours. "Better get some sleep," she said. "You're due back in triage at 0700."

"What about you?" he asked.

"Same," she said. "I'm just about through what's needed before I can go. The night shift can manage by itself if nothing new comes in."

Danny returned to the barracks, exhausted, but too keyed up to sleep. He removed his blood-drenched fatigue shirt and laid on his cot thinking about the day. He'd mostly treated Ninth Infantry Division casualties since arriving in the Nam. The CIDGs were new. He'd only heard about the brown-skinned Montagnards, so different from the Vietnamese. An indigenous people with their own language and culture, they'd been trained and organized to fight the Viet Cong by the Army's Special Forces. Danny had treated several Vietnamese civilian war casualties, CWCs on their charts, when American firepower wounded them.

He'd seen a lot in his first month. Now the Montagnards had come down from the Seven Mountains bloodied and humiliated by the VC. Looked down upon by the Vietnamese, their enmity ran deep.

Before dozing, Danny thought about his friends in the field. He'd just received letters from their families with their in-country addresses. He'd already known Johnny was with the Ninth Infantry but was surprised to learn Palino was too. With different battalions, Danny wondered if they'd crossed paths. Richie was up north with the Air Cav at a firebase. Danny had written to all three.

Waking just before he was due in triage, he rushed into the latrine to clean up. Looking in the mirror, his face and hair had splotches of blood. He took his glasses, wiped specks of the brownish-red off, then walked into the hospital for another day in Vietnam.

When Johnny got back to Dong Tam, there were three letters waiting. He looked at the one from CC, then smiled when he smelled the perfumed envelope. *She must be learning about writing letters*, he thought. He remembered Palino receiving the fragrant note from his girl in Mississippi while they were in training. Johnny hadn't had much time to think about his friends that were also in Vietnam.

He looked at the other two letters, from his father and Danny Holt. He opened CC's first.

Dear Johnny,

I received three letters from you, but they took three weeks to get here, and all came on the same day. I was getting very worried because I had not heard from you. Your father said not to worry as the army probably screws up the mail the same as it does everything else. I cannot believe how much I miss you. It will be a long year without you here to hold me. Make sure you know how much I love you.

Your Girl,
CC

She was hanging in there; Johnny could tell. Her letter eased his mind until he thought about how good their life had been together. His reality would be the Vietnam War for another eleven months, or until Charlie wasted or wounded him. Calroy had completed his tour unscathed, Doc Bernie almost. He had to think he would make it out or his tour would be unbearable.

Johnny opened the letter from his father, the first he had ever received from him.

Dear Son,

I must admit to being worried about not hearing from you. CC felt the same way, and without being totally truthful, I told her I thought the mail was just slow between Vietnam and America. In my war, we had an expression which summed it up--SNAFU--situation normal, all fucked up. It appears the army is incapable of delivering the mail efficiently, but I am thankful you are okay. I am worried they have put you with the infantry, but you must know that everything is fine at home. You must concentrate on what you need to do in Vietnam. I had coffee with Cecelia and her mother, and they are both concerned for you. Benita is very nice, and we have agreed to share any news we hear from you. Please take care, write when you can, and come back to us safely.

I Love You,
Dad

Johnny opened the letter from Danny last. It was a rushed note giving him the mailing addresses of the friends he had trained with. Surprised to learn that Palino was with the Ninth Infantry, he would look him up when he had the chance. Since it was mostly the wounded from the Ninth populating the 29th Evac, Danny wrote that "he hoped not to see Johnny or Palino until after their tours."

The platoon was pulling night ambushes again, but it had been quiet. The mosquitoes were constant, except when it rained, which also caused discomfort. Any night without contact was good. Fully accepted into the platoon now, Johnny marked each day of his tour completed on a calendar he found before embarking on his flight to Vietnam.

With Calroy rotated home, Johnny spent more time with Rafe Johnson. He never tired of listening to him play. His original composition, what he called "Mekong Delta Blues," was an epic poem set to blues music. Lyrically, it often utilized traditional blues phrasing while speaking of the fears, toil and sorrows of doing a tour in Vietnam.

> *Charlie be out watching us tonight*
> *The platoon expectin' a big fight*
> *With the night ambush set*
> *We waited in the dark*
> *Till fire rained down from the sky*
> *Charlie walkin' his mortars step by step*
> *We lost some good men that night*
> *And at dawn we laid them out*
> *Every one of them wasted by the fight*
> *No more, no more, will there ever be*
> *A rest that eternal for the dead*
> *For the men that left us that night*
> *Though the rest of us must stay*
> *No way, no way, no way*
> *Are we ever gonna lose*
> *Those Mekong Delta Blues…*

After crossing off day thirty-seven of his tour, Johnny wrote a letter to Cliff Morris. He had mixed feelings about what he wanted to say.

Dear Friend,

The war is worse than I could have imagined. I have been here a month and the platoon already has four casualties. No KIA's yet (sorry, that is killed in action). This war has become my reality, my life before it a distant dream receding from my memories. Please don't let on to CC how bad it is.

On a positive note, you won't believe who is in my platoon—the grandson of Robert Johnson, the bluesman so influential in much of the music you like. He is the only guitar player I've heard that can play as well as you. He has an original song he calls "Mekong Delta Blues." You have to hear it. If I survive my tour, it would be fantastic to introduce you.

There's a kid in our platoon from Oakland. The guys call him Jungle Boy. He saved the platoon a whole lot of casualties not a month into our tours. We arrived in the Nam on the same day, and he's stuck pretty close ever since. It's hard to explain in a letter. Hope the band is doing well and you hit the big time soon. Write if you get the chance.

Your Friend,
Johnny O

CHAPTER FIFTEEN

Deep into December, Johnny neared two months in the Nam. Any reminders of Christmas depressed him. Shallow attempts at festivities in the war zone only reminded him of what obstacles remained before he could return to his former life. There was only the war and his need to survive it.

They'd made no enemy contact during their stint of night ambushes near Dong Tam. Ordered to prepare for a long stretch in the field, the platoon helicoptered into Soc Trang Province just before Christmas.

Sergeant Morales had re-upped with the army and extended his tour six months. In exchange, he was given a $6500 signing bonus and promoted to staff sergeant. Lieutenant Sanders was pleased. With Morales remaining in Vietnam, more young men might make it home. Twenty-one platoon members left Dong Tam for Soc Trang.

Johnny sensed tension in the first village searched. The thatched dwellings sat along a canal used to irrigate rice fields and transport produce to markets. Johnny watched as a man untethered the mooring on a sampan at the far end of the village and eased it into the muddy waterway. Too far for the platoon to intervene, it glided out of sight.

Sergeant Morales, getting a better look with a set of binoculars, shook his head. "Don't see any weapons on him, LT, but I can't make out if there's anything in the boat."

"All right, let's get the village searched," Sanders ordered.

The villagers gathered outside their dwellings. Johnny noticed how poor they were, clothes ragged on lean frames. Beneath inscrutable expressions, Johnny sensed hatred in the eyes of the elders, like they'd been through this before. He wondered if further into his tour he would react like Toad or Red Robin. They gave no indication they cared if the villagers hated them, or even noticed. Rafe Johnson never said much. Did he equate the treatment of the Vietnamese with the racism he'd experienced at home?

Ten minutes into the search, Johnny saw Morales rush between two huts. A single row of coconut palms bordered the village behind the dwellings. Johnny couldn't see what he chased. Red Robin followed. All eyes were on the pair when they returned with a young Vietnamese man, hands already bound behind his back. Barefoot, and dressed only in shorts, he looked woozy as Red Robin prodded him forward toward the lieutenant.

"Doc," Johnny heard the LT call. "Have a look at him." A wound below his shoulder blade on his back festered. It had been sutured, but some of the stitches ripped apart during the chase.

"That ain't from no thorn in the jungle," Red Robin stated. They were without Nguyen, their Tiger Scout and interpreter, who'd been wounded while with second platoon. An older farmer came forward and spoke the English words all villagers seemed to know.

"No VC, no VC," he began, motioning with his hands as he repeated the words several times.

"Isn't that always the case?" smirked Red Robin. "Nobody is ever VC until they have a loaded gun and are shooting at you."

For the second time since Johnny arrived in Vietnam, Red Robin stood guard while the medic looked at the wound of a Vietnamese.

"Make one move," Red threatened, "and it'll give me an excuse to waste another Charlie."

"We'll have to turn him over to the ARVNs as suspected VC," Sanders stated. "That's an ugly wound he didn't get planting rice."

Johnny deadened the area around the wound and cleaned it before replacing the sutures. "That'll have to do, LT," he said. "The man should be in the hospital, or at least on some antibiotics."

Sanders got on the radio. "Suspected VC captured with a back wound, intelligence value unknown." He placed the mouthpiece back in its cradle. "The ARVNs will have to sort it out," he told Johnny. "It's their country."

The villagers were having their say with stony silence, Johnny thought. *They had no doubt whose country it was.*

The search found nothing more. Johnny fell in behind Red Robin as they left. "Fucking VC village for sure," ranted Red, loud enough for him to hear. "Call in air strikes is what I would do, show the motherfuckers we mean business. Level the whole place. Charlie thinks he can fuck with us. We need to fuck with Charlie."

Jungle Boy continued on point, something he regularly did now. When he came to a stream, he motioned for the lieutenant to post some guards so the platoon could fill their canteens. He continued on the other bank and had gone another hundred meters when he heard three distinct explosions in quick succession. Frustrated with himself for missing something on point, Jungle Boy dove behind the trunk of a tree. No ambush followed the detonations.

Johnny, near the rear of the platoon, hurried forward. Four men were down on the incline on the other side of the stream. Toad lay motionless. Johnny felt for a pulse. Nothing. No sign of the enemy. He saw Rafe Johnson a few yards away.

"Where you hit?" Johnny asked.

"My backside. Motherfuckers got me in the butt."

"You'll be okay, man. I'll be right back."

"I ain't goin' nowhere, Doc."

The third casualty, a kid they called Bama due to his heavy southern accent, was peppered with shrapnel on his right side. Despite the number of wounds, nothing vital had been hit.

"How you doin'?" Johnny asked.

"How the fuck you think, Doc? How would you feel with fifty holes in you?"

Johnny regretted his words as soon as they were out of his mouth. "Sorry, man." Bama was breathing without difficulty and was alert. "I got one more casualty to check. You'll be okay. I'll get you fixed up in a minute, give you something for the pain."

Bama nodded.

Luther Thompson, the son of Indiana schoolteachers, writhed on the ground. Quiet and unassuming, a good platoon member. Not as coherent as Rafe and Bama, Johnny decided to treat him first.

"Just hang tight," he told him. "We're gonna get you out of here, Luther."

"It hurts like a son of a bitch," he responded.

"I know," Johnny said. "I got something for the pain, but I gotta check your wounds first. Stay with me, now."

Luther nodded as he clutched at his abdomen. Johnny ripped his fatigue shirt off and saw the steel balls from the claymore had ripped through his kidney region. He hoped they had missed his liver where the bleeding would be impossible to stop in the field. Johnny applied two field dressings, secured them with an elastic wrap, then gave him a shot of morphine.

Morales appeared and told Johnny the LT already had a medevac on the way.

"Toad's dead," he told Morales. "Luther's wounds are the worst. I've got to get back to Bama."

Johnny knew the best thing he could do for his casualties was get them on a medevac quickly. Bama had learned of Toad's death and had calmed considerably. "Fuck this shit," he said. "In the Nam three months and it seems like I been here forever."

"Dust-off's on the way Bama. We're gonna get you out of here."

"Toad didn't make it?" he inquired.

Johnny shook his head as he concentrated on giving him a dose of morphine. "That will help with the pain," Johnny assured him. "Get you out of the war for a while."

"For good?" a hopeful Bama asked.

"Don't know," Johnny responded honestly. "Maybe."

Johnny returned to Rafe Johnson and found him lying on his side smoking a cigarette.

"Four months to go, Doc, four motherfuckin' months. Toad bought it, huh?" Rafe shook his head. "Son of a bitch. Couldn't stand the motherfucker when I first got to the platoon. Thought he was just another cracker. Funny how that goes. Now I'm real sorry he's gone. Deserved to go home."

"We all deserve to go home," Johnny said. "Medevac's on the way. Should get you out of the boonies for a month, put you that much closer."

While Johnny organized getting the casualties to the LZ, he overheard Sanders on the radio with the captain, nearby with second platoon.

"What kind of a clusterfuck you got going over there, Lieutenant?"

"Sir?"

"What the hell happened?"

"Can't tell for sure, but I think three claymores went off, daisy-chained together, command-detonated."

"You've got to lean on the villagers harder, Lieutenant. Get some fucking information out of them."

"Yes, Sir."

"Stay put," the captain ordered. "I'm coming over with second platoon."

Sanders got off the radio and made sure the LZ was secure for the dust-off. Upset, he wondered how the hell he was supposed to get these kids back home fighting the war this way? Wandering through the Delta, exposing themselves to Charlie, getting picked off a few at a time, the VC choosing when to engage.

Doing all he could for the wounded, Johnny looked after Toad's body. After filling out the field medical card, he wrapped him in a poncho. Not exactly the million-dollar wound Toad had hoped for. Eight casualties in two months, the platoon was down to seventeen men.

After the medevac lifted off, Lieutenant Sanders waited for the company commander. The radio squawked again, and it was the captain ordering third platoon to return to the village. Mason arrived and demanded to know which huts the captured man had run between. Morales came forward and showed him.

"This village is not going to get away with murder, Lieutenant. You've just had one KIA and three wounded within a stone's throw of a VC village. If they think they can fuck with Bravo Company like that, then it's not my company. Your mission is to search and destroy, not let Charlie kill one of your men and get away with it."

Hearing the disturbance, some of the Vietnamese came out of their houses. "Sergeant, remove everybody from these two huts," the captain demanded.

Morales entered with Red Robin and pushed a terrified Vietnamese woman outside with an elderly peasant. Repeating the familiar "no VC, no VC" over and over again, all eyes were on the captain to see what he would do. He went inside the first hut to have a look. Red Robin looked at the Vietnamese with a hatred that burned deep inside him.

"Toad was my friend. All you motherfuckin' VC do is lie and then try and kill more of us."

Mason emerged with a piece of thatch, took a lighter out of his pocket and set the dwelling on fire. Moving to the hut beside it, he did the same. The Vietnamese women were crying and tried to reenter their houses to gather some belongings. Red Robin and the captain blocked their way. Mason turned to Sanders.

"That is how you deny aid and comfort to the enemy, Lieutenant. Is that clear?"

Sanders seethed, but replied, "very clear, Sir."

The platoon dug in for the night, tense, the day's events heavy on their minds. Johnny could tell Jungle Boy blamed himself for not spotting the claymores while walking point. Johnny knew no point man would have seen them.

Any number of possibilities could have gotten the claymores into the hands of the Viet Cong. A staple of every infantry platoon, they might have been stolen or procured on the black market. Deadly at fifty yards, each mine contained 700 steel balls about an eighth of an inch in diameter embedded in a layer of C-4 explosive. Printed on the casing were the words "FRONT TOWARDS ENEMY." They even had a sight built into them for accurate alignment. They would have been easily camouflaged, the detonation cord strung behind the mines with a well-hidden Viet Cong soldier even farther from the platoon triggering the explosions.

"Why was the captain mad at Lieutenant Sanders?" Jungle Boy asked Johnny. "It was my fault Toad got killed today."

Johnny knew better and didn't hesitate responding. "It was not your fault," he began. "Don't go blaming yourself. If you want to blame someone, how about the motherfuckers who started this war. Or the shit tactics created by ticket-punching career officers, the black marketeers, or the clever maneuvers of our enemy. But don't go blaming yourself. The platoon doesn't. The war just got uglier today."

Jungle Boy shifted in their foxhole. For good measure, Johnny continued. "Toad is not dead because you missed something, or those mamasans could have told us anything. Toad is dead because he was out there on the biggest shit detail the army and the country could think up. None of this makes any sense, but it's *definitely* not your fault."

Jungle Boy thought for a moment. "Are you all right, Doc?"

"Just thinking," he replied.

"You think Charlie's gonna mess with us some more?" Jungle Boy asked.

"Until the day we leave Vietnam."

Lost in their thoughts, the two were silent for a while. Finally, Jungle Boy spoke. "You know, Doc, I never had a proper family. Nobody has written to me since I've been in the Nam."

Johnny ached for the kid. His own background was far from ideal, but he had recognized Jungle Boy's close bond with the platoon, how he would rather die than let them down. They were his family now. Maybe the kid had already saved his life by intercepting the ambush on a previous patrol.

"I'll tell you what," Johnny told him. "Neither of us have a brother. Let's make a pact. If we survive the Nam, we are brothers for life. I'm older than you, consider me your big brother. Now don't go doing anything stupid to get yourself killed. We can look out for each other in the Nam."

Jungle Boy beamed. "I know we can," he said.

"Well, little brother, third platoon needs to look after you, too."

"Doc, can we make it official?"

"What do you mean?" asked Johnny.

"Can we be blood brothers?"

Johnny thought for a moment. "I would say we've already been through enough fights with Charlie, seen enough blood, and humped enough miles through the boonies to qualify. And I expect we'll see a lot more."

CHAPTER SIXTEEN

Up before dawn, the platoon readied itself for another day. Johnny sipped on an instant coffee made from what came with his C-rats. Jungle Boy did the same with a cup of cocoa while they shared a package of crackers. Johnny always swapped his packets of cocoa with Jungle Boy for coffee. Tired before the sun rose on the horizon, tension from the previous day had him feeling ill at ease as he checked his gear.

By midmorning, the platoon crossed through a rice paddy near another village and angled toward swampy jungle terrain, which began where the cultivated field ended. Johnny noticed half the crop was prematurely brown as they approached the thicker flora, where patches of dead vegetation contrasted with the lush green of the tropical landscape. Some of the tree trunks were scorched.

"What's that?" Johnny asked Red Robin.

"The agent, orange, with a little bit of napalm thrown in."

"Agent Orange? Never heard of it."

"You haven't been in the Nam long enough, Doc. Chemical defoliants, denying Charlie cover."

"There's always another tree line. You can't spray the whole jungle."

"Fine by me," shrugged Red Robin.

"What about the rice field?"

"Whoops," Red said sarcastically.

On their next break, Johnny looked at the jungle, sicker than at the platoon's entry point. "Why do they call it Agent Orange?" he asked Red Robin.

"It's shipped in barrels with an orange stripe around them."

Still in defoliated jungle near dusk, the platoon dug in for the night.

Maybe the plan is to spray the entire country, thought Johnny. *Perhaps command thought the same as Red.*

Jungle Boy heated a cup of cocoa with a small wad of C-4. Johnny realized it was his comfort food. He felt bad for the kid, who never complained.

"Want some?" he asked Johnny.

"No thanks," he said. Johnny hated the cocoa mixed with water. Jungle Boy would trade the most desirable of his C-rations for more packets of the dark powder. It all tasted terrible.

"Got any ham and lima beans left?" asked Jungle Boy. The kid actually preferred them to most of the other C-rats. "My grandpa used to love lima beans. Don't know why everybody hates them."

"Perhaps because they come in an ugly green can and tastes like all the other shit that comes in ugly green cans—only worse, somehow," answered Johnny.

"Trade you some beef stew for them," Jungle Boy offered.

"Here, take them," he said, tossing the can to Jungle Boy. "Just be careful with that C-4. One of these days you're going to blow us up."

"Naw, Sergeant Morales showed me the exact amount to use."

"Good for Sergeant Morales. I don't think C-4 is the best thing to cook with."

"It works good."

"Blow yourself up, then," Johnny said.

Food was not his biggest problem. He had another matter to tend to. RC had come to him with a bad case of dysentery. Nothing in his aid bag made a difference and his condition worsened. Johnny had gone to the lieutenant and told him Cunningham ought to be sent to the rear. Sanders had been direct with his denial.

"We're already down to seventeen men, Doc, so shorthanded we shouldn't even be out here without any replacements. Can't spare another man to a case of the shits."

RC humped on the next day, his gut on fire and his diarrhea running down his leg, so miserable he wished Charlie would put a bullet in his brain. Tut and the squad helped by packing some of his gear, but they were already weighted down. Tut pulled RC's guard shift hoping the extra rest would help his friend recover. It didn't.

Tut returned to his foxhole and found RC shivering. He appealed to Johnny one more time. "Can't you get the LT to reconsider? There's nothing else you can give him?"

Johnny had given RC as many aspirin as he thought safe and decided to start an IV. "This will help replace some fluids," Johnny told him. "I'll have another look first thing tomorrow, Tut, but the LT is not going to send for a medevac tonight. I'll talk to Sanders again in the morning, try and get him to reconsider."

A light drizzle began just before dawn, adding to the platoon's misery. The damp jungle emitted a chemical smell from the defoliants. Johnny huddled beneath his poncho. Unable to sleep much, he checked on RC at first light.

"No change, Doc." Tut had his friend wrapped in layers of poncho liners borrowed from his squad. Johnny found RC feverish and still shivering. There was no way he could continue on the patrol. With increased resolve, Johnny went to speak with the lieutenant. On his way, a single shot reverberated through the early morning sound of the drizzle falling. Startled, the platoon reached for weapons and took cover in their foxholes. King Tut emerged from his.

"No, no, no," he repeated in agony, his hands on his head as he stumbled forward. "Not this way. He just wanted out of the Nam."

Johnny rushed past Tut and found Cunningham motionless, a self-inflicted gunshot wound to his skull. Kneeling beside him, Johnny took the M-16 out of his hands and covered what was left of RC's head with a poncho liner. He noticed a note tucked between the dead man's legs. Printed with a shaking hand, it read:

> *King, you have been a good friend.*
> *Just can't take any more of this*
> *fucking war. Good luck.*

Johnny tucked the note into his pocket. He would give it to King Tut later. For now, he had a field medical card to complete. A medevac would be dispatched now to retrieve the body. Numb, Johnny found RC's dog tags for the information needed. He felt the eyes of several platoon members standing above him as he worked. His own hand shaky, he completed the card and wrapped the body in a single poncho.

Sanders watched the medevac approach the LZ. He felt responsible for Cunningham's death. His judgement distorted because of the growing tension between him and the captain, he should have looked after RC first and dealt with the skipper's anger later. Sanders spoke with Mason on the radio. Incensed, the company commander had lost patience with the platoon leader.

"You're telling me you've lost another man, Lieutenant, without any contact with the enemy?"

"Suicide, Sir."

"What kind of a platoon are you commanding, Lieutenant? You've lost five men to the rear, two of them dead, and only have one captured VC suspect to show for it. Better tighten things up with third platoon."

Sanders' priority of getting the young men under his command home safely had turned to shit.

Jungle Boy was still reeling from not spotting the claymore mines that had killed Toad, and King Tut paced back and forth not knowing what to do with himself.

When the dust-off touched down, Johnny had Jungle Boy help him load RC's body. When the Huey left, they would have to pick up their gear and continue with the patrol.

Tut thought of all the ways it could have ended differently. *Why didn't the LT just call for a medevac? Hell, I would have shot him in the foot if it would have saved RC's life.*

A troubling somberness descended on the platoon as they assembled their gear and proceeded with the day's hump. For the first time there were grumblings about Sanders' leadership. "What was the LT thinking? RC was sick, man, can't hump with eighty pounds through this muck in that condition."

A Huey resupplied the platoon after the day's patrol and dropped a mailbag. Johnny tucked a letter from CC into his aid kit. He'd read it later. He helped Jungle Boy dig in for the night, then went to check on Tut.

He found him sitting on the ground next to his foxhole smoking a cigarette.

"How you doing?" Johnny asked.

Tut exhaled and then ground the cigarette out in the dirt. He took another from an opened pack, then tapped the unlit end on his boot before lighting it.

"How would you be doing if you just lost the best friend you ever had, the one you had humped through all the shitholes in the Delta with? The same friend who was gonna introduce you to his pretty sister back in the world because he thought she deserved a good guy for a boyfriend? How do you think that pretty sister is gonna be feeling now? You been here long enough to be one of us, Doc. I got to tell you, it's a motherfucker."

"I let him down twice," Johnny said. "Couldn't stop his dysentery and couldn't convince the LT to get him on a medevac."

Continuing to stare straight ahead at nothing in particular, Tut took another cigarette and began tapping it on his rifle. "We all let him down," he said in a flat monotone. Before lighting up, and while still staring straight ahead, he told Johnny. "Like I said, it's a motherfucker."

The next day, the platoon came to the end of the defoliated jungle. Dissatisfied with his lieutenant's performance in the villages, Captain Mason had third platoon searching for an enemy base camp intelligence reported operating in the vicinity. Sanders had the men break for the night within sight of the undamaged tree line. It's where he would set up an ambush.

Sanders conferred with Morales. "At 0100 I want you and Red to follow the contour of that ridge and enter the jungle about 200 meters east of our position. Work back towards the spot where that clump of brush sits next to the stand of trees." Sanders pointed to the terrain straight ahead of them. "It's where I would set an ambush. Take the starlight scope with you."

Packing only their M-16s and bandoliers of ammo, the two moved quickly and entered the cover of the tree line. Moving cautiously, they proceeded west towards the designated site, stopping every few meters to listen and scan the area ahead. Every sound amplified in their ears, the starlight scope giving them a green-tinged look at the topography. One mistake could expose them.

Utilizing the starlight scope, Morales came to the dense flora beside the entry point the platoon would use the next day. He could not see through the undergrowth but detected a faint odor of perspiration and feces in the air. Making sure, he motioned to Red and tapped his nose twice. His partner nodded in agreement.

Morales signaled he wanted to skirt the thickest part of the scrub and go deeper into the jungle and approach the position from the rear. No longer doubting his nose, he wanted to make sure the VC were still there. Detecting movement through the night scope, he froze as he watched a guard look in his direction. Morales worried their presence disrupted the usual sounds of the jungle and that the sentry had heard the change. Not moving for several minutes, the guard finally turned and woke a soldier sleeping in a foxhole. Morales breathed easier and watched a routine change of guard.

Not needing further clarification, Morales and Red Robin carefully crawled backwards and then retraced their route to the platoon. By 0400 they were speaking with the lieutenant.

"You were right, LT, Charlie's just inside the tree line and waiting to spring an ambush. We couldn't get a count, but there's no doubt the gooks are there." Red Robin nodded in agreement.

"Good work," Sanders told them. "I'll radio the coordinates and get some air support."

At dawn Johnny heard the rotors of the gunships approaching. Smoke had been popped just beforehand to help guide the helicopters towards the Viet Cong position. Johnny saw Sanders on the headset in communication with the pilots. The platoon was ordered to advance after two passes by the Cobras.

Ten bodies were strewn in a pocket of destruction where the deadly arsenal had ripped to shreds every living thing, including shrubs and trees. The horrid stench of blood, intestines, chewed earth, and tree sap filled Johnny's nostrils. In a repeat of an ambush prevented a month ago, dead soldiers lay in grotesque and unnatural positions in the killing zone. They found no survivors.

"Great work out there guys," Sanders complimented Morales and Red Robin in front of the platoon.

"Thanks," Morales responded. More agitated, Red gave more detail.

"We could smell the motherfuckers before we saw them, LT. Eating all that gook supper is what did Charlie in. It stinks before they eat it and smells even worse coming out the other end."

Ten bodies would get the captain off Lieutenant Sanders' back, at least for the time being. It also restored confidence in the LT's leadership within the platoon.

The day's hump provided nothing more than a grueling patrol through the jungle. Captain Mason, greedy for more success, had third platoon still searching for the elusive VC base camp. When they dug in for the night, Johnny remembered the unopened letter from CC tucked in his aid bag. He noticed a thumbprint of dried blood on the envelope. He must have touched the letter after checking the VC bodies that morning. Opening the note before it got too dark, he sat on the ground and read.

> *Hi Johnny,*
>
> *I have some exciting news. Big Rock just signed a recording contract with Capitol Records. The band is so happy. The record company wants to release a single of one of Cliff's original songs, "Something About Love." Then they'll record a whole album. Cliff and Suzi said to say hello. He plans on writing to you when he gets a chance. He was very excited to hear Robert Johnson's grandson is in your platoon and would like you to introduce him after the war.*
>
> *Johnny, please be safe and come home to me. I love you and miss you so much.*
>
>

Your girl,
CC
>

Jungle Boy noticed the letter in his hand. "From your girl?" he asked.

Johnny nodded.

"How come you never talk about her, Doc? I bet she's pretty. I think I'll have a pretty girlfriend someday. Hope so anyway."

"She is pretty," Johnny said. "Maybe too pretty to keep."

Jungle Boy thought for a moment, wanting to say something to make Johnny feel better.

"How long we been here, Doc?"

"Two months."

"Not even a year left on our tours."

"Our tours are a year. We weren't here a week before we saw our first combat. We have a long way to go."

"We'll make it, Doc. You'll see."

The kid had grown on Johnny. He put CC's letter back in the envelope, tucked it into his rucksack and smiled. "You think so?"

"I know so," Jungle Boy replied.

CHAPTER SEVENTEEN

The platoon continued searching for the VC base camp. On Christmas Day, a Huey arrived with individual kits containing a feast of turkey, mashed potatoes and fresh peas topped off with apple and pumpkin pie. Other than a good meal, the holiday went unacknowledged. *Just as well*, Johnny thought. The Season only made him more homesick.

The grueling three and a half weeks on patrol ended in mid-January when the captain grew frustrated without any further body count. When they returned to Dong Tam, the barracks were noticeably subdued. Rafe Johnson was not in his hooch playing the blues, and Toad wasn't around to feign giving Red Robin a hard time. Johnny used the stand down to search for Don Palino, whose address in Vietnam listed the Fourth Battalion of the Forty-Seventh Riverine of the Ninth Infantry. They went looking for Charlie aboard the Navy's Tango boats, heavily armed troop carriers large enough for an entire platoon and their gear.

Johnny found Palino's unit bunking on a barge floating in the My Tho River. Standing beside the massive waterway, he asked groups of soldiers waiting to board a tiny army boat ferrying soldiers to and from the floating barracks. Delta Company had also just returned from patrolling the rivers and canals of the Mekong Delta. A soldier with three day's growth of stubble but wearing a clean set of faded jungle fatigues stood waiting to board the small craft. He responded to Johnny's inquiries.

"A Doc named Palino? I guess that would be my platoon's medic. Lives on that barge out there in the river when he ain't humpin' his ass off in the boonies. We're in for a day or two."

Johnny waited his turn, and the little boat ferried him to the barge. He found Palino in his hooch drinking whiskey straight from a bottle.

"Well for fuck's sake," he said when he saw Johnny. "How is the big O?"

"Just back from three and a half weeks in the bush. I hear you travel around on boats now, riding high just like a big shot."

Palino laughed. "Well, let me tell you, it's a motherfucker," he protested in his familiar Mississippi drawl. "If I wanted to fight on the water I would have joined the Navy. I hate the water, and the Mekong Delta is full of it. And the leeches, can't wade through so much as a puddle without them sucking blood from you. Spent ten minutes picking them off me after my first patrol while my platoon members laughed. Squirted bug juice all over me to help and that burned for two days."

"Besides that, how are things with the Riverine?"

"Didn't someone say, 'war is hell?' It's much worse than that. We find Charlie by waiting for him to take a shot at us. We are cannon fodder, bait. You think that's a winning strategy?"

Palino was drunk, slurring his words. "Hard to get a perspective on this shithole. I have some scores to settle if I make it out of here. Remember my girl, Stormy Beth, with the daddy so rich that the ugly son of a bitch could still marry a beautiful woman? The girl who was swearing off sex for a year, saving up her passion for when I got back? Wrote me a letter saying she hopes I understand, but she's fallen in love with somebody else. Hopes we can still be *friends*. What am I to understand, *exactly*?"

Palino got to his feet and smiled. Holding the bottle of whiskey in the air for a moment, he took another swig. "Forgive me," he bowed, "I forget my manners." He passed the bottle to Johnny.

He took a swallow and handed it back to Palino. "I don't know, man, I just want to get back home to my girl."

"You still have a girl? That's pretty good longevity for the Nam. The Drill Sergeants weren't kidding about Jody."

"Or Vietnam," Johnny added. "I wonder how many of them are back over here? My platoon sergeant just re-upped on the condition that if he extended his tour for six months, he would not be redeployed overseas for at least a year."

"The man drives a hard bargain."

"I guess you've heard from Danny," Johnny said.

"Yes. The kid is too nice and innocent for the Nam. Says he's in a real meat grinder at the 29th. The war never stops."

"We hitched planes together to get to the Delta. Had to part ways at the Can Tho Army Airfield. They'd just had a sapper attack and were overrun."

Palino, sitting again, leaned forward and stared at Johnny. "So, what's your real story, O? A smart guy like you winding up in Vietnam."

"I'm not so smart, wasn't paying attention. Never heard of Vietnam before the war started. Never registered for the draft."

Palino smirked. "There's more to it than that. I was registered and in school with a deferment."

"And?" Johnny questioned, hoping to divert Palino from his probing.

"I fucked the wrong man's daughter." Palino paused for effect and gauged Johnny's reaction.

"There," he continued, "I've told you more of my story. What really happened to you?"

"I don't like to talk about it. Not much we can do now. Number one, I'd like to survive my tour. Number two, I'd like to still have my girl when I return."

"So, what are the odds?" Palino pressed.

"Not good. My platoon commander is excellent, the company CO is a career-pushing jerk always willing to put our lives at risk. On the home front, who keeps a girl for a year?"

"Thoughtful answer. You know I was attending the University of Mississippi?"

"Yes, what happened?"

"You know I liked to party, meet women, but I was keeping up with the course work. I did know there was a war going on. Professor William Kittleson is what happened. I flunked his statistics course."

Palino, appearing more sober with the serious topic, took another swig from his bottle.

"I knew something was fishy because I studied the material well enough to pass, but the final exam had questions the course didn't cover. When I asked my classmates, I realized I wasn't given the same exam. Next thing I know, the draft board notifies me I've not earned enough credits to maintain my student deferment. It's one of the scores I have to settle. I'm sure Big Daddy McTeer is behind it somewhere."

Palino peered at Johnny. "There's more. I come from a little town near the border with Alabama called Birdsview. Pretty little place once you get past the poverty on the east end of town. That's where I come from. The Blacks have their poor section, and the Whites have theirs. My mother is a beautiful woman. She is also one-eighth African American. That makes one-sixteenth of me with nigger blood. My mother easily passes for a White woman, but it's in the genealogy. I'm sure Daddy McTeer had it all checked out. It called for a primitive response."

"You can't be serious?" Johnny questioned.

"Believe it, brother, because it's the truth. Things haven't improved all that much in Mississippi, not for people the McTeers don't like."

Palino passed the bottle to Johnny. "There, I've told you my story. How about the rest of yours? You kill somebody?"

"Nothing bad enough to deserve the Nam."

"Who does deserve the Nam? The dumbfucks who support this war, for sure. But none of their sons are here. Figure that."

"So how is it really going for you in the field?"

"Like I said, we patrol the rivers and canals waiting for Charlie to take a shot at us, then rush ashore chasing him and become grunts again. Since I've been here, we've had one KIA and three wounded. That should wipe us out over the course of my tour. Of course, there will always be replacements, others like ourselves. We're completely expendable. I think we made a big mistake getting on that plane and coming over here. I'd like somebody to pay for that."

Johnny nodded. "I know, I know. We're at six wounded and one KIA and it's not been three months since we arrived in country. Just be careful, man. Don't let your anger get you in trouble."

"You're not angry about being here?" Palino asked in a raised voice. "How big of a shit detail does it take to get you mad? I can't get past wanting to even the score. In the meantime, I drink and go fuck the whores when I can. Spend all of my combat pay on five and ten-dollar good-time girls. That's not much fucking, really. How far does sixty-five dollars a month go? What is a life worth in Vietnam? It doesn't seem like sixty-five dollars covers it." Drunk again, he held up the bottle in a mock toast. "At least the women here are cute. Not much hair on their pussy, but they are beautiful. Care to join me?"

"I can't, man," Johnny said. "Can't we just get a meal somewhere and drink a little more?"

"In Dong Tam? It's good to see you Johnny O, but I need to go meet my good-time girl. Not many chances for fun as a grunt medic in this war. Good luck with keeping your girl. I've already lost mine to some privileged shithead who won't have Vietnam in his future."

Johnny said goodbye and waited for the tiny boat to ferry him back to shore. Ill at ease after his conversation with Palino, he considered what to do with the day. *Should he return to his hooch and catch up on some letters? Jungle Boy would be in the barracks. Maybe they could catch the evening meal in the mess hall? What would they be serving, rehydrated potatoes and canned peas with a pulverized cow pressed into some semblance of a meatloaf? Better than C-rations, but nothing to rush back for.*

Johnny decided to wait for his friend, follow him, and keep him out of trouble.

* * *

The American Texas Bar was a whorehouse masquerading as a saloon. Off-limits after dark, it did a thriving business during the day. Already very drunk, Palino took the ferry to shore. Johnny followed him to the bar and waited a few minutes before entering.

Full of grunts in from the field wanting to drink and find a woman, the saloon was similar to any at home. Tables and chairs filled the main room, and a long wooden bar ran the length of one wall. Two Vietnamese bartenders, with cigarettes dangling from their mouths, served drink orders from behind it. Scantily clad saloon girls brought the drinks to the tables where American soldiers sat in their jungle fatigues. The women flirted with the men and sat on their laps looking to do more than bring them whiskey.

Palino found a seat and ordered. A pretty Vietnamese girl in a short white skirt snuggled up to him and ran her fingers through his hair. She whispered in his ear. "You *beaucoup* boom-boom with me GI? Give you good time. Not rush for number one GI."

Like most Vietnamese women, she was slender, small-breasted, and very pretty. Her long hair hung to her waist. A sleeveless white blouse contrasted with her smooth, sensuous and pale skin. Lips accentuated with bright red lipstick insinuated availability. She brought Palino his drink and sat on his lap, snuggling into his body. He ran his fingers over her bare thighs.

"So, what is your name Miss Pretty Boom-Boom?"

"My name, Wuby," she said, having trouble pronouncing the "r."

Palino found that amusing. "Tell me your real name in Vietnamese."

"My name Wuby," she reiterated petulantly. "GI want to talk all day or boom-boom Wuby?" She pouted.

Palino sipped his whiskey. "All right, all right, let me finish my drink, and then we go upstairs."

"You want go upstairs, Wuby take you, show you good time. Maybe boom-boom first, drink later."

"Why so fast?" asked Palino. He was enjoying her forwardness and petulance.

"Why GI no want boom-boom with Wuby? Maybe GI *dinky dau*," using the Vietnamese word for crazy.

Palino laughed. "GI *dinky dau* for Ruby, *dinky dau* for whiskey."

She didn't understand and got angry. "What you say, GI, come to Texas Bar and no want boom-boom?"

When Palino laughed, Ruby stood and went to another table. A platoon member noticed and waved to him. "Way to go, Doc. I see you have a way with women."

Palino waved back and sipped on his whiskey. Ruby sat on another soldier's lap.

Johnny, feeling ridiculous while in the bar spying on his friend, joined Palino at his table. Acting unsurprised to see him, Palino asked: "Change your mind?"

"Not exactly," Johnny said. "Just following you to make sure you stay out of trouble."

Palino squinted at him from behind his drunken haze. "Perhaps you can follow me out to the field and keep me out of trouble there. But wait, you already are a grunt medic in a platoon. You consider the American Texas Bar more dangerous?"

"Just didn't want you doing anything foolish because you're drunk."

"Not on this watered-down whiskey. At least have another drink with me now that you're here."

They sat in silence for a while. None of the bar girls joined them after Ruby's experience with Palino. "Gee, you're a bundle of fun, Ornowoski. You really know how to liven up a party."

Johnny smiled sheepishly and raised his glass to Palino.

When Johnny returned to the barracks, he found Jungle Boy sharpening a long-bladed knife he hadn't seen before.

"What's that?" he asked.

"Sergeant Morales thought I should carry this since I walk point so much."

Jungle Boy always followed the sergeant's advice. If Johnny was like an older brother, Morales was an uncle, someone to admire and emulate.

"Three new guys in the platoon," Jungle Boy stated. "One of them is really scared. Name's Billy Warrington. Some of the guys are already calling him Billy War. How scared were you, Doc, when we got here?"

"Scared enough to know it would be a long year."

"I was scared," said Jungle Boy, "but never going to show it."

"Natural enough," Johnny responded.

"We're out on ambush tomorrow night," Jungle Boy said.

"You on point?"

"I like walking point."

"Maybe you should let someone else do it once in a while."

"Why?"

"Because it's dangerous."

"How would you know, Doc? As the medic, you never walk point."

"All right, all right," Johnny conceded, "but must you walk point every time we go beyond the wire?"

"I guess I could cut back a little."

"Just a little?"

"Don't want to lose my edge. Sergeant Morales says he has seen it before. A guy goes on R&R or something and he loses his edge."

No sense arguing with Sergeant Morales, Johnny thought. *Jungle Boy accepted every word of his as the Gospel Truth.*

Late the next afternoon, the platoon assembled to go beyond the wire. Rockets, which had a range of eleven kilometers, were hammering Dong Tam every night. Instructed to travel several klicks and set up on ambush, the platoon would continue patrolling the next day and establish a different position the following night.

Lieutenant Sanders assigned the new kid, Warrington, to Tut's squad, reasoning he would adjust better to his leadership. Red Robin would not tolerate the degree of fear the new guy exhibited. Tut's squad would also be the last out for the first night of ambush. Sanders had asked Johnny to walk behind Warrington in the formation and help him get through his first patrol.

The new kid labored with the gear he packed. His slight frame sagged at the shoulders. Whether from fear or physical exertion, he gasped for air. His helmet looked too heavy for his head and tilted to one side. Johnny considered intervening and giving Warrington a placebo to ease his anxiety. He worried the kid was making too much noise while hyperventilating. The pace slowed in the dark, and Warrington fell into a better rhythm. Johnny breathed easier.

A light drizzle began falling shortly after dark as the platoon got close to the ambush site. Billy Warrington shivered as they set up. Johnny sat next to him. "First, let's get you warmer," he suggested. He adjusted his poncho for him to keep the rain from penetrating and showed him how to situate his rifle for quick access.

"Where you from?" Johnny asked.

"Boston," Warrington answered.

"Drafted?"

"Yeah, couldn't afford to stay in school. All of my friends have deferments."

"Mine, too," Johnny told him. "Don't know how we lucked out. Well, I do, but it's a long story."

"Yeah, with me, too."

"Listen, it will get better. If you have any questions, don't be afraid to ask me. Tut will help you as well. It's good you're in his squad. You met Jungle Boy yet?"

"I know who he is. He likes walking point?"

"He does. Red Robin is good at it, too, and Sergeant Morales before he became platoon sergeant."

"Why do they like walking point?"

"They feel more in control. Jungle Boy just told me nobody has been wounded walking point since we got here. They won't expect you to walk it until you've adjusted to the Nam. You have a lot of guys looking out for you."

Warrington nodded.

"Just keep your concentration and your rifle ready. Watch how the experienced guys react. Charlie might be tough, and he's crafty, but he ain't superman. Bullets don't bounce off him."

Johnny stayed near Warrington during the night. The rain lifted, and it helped revive the new kid. Rockets began slamming into Dong Tam from a far-off sector. Nothing third platoon could do about that. Afterwards, the jungle quieted to the normal sounds of nocturnal creatures chirping and croaking. At dawn, the platoon readied itself for the day's patrol.

CHAPTER EIGHTEEN

29th Evacuation Hospital
Binh Thuy

Rafe Johnson sat on the side of his bed in the ambulatory ward and joked with a group of patients gathered around him. Nearly recuperated from their wounds, they would be returning to their units soon.

Charlie had mortared the hospital compound the night before and scored a direct hit on the morgue. The soldiers mocked his prowess.

"I just never seen Charlie as stupid before," laughed Rafe Johnson. "Guess he just really wanted to make sure the dead is dead."

"Makes sense, I guess," added Hank Griffiths in the next bed. "Not his best shot." He'd moved near Rafe when they discovered they were in sister platoons of Bravo company.

"I mean, why the fuck is Charlie mortaring a hospital?" chimed a third grunt. "He's already got everybody taken out, at least for a while."

"Maybe we's just easy pickins, like sitting ducks," Rafe continued.

During the attack, nurses and medics had patients lying on the floor next to the walls with mattresses over them. The ward, protected by sandbags stacked three feet high on the outside wall, would need a direct hit to harm anyone. The grunts, appreciating the gesture, would have felt more comfortable with their M-16s. The barrage ended when gunships raked fire on the VC's position, Charlie vanishing as quickly as he'd arrived.

Danny Holt witnessed the attack from the corner guard tower on the northwest side. He had drawn the 1100 to 0300 watch, the worst, because he had trouble sleeping before and after the shift and was due back in triage at 0700.

Danny saw the flash from the mortar tubes as the VC lobbed several rounds at the air force base, the enemy's exact location hidden in the reeds between the two compounds. Before the gunships arrived, Charlie fired three mortars at the 29th. Incredulous, Danny watched the last round explode when it hit the morgue, a small building standing by itself near the helipad.

Armed with an M-16 and two magazines, Danny fired 19 shots towards the muzzle flashes. When the gunship arrived, the mortars ceased. A solid red line appeared when the Cobra's Gatling guns rained fire on the VC team's suspected position. Unable to see the helicopter in the night sky, its tracers created a bolt of red lightning thick and uninterrupted with every sixth round emitting a trail of fire.

Danny had no idea that he'd treated three of the casualties from Johnny Ornowoski's platoon late in December. Only Rafe Johnson remained at the 29th. Luther Thompson and Bama, their wounds more serious, were recuperating at a larger facility in Long Binh.

Rafe Johnson would be back with third platoon in a few days. He'd attracted the attention of two medics who played guitar. Gregarious by nature, he was happy to show them several blues riffs. In the evenings, he began playing on the ward, attracting a larger audience each night. A nice diversion for everyone, Rafe worked on a new song.

"I call it 'Comin' Home in a Box Blues.' You've healed me up pretty fast and now it's time to return to my platoon. Good luck to all of you here at the 29th. A big *thank you* for all you've done."

> *Arriving in the Nam, down in the Mekong Delta*
> *Through the jungle, swamps and paddy dikes*
> *Lookin' for Charlie spoiling for a fight*
> *Got rocked so hard my mama heard me cry*
> *Don't you let me die, brother, die*
> *Not in this Delta swamp*
> *Make any man regret why he'd come here to die*
> *I be lookin' for an answer, lookin' far away*

Back to my home in Georgia, amongst the pines so tall
Where they be layin' down my body deep beneath the earth
Just be comin' home too early, a bullet through my heart
I be comin' home too early, comin' home in a box
My family be gathered as they lay me in the ground
While my mama be a cryin' and my father be so sad
Sister Greta and her husband be holdin' one another
Little sister, Esther, will never understand
Why her big brother comin' home so early
Comin' home in a box and laid beneath the earth
Laid to rest with a bullet through the heart
Comin' home in a box, comin' home in a box
Comin' home in a box blues...

Muriel Tandy wept softly at the end of the song. She'd stopped by with Danny Holt after their shift in the ER. Nine months in triage, she'd seen every kind of misery. She'd not had one shift without casualties. All those young men arriving in pain, their mangled bodies in pieces. Coated with blood and Mekong Delta mud, no end to the war in sight. It wasn't just the lyrics that touched her deeply, but the mournful style of blues, every person silenced by the accumulated memories of their tours. Everyone listening in the ward had experienced the worst of the war.

Danny struggled with his emotions. He'd just received a letter from Richard Cordero's father. Richie's firebase sustained a heavy barrage of rocket fire and was nearly overrun in the subsequent ground attack. Wounded treating a casualty, Richie died before a medevac arrived. His father, distraught at writing such a letter, did so out of an ingrained courtesy for a friend of his son who promised to stay in touch. Danny had been more worried about Johnny and Palino, but it was Richie who was dead, not four months into their tours.

Danny noticed Muriel crying next to him. She didn't know it, but Danny had a giant crush on the nurse from Montpelier, New Hampshire. Working side by side, Danny didn't understand his infatuation, a romance that could never develop. Nurses were officers, and medics were not allowed to fraternize. Not a lot of saluting or military decorum at the evac hospital, but the differences in background and education contributed to the separation. Muriel, older, taller and forty pounds heavier, addressed Danny as "Holt" most of the time, hardly a romantic moniker.

Several nurses were paired with doctors. Muriel, rumored to date a medevac pilot, kept her personal life private. Always dressed in jungle fatigues, standard for all medical personnel at the hospital, Danny wondered what he found so attractive about the buxom nurse with the red hair. Most competent in the ER, she worked with sleeves rolled up exposing powerful forearms. Not pretty in a conventional sense, Danny knew his interest would not be reciprocated in Vietnam. What might be possible in the privacy of an officer's hooch, could never happen in the medic's barracks. Crowded, hot and noisy, sound systems blared as medics relaxed between shifts. Danny hardly noticed anymore. Usually exhausted enough to catch four or five hours of sleep, the stresses of the Nam prevented more.

After hearing Rafe Johnson play on the ward, he returned to the barracks to a sound system cranking out Country Joe and the Fish singing their "Vietnam Song." A favorite among the medics, Danny normally didn't mind the tune. After a day in triage, then listening to Johnson's playing, he wasn't in the mood for Country Joe telling him about Vietnam. On this night, he found the sarcasm clownish and grating, and jarring his nerves. *What the fuck did Country Joe know about the Nam?*

Wanting to clear his head, he walked outside and found a quieter spot. Never silent in the compound with the generators running, he sat with his back against the sandbags surrounding a bunker. In the last twenty-four hours he'd learned of Richie's death, been exposed in a guard tower during a mortar attack and had a busy shift in the ER.

He would have to write to Johnny and Palino. With every medevac arriving from the boonies, he worried one might bring a friend on a stretcher.

*   *   *

Rafe Johnson had a small bag packed and prepared to leave the hospital. Always the gentleman, he bid farewell to his fellow casualties on the ward before saying goodbye to some of the nurses and medics who'd cared for him.

"Wish I could stay longer, but Victor Charles awaits my return. Starting to get short now, so I hope he appreciates that."

"Don't count on it," retorted Hank Griffiths. "Charlie don't appreciate nothin' till he greases your ass. Be careful, man, and we'll see you back at Dong Tam."

Part of Rafe wanted to get back to the platoon. During his recuperation, he'd had little news about how the guys were faring. Walking the halls of the hospital every day and the endless banter amongst the patients grew boring.

Catching a ride to Dong Tam at the Can Tho Army Airfield went smoothly. Finding the barracks empty with third platoon on a company sweep, Rafe settled into his hooch and worked on a new verse to "Mekong Delta Blues."

All along the Mekong, its jungles, swamps and rivers
So far, far away from the home that I knew
The night so thick with dark I cannot see
Until Charlie lights the night with an ambush
A mortar round or rocket flashing through the sky
Then I see, brother, see, how it's forever gonna be
For I ain't ever gonna lose those Mekong Delta Blues
No, never going to lose the Mekong Delta Blues.

The song grew. He played the blues because they spoke to him, connected him to a deep well of common experience, mostly Black, but also universal and evocative of the human experience. Many peoples suffered in Vietnam, including his own. He had no real quarrel with Charlie. He fought him to survive. There were many enemies in the world at a great many levels. He hadn't started this war and knew he wouldn't be here when it ended. A little over three months to survive, then he could go home and fight his battles there. Nearly a month at the 29th, and he hoped he hadn't grown too soft. It was nice getting away from the combat for a while. Now he had to refocus and get through the rest of his tour.

✳ ✳ ✳

Raphael Johnson, born in Natchez, Mississippi, had mostly grown up in

Georgia. Raised by women, not because his father had disappeared, just on the road constantly as a long-distance truck driver.

His Aunt Corinne had a stack of records that fascinated the boy. When she wasn't listening to the blues on the record player that held a stack of 45s, she had the radio tuned to a Black station playing Howlin' Wolf, Muddy Waters and Jimmy Reed. At a young age, he got his own guitar and started playing. Before that, he spent hours imitating Little Walter and Sony Boy Williamson on harmonica. On his first guitar, he copied the rhythms of John Lee Hooker and Mississippi Fred McDowell. Later, he plugged in and played an electrified blues.

By the age of sixteen, he performed in local clubs with older musicians. They'd sneak him in the back door, put a snazzy hat on him to make him look mature, and play rhythm and blues into the wee hours of the morning.

Of course, there was the family connection to Robert Johnson. Neither his father nor Aunt Corinne had been raised by the great bluesman, but Rafe always figured he was in his genes. He loved playing, and it came naturally. Raphael had never known his grandparents and the family information was skimpy. He could never separate the legends from the man. Myths were created from the song "Crossroads," where Robert Johnson sold his soul to the devil to become a great blues guitarist. So, he studied his grandfather's music. His personal collection included "Come on into My Kitchen," "Kindhearted Woman Blues," and "I Think I'll Dust My Broom."

By the age of eighteen, Rafe played professionally with the Curtis Brown Band, touring the South on a regular circuit, playing mostly Black clubs, but sometimes crossover audiences at larger venues. Curtis took the younger musician under his wing and taught him about the blues and playing professionally. He believed in putting on an entertaining show. Disciplined and old school, Curtis demanded his musicians stay sober and show up on time. Rafe loved playing with the band.

On the road, he had no fixed address. When the band wasn't touring, Rafe sometimes stayed at the house of his mentor. On a return trip to Georgia to see his mother and Aunt Corinne, he found his draft notice in an envelope the women were afraid to open. The army inducted him at the age of nineteen.

CHAPTER NINETEEN

Villagers gawked at the platoon from the shore of the canal. Palino looked over the side of the troop carrier and detected glimmers of hatred behind the stares. The Americans readied to return fire if attacked. Palino now understood the phrase "inscrutable Oriental." The Vietnamese always knew so much more than they let on.

The medic, frustrated by the tactics in the war, cruised the canals of the Mekong Delta with his platoon daring the VC to take a shot at them. He'd heard all the arguments for the war in university, the domino theory and how strategically important Vietnam was for stopping the flow of communism into the region. *It's all bunk,* he thought. *How could these poor villages and the ragged people who inhabited them be of any vital interest to the US.?*

Palino's opinion about his company commander was the opposite of Johnny Ornowoski's. Captain Ramsey had a special regard for his medics. Also from the South, he had the easy-going manners of a gentleman. Career army, he understood that most of the young men under his command were not. As a lieutenant with the 173rd Airborne during his first tour, a young medic he'd grown close to was killed. Now a captain and commanding a company, regard for his medics remained.

He joked with Palino about being from the deep, deep South in Mississippi, while the captain was an Arkansas boy with family roots back to the days when moonshine whiskey kept the family farm going until more prosperous times arrived.

Palino's platoon leader, Lieutenant Womback, was as crass as his company commander was refined. In the medic's eyes, the son of a bitch was undereducated, violent, and proud of it. Always ready to "rock and roll," his term for combat, his reckless pursuit of the enemy created tension within the platoon.

The lieutenant's performances in the villages were pompous spectacles. Strutting arrogantly, barking orders, and ogling the young women only made more enemies. Palino seethed as Womback made an ass of himself.

"Just letting them know who's in charge," Womback commented. "There's a war going on and I'm not here to coddle the goddammed VC sympathizers in the villages. You're either with me or my enemy. Understood?" Anything in the middle was an unnecessary complication for higher command to sort out. Womback wasn't about to let it interfere with the way he led his platoon.

As part of the Ninth Infantry's Riverine Force, Palino's unit cruised the rivers and canals on fifty-six-foot troop carriers operated by a Navy crew of seven. With a reinforced hull and landing ramp in the bow, the boats were designed so troops could quickly engage the enemy on shore. Called Tango boats, mounted thirty and fifty caliber machine guns, rapid-fire grenade launchers, and twenty mm canons comprised the craft's arsenal.

The morning's monotony broke into chaos when the Tango boat triggered a mine just past a village. The explosion rocked the ship hard, but the hull held. The VC opened fire the moment the mine detonated. Regaining control of the boat, the Navy crew unleashed its arsenal at the enemy, while the infantry troops rushed ashore on the lowered landing ramp. The VC fled the Navy guns returning fire.

Palino stayed on the carrier to treat three casualties from the initial attack. Thrown in the air by the explosion, a soldier sustained a gunshot wound to the head, killing him instantly. Another took a round in the shoulder and a third was incapacitated by a nasty blow to the side of his head when thrown into a gun turret.

Palino ran ashore after treating the wounded aboard the boat. In the pursuit, Womback led the platoon into a classic L-shaped ambush. As the medic raced to catch up, he saw several men down. That's the last thing he remembered. The man ahead of him tripped a booby trap and took the brunt of the shrapnel, but one of the fragments slammed into the side of Palino's helmet with enough force to knock him unconscious. A smaller piece of metal sliced through his cheek, dislodged several teeth, and wedged against his tongue.

Palino regained consciousness in the medevac on the way to the 29th Evac, his head on fire with pain. He watched as the dust-off medic treated his fellow platoon members. When he got to Palino, he hollered above the noise of the rotors.

"Head wound," he said, "can't give you nothin' for the pain. Hang in there. We'll be at the evac hospital in a few minutes. More help is on the way."

At the landing pad, Palino was eased onto a gurney and taken into the ER. The bright lights in triage caused a surge of new pain. Closing his eyes, he felt the medics cutting his clothes off, taking his blood pressure, and getting an IV started. An hour later they wheeled him into surgery.

Daniel Holt arrived for his evening shift in the ER. Two soldiers with minor shrapnel wounds remained waiting for available spots in the operating room. Triage showed signs of a busy afternoon with blood pooled on the floor and discarded piles of fatigues scattered about the room. Shelves depleted of medical supplies needed restocking.

"Busy afternoon?" Danny inquired.

"A riverine platoon got chewed up pretty bad. Took two medevacs to get everybody here. These two are what's left to go into surgery." Kenny Fromm nodded in the direction of the casualties on the stretchers.

Overhearing, one of the wounded men added: "No shit we got chewed up pretty bad. Charlie was just waitin' for us after we passed by the village. Nearly blew our boat out of the water. I knew somethin' was comin' just by the way them gooks was eyeing us from the shore. Can't trust nobody in the villages. They're all VC."

Kenny walked out of earshot and spoke softer. "Three KIA in the morgue." A new one had been constructed after the mortar attack. The mortician in charge was just a kid who'd had training in a funeral home before being drafted. He'd not been in the building during the attack. A bit of a pothead, he and his buddies liked to smoke weed in the airconditioned facilities where the officers rarely hassled them.

Danny looked at the casualty list. "Oh, no. You remember treating a medic from Mississippi?" he asked Kenny. He knew it was a stupid question. They were always too overwhelmed to remember the names on their charts.

Overhearing again, the talkative casualty on the stretcher blurted out: "Doc Palino's from Mississippi. Got some kind of head wound. Knocked him right out. Motherfuckers were just waitin' for us. Ambushed us and disappeared again…"

Danny tuned out the rest of his remarks. He caught up to his friend, Kenny, before the end of his shift. "Can you cover me for a few minutes?"

"Sure, what's up?"

"A friend came in with the riverine casualties. I want to check on him."

Danny saw an OR tech coming out of surgery. "You assist on a head wound today?"

"Yeah, just finished. He'll be okay. Nasty frag wound on his face, probably leave an ugly scar. Had a concussion, too, but he's stable."

Palino awoke on the ward, groggy and confused. His head throbbed while his ears rang with a high-frequency whine. His tongue swollen in a painful mouth, he raised his hand and felt sutures on the outside of his cheek. A nurse noticed him stirring and arrived at his bedside.

"You've been wounded and are at the 29th Evacuation Hospital. You've only been out of surgery a few hours. Are you in pain?"

Palino nodded, sending a surge of lightning through his brain.

"We'll adjust your medication to make you more comfortable. For now, lie as still as possible. The doctor will see you this morning."

Palino felt his face again. His right side swollen, a line of sutures ran from his cheekbone to his jaw. Nauseous and dizzy, he closed his eyes, but the room continued swirling in his head. He only remembered gliding by the village as Vietnamese stared from the shore, the boat rocking in the dirty canal water after the explosion, and running to catch up to the platoon.

He dozed, awaking when he overheard a doctor discussing his condition.

"He sustained a concussion from a hard blow to the head. His helmet must have saved his life. Was he in a lot of pain when he woke?"

The nurse nodded.

"Then let's keep him comfortable with his medication and give his brain time to heal. Administer what he needs for the pain but monitor his vital signs closely to make sure no complications arise. I'll speak to him about the wound on his face."

Palino stirred. The doctor, a drafted surgeon, loomed over him and examined the sutures on his cheek. "I'm sorry to have to tell you, but the wound on the side of your face will leave a scar. Doctors may be able to improve your looks after it heals, but the shrapnel tore right through your cheek and damaged a lot of tissue. You are fortunate to be alive."

Angered by the last comment, Palino seethed. *And aren't we all lucky to be in Vietnam,* he thought. More pain shot through his brain with the agitation. He attempted to speak. With his tongue swollen and mouth sore, he had difficulty forming words. "Can anybody tell me what happened?"

"Your platoon was ambushed and sustained heavy casualties. Other than that, I don't know. In a few days you'll be up and about and can speak with some of the other wounded. Perhaps they can give you more details."

Palino closed his eyes. Feeling weary, he dozed again.

Danny Holt came by the ward after his night shift. Finding Palino asleep, he didn't disturb him.

"How's he doing?" he asked the nurse on duty.

"His vitals are stabilized, but he sustained a concussion besides the wound on his cheek. You know him?"

"We trained together and arrived in-country at the same time. He's the medic with the riverine platoon that got ambushed yesterday. Four of us came over together. A buddy up north has been killed."

"Your friend will be okay," she said. "He just needs some time to recover."

Danny thanked her and left to get some sleep before the barracks warmed to uncomfortable levels.

Palino asked for pain medication frequently. The pounding in his head continued. Danny found him awake on his third day in hospital.

"I wondered when I'd bump into you," Palino said, attempting a smile.

"You sleep quite a bit," Danny responded. "How you feeling?"

"Like somebody took a sledgehammer to my head. Hurts like hell whenever I make the slightest move. They took another set of X-rays to make sure they didn't miss anything, but they came back negative."

"Hang in there; the nurse told me it'll get better with rest."

"I still don't remember much of what happened," Palino mumbled.

"I checked on your platoon members," Danny said.

"How bad was it?" Palino shifted on his bed and winced.

"Here," Danny said, "Let's get you more comfortable." He eased another pillow behind his friend and pulled a chair closer.

"One of your guys, Paul Abrams, saw you get wounded. He told me Nunez tripped a booby trap that killed him and caused your wounds. They thought you might be dead, too, but found you unconscious and breathing."

"Son of a bitch," Palino exclaimed, remembering more. "Womback the ignorant, my LT, must have walked the platoon into an ambush. Is he in here?"

"I found no Womback on the casualty list."

"I remember Johnny Corsair getting shot on the boat."

"He's one of your KIAs. There were three. Lisky was the third."

Palino looked away for a moment, like he was digesting the information. "I didn't know Lisky well. We both kept to ourselves."

Danny nodded. "I'm sorry, Don." He wasn't sure it was the right time to tell him about Richie Cordero but decided he should.

"I have some other bad news," he began. "Richie's been killed up north with the Air Cav. I received a letter from his father."

Palino looked like he didn't comprehend. "Richie? How? Stupid question," he recovered, returning to his anger. "This is Vietnam, the stupid war." His head continued pounding. "Everything here turns to shit. Have you noticed that? The people hate us, and we keep getting killed. I would like to know one thing we've accomplished."

"I'm sorry, Don," he repeated. "He was our friend. I just heard a few days ago. His firebase came under a rocket barrage and was nearly overrun. I haven't had a chance to write to you or Johnny. Have you seen him?"

"I have. Johnny came by my barracks when we were both off operations. His platoon is in the boonies a lot. I'm not sure I was the best host. I'm mostly drunk when we're in Dong Tam standing down. Vietnam changes everyone, but he's okay. His platoon's seen a lot of combat."

Danny felt the gloom of someone who knows how hopeless his sentiments are against the tide of events out of his control. "How could any of us have known what we'd be facing. You speak of the hatred of the villagers. We see civilian war casualties in here all the time. We only treat those we've wounded with our firepower."

"I'm in a lot of pain and my face is disfigured. Not good for someone who likes women as much as I do. Can you ask the nurse to get me some medication? It's good to see you, Danny. Come back tomorrow after your shift."

CHAPTER TWENTY

Johnny returned to Dong Tam with third platoon. Exhausted and filthy, the mud of the Delta had dried and turned to powdery dust where it hadn't formed cakes on his skin from perspiration. He barely had the energy to unlace his boots. His feet were infected with jungle rot, and he needed to dry them. His entire body was sore from the exertion of humping seventy pounds of gear through the swamps and rice paddies. Boils erupted on his skin from poor nutrition and unsanitary conditions in the field. Too weary to clean up before resting, he eased himself onto his cot and stretched out. A familiar sound emanated from the far end of the barracks—Rafe Johnson playing the blues.

Before dozing, he listened to the rhythmic chord progressions of the talented bluesman. Hearing Rafe Johnson play was the only time he was able to forget he was in the Nam. The blues, music and lyrics, spoke of pain and loss. It soothed because suffering was part of living and evoked a shared experience in a way that made a person feel they were not alone. Johnny could barely hear the words from his hooch, but he derived meaning from the mournful harmonica in between the words which cried out about the loss all around them.

> *Been fighten' in the jungles and the swamps*
> *Been makin' time, brother, time*
> *Jus' puttin' in my tour, brother, tour*
> *Until I be finishing my year.*
> *When I can say bye, brothers, bye*
> *And bid you all farewell*
> *About to return from humpin' in this hell*
> *From fighten' along the Mekong and the mighty My Tho*

Muddy waters of grief and rivers of pain
Be leavin' this fight, soon, brothers, soon
Jus' lookin' for some peace, brothers, peace
Not sure I'm ever gonna lose, brothers, lose
Those Mekong Delta Blues
Need to lose, brothers, lose
Those Mekong Delta blues...

When Johnny woke it was quiet except for the normal sounds of the barracks, guys talking, a radio playing a rock and roll hit from home. He rose and walked toward Rafe Johnson's hooch. He found him lying on his cot, hands behind his head, staring at the ceiling.

"Jus' thinkin'," he said, breaking into a grin at seeing the Doc.

"I don't know if I should welcome you back or not," said Johnny. "How was the 29th?"

"A lot quieter than around here, but Charlie is on to them, too. Took out the morgue with a mortar while I was there. What's the news here?"

"Same old shit. Third platoon was deep in the bush when Tet hit, so we missed it. Charlie's been laying low ever since."

"You mean I didn't even miss any combat while I was gone?"

"Not much. Jungle Boy got separated from the platoon during a firefight. Nobody got hit. I think we sort of surprised each other when our paths crossed." Johnny sat on Rafe's cot before continuing.

"The LT's starting to get short. Everybody's anxious about who will replace him. We're standing down for at least a day. After that, your guess is as good as mine. Anyway, it's good to have you back, at least for the rest of us."

"Not the million-dollar wound we all hope for, but it gave me a rest," Rafe said, getting up from his cot.

After visiting with his friend, Johnny returned to his hooch to write some letters. On their last operation, they'd patrolled through villages where they'd been before. The LT had him set up a medical clinic in a hamlet less hostile to their presence. Johnny spent a morning conducting a sick call.

Their new Tiger Scout, Pham, interpreted and assisted him. He liked the young Vietnamese, who was bright and quickly learned English and medical procedures. Johnny wasn't comfortable doling out medications in this setting. Not trained in internal medicine, he had picked up medical knowledge beyond treating battlefield wounds, but there was never any follow-up in the villages. He saw lots of skin ulcers and rashes, treatable cuts and infections, and symptoms of internal parasites.

Feeling he'd done some good for the day, a mother near the end of the line handed him her baby girl. The year-old child had a badly deformed cleft palate and a hand without all of its fingers. The woman stood before him hoping for a miracle that might transform her daughter.

Johnny examined the girl's face. Her upper lip, split all the way to a nostril, exposed gums that were also deformed. Johnny looked at Pham and shook his head.

"Tell this mother I'm sorry the baby has these deformities, but there is nothing that can be done in the village. She must see a doctor in a hospital some day, and they can operate on the child."

Johnny knew the advice was useless. The young mother, obviously poor, and with the war going on, would not have the option of medical treatment for her child. It's what he disliked about the clinics in the rural areas, called MEDCAPS, the acronym for Medical Civic Assistance Program. He had no way of helping the worst afflictions he saw.

Johnny considered the platoon's new Tiger Scout, Pham, a big improvement over the dour and hostile Nguyen. Whenever possible, he hung around Johnny and showed an interest in assisting the medic while he interpreted. The young Vietnamese Tiger Scout told him his story.

Pham's father, the headmaster of a rural school, believed that education was an essential component of "moving the country forward," a phrase that he inculcated in his son.

As a patriot, he believed his teaching talents were best applied in the countryside where the nation had the most need. Others like him would be doing the same in many villages throughout Vietnam. He felt that learning began with literacy and that it bettered the people's lives by providing a means to solve the nation's problems. His political views were derived from how to improve the lives of the people. He considered the pursuit of knowledge among a person's highest virtues.

The Viet Cong arrived in Pham's village and convened a political meeting in the schoolhouse. They explained why the people must support them in defeating the oppressive Saigon regime and their American puppet masters.

They conscripted Pham and several other young men and sent them to training camps that evening. Pham was seventeen. The day after, the head cadre in charge of political matters barged into the school and confiscated French textbooks from the colonial era and any written in English. After berating the teacher in front of the students for poisoning young minds with false ideas, the books were burned. When the headmaster protested, the cadre accused him of harboring sympathies for the mad dog Americans intent on destroying the will of the people. The ideologues firmly in control, Pham's father was put on trial, Viet Cong style, the cadre whipping the tribunal into a frenzy with false accusations. Taken to the middle of the village and shot, the family was not allowed to remove the body for one day.

The ideologues were not through. Pham's older sister, pretty and unmarried, was taken to be "reeducated" in matters necessary to the people. Held in a bunker complex not far from the village, she was forced to provide sex to the Viet Cong in charge of her "education." Strictly prohibited according to official Viet Cong policy, the hardliners justified their actions by claiming she was incorrigible and an enemy of the people. Filthy from their defilement, and no longer desirable, the cruelest cadre took his knife and slashed her cheek before sending her back to her village.

Pham knew none of what had happened. Accepting the political dogma during his training, he joined a mortar team and participated in several operations. Only by chance did he learn the fate of his family.

At a camp deep in the jungle, Pham recognized a boy from his village. At first, he could not believe what the young man told him. *His father executed for betraying the people he only wished to educate? How could that be?* His fellow soldier provided more details when they had a chance to speak privately.

On his next mission, Pham used the cover of night to separate from his team and returned to his village. His mother, still mourning, confirmed the boy's story of the execution. Aghast at seeing his sister, a scar running the length of her cheek on her once-pretty face, he was ashamed and vowed to fight the people that had done this to his family.

Johnny listened to Pham's story and saw it as the cruelty of the war. He'd already crossed into a survival mode that he recognized in Red Robin, Sergeant Morales, Rafe Johnson, King Tut and Lieutenant Sanders. Resigned to his tour, he focused on surviving it.

CC was no longer part of his world in Vietnam. She wrote to him and assured him she was still his girl. It was Johnny who recognized the changes in himself. Nothing he could explain in a letter. He'd never known such physical and emotional exhaustion. It took all his efforts to carry on. He feared missing CC too much. Maybe he was afraid of losing the edge Sergeant Morales had warned Jungle Boy about.

The kid was still walking point, and the platoon liked having him out front. He'd prevented more casualties on two recent patrols, but he'd also had a close call.

Leading the platoon through a swamp at the edge of a rice paddy, Jungle Boy spotted two trip wires submerged under water.

"How'd you see them?" Johnny asked later. The medic couldn't detect them until Tut cut the wires and inactivated the danger of tripping them.

"Rather clumsy setup of Charlie's," Jungle Boy replied. "Could see the wires where they came out of the water. Plain as day."

Then, there were the snipers in the trees. One of them had taken a shot at Billy Warrington and just missed the kid's head. Instead of worsening his fears, it had the opposite effect. War became more confident, functioned better, and accepted by the platoon.

Jungle Boy shot the VC who had fired at Billy, and he fell, dangling from the tree by a vine tied around his ankle. A second sniper froze in his perch, terrified, hoping to go unnoticed. Jungle Boy spotted him, and the platoon put a hundred rounds into his body.

On the same operation, a squad of VC intersected with third platoon's single file movement through a thick stretch of jungle. The Viet Cong had walked into them from the side. An intense firefight erupted at close range while they each tried to gain an advantage.

On point, Jungle Boy had not noticed anything unusual and was surprised by the firefight to his rear. He circled back to see if he could find the VC flank and return fire. The smaller enemy unit, already retreating, was pursued by King Tut's squad. Jungle Boy had not circled deep enough to flank the VC. Tut's men noticed movement in the foliage, and they all fired their weapons into the trees.

In the thick brush, Jungle Boy knew he'd been mistaken for the VC. Dozens of rounds whizzed overhead and slapped into trees. He was fortunate to be on higher ground and worried the M-79 would start lobbing grenades at him.

Jungle Boy's absence was noticed when Sergeant Morales sent Red Robin to check on the point position. There was some fear he might have been wounded and captured. Instructed never to cry out for help when separated from the platoon, Morales had told him: "We'll come get you. Yelling for us also gives your position to Charlie."

Red returned without finding him. Everyone, on edge after the initial firefight, heard Tut's squad putting rounds into the trees. Maybe the VC had circled back and set up a position on third platoon's flank. During the first lull in the firing, Jungle Boy hollered.

"If you stop shooting at me I can come out."

"Jungle Boy?" Tut responded. "What the fuck is he doing up there?" he asked of nobody in particular. "We almost greased your ass," he said with a sense of relief when the kid appeared.

"You're telling me?" Jungle Boy said. "If your squad could shoot better, I'd be dead."

Billy Warrington found that funny and started smiling. It broke the tension.

"Fucking Nam," is all Tut said as they walked back to rejoin the rest of the platoon. Billy Warrington fell in beside Jungle Boy on the way back. He'd just survived another firefight. Hundreds of rounds had been fired. Nobody from third platoon had been hit.

CHAPTER TWENTY-ONE

Palino stared at his reflection in the mirror in the ward's washroom. The gash across his cheek, still swollen and tender, had distorted his once-handsome face into a contorted disfigurement. The frag wound had damaged a considerable amount of tissue when it put a hole through the side of his face, leaving a gaunt and strained facial expression after the surgery. Not liking the image staring back at him, Palino turned away and returned to his bed.

After two weeks, the headaches were still intense, requiring heavy doses of painkillers to alleviate. Unable to walk far without triggering more pain, Palino sat on a chair outside the ward before the daily temperature rose to an uncomfortable level. With not much to see, he stared at the sandy soil in the compound, where not a blade of grass grew. *An artificial desert created by the sprays within the nondescript compound,* he mused, *taming the tropical vibrance of the Delta.*

Beyond the fenced hospital perimeter, army trucks rumbled alongside the commercial activity not consumed by the war. American dollars stimulated the local economy. Vietnamese civilians took jobs cutting American hair, laundering their jungle fatigues, cleaning hoochs, and supplying an array of goods necessary for a functioning army half a million strong. Lurking beneath the legitimate an underworld also existed. Barely concealed, the illicit trade in weed and opium thrived, and the black market profited. Bars catering to lonely soldiers reaped fortunes by Vietnamese standards for barmaids with even a modicum of charm.

Concerned about his inability to shake the headaches and dizziness from the blow to his head, and increasingly bitter about his marred face, Palino fumed. Bored out of his mind, he couldn't even read without triggering more pain. With no interest in the typical banter amongst the recovering patients, his days became monotonous ordeals.

Morose, he feigned sleep to avoid interaction with others. Palino became anxious when he overheard a conversation between his doctor and the day nurse.

"He's still asking for pain medication during the day? Better start lowering the doses. We don't want him addicted or dependent on them. All his tests are negative. The pain should be subsiding by now. See if you can't get him up and about more. How is his appetite?" The doctor continued with his assessment.

"He sleeps a lot," the nurse said, nodding in Palino's direction. "He says he can't walk far without the headaches recurring. He eats very little."

"Okay, keep me apprised. Any chance he's malingering? We should be getting him back to his unit soon."

Not faking his headaches or the dizziness, it never occurred to Palino he might be sent back to his unit prematurely. *They should put seventy pounds of gear on the doctor's back and send him packing through the muck. The irritating nurse can go with him, get a taste of the real Vietnam.*

Noticing the efficacy of his meds declining, and worried about being released from the hospital, Palino attempted longer forays into the compound. Any exertion made him nauseous, and the sun gave him the sensation of burning through his eyes to a pain center in the brain. He was in no shape to return to his platoon.

Catching a whiff of marijuana on an outing, he approached three men huddled together with their backs leaning against the sandbagged wall on the shaded side of a bunker.

"Mind if I have a toke?" he asked. "My head's still ringing from the frag that knocked me out."

"I remember you," said one of the men. "I was the OR tech for your surgery. Still not feeling well?"

"Can't shake the headaches. This should help." Palino inhaled deeply from the joint. "Thanks," he said, handing it back.

"How long you been in the Nam?" Palino asked after exhaling.

"Ten months," the OR tech told him. "Getting short, I guess. Feels like I been here longer. In the OR the whole time. Lots of grim shit in there. Shouldn't complain. Must be worse for you guys in the field. How about you?"

"Five months in the Nam now. You know Danny Holt?"

"In triage? Sure."

"We trained together."

"No shit. I had to sign on to four years to become an OR tech. Still wound up knee-deep in the war. Still, nothing like you must experience with the Ninth."

"It's all pretty shitty. Thanks for the tokes. Know where I can get my own supply?"

Palino returned to the ward and found a tray of food on his bed. Picking at the beef and potatoes, not even the marijuana improved his appetite. A nurse approached.

"You should eat. You have to get your strength back before…"

"Before what?" he interrupted. "I go back to the field. You know what it's like out there?"

She shook her head.

"Perhaps you should find out before you send people back."

"You need to eat, regardless of where you are," she recovered.

She was kind of pretty, but Palino didn't like her. He pegged her for one of those patriotic types blinded by the empty concepts of freedom and democracy that didn't apply to the Nam. She didn't know shit.

He shoved the tray away and glared at the nurse. "I'd like something more for the pain."

She glared back. "The doctor says he doesn't want you becoming dependent on the meds."

"Then how am I supposed to get rid of the pain?"

"He says you shouldn't be experiencing as much pain as you claim. All your tests have come back negative."

"So now he knows how much pain I *should* be feeling? I'm only allowed so much?"

Angry, the nurse grabbed the tray, started to walk away, but then turned to face Palino again. "We try to look after you boys, but some of you are just so bitter."

"You look after us boys, do you?" he shouted. "Do you know how we find the enemy? *Us boys* ride around in boats waiting for Charlie to take a shot at us. *Us boys* is bait, cannon fodder. I was wounded and want something for my pain," he demanded.

The nurse shoved the tray of food back at him and walked away in a huff. "Take it up with the doctor," she shouted over her shoulder.

Palino raged. "My fucking head hurts, and I want it looked after."

Danny arrived on the ward to visit. Noticing his friend's agitation, he asked what was wrong.

"That asshole, Cornick, thinks I'm faking my pain. They're going to send me back to my unit soon."

"Dr. Cornick? They can't send you back if you're having headaches and are dizzy."

"Sure they can, if they think I'm faking it."

"With a head injury. No way."

"I can't go back to the boonies feeling like this."

Rick Renault, the OR tech, arrived on the ward, interrupting the conversation. He nodded hello to Danny. "I hear you and Don trained as medics together."

"We did. Listen," Danny said to Palino, "we'll figure something out. I'm due in triage. I'll see you right after my shift."

Renault handed what looked like a package of cigarettes to Palino. Inside were several joints with a dark tar-like substance coating the papers they were rolled in.

"Opium. That ought to help. The only thing I'm going to miss about the Nam." Renault sat on the chair vacated by Danny. "I've got a day off scheduled for Thursday. If you can sneak off the ward for three or four hours, I can take you into Can Tho and show you around. We can get resupplied, maybe get laid."

On Thursday morning, Palino waited for Renault. He had a set of jungle fatigues and changed into them in a supply room on the way out of the hospital. The OR tech had already stashed a set of boots inside.

Military personnel were not allowed out of the compound in civilian clothes. Dressed in standard fatigues, getting off the hospital grounds was as easy as signing a log at the gate. The bored MPs were more concerned with who came into the compound than who left.

Palino smoked an opium-laced joint before meeting Renault. The dope numbed the throb in his head to a manageable level, and he looked forward to getting out of the hospital for a few hours. He let Renault organize getting to Can Tho.

The OR tech had them on a deuce and a half within minutes of leaving the compound. Palino sat in the canvas-covered back of the truck as it rumbled towards Can Tho. In his opium-induced state, he viewed the teeming activity of the road. Open-fronted shops sold everything from colorful ceramic wares to wooden coffins. Cycle shops, strewn with parts, serviced the numerous motorbikes zipping in and around the lumbering trucks and slower cyclos powered by bicycles, relics of the Chinese rickshaws in use for centuries. The opium produced a passive contentment that had Palino observing from an internal quiet spot that only saw things as they were, devoid of placing values or imposing his receded will as an active participant.

In his timeless state, the bustling of Can Tho appeared before Palino as the truck dropped them off.

"Most of the activity revolves around the marketplace along the river," Renault said. "We can go have a look, secure some dope, and head back in a couple of hours. How's your head doing?"

The sun's glare caught Palino by surprise after riding in the canvas-covered truck. "I could use another hit of opium. Is there someplace we can sit down and smoke a joint?"

Renault led him to a park a block from the Hau River. Mostly deserted, they sat beneath a large tree that blocked the direct sun.

"How often do you get to Can Tho?" Palino asked.

"Once or twice a month. We usually get a day off when switching shifts. Two if we're lucky."

"Are the bars open yet?"

"All day. They close at night, at least to the Americans restricted by curfew."

"I think I'd like a whiskey. Where do you usually go?"

"You can decide. The brothels are the only places to get a drink off the bases. They're all in an area just past the market."

The cyclos, prevalent in the city, were off-limits to American troops, but Palino didn't want to walk. Approaching a driver parked and sitting in his bicycle-powered rickshaw, Renault spoke the name, "Garden of Eden. Everybody knows where it is," he told Palino.

Skirting the main market area, the cyclo took them through a modestly prosperous Vietnamese neighborhood. The houses, small by American standards, were reminiscent of the French colonial presence in the country. White stucco prevailed, and painted wooden shutters were open on the windows facing the street. Large trees lined the paved roads, wide enough for two-way traffic but lacking the bustle of the main commercial center of the city.

In minutes, the driver had them at the bar district where the names of the establishments reflected their clientele. The New York Go-Go Bar's garish purple sign competed for attention with the bright red of the Hollywood Saloon. More tasteful on the outside, the Garden of Eden sported green shutters on a colonial-style two-story building. The name appealed to Palino.

"I'll be in there," he told Renault.

"I just have a couple of things I want to pick up. I'll be back when I'm done."

Palino entered the darkened bar. When his eyes adjusted, he could see a few soldiers sipping alcoholic beverages while scantily clad barmaids brought them drinks. Taking a seat at an empty table near a wall, he watched a girl walk to his table to take his order. "Whiskey," he told her.

She returned with a tray of drinks and placed it on the table. Slender, and unusually large-breasted for a Vietnamese, she leaned over Palino and lingered for a moment with her low-cut dress exposing the tops of her breasts. Noticing his wound, she touched it gently with her delicate hand.

"GI hurt," she said. "Maybe boom-boom make GI better."

"Maybe next time," Palino said. He was getting hooked on Vietnamese women but had another purpose for the day's visit. "Just bring me whiskey," he said, touching her arm.

Faking offense at not wanting to negotiate a fee for taking her upstairs, she pulled her arm away. "No can touch without boom-boom," she said, collecting Palino's money for the drinks.

"Not today," he reiterated, leaning back in his chair while watching the comings and goings of the bar's patrons.

"You've been drinking," the nurse scolded him.

"And not feeling any pain," he shot back. "I'm self-medicating. You got a problem with that?"

"Several," she huffed. *Another of the uppity nurses on the ward,* Palino fumed. Danny spoke highly of most of them, but the wounded medic had managed to piss them off. *She's upset that I would take a drink in Vietnam, but not concerned that I've been wounded and in pain. Am I the only sane person in this war?*

"Where have you been all day?" the nurse pressed. "If you're healthy enough to be off the ward drinking, I'd say you're healthy enough to return to your unit."

Palino held his temper and mused inwardly. *She has no idea I've been in Can Tho. That would really get her going.* "I'm the only one who knows whether I'm in pain or not," Palino shot back.

Danny stopped in. He'd also noticed Palino's absence during the afternoon. On the day shift again, he popped into the ward in the lulls between casualties.

"I couldn't find you," Danny said.

"That's because I was in Can Tho."

"You're kidding? Have you been drinking, too? Be careful, man, this could end badly for you."

"It already has. I can't go back to my unit. I need out. It's too crazy."

"We can still get you some time to recover, Don. At least try."

"I can't go back," Palino stated matter-of-factly.

"You could be court-martialed, and in the Nam that could mean LBJ."

The abbreviation stood for Long Binh Jail, the same initials as the president who had been responsible for the massive build-up of American troops in Vietnam, Lyndon Baines Johnson. The facility had a fearsome reputation, a prison within a prison, full of racial tension and violence.

"Richie is dead, I came close to dying, and Johnny's seeing lots of combat. At this rate, you might be the only one of us to survive. From my perspective, Long Binh Jail's not looking too bad."

Kenny Fromm appeared on the ward to fetch Danny. "Sorry, man, medevac's on the way, ten minutes out. We need you in triage."

Palino spent the next two days writing letters. He asked if it was possible to make a phone call to the US. Not easy, but possible.

He stopped complaining about his headaches and became a model patient. He made one more foray into Can Tho and visited the Garden of Eden but not to drink or see any of the girls.

Receiving his release from the hospital, he packed his few belongings and looked for Danny.

"Goodbye for now," he began. "Can you do me a favor?"

"Of course."

"Let Johnny know what's happened to me."

"What do you mean?" Danny wasn't sure what his friend was asking.

"I'm going AWOL, not back to my unit. You won't turn me in, will you? It would be nice to get a head start." Palino smiled slightly. Despite the circumstances, he retained a flair for the ironic.

"Of course not, but are you sure?"

Palino shrugged, leaving Danny conflicted. He understood his friend's reluctance to return to his platoon not fully healed. Either path was fraught with uncertainty and serious consequences. "We're all trapped in this war, Danny. I have a bad feeling I won't survive it."

"Then take care, my friend. I'm so sorry for the way it's turned out."

CHAPTER TWENTY-TWO

Johnny and Jungle Boy gathered with several platoon members to say goodbye to Red Robin. Standing in his hooch, the smiling grunt nodded hellos and shook hands with everyone. A short-timer's party brewing, the seasoned infantryman accepted a bottle of Jack Daniel's from an outstretched hand while Rafe Johnson opened the lid on a cooler of beer.

"Congratulations, Red," Johnny began. "I speak for the platoon when I say we're sorry to see you go but glad you made it through your tour."

Not one for modesty, Red Robin addressed the group. "Now that I won't be there to save your sorry asses next time Charlie figures to grease one of them, you watch yourselves, you hear."

"We'll do our best," Jungle Boy responded.

"And speaking for this cherry, I expect you'll not let him go his full tour without losing him his virginity." Red had his arm around Jungle Boy's shoulder. Even a trimmed-down Red at the end of his tour dwarfed the platoon's smallest and youngest member. Not releasing his grip, Red continued.

"I would have taken that task on myself but for all the other things they've had me doing over here."

A blushing Jungle Boy, at a loss for words, grinned awkwardly.

Johnny rescued the kid from Red's grip by handing the departing grunt a gift from the platoon, a brass belt buckle with the Ninth's insignia on the front. Custom engraved on the back were the words: "GOOD LUCK BACK IN THE WORLD, RED. THANKS FOR BEING THERE. YOUR BUDDIES IN THIRD PLATOON."

Obviously touched by the gesture, Johnny thought one of the toughest platoon members might cry. Instead, he fetched a package of plastic cups and handed them out. Breaking open the bottle of whiskey, he poured some into everyone's glass.

"To Toad," Red Robin raised his cup, "and RC, and everyone else who didn't make it out of the Nam. Make sure you all do."

"To Toad and RC," everyone repeated before downing their drink.

Red Robin wasn't the only platoon member leaving. Lieutenant Sanders and Sergeant Morales were also short. Their looming departures meant a change in leadership, something that concerned everyone.

Johnny had seen what poor command meant in the Nam. Just in from a patrol that lasted five days, he would use the brief stand down in Dong Tam to check on Palino, whose lieutenant had carelessly rushed his platoon into an ambush. Johnny wanted to verify the news that he'd not returned to his unit.

He didn't stay long at the party. He had mail from CC and wanted to write some letters. Permanently exhausted as he approached the halfway point of his tour, sores peppered his body, and jungle rot ate at his toes. Stretching out on his cot, he fell asleep with the scent of his girl's unopened perfumed envelope mingling with the boisterous sounds coming from Red Robin's hooch.

Dear Johnny,

I miss you so much. Life is not the same without you. Please be safe and come home to me.

I have some terrible news. Ralph Barnes was arrested and is in jail waiting for his trial.

There is so much I wish we could talk about, but it is difficult in a letter. I want you to hold me and make me feel safe in your arms again. I won't ever let you out of my sight when you return. Until then, love and kisses from your girl.

Forever Yours,

CC

CC didn't mention the possible implications of Ralph's arrest. Her dealing amounted to very little, but if the authorities were watching her supplier, they would likely know about her. She desperately wanted Johnny to come home but had six months to wait. CC also needed to get her own situation in order before Johnny returned.

When he set out for the barge that acted as Palino's barracks, Johnny only knew what Danny Holt had related in a letter.

> *Johnny,*
> *Our friend, Don Palino, has asked me to inform you of his situation. About a month ago, he was wounded and medevaced to the 29th. He suffered a concussion from a frag hitting his helmet, along with a bad facial wound. While recuperating, he suffered severe headaches and dizziness, despite all X-rays and tests coming back negative. The doctors cut his pain medication back, and he began self-medicating with opium and alcohol. After his release from the hospital, he decided not to report back to his unit. Rumor has it he is in Can Tho. I'm sorry to have to inform you of this news, especially so soon after Richie's death. I don't know how things have gotten so crazy. I'm very worried about you. Don says your platoon is seeing lots of combat. Please take care and write when you get the chance.*
>
> > *Your Friend,*
> > *Danny*

Johnny knocked on the door of Palino's hooch. A stocky dark-haired kid in new jungle fatigues appeared.

"I'm looking for Doc Palino," Johnny said. "I believe this is his hooch. Can you tell me where he is?"

"*Was* his hooch," the soldier answered. "I'm his replacement. Nobody has a clue where he is. I can tell you one thing, though."

"What's that?" Johnny asked.

"He's in deep shit if he does return."

"Let me tell you something," Johnny responded, suddenly angry. He didn't like the kid's attitude. "You're the one who's in deep shit. Welcome to the Nam."

When he returned to the company area in Dong Tam, Johnny found Lieutenant Sanders writing a report for the captain on the small desk provided in his hooch.

"What can I do for you, Doc?"

"I need to get to Can Tho for a couple of days." He'd decided to level with the LT as much as possible. "A friend of mine is missing, and I'd like to try and find him."

"That's asking a lot," Sanders responded.

"I know, LT, but I figure I'm just about due for an in-country R&R. Surely we'll stand down for a couple of days during the transition when your replacement arrives. Perhaps then?"

"Tell me more. I can't just give you permission to wander the war zone looking for someone missing in action. It's too dangerous. And how do you expect to find him? Isn't that his platoon's responsibility?"

"Sir, he's not MIA, just gone."

Sanders looked perplexed. "AWOL?"

"It could be, but there's more to the story. He was wounded and suffered a concussion. It may have affected his judgement."

"How do you know this?"

"A fellow medic at the 29th Evac wrote to me. The three of us trained together."

"You have a lot of friends."

"Yes, Sir."

Sanders thought for a moment. He admired the Doc's loyalty. He'd been fortunate to have two good medics while commanding the platoon. As weary of the war as any of his troops, he decided to help Johnny look for his friend.

"You know I'll have to bend the rules to grant your request."

"Yes, Sir."

"We could both be in a pile of shit if something goes wrong."

"Yes, Sir."

"I'll see what I can do."

A few days before the LT's scheduled rotation date, the lieutenant summoned Johnny. He found Sanders with a compact blonde man in newly issued jungle fatigues.

"Doc, I'd like you to meet Lieutenant Howitz, my replacement."

"Welcome to third platoon, Sir. We hate to see the LT go but are glad for him. If there's anything I can do to help familiarize you with the platoon, just let me know."

"Thanks," said Howitz.

"And, Doc, about that in-country R&R," Sanders said, "your orders are in the orderly room. Better hurry and fetch them before the captain changes his mind. It was a tough sell."

Johnny thanked the lieutenant and hurried to the orderly room. Fortunately, the captain was not there. The company clerk handed him his orders.

"Make sure you don't screw up, Ornowoski. The captain and Lieutenant Sanders don't see eye to eye on this one."

Johnny ran to his hooch and packed a few items for his trip to Can Tho. He stopped to see Jungle Boy on his way to the airstrip.

"Walk with me and I'll fill you in. The LT has gotten me three days' leave in Can Tho to find a friend. Promise me you'll stay out of trouble while I'm gone."

"How would I get into trouble?" Jungle Boy asked. "We're standing down for a few days during the transition."

"Don't go volunteering for anything. Stay put so you can let me know what's been going on when I get back."

"War and I were just going to catch a movie they're showing tonight." Jungle Boy and Billy Warrington had formed a close bond as the new grunt had adjusted to the Nam. Once derogatory, his nickname had stuck, but no longer carried a negative connotation.

"Sounds like there's more chance of you getting into trouble than me," Jungle Boy continued.

Johnny shrugged. "Okay, okay, I get your point. We'll both be careful, right?"

By hitching a flight out of Dong Tam before dark, Johnny gained half a day. A Huey returning to the Can Tho Army Airfield had him there within an hour. The same leaning air control tower hovered over the terminal, and the same skinny kid inside coordinating flights gave him directions.

"If you hurry, there'll still be some army trucks heading in the direction of the 29th Evac." Johnny walked to the main road and stuck his thumb out. A jeep pulled over to pick him up. Surprised to see a woman in jungle fatigues in the passenger seat, Johnny asked: "You going anywhere near the 29th Evac?"

"It's where we live," responded the red-haired woman, who had lieutenant's bars on her collar. "What brings you to Binh Thuy?"

"I'm trying to find a friend of mine, Danny Holt. You know him?"

"Danny? I work with him in the ER. Muriel Tandy," she introduced herself, extending her hand. "We'll take you right to him. The chaplain and I are just returning from the orphanage in Can Tho. I spend some of my days off there. I'm afraid business is booming in the war zone. I go as much for myself as the children. Some of them are so traumatized they just crawl into your lap and want you to hold them all day. It's run by an order of Catholic nuns. Chaplain Brandt is organizing donations from the US."

The chaplain, a captain, glanced at Johnny while driving. "How is it you know Danny?"

"We trained together." Johnny didn't elaborate.

When they arrived at the compound gate, an MP took a quick look under the jeep with a long-handled mirror and waved them through. Captain Brandt pulled up to the entrance of the hospital and parked. A nondescript sign atop the facing on the awning simply read: 29th EVACUATION HOSPITAL. A red cross and the unit's insignia the only other items visible on the painted plywood.

"Come with me," Muriel Tandy told Johnny. He followed her through the entrance and into a long covered hallway which ran the length of the hospital. On both sides were double doors that opened into the individual Quonsets, which comprised the hospital. Muriel walked through the second set on the right, and they were in the emergency room.

"I thought you might still be here," Muriel said to a medic cleaning up. "Someone's here to see you."

Johnny looked past her and saw a skinnier version of Danny Holt, who squinted at him from behind his glasses. Taking a moment to recognize Johnny, he asked: "Are you okay?"

"What do you mean?" said Johnny.

"I mean, you're not hurt?" Danny stepped toward Johnny to have a better look. "What are you doing here? You're so thin. Have you been sick?"

Johnny looked at Danny. His fatigues hung on him and were splattered with blood. He could see specks of blood on his glasses. "I'm fine," Johnny said. "I've come to help you find Palino. Have you heard from him?"

"No word at all," Danny said, beginning to comprehend the reason for Johnny's visit. "I thought you must be hurt to just show up unexpectedly. Everybody we see is either wounded or sick. We don't get visitors."

Johnny smiled at him. "Of course. This is where the guys I put on a medevac wind up." He looked around the triage unit. No casualties remained, but two piles of discarded fatigues, bloody and dirty, were on the floor. Another medic mopped pools of blood from the floor.

"The helipad is just out there," Danny said, pointing to the opposite set of doors from where Johnny had entered from the hallway. "I worry I might see you on one of them. I wasn't here when Don came in. I wasn't able to help him much."

"We'll try and figure something out," Johnny said. "First, we have to find him. I've only got three days."

"Help me clean up," Danny said, "then we can go sit in the mess hall and talk. My shift ends at seven."

Danny grabbed a cup from a tray and filled it with coffee from an urn. "Grab something to eat if you like," he said to Johnny. "I'm usually not too hungry after my shift." Johnny filled a cup, and they found a table out of earshot in the sparsely filled mess hall.

"One of the OR techs went into Can Tho with Palino," Danny began, "and dropped him off at the Garden of Eden, a local brothel. It's owned by an expat Frenchman and his Vietnamese wife. A known hub of illicit activity going way beyond prostitution, it's rumored that anything can be bought for the right price. None of it legal."

"Anything?"

"Pretty much. Opium, heroin, guns, ammunition, it's all available. The brothel is just a front. I suspect Don's trading on the black market. That's all I know."

"I have no days off scheduled for a while. We're short medics in triage. We'll go over to the barracks later and see if anyone's going into Can Tho tomorrow. Someone can show you where to start. The street kids may be able to help, for a fee. Make sure you pay them *after* you get the information you need."

By seven the next morning Johnny was out the gate. Danny had told him everything he knew about what led to Palino's AWOL. They had breakfast in the mess hall before Danny's shift.

Johnny had decided to get an early start. After getting detailed directions, he went into Can Tho by himself. Too early for the brothels to open, Johnny poked around the open market. Walking toward the red-light district, he soon attracted some of the street kids Danny had mentioned.

"Hey, GI, you want number one girl?" Soon he had a small crowd of young pimps all offering number one girls.

"I have a job for the kid who speaks the best English," he said. "I'm not looking for girls," he continued. "I need to find a friend of mine. He has a scar on his face." Johnny drew a line across his cheek with a finger.

"I speak English," one of the kids offered. Skinny, and with a slightly protruding set of buck teeth, the boy was dressed in a dirty yellow T-shirt and black shorts. "What you want, GI?" he asked suspiciously.

"Only to find my friend. Can you help?"

"Why you need see?" the kid asked.

"You know who I mean?" Johnny said, redrawing the line across his face.

"Maybe." The kid gave nothing away. "What you pay?"

"Same, same boom boom," Johnny said, "except you keep all the money." Johnny held up two five-dollar MPC notes and gave one to the kid. "You deliver a note to my friend, get him to send a message back, and I give you the other five dollars. You arrange a meeting with my friend, and I give you more. Understand?"

The kid nodded. "Lanh go now and find friend. Be back here one o'clock."

Johnny decided to wait in the Garden of Eden where he might obtain more information. He sat on a stool at the counter after his eyes adjusted to the darkened room. A few patrons were at tables in the main part of the establishment.

"I'll have a beer," he said to the Vietnamese bartender, a slight man with several days' growth of stubble. Johnny nodded to a middle-aged sergeant sitting toward the other end of the counter. A bar girl appeared and brushed against him.

"You want goodtime boom-boom, mister? Ten dollars we go upstairs."

The girl pulled the nearest stool close to his and sat, exposing her thighs underneath a short purple dress. Johnny inhaled her floral perfume while he took a sip of beer. Not wanting to appear too anxious, he waited a minute before pulling ten dollars out of his pocket. The girl took it and tucked it into her bosom.

"You'll watch my beer?" he said to the sergeant sitting nearby. The man nodded slightly and smiled.

The girl took Johnny's hand and led him to a room upstairs. A ceiling fan whirred lazily overhead, and two geckos, motionless, clung to a wall. Without hesitation, the girl began to unzip the pair of patent leather boots that came to her knees.

Johnny stopped her. "I just want to talk," he said. Immediately suspicious, the girl stepped back into her boot. "I'm trying to find a friend of mine," he continued. "I know he's been here. He has a scar on his face." Johnny repeated drawing an imaginary line down the side of his cheek.

Agitated, the girl reached into her bosom, withdrew the money Johnny had given her and threw it on the bed. "No want trouble, mister. No want talk."

"I just want to find my friend,' Johnny reiterated.

"Maybe friend not want to see you, mister. We go downstairs now. Pretend short-time over."

Johnny didn't push it. The girl's reaction told him she knew about Palino. He would take another approach.

He came downstairs, grabbed his beer and took a long draft. Moving closer to the sergeant, he sat down again. "I'll have another," he told the bartender. "That was something," he exclaimed. "Six months in the boonies without any, if you know what I mean," he said, looking at the sergeant.

The older man took the bait. "I see you're with the Ninth Division. What brings you to Can Tho?"

"My company sent me to IV Corps Headquarters trying to requisition some stuff we never have enough of in the boonies." He took a swig from his beer. "Time for some relaxation, too, I say."

"What are you looking for. Maybe I can help. Sergeant Keenan," he said, extending his hand. "I work in supply. You know the army. Too much of some stuff, but not enough of what you really need."

"Amen," said Johnny. He decided to take a chance. There was something odd about the supply sergeant, a little too old, the hair too long, sitting in a brothel drinking at ten in the morning.

Johnny leaned closer and lowered his voice. "Actually, Sergeant, my unit is full of potheads and their supply is much diminished. My point man also needs some oddball ammunition for the zip gun he likes to carry when he's out front. Personally, I much prefer a beer and a shot of whiskey, but the weed tends to calm the crazy motherfuckers in my platoon."

Keenan smiled. "Perhaps I can help with that, too," he said quietly.

"We're willing to pay, Sergeant. It's not like my guys are the only potheads in the Nam, now are they? I don't dare come back empty-handed."

"How much you looking for?"

"Fifty pounds, Cambodian Red. Need a bit of opium, too. Mellows some guys right out."

"I'll have to check on the supply. How long you in Can Tho?"

"Two more days, Sergeant. Gotta go for now. Will you be here tomorrow?"

"Sure thing," he said. "Check back around noon."

Johnny walked two blocks to meet with Lanh. Right on time, the kid appeared. "Friend say to read letter. Now you pay Lanh." He handed him the folded note.

Johnny,

I think it's best not to see one another right now. What is it you want? I'm not going back. Just to verify it's you, what is my girl-friend's name?

Yours,
Donald

Johnny took two five spots out of his pocket. He handed one of them to Lanh. "That's what I owe you for finding my friend. There's five more if you deliver another message and return with one." He scribbled a reply.

Don,

I don't have long. I've gone to a lot of trouble to find you. I have come on my own. You know I would never turn you in. Your girl-friend's name is Stormy Beth. Just to make sure Lanh is on the level, where is Danny from? He's worried about you, too.

Johnny

He handed the new message to Lanh. "Can you be back by three o'clock?" The kid nodded a yes. It was his lucky day. His cut might be ten percent for arranging a girl for a soldier. Delivering the mail was lucrative business.

Johnny walked toward the waterfront and sat down at an outdoor café. He ordered vegetables with steamed rice. Noticing the locals consuming bowl after bowl of a watery soup, he tried some. The *pho* quenched his thirst.

Once more, Lanh arrived on time and bearing a note.

Johnny,

You are persistent and making this kid a lot of money. Danny is from Colorado. I've set something up for tomorrow. You can appreciate how careful I must be. I will send the kid to fetch you at nine in the morning.

Donald

CHAPTER
TWENTY-THREE

Right on time, Lanh waited for Johnny at the designated street corner in Can Tho. Without a watch, the kid had managed an accurate schedule. Still dressed in his dirty yellow T-shirt and black shorts, Johnny wondered if the boy even had a home. Lanh got right to the point.

"Friend say follow Lanh to river. Take sampan. Pay Lanh five dollars."

No note from Palino. Johnny followed the kid on a path through a slum on the outskirts of Can Tho. Tiny, thatched huts were crowded next to tin shacks of corrugated metal tacked onto poles embedded in the ground. Young children, with no underwear and pants, eyed him warily as he followed Lanh. Women crouched over charcoal fires, while others washed clothes in large plastic tubs. Older women chewed betel nut, which left stains on their crumbling teeth. Every pair of eyes were on him as the neighborhood continued its morning activities. Nobody spoke.

They moved on the path toward the river, away from the floating market at the center of Can Tho. The great expanse of the Hau River appeared after a trek of half a mile. The huts, sparse now, gave way to jungle that grew to the river's edge. A sampan, moored to a simple stake pounded into the ground, bobbed in a small eddy created by silt deposited by the massive river system emanating from the Mekong. A Vietnamese man and his young daughter waited nearby.

"You take sampan now, cross river. Give five dollars to Lanh. Lanh go now."

A tiny motor propelled the small boat across the waterway. The man stood in the bow with a long pole intently watching for floating debris. The girl, wearing a *non la,* the ubiquitous conical hats woven from bamboo and palm leaves, controlled the rudder in the stern. Johnny sat in the middle on a four-legged stool raised only inches off the boat's curved floor and looked at the expanse of the river. The opposite shore, barely visible when they started, came into view. Palm trees lined the river, and a cluster of thatched dwellings formed a tiny village. More prosperous-looking and ordered than the poor section of Can Tho, the sampan glided to a stop against a sandy bank in the river.

A boy in his teens, slightly older than Lanh, met them when they landed. Without speaking, he motioned for Johnny to follow. They walked along the shore, taking a path leading from the river to another cluster of dwellings concealed by the tropical foliage.

A storefront appeared in a concrete building. Not as congested as Can Tho, the commercial activity continued at a slower pace on this side of the river. Johnny followed his guide through an open door. Bins of un-processed herbs and roots of many shapes filled the air with medicinal pungency. Brightly colored packaged goods, with yellow and red lettering in Vietnamese, lined the shelves.

Another door at the back of the small shop opened into a lovely garden with flowers in bloom. A cobbled stone path through the cultivated flora led to a stucco hut. The boy motioned for Johnny to enter, then took his leave.

Palino sat at a wooden table, his chair facing the entrance. Johnny noticed the horrible scar on his right cheek. No longer confined by army regulations, he'd grown a beard that he kept trimmed but was too sparse to hide the disfigurement of his wound. Dressed in civilian clothes, he greeted Johnny.

"You are persistent in the pursuit of your friends. I'll interpret that in a positive way." His Mississippi drawl intact, charming and urbane at the same time, just as Johnny remembered it. "Life takes us down many unexpected paths on the way to hell, is how my grandfather expressed it."

"I'm afraid I don't come from such eloquence," Johnny responded, "just a long line of plodders toiling away at life." He looked around the room, simply furnished with only a table with chairs. An enclosed cabinet stood near the entrance to a second room, and a window provided a view of the garden.

"Please have a seat," Palino gestured. "I won't forget my manners now that we meet a second time in the war, especially since you have gone to great lengths to find me. As you can see, I am sober, but this calls for a drink. Nhung," he called, "please bring us some whiskey from the cabinet." He made a drinking motion with his hand when a pretty Vietnamese woman appeared from the other room.

Tall for a Vietnamese, her long black hair reached well below her shoulders and accentuated her elegance as she moved to fetch the bottle of whiskey and two glasses. When she placed the whiskey on the table, Johnny, startled, noticed a scar of her own on the side of Nhung's face. Palino smiled when he observed Johnny's reaction.

"She is a beauty. One can ignore such an imperfection when beset with a disfigurement of my own." He touched the wound on his face.

"First, Lanh shows up, and word quickly follows that you are looking for me at the Garden of Eden, a misnomer of gigantic proportions, unless you factor in the biblical Fall of Man. Sergeant Keenan tells me about some hick grunt with ORNOWOSKI on his name tag looking for fifty pounds of weed. Said you needed it for the potheads in your company. I had to laugh. I guess you picked up on the fact he's no sergeant. Very clever, though nothing's impossible in the Nam. It reveals more of your story than you've told me. You tracked me down rather easily."

"I wasn't sure Lanh would be able to find you. I was just pursuing another option. It's rumored you're doing business on the black market."

"Is there a better place for business than a war zone? A country opens up its pocketbook to fight one. As for Lanh, where do you think he has learned his English? He will go far if given the chance."

"Pimping girls in Can Tho? He is clever and gave nothing away," Johnny said.

"Yet another form of casualty in the war zone. Is it more vulgar than the killing we've experienced? Everything is corrupted by our presence here, but you didn't come all this way to have a chat about the morality of the war."

"No," Johnny said, "we are all trapped by it."

"And finding our own ways of surviving," Palino added. The hint of a smile formed at the corners of his mouth.

"So, what are you doing here on the other side of the Hau River?"

"We don't live here. The older man in the shop is Nhung's uncle on her mother's side. As a Buddhist monk, he took an interest in herbal medicine. Aware of his niece's difficulties, he offers refuge when necessary. He's also trying to help with my headaches, which are persistent. He's wise in ways that defy the situation in Vietnam."

"Isn't it dangerous for you, an American on the run in the Mekong Delta? What about the Viet Cong?"

"I fear the ideologues on both sides. Most of the Vietnamese realize the war will end and one side prevail. A strange tolerance exists in the culture. Apart from the hardcore VC, and the corruption amongst the elites in South Vietnam, most people hope to avoid the revenge they know will follow after the war, whichever side wins."

Palino took a sip of his whiskey and continued. "Take Nhung's uncle, a benevolent man at heart. He has no sympathy for wealthy landlords that keep the people poor. But he also sees through the propaganda of the communists. Whose side would he be on? Most Vietnamese are nation-alists who would like the Americans to leave, so some side with the Viet Cong to that extent. You have seen how we go into the villages armed and hostile while we search the meagre belongings of poor farmers. How would Americans like that, so puffed up with our sense of freedom and rights to our property? Our arrogance defies description."

"What will you do?" Johnny asked. "How do you see all of this ending?"

"Tragically, no doubt, but is it any more appalling than trying to keep dying grunts alive in filthy rice paddies, and dying there myself? How long do you think I would last back in my unit with my headaches and dizziness and packing seventy or eighty pounds of gear?"

"How did it come to that? You have a head injury."

"They started to believe I was faking my symptoms to avoid going back to the field. I wasn't, but given the circumstances, it would have made perfect sense. They have no idea what it's like out there. You would not believe the head nurse on my ward. Talk about being puffed up with a sense of self-importance and righteousness. As long as wounded grunts idolized her as Florence Nightingale, they were great. She could be pretty and tend to *her boys*. I was angered and offended by all of the pretending going on. Every aspect of this war reeks of hypocrisy."

"What if we could prove you were suffering from the effects of the concussion? Danny said all the tests pinpointed nothing, but head injuries are tricky. I don't understand why that didn't factor into the diagnosis?"

"Poor Danny, he was so astonished by the unfairness of it all. He thinks highly of most of the nurses. I think he's in love with that large red-haired nurse he works with. The inequities began a long time ago. Who do you think you're slogging through the boonies with? Do you think any of them have a quarrel with Charlie? What the fuck do any of them care whether the villages are communist or not?"

Palino looked at their glasses, empty now. Pouring from the bottle, he filled them and nodded at Johnny to have another drink.

"Did you know that many nurses are paired with doctors? Someone who likes women as much as I can hardly object to the morality of a little sex for comfort in the war zone. It is the inflated sense of self-importance that offended me. The complete and utter blindness to put any of the war into a sane context. So, I drank some whiskey and smoked a little pot to dull the pain in my head. They weren't giving me enough meds to control it, but the whiskey offended them. Sending me back to my unit did not. She was fucking my doctor, you know, and complaining to him what a lousy patient I was."

"What will you do?" Johnny asked. "You can't stay on the run in Vietnam forever."

"Make a lot of money to start with. I won't deal in guns; there are too many already. Everything else I consider fair game. I have a growing list of contacts. Sergeant Keenan is really an American civilian here to make his fortune. Initially, he came over with a private firm providing building supplies for the military. He liked the availability of the women and found he could make a fortune on the black market. Nhung and I will probably wind up in Thailand where the money I make here will last a lifetime. She helps soothe the demons raging in my soul. I hope I am good for her."

"She was wounded? Danny says he sees a lot of civilian war casualties in triage."

Palino laughed sarcastically. "Wounded? Hardly. The morally superior VC took a knife to her, that is after they grew tired of raping her and she no longer appealed, the stink of themselves all over her. Also, after they killed her father, the headmaster of a rural school."

Johnny looked at Palino across the table. "She has a brother named Pham?"

Startled, Palino stared intently at his friend. "How could you possibly know that? Nhung had to leave her village to seek work. I found her in the Garden of Eden doing drunken soldiers for half the going rate. The last time she saw her brother, he'd deserted from his Viet Cong mortar team."

"And came over to our side as a Tiger Scout. He's with my platoon," Johnny said. "Tell Nhung I can take a message back for Pham if she wishes."

Sensing the conversation involved her brother, Nhung returned and whispered in Palino's ear. "She will get her uncle to prepare a letter for Pham. Their mother is very sick and has not known where to find her son." Nhung bowed slightly and went to see her uncle. "Once again our paths have converged," Palino said. "Enough about my life. You still have your girl? CC is it?"

Johnny nodded. "To keep a girl, you also have to remain alive. I have a bunch of war to get through."

"What are the odds now, since we're all gambling with our lives?"

"I've stopped calculating," Johnny said. "Some of our guys have rotated home without being wounded. I have to try and be one of them."

"Why aren't you angrier?"

"Maybe that will come later. I look at the guys in my platoon, and it is like you say, most of them getting the short end of the stick. I guess as the medic, I feel a responsibility toward them. There is this kid we call Jungle Boy. The same shitty background as a lot of us, but he has heart. Likes walking point. Would rather die than let the platoon down. Just a little guy packing all that weight. For him alone, I have to stay.

"When I looked you up on the barge, you kept pressing me about my past, sensing there was more to my story. Well, I promised myself before I left for Vietnam that if I survived, I was done living on the fringes, never in control of my life. Who has any guarantees in the Nam? I didn't expect it to be this bad, but my only path forward is through the war."

"A noble but naïve sentiment," Palino commented. "You were in trouble with the law?"

"Prison or the army," Johnny stated. "We'll see if I made the right choice."

Nhung reentered the room and spoke in Palino's ear. "She says her uncle is writing a letter and preparing a package for you to take back for Pham, if that's okay?"

"Of course. Is there anything I can do for you?" Johnny asked as a last attempt to find a solution for his friend's dilemma.

"There is no going back," answered Palino. "And now, I would never leave Nhung."

She stood at his side. She was beautiful, even with the scar on her face.

Johnny rose. "I must go. Any messages you want me to deliver?"

Palino shook his head. "Just tell Danny not to feel badly. None of this is his fault. The world was a shitty place long before he arrived in it."

Johnny stepped forward as Palino stood and looked into his eyes. "I guess this is goodbye," he said, before wrapping his arms around him. His eyes misted, but Palino's gaze remained steady without showing emotion.

"We will meet again," smiled Palino, always sardonic, "somewhere on that path to hell."

On the morning of his departure, Johnny sat with Danny in the hospital's mess hall.

"I don't know how I feel anymore," Danny began. "You see how I spend my days. I guess when Palino was here I thought I might be able to help a friend. In the end, I wasn't able to. I saw a side to a couple of the nurses and doctors I hadn't seen before."

"He knew you'd be feeling guilty; told me to tell you not to," Johnny said.

"He said that? I guess it's hard to put it all into perspective. I spend most of my time in that cramped little room never knowing what's coming next, scrambling to keep people alive who were shot, mortared, booby trapped, or messed up in ways I couldn't even imagine before Vietnam. Then I go off shift, wash the blood off, maybe pull four hours of guard, catch a bit of sleep and start all over the next day. Sometimes the doctors are cranky with me, or the nurses, and I was powerless to help a friend when he came through triage. Tell me how I should feel about things?"

"I can't. I'll tell you what, though, if I manage to make it out of the Nam, I'll take you with me," Johnny said, attempting to inject some levity into the conversation.

"Don't even joke about it. I don't want to see you again until the end of the war. First, Richie, and then Palino, all of our fears from training are coming true. I just can't believe what's happened to Don. He's really not coming back?"

"No. I guess I had to hear it for myself. He always impressed me how urbane he sounded with that Mississippi drawl. I knew he was intelligent, but now he has me thinking that maybe I'm the stupid one for going back. But I have to. Maybe I've been more fortunate than him. There are guys in my platoon I've gotten close to. Then, there's my girl. I want to go home and live a normal life. His girl has broken it off with him."

Danny picked at his food, rubbery scrambled eggs and toast. "So, how bad is it out there?" he asked.

"It depends," Johnny said. "It's uncomfortable because it's so hot, or raining, and you're always sweating carrying all that weight. It's boring, then terrifying when you make contact. With every step you are looking for where to find cover if ambushed, yet sometimes you wish for a little contact just so you can put your gear down. The mosquitoes are a constant, except when it's raining hard, and the Delta is full of leeches, snakes and booby traps. Given all that, I don't see blood every day. When I do, I worry I won't be a good enough medic because it's just me out there with my aid bag."

Kenny entered the mess hall. "Sorry to interrupt, man," he said to Danny. "A medevac's on the way with five casualties, an ETA of ten minutes."

"Be right there," Danny acknowledged. He looked at Johnny. "Guess I better get back to the war."

"Me too," said Johnny. "Come on, I'll walk with you back to the ER."

CHAPTER TWENTY-FOUR

Returning to Dong Tam, Johnny dropped his bag in his hooch and went to find Jungle Boy.

"Any news?" he asked.

"We're back on night ambush tomorrow with Lieutenant Howitz. Three new guys in the platoon. Sergeant Morales' replacement is due any day."

At the halfway point of Johnny's tour, the platoon was changing. Red Robin was gone. After Sanders, Morales would rotate home, and Tut would be next, Rafe Johnson soon after. All eyes would be on the new LT and the platoon sergeant replacing Morales.

The captain eased Howitz into his command by sending the platoon on night ambushes near Dong Tam. Johnny observed the lieutenant conferring with Sergeant Morales before going beyond the wire. Average height, and close-cropped blond hair, their new leader exhibited a reserved personality difficult to assess. *Definitely not brash or a know-it-all,* Johnny observed. Howitz moved with ease under the weight of his gear, appearing confident without the arrogance of someone needing to validate his authority by barking orders.

A graduate of West Point, the new lieutenant came from Iowa, where he grew up on a farm and excelled at long distance running. He held the state high school record for the mile and ran cross country. It helped him with the rigors of military training at the academy. The ultimate test of his abilities in the infantry would surface with the stresses of combat.

The platoon's first night on ambush passed without incident, and the unit breathed a collective sigh of relief. Howitz relied on the guidance of

Sergeant Morales during the patrol and showed no inclination to disrupt the platoon dynamics established under Sanders' command. No contact with the VC occurred as Morales completed his tour. Everything changed with the arrival of the new platoon sergeant.

The captain assembled the platoon to introduce Sergeant Magruder. Pleased to have an experienced NCO paired with the inexperienced Howitz, the company commander iterated Magruder's combat record from his previous tour. Adorning the sergeant's right shoulder, the word "airborne" appeared above the unit insignia of the "screaming eagle" of the 101st Infantry Division. A combat infantryman's badge, also in black, was sewn above the pocket of his fatigues. Looking bored and unimpressed during the introduction, Magruder had arrived in Dong Tam in a nasty mood but ready for more war.

He would have preferred another tour with the 101st. Rumors of an incident in a northern village followed the sergeant to Dong Tam. In a rage near the end of his tour, he'd broken the jaw of a Vietnamese civilian with the butt of his rifle while questioning him. Witnessed by a South Vietnamese official with ties to the provincial chief, the army whisked Magruder out of the country and promised disciplinary action. Wishing to re-up and return to Vietnam, but not with a stain on his military record, the charges quietly disappeared. Magruder interpreted his assignment to Dong Tam as a demotion from an elite unit.

Johnny noticed the coldness in the sergeant's hazel eyes tinged with an unusual amount of yellow. Magruder's gaze unsettled Johnny, like a cat sizing up its prey. Something in his southern drawl, harsh and with a sarcastic twang, so different from Palino's gentlemanly lilt, made him wary. Magruder exuded an overall impression of nonchalance, but with menace, which might be doled out on a whim.

By the time Magruder arrived, the captain was comfortable sending third platoon on a longer patrol with Howitz in command, especially with the combat-experienced platoon sergeant.

Johnny got a glimpse of Magruder's leadership under fire within minutes of their first contact. Flying into a hot LZ taking light arms fire, one of the new guys jumped off his Huey too early and injured his ankle. Magruder, unhappy with the inexperienced move, literally hauled the terrified grunt to the tree line, where he insisted the injured man fire back at the VC with the rest of his squad.

Johnny, in the third Huey, and watching the kid hobbling and being dragged into position, moved forward to treat the injury and arrived in time to hear the sergeant screaming. "If you aren't more scared of me than the fucking gooks, then I ain't doing my job."

Inserted, and with the last Huey out of the LZ, Howitz had the artillery shelling the enemy. With the VC retreating under the barrage, Magruder organized the platoon to go after them. Howitz informed him that gunships were on the way and would take a pass before the platoon proceeded.

"Anything you say, LT," Magruder replied with a trace of contempt. He turned and walked off in a huff, frustrated by the overcautious approach.

When the platoon proceeded, they found several bodies where the artillery and gunships had shredded the trees. Searching the dead soldiers' pockets, Magruder found a photograph of a Vietnamese woman staring self-consciously at whoever had taken the picture.

"Fuckin' gook women," he commented. "This one's ugly as shit. Must be the wife or girlfriend of this bastard." He kicked the body hard and stuffed the photo into his own pocket.

Johnny wasn't sure if the new guy's ankle was sprained or broken. Regardless, he would need a medevac. After arriving in the landing zone with the Huey's M-60s pouring rounds at the enemy, and the platoon's firepower after insertion, Charlie had managed to inflict only a minor wound. A bullet had taken a chunk of flesh out of the forearm of a grenadier named Sampson. With the platoon for a couple of months, Johnny had not gotten to know him. Without realizing it, Johnny had begun to withdraw. With one exception, he avoided getting close to the new guys arriving in the platoon.

✳✳✳

Jungle Boy and Billy Warrington had formed a bond. "War," as he was known by the platoon, had learned to function. Adjusting to Vietnam had been difficult. Unused to hardship, Jungle Boy had helped him adapt, explaining things and giving him confidence through his unwavering support. Protective of his new friend, Jungle Boy was in awe of the fact Billy had attended university in Boston before family circumstances caused him to miss a semester. The draft intervened in the interim and nabbed him.

Billy admired Jungle Boy's courage and how he'd helped him come to grips with his fear. How he gave him hope about surviving the Nam. The friends admired the qualities in each other they individually lacked.

Jungle Boy had never had a friend that had been to university. Billy knew stuff that impressed him and encouraged him to use his "smarts" after the war. Jungle Boy, amazed that somebody found him intelligent, realized Billy had also given him confidence in ways he'd never considered. Always transparent with the Doc, he approached him in their foxhole.

"You finish high school?" Jungle Boy asked.

Sensing the kid wanted to sort something out, Johnny kept his answer simple. "No," he said.

"Me neither. You going to?" he continued.

Johnny shrugged. Jungle Boy, more certain they'd survive the Nam, never wavered in that belief. "I suppose I might."

"War says I'm smart enough for college, if I want to go."

Johnny thought of Cliff Morris telling him something similar. Yet here they were in a damp foxhole halfway through their tours. Nothing but Vietnam seemed real. *There's too much war to get through before I can make plans,* Johnny thought. "Sure, you're smart enough," Johnny answered. These conversations with Jungle Boy made him melancholy, but the last thing he wanted was to thwart the kid's unshakable faith that they were both making it out of the war. Maybe that gave him hope as well.

"I always thought I'd stay in the army," Jungle Boy stated.

"You're only eighteen," Johnny said. "You don't need to make that kind of decision now."

"Almost nineteen, Doc. You know, when I was still in Oakland, I used to walk down to the recruiter's office just to look at the posters they had on their windows. I really wanted some of that."

"Some of what?" Johnny asked.

"The respectability, I guess. I wanted to wear that uniform and be proud. But War is saying that maybe we can go to college together. Think that's a good idea, Doc?"

"Better than staying in the army. How many tours in the Nam do you think you can survive?"

"Sergeant Morales survived more than one."

Of course, he did, thought Johnny. *And who's he to argue with Morales.* "Well, I'd think about it carefully," he told Jungle Boy. "Make sure it's really what you want to do."

After the medevac arrived and left with Sampson and the new guy, the platoon moved beyond the shredded terrain and encountered thicker scrub brush. Still convinced a VC base camp existed in the area, the captain had his platoons searching for it. Masters of camouflage, the VC were adept at hiding but would likely make a stand if discovered.

Jungle Boy walked point as the platoon moved deeper into the brush. Howitz ordered a break on high ground that overlooked a swampy terrain. Magruder motioned for Jungle Boy to have a word.

"How often you walk point?" he asked.

"Most of the time, Sergeant."

"You ought to let some of the other guys get some experience with it."

"I like walking point," Jungle Boy said.

"Maybe so, but we're gonna start rotating it more regularly."

"Okay, Sergeant, but I think the platoon likes having me on point."

"Like I said," replied Magruder, "we're gonna start rotating the point position."

On their next break, Johnny approached Jungle Boy. "What did Magruder want?"

"Says he wants more rotation on the point position."

"Maybe not a bad idea. I don't like the feel of this operation."

"Exactly why I should stay on point," said Jungle Boy. "Tut's squad is up front tomorrow."

The platoon moved out in the morning with Tut on point. With new guys in his squad, he felt obligated to take the lead. He'd gone a klick when the swamp brush thinned, and visibility improved. The terrain had been sprayed with chemical defoliants, not recently, but a few months prior. Thinner and sickly, the foliage struggled to regain vibrancy.

Tut halted when he saw a bunker complex constructed of logs and mud no longer concealed by the languid flora. He motioned for Magruder to come and have a look.

"Bunker complex, Sergeant, better let the LT know it's here and see what he wants to do."

"What for?" Magruder responded. "The platoon's got to check it out anyway. I'll take half your squad and move into position from the side. Set up the M-60 with a clear field of fire and open up on its front when you see me make my move. I'll toss a grenade through the peep slot on the right."

Magruder took three of his guys and skirted around to where he could approach the bunker from the side. Without hesitating, he ran twenty-five meters from his position and tossed a grenade through the first firing slot. Moments later, the grenade detonated, instantaneously setting off a series of secondary explosions from within the bunker. Mud walls heaved as logs a foot in diameter lifted and crashed into the disintegrating bunker.

Magruder ran a few steps and dove to the ground when flying debris sent clods of dirt and wood splinters hurtling in all directions. Tut watched as the bunker lifted slightly and collapsed while the arms cache stored inside continued cooking off. From his position near the rear of the platoon, Johnny heard the explosions and rushed forward. Expecting the worst, he was relieved to see Jungle Boy unharmed by the detonations.

Lieutenant Howitz saw the collapsed bunker and correctly assessed the situation. Controlling his anger, he marched toward Magruder brushing himself off after the munitions had finished exploding.

"That's not your call, Sergeant."

"Just thought I was doing my job, Sir," Magruder said, a thinly veiled sneer in his voice. "Didn't want to lose the element of surprise, but I will check with you next time before I do anything." Magruder's tone left nobody wondering how he felt about being told what to do by a green lieutenant.

Howitz took two steps toward the sergeant. All eyes were on what he would do.

"Nobody is denying your combat experience, Sergeant Magruder. But as long as I am in command of this platoon, the well-being of the men comes first. You will not take unnecessary risks with their lives. Understood?"

Magruder locked eyes with Howitz. "There is a war going on, Lieutenant. If this unit is not prepared to fight it, then none of us should be here." Magruder paused, letting his comments hang in the air. Nobody hearing his tone, viewing his body language, doubted what he truly meant. *Third platoon is a bullshit unit led by a green lieutenant.*

Johnny, close enough to listen, and uneasy with the tension, had never witnessed this kind of friction between Sanders and Morales. It didn't bode well for the platoon.

Howitz, having made his point, addressed the situation at hand. "All right everybody, listen up. The captain says intelligence suspects a VC base camp is in the vicinity. The bunker may be the first sign of something. If so, they know we're here. Stay alert. Sergeant Magruder and I will have a look at the bunker, and then we'll saddle up."

Johnny took a drink from his canteen and found Jungle Boy. "Watch yourself," he cautioned. "I don't like the *feel* of this. If the VC are around, they know exactly where we are."

Johnny saw the lieutenant and Magruder having an animated conversation at the destroyed bunker. Johnny worried how deep the brewing dissension would go.

The defoliated area continued for another klick before the density of the swamp impeded the platoon's progress. Tut crossed a trail, unsure if it was animal or in use by the VC. He halted the platoon. Howitz took charge and sent four-man patrols in both directions for 200 meters to see what they could find.

"Nothing, LT," Jungle Boy reported for one of the patrols. "The VC are good at covering their tracks, but we didn't see any signs of them."

After another hour of humping, Howitz had them dig in for the night. Uncomfortable in his damp foxhole, and hounded by the mosquitoes, Johnny went and saw Tut.

Smoking a cigarette before dark, Johnny sat down next to him. "What happened out there today on point?"

"Magruder took charge without conferring with the LT. Said we could handle it ourselves."

"It sounded like all hell broke loose. I was sure I'd be needed up front."

"No shit. Magruder was none too happy when the LT got after him. We got enough to worry about without him coming in and stirring things up. I think Howitz is okay. A little early to tell, but I think he gets it. Magruder's going to make trouble for him. I'm too short for this."

"And for walking point, Tut. Let one of the other guys do it next time your squad's in the lead."

"Yeah, maybe. I been here so long it's like home is just a fantasy my mind has concocted. It's not even real anymore." Tut paused for a moment and took a drag on his smoke. "What do you suppose a guy like Magruder gets out of the Nam?"

"Another fight, one he gets to have for keeps," Johnny said.

"Did you see him with those dead bodies? I mean, at this stage I ain't exactly shedding tears for Charlie. It's either him or me. Guess I'm just sick of the killing."

Johnny nodded.

Rafe Johnson's squad was scheduled to be in the lead the next day. Angry from his run-in with Howitz, Magruder came and spoke with him.

"You taking the lead tomorrow, Johnson?"

"You know Jungle Boy usually walks it for our squad, and he's good at it. Some guys just don't like it."

"How about you, Johnson, you like it?"

"We already have a good point man," he evaded the question.

"I was askin' *you*," Magruder pressed.

"No, Sergeant, I don't like walkin' point. I'm getting too short for it, if you're askin' me."

"No, Johnson, I was askin' if you *liked* it, not for a commentary on how short you are."

"I thought you were," he said, not backing down.

"Every man in this platoon should be able to walk point. Makes for a chickenshit outfit when they're not. Nothin' to get spooked about."

"I seen lots of shit with third platoon, Sergeant. Nothin' wrong with wantin' to get home again."

Magruder stared at Johnson. "Just because you're short don't mean you get special privileges, Johnson. Make sure you remember that and hold up your end."

Two more days of humping through the swampy terrain and no signs of the enemy. On edge, the whole operation had an eerie feel to Johnny, like trouble was just ahead, but nothing happened.

The platoon, exhausted and uncomfortable in the damp conditions, fought off the mosquitoes and pulled leeches off on every break. Nobody could keep their feet dry. Johnny couldn't control the jungle rot. Called trench foot in previous wars, they all needed to get their feet dry.

Rafe Johnson came by Johnny's foxhole after they'd dug in for the night. He offered Doc a cigarette and rested his back against a sapling.

"What's up with Magruder?" he asked. "The man's messin' with stuff he should be leavin' be."

"He's got everyone on edge," Johnny said.

"Came close to callin' me chickenshit," Rafe continued. "Disruptin' the whole platoon, and right in front of the LT. Where's the Jungle Boy?"

"Setting up for first watch."

"How's he feelin' about stuff?"

"He's not saying much. Thinks it's a bad idea having so many different guys walking point, especially when we're looking for a VC base camp."

"Magruder's trouble, stirring up shit from the moment he arrived."

"He's making things difficult for the new LT. We've got enough to worry about without that kind of friction."

"Things'll come to a head, Doc. Somethin's gonna give."

Two days later, a rice paddy appeared at the edge of the swamp. Delaware, the point man for the day, conferred with Magruder and the LT.

Magruder pointed to a village half a klick away, a row of palm trees swaying above the thatched rooves on the dwellings. "I think we should check it out."

"Okay," said Howitz. The sergeant had been difficult, but he tried not to let it affect his judgement. He got on the radio with the captain, nearby with first platoon.

"We're out of the swamp, Sir, and into a paddy. Would like to check out the next village."

"Roger that, Lieutenant. Charlie can't be far. Second platoon's got one KIA, booby trap."

"Yes, Sir."

Second platoon's casualty was gruesome. Their point man tripped a wire that released the tension on a sapling, sending a set of sharpened bamboo stakes into his chest. Embedded, and still attached to a base, the medic had to cut through each stake before pulling them out one at a time.

The platoon, without Pham, their Tiger Scout, prepared to enter the village. Johnny knew the reason for his absence. When he had given the young Vietnamese the letter from his sister after seeing her with Palino, Pham had wept. Unusual for a Vietnamese to show such emotion in front of a foreigner, Johnny could only imagine the pressures the young man faced. His father executed by the VC, his sister raped and discarded, and now he learned of his mother's illness. His whole country torn asunder with divided loyalties, Pham vanished without saying goodbye.

When they entered the village, the Vietnamese stood outside their huts and stared blankly at third platoon. Dressed in rags, they stood motionless, passive in their resistance to the intrusion. Their response enraged Magruder.

"What you say, papasan," he turned to an older man standing outside a dwelling, "VC village?"

"No VC, no VC," he protested.

The sergeant looked at the point man, Delaware, and smirked. "Motherfuckers never know where Charlie is, ain't that right, papasan." His tone menacing, he got right in the man's face and glared at him before speaking again. "Can't stand the motherfuckers. We're over here trying to help them out and all they do is lie and stab you in the back. Can't trust a one of them." He pushed the man, hard, and he stumbled backwards.

"Have you found something, Sergeant?" Howitz intervened.

Magruder turned and momentarily gazed at the lieutenant, careful not to challenge him too directly but allowing his glare to linger a moment before answering. "Just tired of the lying, LT," he said. "I'd wager the papasan knows exactly where the VC are and every booby trap in the area."

"Let's get on with the search," Howitz instructed.

Johnny sensed the lieutenant's frustration with Magruder coming to a head. There were grumblings in the platoon and unease with the tension building. The patrol, into a second week, had everyone exhausted. Morale was low. Magruder didn't seem to notice, or care.

CHAPTER TWENTY-FIVE

King Tut gathered his squad after the platoon had dug in for the night. Squatting by his foxhole, Tut was weary, the strains of his tour evident in the lines around his eyes. Squinting from the smoke of a lit cigarette, he took a final drag before speaking.

"Our squad is in the lead tomorrow," he began, "and I gotta be straight with you. I'm so short I'm spooked about walking point."

"You done your share, King," said Half Pint. "Let one of us take a turn."

"You volunteering?" ventured Morgan.

"No," answered Half Pint, "just sayin' King shouldn't have to do it if he's feelin' spooked. Maybe we should draw straws."

Tut nodded his approval of the suggestion. "I'm sorry guys. I just can't do it anymore, not with just one week left. We're all agreed, then, to drawing straws?" Nobody objected. "Short straw walks point tomorrow."

He turned his back and took out four matches. There were only five of them in the squad, shorthanded as usual. "You go first," he said to Half Pint, "you been here the longest." He offered his hand with the matchsticks.

Morgan drew next, then Billy Warrington. The newest squad member, a kid named Eli, trembled as he took the last match from Tut. They showed their draws to each other by holding them in their palms.

"Looks like you're on point, War," said Half Pint. "Watch yourself out there."

"We've got your back tomorrow," Tut assured him, but the decision nagged at him.

✳ ✳ ✳

The platoon moved toward a village to begin the day. Crossing on the dikes surrounding the flooded paddies, War led the procession of infantry troops. Tut worried about booby traps. The hamlet entered the previous day had an underlying hostility, *a VC feel to it,* thought Tut. Having second thoughts, *maybe I should have just walked point. No way I would have let the newest guy, Eli, walk it. Maybe War isn't ready.*

Relieved that most of the morning would be consumed by the search, War breathed easier. There would be no dense brush or jungle to conceal an enemy ambush. The time spent in the village relieved the pressure that he might miss something and endanger himself and the platoon.

More openly hostile than the village searched the previous day, Johnny felt uncomfortable as the Vietnamese stared straight ahead, brows furrowed and eyes squinting from the strain of suppressing their thinly veiled anger. Their resentment was palpable, just beneath the surface. No pretending in this village as third platoon rummaged through their dwellings, sifting through baskets of stored rice and checking beneath floor mats woven from the fronds of palm leaves. Tin pots clanged from the barrels of rifles tapping on them, lids lifted whenever duller sounds suggested stored contents inside. Standing outside, the women spoke Vietnamese in sharp tones amongst themselves. Small children clung to the legs of mothers and grandparents, the younger men in the rice fields, or away waging war with an assortment of armies to choose from in Vietnam.

Magruder never stopped glaring with those cold, yellow-tinged hazel eyes, ready to erupt at the slightest provocation as he strode by the clusters of villagers standing outside their huts. Offended by the tone of a woman shouting, he got in her face before bumping her. "You VC, mamasan? Shut the fuck up. That goes for all of you." He turned from her and scowled. The groups nearby quieted.

The search took most of the morning. They found nothing but had disrupted the entire village. Angrier than when the platoon arrived, there was no mistaking it on the faces of the Vietnamese, who stood and watched as the Americans left. Behind Magruder in the formation, Johnny heard him mumbling curses about "needing to teach the gooks some serious fucking lessons."

He really hates them, thought Johnny. Not liking the situation, they trudged through the paddies adjacent to the hamlet. Johnny watched War assume the lead again. The tension of the confrontational search and an angry Magruder had him on edge.

The platoon reentered jungle after their midday break, and the pace slowed. By 1500 hours the growth had thickened, the platoon's progress at a crawl. War came to a bamboo thicket and entered after looking back towards Tut, who nodded. Keeping a safe distance behind the point man, Tut watched Half Pint enter behind him. Seconds later, Half Pint reemerged from the bamboo and shook his head while motioning for Tut.

"I've lost track of War," he said, "and can't pick up his trail. You better have a look. He entered right here," Half Pint told him. "It was right here; I'm sure of it."

Concerned, Tut walked into the thicket and found no trail. He suppressed his anxiety as he searched in all directions for a sign of Billy. Nothing.

Reemerging from the bamboo, he saw Magruder approaching.

"What's the holdup, Tuttley?"

"No sign of a trail after Billy Warrington entered the bamboo, Sergeant. It's like he just vanished."

"Not possible," Magruder exclaimed. Still frustrated from not finding anything in the village, he strode toward the thicket. Half Pint stood where War had entered. Striding past him, the sergeant had a look for himself. Tut followed, his uneasiness growing.

"Get your squad spread out," Magruder ordered, "and proceed through the bamboo. Nobody can just vanish. Make sure none of the rest of you get separated. I'll alert the rest of the platoon."

Tut took a position to the left of Morgan and Half Pint, with Eli on his other side. Twenty feet in, impenetrable stands of mature bamboo grew, their thicker trunks, stout and growing tight against each other, reached high into the sky seeking light. Darker in the dense flora, the decreased visibility made picking up a trail difficult. Losing sight of Morgan, Tut could hear him thrashing through the thicket. With no end to the bamboo grove in sight, a cry from Half Pint alerted them.

"Over here," he shouted, "I've found a trail." Running diagonally through the rest of the grove, it widened and opened onto a clearing. Morgan followed Half Pint into it. Worried Eli might get separated, Tut made sure he followed.

Just as Tut emerged from the bamboo grove he saw Half Pint cutting the vines wrapped around a tree. His back obscured Billy Warrington strapped to the gnarled trunk. About to shout a warning, Tut heard an explosion. Half Pint took the force of the blast standing, then crumpled. Morgan, having seen a grenade fall on the ground after the vines holding Billy Warrington's body were loosened, dove away from the grenade as it detonated.

Tut arrived to find Half Pint writhing on the ground uncontrollably. Billy's body slumped against the loosened vines binding him to the tree, his legs twisted into an unnatural position beneath him from the explosion. Morgan, dazed, raised himself on his elbows and looked toward Tut, who kneeled beside Half Pint. He had seen this before, booby-trapped bodies. Unable to warn Half Pint in time, the squad leader struggled to function. He hovered over Half Pint not knowing where to begin, hoping Doc Woski would arrive soon.

Half Pint oozed blood and tissue bandages wouldn't seal. Dying a painful death, his entire abdomen and groin a mutilated mess. Shrapnel had penetrated his chest and he was having trouble breathing. Tut stood and looked at Billy. The kid had been tortured, but the grenade had obscured his new injuries from the old. Out of the corner of his eye he saw Eli vomit.

Hearing the explosion, Johnny rushed toward the sound. Without saying anything, he bent over Half Pint and opened his aid bag, withdrawing a tube of morphine. After injecting all of it, he rose and took a quick look at Billy.

"Half Pint found him tied to the tree," Tut said. "They booby trapped the body."

Johnny nodded. "He won't make it," he said quietly. "Stay with him while the morphine takes hold. There's not much you can do. I've got to have a look at Morgan."

Johnny cut the shredded fatigues from his bloodied legs and bandaged them. Morgan's pack had protected his upper body from the shrapnel when he turned away just before the explosion. "I saw the grenade just in time," he said, still in a daze. "How bad is Half Pint?"

Johnny shook his head. "It looked like War was already dead," Morgan continued. "He just disappeared on point. We couldn't find him."

"You want something for the pain?" Johnny asked. Still dazed, Morgan looked at Half Pint. "You better see how my partner's doing."

Not sure Morgan comprehended Half Pint was dying, Johnny took another tube of morphine and injected part of it into his arm. "That will see you through the worst of the pain," Johnny told him. "Half Pint's not gonna make it." Morgan stared at Johnny but didn't say anything.

Magruder arrived just before the lieutenant. Half Pint died while Johnny knelt beside him. He pulled the poncho liner that covered his body over his face. Looking up, he watched as Magruder swore and looked for signs of the VC in the trees where the clearing ended. Howitz got there and took charge.

"Let's check out the tree line and get some guards posted. Medevac's on the way. Pop some smoke to let them know our exact position." The LT looked at Johnny.

"Two KIA, Sir, Half Pint and War. Morgan will be okay, multiple shrapnel wounds on both legs."

Johnny organized the bodies and tended to Morgan while he waited for the dust-off. Numbed by Billy Warrington's death, he mechanically filled out the field medical cards required of him. He worried about how Jungle Boy would react to Billy's death. The kid had naively assumed they would all survive the Nam and be friends forever.

Billy had been tortured. The grenade made a further mess of his body, but there were other signs on his face. An ear missing, and a slash across his throat. Johnny agonized about the ways he might have suffered. Almost certainly dead before the grenade went off, but that didn't tell him much.

As he gathered Billy and wrapped him in a poncho, a leg detached itself. Johnny picked it off the ground and put it with the body in the poncho. After folding it around Billy and securing the ends, Johnny noticed an ear beneath the tree. Vietnam made for strange decisions. Unsure what to do for a moment, he dug a shallow hole with a knife and buried it. Weary of the carnage, *did it matter that Billy left an ear behind next to a bamboo grove in Vietnam?* Johnny had no idea. *Dead is dead and none of it would help or mean anything to Billy. It was all about the living, and Johnny was hanging onto life by a tenuous thread.*

Tut found a spot in the clearing and sat. He was done functioning in the Nam. Eli stood behind him, not sure what to do.

"Tut," he called out softly, "Tut, what should I be doing?"

Tut heard him, but the voice was disconnected from his inward reality. In making a mess of his final patrol, he had nothing left to give. He should have just walked point. He knew that if Eli, new in-country, had drawn the short straw, he wouldn't have let him take the lead. *So why did he let Billy? The kid had come such a long way but look at how he died.*

Tut took a cigarette and tapped it several times against his rifle stock before attempting to light it. Noticing he'd smashed it in the tapping, he took another and lit it. His hands shook, and he heard Eli's voice behind him. He could only focus on an internal dialogue.

Too spooked to walk point myself, I've played Russian roulette with my squad. War had no business being out there, not yet, perhaps never. This will be my last patrol, but it hardly matters. Vietnam is a part of me forever. I should have just walked point. Dead or alive, I'll be leaving. It really doesn't matter. I've realized too late that I can leave Vietnam, but the Nam will never leave me.

Jungle Boy kept his feelings to himself as they dug in for the night. The kid was so transparent that his silence worried Johnny. *How did any of them keep functioning,* Johnny wondered. He was beyond tired of the war, emotionally drained and physically exhausted. His whole body ached as he struggled against the futility of the war. Billy's death depressed him. He'd advised Tut against walking point, was relieved Jungle Boy was out front less, but now Billy was dead, and Tut was going home an emotional mess. Johnny seethed at Magruder for disrupting the platoon, but he also assumed some of the guilt about what had happened.

Finished with their foxhole, Jungle Boy spoke. "Billy was a friend of mine. I don't have many friends. He wanted me to meet his mother after the war, you know. I guess that will never happen. Billy wrote to her about me, and she thanked me in one of her letters to Billy for helping him out. I guess I let him down."

"You didn't let him down," Johnny interjected. Angry and demoralized like everybody else in the platoon, he struggled with what to say.

"Don't go blaming yourself again for something that happened in a war you didn't start. There's plenty of blame to go around for what happened to Billy and none of it leads back to you. This platoon is getting as fucked up as the war."

"You think any of this would have happened if I was on point?" Jungle Boy asked.

Johnny shook his head, looked at Jungle Boy for a moment, then stared straight ahead. "Don't know. What I do know is that you've done more than your share for this platoon. Keep that in mind before you go volunteering for anything or blaming yourself for things you can't control. We've got five months left on our tours. Not exactly short, but we're over the halfway point."

Jungle Boy sat down next to Johnny in the hole they'd just dug. Water began to seep into the cavity. *Typical Delta shithole,* thought Johnny. "How are your feet holding up?" he asked.

Jungle Boy shrugged. "They're sore like everybody else's."

"We've been out here too long. Try and dry them out at least once a day if you can. You got dry socks?"

"Is anything dry in the Delta?"

"I guess not," Johnny said. "I'll have a look at them later." Seeking a few peaceful moments, he pulled his poncho tightly around himself. "You okay if I doze for a few minutes?"

"Sure thing, Doc. I could use some time to say goodbye to Billy."

The platoon returned to Dong Tam the following afternoon. Badly shorthanded, and exhausted from the long patrol, they would stand down for a few days to recuperate.

Rafe Johnson came by Johnny's hooch. "Some of the platoon is having a meeting later. The guys think you should be there."

"What's up?" Johnny asked.

"Later," is all he said. "Can't tell you more than that."

Johnny tried finishing a letter to CC but had to put it down. His thoughts drifted to Billy Warrington, but he couldn't think of what to say. *I'll finish it later,* he thought. He dozed for a couple of hours. Having drifted into a deep sleep, he awoke feeling vulnerable, like he'd let his guard down by sleeping too deeply. Unable to formulate any small talk in the letter, he wondered what CC was doing at that exact moment. She'd become a dream from another world that was fading into obscurity. His letters were vague attempts at holding onto that world, uncertain it even existed. Only the war was real.

Rafe came by after dark, and they walked to a deserted area by the airstrip. In the open and out of earshot, they were met by three members of Rafe's squad. Ben Moses, a brother from Cleveland, sat on the ground next to Delaware and Wheels. The latter grunt had arrived with Billy as a replacement. Rafe got right to the point.

"I guess I'll start," he began. "We got some of you together because Magruder's got to go, and we need to make that happen." He looked at Johnny. "Sorry to involve you, Doc, but we figured you'd better be in on it since you'll be the one treating the motherfucker's wounds."

"Or putting him in a body bag," Wheels added. "Can we trust you?"

"Hey," Rafe interjected, "the Doc don't need to prove his loyalty. He's been there for the platoon since he got here."

Johnny had no idea how the brash young man had gotten his nickname, but the Nam had not improved his personality. "What is it you want from me?"

"To look the other way, not raise any issues with the nature of his wounds," Rafe responded.

"You know I won't be turning anybody in, but are you sure you want to do this, Rafe? You're awful short."

"The plan is to do it in a way nobody knows who pulled the trigger," Rafe answered.

"When?" asked Delaware.

"Our next firefight. Whoever is in a good position to shoot Magruder gets it done."

"Shooting to kill or wound?" asked Delaware.

Rafe shrugged. "I say we take a vote."

"Motherfucker as good as killed Billy himself," Wheels said. "I say he dies. An eye for an eye."

"You gettin' religious on us, Wheels?" Ben Moses said, the Black preacher's son from Cleveland.

"You sure you want to kill him?" Johnny added. "That could get serious."

"Put him in a wheelchair just like his twin brother," Delaware said. "He's always bragging about how good it was with the 101st Airborne. Wasn't so good for his brother now was it?"

"Might be difficult to pinpoint a shot during a fight," Rafe said.

"And we be takin' away a gun during it," Moses added. "Could just throw a grenade in his hooch."

"No," Rafe said, "we do that they know for sure it's one of us, and the army won't let that one rest. I say we take a vote on whether to wound or kill Magruder."

Five men sat with their legs crossed in a tight circle. Nobody objected.

"Okay," Rafe said, "secret ballot." He took a pack of cigarette papers and gave one to each man. "Put a 'K' or a 'W' for wasting or wounding the son of a bitch."

Five men marked their votes and handed them back to Rafe Johnson. He held them in his palm after the count. "Three for wounding against two for killing. Guess that decides it."

"What about Howitz?" Wheels asked. The LT hasn't stood up to Magruder. Lets him run the platoon."

"Too risky," said Rafe. "I think we see a different Howitz without Magruder around undermin' every decision the LT makes."

"Howitz is sick of Magruder," Johnny added. "It will be a different platoon without him. I don't think we want a complete change of leadership again."

"All right," Rafe said, "nothing leaves the group. Everybody swears to secrecy?"

All heads nodded. Rafe took the papers with the votes and burned them.

"One more thing," Johnny said.

"What is it, Doc?" Rafe responded.

"We've all sworn to secrecy." He looked at the others nodding. "Jungle Boy is kept out of this."

CHAPTER TWENTY-SIX

Deep into June, the southwest summer monsoon rains filled the canals and swamps of the Mekong Delta. Beneath the saturated landscape the water table rose. The low-lying areas overflowed, and the canals and rivers threatened to rise above their banks. Sampans transported enemy weapons more efficiently than any land routes in the Delta.

The waterlogged conditions made third platoon's field operations even more miserable. Foxholes filled with water, and frequent downpours kept every man wet. Patrolling a canal near a tributary of the Cuu Long River, Johnny's boots sank in the mud with every step, soaking his feet and requiring energy-sapping effort to pull each foot out of the muck. He knew the entire platoon would have foot problems because of the damp.

On a midday break, the platoon was alerted to a squad of Viet Cong fleeing a sampan damaged in an encounter with a Navy patrol boat. The enemy soldiers fled on foot where the canal branched off the river and headed toward third platoon's position. Howitz set the unit into an ambush formation along the opposite side of the waterway. Hidden behind the brush and river debris deposited when the canal banks had overflowed, they waited. In communication with an observational helicopter, third platoon had the advantage.

Howitz waited until five VC appeared on the opposite bank before firing a shot that signaled the beginning of the ambush. Four soldiers went down immediately and the fifth, wounded, crawled into the brush for cover. Grenades were tossed by the strongest arms and the grenadier carrying the M-79. The concussions sent mud and splinters in all directions.

A small sampan washed ashore in the flooding made crossing the canal possible. Holding four men and their gear, Delaware, on point for the day, crossed with Howitz and two others. Magruder followed in the next boatload. Four VC were dead on the bank. Their rifles had not fired a round. Delaware found the fifth soldier in the undergrowth, having only crawled a few feet before the grenades had inflicted his final and lethal wounds.

Tensions had not eased between Howitz and Magruder. The lieutenant had thought long and hard about how he should approach the sergeant. He concluded nothing short of bringing him into line was acceptable. He was willing to risk his command over it. He might be an inexperienced lieutenant with his first combat assignment, but he would no longer defer to decisions made by Magruder if he thought they were inappropriate. During the platoon's previous stand down he had confronted the sergeant.

"The platoon is not comfortable with the changes you've made to the point position, Sergeant. Neither am I."

Magruder looked at Howitz and glared. "I've seen more combat than this chickenshit outfit combined, Sir," he said with unhidden contempt. "If you are giving me an order to pamper these men instead of going after the Viet Cong as hard as we can, then I disagree."

"I don't see how putting inexperienced young men on point is good for the platoon or going after the VC, Sergeant. It caused the death of two men and put another in the hospital without inflicting a single casualty on the Viet Cong."

"All because they've been pampered and poorly trained, Lieutenant. It's my job to see they're fit for combat with an enemy that is kicking this platoon's collective ass. I'm here to change that."

"Nobody is disputing your combat record, Sergeant, but going forward I will be in charge of who walks point. Warrington's death was unnecessary and has left the platoon demoralized. Is that understood?"

Magruder stared coldly at Howitz as he responded. "Perfectly." He hesitated before adding "*Sir*" in a derogatory tone.

"Then that will be all, Sergeant."

✷✷✷

After checking the bodies, the platoon retraced the path taken by the VC before the ambush. Delaware remained on point. As they moved along the bank the brush along the canal grew dense. Delaware consulted with Howitz before proceeding. Continuing in the direction where the VC had fled their damaged sampan, Delaware skirted the impenetrable brush as the fleeing VC must have. Wading through standing water as he continued, he sunk to his knees in mud. Contact with the VC was reestablished when three rounds to the point man's chest dropped him, killing him instantly.

The counter ambush resulted in a fierce firefight. Charlie had regrouped and linked up with a squad-sized unit in the vicinity. Spread out and firing at third platoon from the swamp, they were well hidden but without effective cover. Third platoon, even more exposed initially, found cover in the brush Delaware had skirted. Howitz moved forward with the rest of Rafe Johnson's squad and took a position behind a growth of palms twenty meters forward and to the right. Wheels had the M-60 firing bursts at the VC from that position, while the rest of the platoon fired steadily from their cover closer to the canal.

Magruder advanced toward the VC and fired from behind a mound of earth that looked like a giant anthill sticking out of the swamp. Johnny reached Delaware using the steady small arms fire of the platoon as protection. Finding him dead, he lay prone in the water behind the body. He hadn't really gotten to know him. From there, he watched Magruder. *He might be a hateful son of a bitch,* thought Johnny, *but he was no coward in a fight.*

Howitz shouted coordinates into the radio headset as he called for artillery support. A minute later, a marker round landed beyond the VC's position. Adjusting the coordinates, a series of shells exploded closer to the target. The VC, firing sporadically, were disengaging. Still putting rounds into the brush, the platoon advanced. Johnny saw Magruder go down. Johnny got to him without difficulty and found him cursing the platoon. Bullets had riddled the back of his legs and destroyed one of his knees. He knew instantly what had happened.

"You in on this Woski?" he ranted. "You think you chickenshits are going to get away with this? You think I don't know what's going on?"

Magruder writhed in pain while Johnny ripped his fatigue pants, exposing his wounds. Bleeding profusely from the leg that no longer had a functioning knee, Johnny applied a tourniquet above it before bandaging the wounds. A final burst from an AK-47 passed above the knoll they crouched behind.

Magruder continued to curse the platoon. Johnny took a tube of morphine and injected a heavy dose to calm him. By the time he'd finished bandaging his legs, the sergeant had quieted.

The worst of the firefight ended once the artillery barrage began. Two more dead bodies were found to add to the count. Battalion would be pleased. Howitz proved cool under fire.

Johnny surveyed the shattered landscape, ugly in the aftermath of the fighting. He looked for Jungle Boy, thankful he'd not been on point. A drizzle began to fall as the sky darkened. Johnny was chilled by more than the rain.

Back in Dong Tam, Rafe Johnson came to see Johnny.

"How you think it went down, Doc?"

"Magruder was cursing the entire platoon. He knew it was one of us who shot him. Be hard to prove, but I expect he'll raise a fuss."

Rafe nodded. "I expect so. Will his wounds give anything away?"

"Not likely. You know how many rounds are flying in a firefight. Magruder can suspect all he wants, proving something is another story."

"Howitz did good out there," Rafe added.

"It's his platoon now. Our chances of getting home have improved."

"Yeah, we're back outside the wire tomorrow. Not much of a rest."

The platoon returned from a four-day patrol wet and tired. No contact had occurred. Caked in mud that covered their boots and fatigues, faces and forearms where sleeves were rolled up, they reeked of the jungle, bug juice and sweat. Everyone had four days of stubble.

Gawking at them, and standing next to the captain, a sergeant stood in pressed fatigues and a new pair of jungle boots. Thinking only of rest and getting clean, nobody paid him much mind. The platoon filed by the captain thinking the man a Dong Tam REMF conferring with their company commander about a mundane matter that wouldn't concern them.

Jungle Boy, with a darkened face and a green sling he used as a bandana to cover his blondish hair, had his helmet slung over his rifle now that they were inside the wire. Wheels glanced at the sergeant and smirked, the bull's-eye drawn in black on his camouflaged cover attracting the man's attention. Eli, in a new squad now that his old one had been wiped out on the operation that had killed Billy Warrington, wore a helmet expressing an infantryman's disdain: WHAT ARE THEY GONNA DO, SEND ME TO VIETNAM?

Captain Mason pulled Howitz aside and introduced him to their new platoon sergeant, Cedric Cantwell, the army's answer to the NCO shortage. Fresh out of the Noncommissioned Officer Course, derogatorily referred to as "Shake and Bake School."

The army needed grunt NCOs. Their ranks were depleted by the war, discharge, and changing infantry MOSs to avoid multiple combat tours in Vietnam.

Lieutenant Howitz introduced Cantwell to the platoon the next day. Still in his crisply pressed jungle fatigues, the men were incredulous as he stiffly shook hands. Johnny mumbled a feeble "welcome to third platoon."

Some of the others were not so kind. Still smirking after the new sergeant left, Wheels commented. "Gee whiz, I wonder how he'll cope when he gets his new fatigues dirty?"

"Are you shittin' me?" Rafe Johnson exclaimed. He had never heard of the school for creating instant sergeants. "That's our new NCO? Welcome to the Nam."

"Get me the fuck out of here," mumbled their RTO, who packed the radio for Howitz. "First Magruder, now this. What the fuck?"

"Mail call," someone shouted, breaking off the conversations about Cantwell. Most of the platoon assembled on the first floor of the barracks.

The mail clerk, who provided a running dialogue as he read out names and distributed the letters, waved the first batch above him to quiet the banter.

He called out "Ornowoski" near the end of the first stack. "Umm, umm," he mused, "be nice to see the woman behind that fragrance." Johnny ignored the comment as he accepted the perfumed envelope. More interested in reading the contents than smelling them, he didn't take the mail clerk's banter personally.

"Jungle Boy," the clerk called out, looking surprised. "Even your people at home call you that?"

"I'll get it to him," Johnny spoke. The kid wasn't around for mail call because he never got any.

"Can we get on with this without the running commentary?" Wheels protested. "Fucking REMF shouldn't need to give a speech with every letter."

"Touchy, touchy," the clerk shot back. He pointed to the combat infantryman's badge above his shirt pocket. "Been in the shit already, man. Just recuperating before the man sends me back out, so watch who you're calling a REMF."

"Can we just simplify this?" Wheels continued. "Have I got any mail?"

"What's the name?" the clerk relented.

"Russo," he answered. "Art Russo, Brooklyn, New York."

"Sorry, man, nothing here."

Johnny looked at the letter for Jungle Boy, using his nickname, the return address from a Beverley Morrow in Boston. Johnny walked over to his hooch so he could give it to him.

"Got something for you."

"A letter?" Jungle Boy asked, surprised. "Who from?"

"Don't know. It's addressed to Jungle Boy. Sent from Massachusetts."

Jungle Boy sat up quickly. "That's where Billy was from." He took the letter and looked at it carefully, making sure it really was for him. "You know I never get any mail. This is my first letter," he said, opening it.

> *Dear Jungle Boy,*
> *I hope you don't mind my writing to you. I am Billy Warrington's mother. I am so lost since my son's death and really need a connection to him. Billy wrote to me about what a good friend*

you were and how much you helped him in Vietnam. That was very kind of you. If it is all right, I would really appreciate staying in touch and would very much like to hear from you, maybe even meet after your return from Vietnam. Losing a son in war is the hardest thing a mother has to endure. Please take care over there and come home safely.

Yours Very Truly,
Beverley Morrow
Billy Warrington's Mother

PS: What is your actual name? I would love knowing more about you.

Jungle Boy put down the letter. Tears were forming in his eyes.

"It's from Billy's mother… She says she would like for me to write to her, maybe even meet after the war. Can you help me with that, Doc? I'm not so good at writing letters. I've never done it before."

Johnny nodded. "We can get one off this afternoon if you like. Nothing to them once you get the hang of it." Not totally truthful, given the difficulty he had writing to CC.

That afternoon they sat in the kid's hooch and composed a letter. Jungle Boy fretted over every sentence, wondering if he was too formal or casual.

Dear Beverley Morrow,
I was pleased to receive your letter and wanted to respond right away. Billy was a good friend of mine, and I am still grieving his loss, as you are. I wish we could have met someplace other than Vietnam, but I am so glad to have had him as a friend.
My real name is Delbert Kincaid. I would be pleased to stay in touch and meet one day.

Billy's Friend,
Delbert Kincaid

"That's a fine letter," Johnny said as they posted it.

CHAPTER TWENTY-SEVEN

Two days before his scheduled rotation home, Rafe Johnson stood at attention in the captain's office. The company commander suspected he'd had something to do with Magruder's wounds. The sergeant was not going quietly into the realms of the disabled. Naming names, Johnson's was at the top of his list.

"What happened out there, Johnson?" Captain Mason pressed. Stern and threatening, he attempted to obtain a confession.

"You think you can get trigger happy because, what, your platoon sergeant looked at you the wrong way? That's not how my company operates, Johnson, and that's not how my army goes about its business." Mason stood erect before leaning forward with a hard stare into Rafe's eyes. "Why don't you come clean, tell us what really happened so you can go home as scheduled."

Rafe was having none of it. Suspecting the captain was bluffing and fishing for a confession, he would admit nothing.

"The firefight was intense, Sir. I shot at the enemy. Someone would have to be crazy to take out one of our guys when Charlie was shooting at us like that."

"Sergeant Magruder thinks otherwise, Johnson. You think a man with his combat experience can't tell where the rounds came from that wounded him? And guess whose name keeps coming up?"

"I don't know, Captain. We've all seen a lot of combat. I didn't see anything out of the ordinary, and I certainly didn't shoot Magruder."

"That's Sergeant Magruder to you, Johnson. You think I'm unaware of the tension in third platoon? You know what I think, soldier?"

"No, Sir, I don't."

"I think a bunch of you planned this, and I'm going to get to the bottom of it."

"Why would we do that, Captain?"

"I'm asking the questions here, Johnson. Don't think that just because you're about to go home that we don't know how to find you. Think about that, soldier. Come clean now and it will go a lot easier on you."

The captain paused long enough to make Rafe uncomfortable, his eyes staring coldly at him the whole time. Johnson avoided eye contact by staring at the wall.

"Is that all, Sir?" he finally asked.

"For now," Mason answered. "You're dismissed."

Rafe saluted the captain. He was careful not to be goaded into showing any attitude. Intentionally wounding Magruder would be difficult for the army to prove. Impossible if nobody confessed.

Jungle Boy and Ben Moses put the final touches on a short-timer's party for Rafe. Blocks of ice were scrounged and crushed in steel drums cut in half for cooling cans of beer. Rafe would leave Dong Tam in the morning to begin his journey home. In his hooch, he finished the last verse of "Mekong Delta Blues."

> *All along the Mekong, where the mighty river flows*
> *The bottom of that river reaches into hell*
> *I crossed the river Mekong and touched the shores of death*
> *For the Devil's in the Delta and he's showin' us the way*
> *All the paths go through Hades and end up in hell*
> *I've been twelve months in the Nam tryin' to break the spell*
> *Should have never crossed that river, the mighty Mekong into hell*
> *I been twelve months in the Nam, just tryin' to get back home*
> *Before the Devil comes and takes me, drowns me in the river*
> *Down along the Mekong, twelve months in the Nam*

I've had my glimpse of hell, all across that river
Been in the Nam too long, I've had my taste of hell
And when I cross that river for a final time
I won't be lookin' back, no way no way no way
But I'm never gonna lose those Mekong Delta blues
No I'm never gonna lose those Mekong Delta blues.

The song had thirty verses now. Begun early in his tour after a firefight in Tra Vinh that had been Rafe's bloodiest battle in Vietnam.

He remembered the pouring rain and hoped the downpour would deter Charlie. Instead, Rafe learned how well the enemy could fight in wet conditions. The VC started with mortars. They had the platoon's position pinpointed, and the rounds fell on top of them. A ground assault followed. Charlie had used the rain to sneak up to their perimeter and place third platoon's claymore mines in the opposite direction. When they detonated, the steel balls wounded and killed several of their own men. The fighting turned close and intense. By morning, half the platoon was dead or wounded. Seven body bags were needed. Rafe stood shivering from the wet and the fear, wondering how he could survive twelve months in Vietnam. The mournful blues riff had come to him when he picked up his guitar back in Dong Tam. The harmonica added perfectly to the melancholy of the song.

Johnny listened as Rafe played into the night. A somber mood overcame the group. There would be no more Rafe Johnson playing the blues in his hooch or leading a squad in the field. Johnny dared not think too far ahead, knowing he and Jungle Boy had beaten the odds so far. That meant nothing until they could say that after twelve months.

Rafe pulled him aside and said, "You look after my man now, ya hear?" Meaning Ben Moses, who had grown close with Rafe as Jungle Boy had with Johnny. The medic gave him assurances, but they both knew the Nam was a roll of the dice, a crap shoot. Sometimes a bullet and someone's head simply intersected space at the same time. There were hundreds of rounds fired in every fight.

"And Doc, this is where you can get in touch with me. Don't let them intimidate you about our friend. You had nothing to do with it." That was all he said. They'd agreed not to discuss Magruder after he was gone. Rafe handed him an address written on an envelope. "See that you and Jungle Boy make it out of here. Got it?" Johnny nodded and realized that he and Jungle Boy would now be the longest-serving platoon members.

The rainy season didn't curtail their field operations, just made them more miserable. Booby traps and ambushes remained their biggest concerns. Johnny always had the feeling that eyes were on them during patrols, but he also watched for trench foot, malaria and heat exhaustion in the men. He shivered at night with the damp, but when the sun shone between frequent downpours, they all sweated in the humid heat. Clouds of mosquitoes sought their blood and had ample breeding grounds in the pools of water so plentiful in the Delta.

New guys were susceptible to heat exhaustion until they were acclimated. Johnny watched Minnesota struggle with the weight of his gear on his first patrol. Cantwell told him to pack lots of ammo, and he was weighted down. Johnny was summoned to have a look at him when he complained of muscle cramps. Clammy to the touch, Johnny loosened the straps on Minnesota's pack and removed the bandolier of M-16 mags and laid the extra 200 rounds of M-60 ammunition everybody packed on the ground. Opening his fatigue shirt, he doused him with water from his canteen and wiped it with a cloth. Johnny gave him a handful of salt tablets, got him to drink some water and catch his breath. That was the best he could do until they came to a stream. That seemed to revive Minnesota enough to continue until they dug in for the night.

Cantwell, the new platoon sergeant, also struggled but was not about to show any weakness or fear. Johnny figured the army must have some screening process for the "shake and bake" sergeants but knew Cantwell would get worn down by the war like everybody else.

Johnny's own body was a mess. He'd lost thirty pounds and had infected lumps from the leeches, thorns and insects. A bout with a colony of red ants was surprisingly painful and left a numbing and lingering pain where welts from the bites formed.

Still looking for the elusive VC base camp the captain wanted one of his platoons to find, they trudged on. Mud became a problem. On point, Wheels sank nearly to his waist, and the platoon had difficulty freeing him. Jungle Boy, lighter, retrieved his gear and took it to higher ground before returning to try and pull him out. The more Wheels attempted to move, the deeper he sank. Like quicksand, he worried about sinking further. Vines were found and placed together like ropes, and the point man was finally dragged out of the muck. Filthy and exhausted, they had all used precious energy fighting the mud.

Lieutenant Howitz spoke with Johnny about the new guys. He checked with him daily about any medical conditions. During one of their conversations, he raised the issue of Magruder.

"Battalion is inquiring into what happened. Magruder claims it was someone in the platoon who shot him. What did you see when you treated his wounds?"

The question didn't catch him off guard. He also suspected the LT was as glad as the rest of them to be rid of the disruptive platoon sergeant. "You have been in enough firefights now, Sir, to know how many rounds are fired. I didn't see him go down when he got hit. The firefight was still intense, and I was trying to get to Delaware. After finding him dead, I was under fire and laid behind him in the water. That was when I noticed Magruder had been hit. His knee was badly damaged, and he was in a lot of pain. None of his wounds were life-threatening if I got the bleeding stopped. Once I got that under control, I gave him a shot of morphine."

"So nothing unusual about the wounds?"

"No, Sir."

"Be prepared for more scrutiny on this one, Doc. The army doesn't like losing NCOs with Magruder's combat record. He's probably disabled enough that he'll be discharged."

Johnny interpreted the lieutenant's remarks as a warning more than a threat. It was the lieutenant's platoon now. The men were comfortable with his leadership, and with the inexperienced Cantwell as platoon sergeant, nobody was interested in challenging the LT's authority as long as things were running smoothly.

Johnny remembered Rafe Johnson telling him: "The army loses one of its own in Magruder, and the man be all over that one. Dumb bastard gets Billy Warrington killed, there's not a peep."

I think the LT knows, Johnny thought, *or at least suspects, but just wants the issue to fade. Not one member of the platoon was sorry to be rid of Magruder.*

Jungle Boy heated one of his concoctions out of the C-rats he'd traded for. After feeding both of them, he wanted to talk. Five days into yet another stint in the field, they were bunkered at a fire support base running ambushes and day patrols protecting an artillery unit.

A month had passed since he'd written to Billy's mother, and Jungle Boy kept looking for a reply. He reread Beverley Morrow's letter for the hundredth time.

"She says right here near the end she would be pleased to know more about me. Do you think I should have told her more in my letter?"

"I think you'll hear from her again," Johnny assured him. "Then you can think of more to say. It was important to respond to her quickly. We've been out here a long time, and won't be back in Dong Tam for a while. You know how sporadic the mail is. There's probably a letter waiting to catch up to you. And besides," he added, "we're getting short. It's best to keep focused on going home alive."

"Uh, uh," Jungle Boy said. "You know this is the only letter I've gotten since I been in the Nam. Even my own mother hasn't written. I just want to make sure I don't miss one from Billy's mom."

"You won't. I expect you'll get one any day. And just remember, once you get home, you can go and see her yourself. She says in the letter she'd like to meet you. Just keep in mind you have to be alive to do that."

Jungle Boy folded the letter and put it back in the envelope. Johnny could tell the kid was thinking about what he'd just told him. It seemed to brighten his mood.

CHAPTER TWENTY-EIGHT

The helicopter skimmed the treetops as Johnny gazed out the open door of the Huey. The top of the jungle whipped by as they rushed to a predetermined LZ, a hot one. Second platoon, already engaged with Charlie in an intense firefight, needed help. The Viet Cong had decided to stay and fight.

Johnny's stomach tightened as they neared the landing zone. The door gunner fired into a tree line as they approached the drop point. Jumping to the ground before the helicopter touched down, Johnny rushed to find cover behind a tree felled by an artillery strike before they were inserted. Howitz was on the radio and calling for more after the last helicopter had deposited the final six men of the platoon. Rather than dislodging Charlie, it had the effect of disturbing a hornet's nest. The VC base camp had been discovered. The enemy was dug in and not retreating. Their fortified bunkers had withstood air strikes and artillery shells.

The stalemate lasted the daylight hours. Third platoon sustained two shrapnel wounds and a leg injury from the jump out of the Huey. Inserting troops into a hot LZ required precise coordination between the helicopters with room for only one landing at a time. Some never touched the ground as infantrymen jumped from the aircraft running. Crews and grunts were vulnerable during the drop and wasted no time.

Johnny looked at the new guy's leg, the first injury of the day. In his first firefight, rattled by the noise and the urgency, the sounds of the door gunner's M-60 in his ear, and the AK-47s firing from the tree line, he panicked and jumped too soon. Landing with seventy pounds of gear, something snapped in his leg. He would be unable to hump.

The shrapnel wounds would not require immediate evacuation. Bandaging them took no special skills on Johnny's part. Second platoon had not been as fortunate. Johnny was summoned to help with their wounded.

Their medic, Tommy Brandt, had a wound in his upper arm. A bullet had taken a chunk of flesh with it as it passed through. Able to function for most of the day, the arm stiffened and was too sore for him to continue. He would need to be evacuated with the first load of wounded.

Johnny rebandaged Tommy's arm and helped organize the casualties. Two dead soldiers lay side by side wrapped in ponchos.

"Charlie was just waiting for us," Tommy said as Johnny looked at his wound. "Flew right in on top of him and the motherfuckers were not budging. Hottest LZ I ever landed in. Guess I'll be out of it for a bit. Not even halfway through my tour yet. How about you, Doc?" Even the medics called each other by the nickname they shared.

"Six weeks to go," Johnny replied. "Plenty of time for something bad to happen."

"Thanks for helping out," Tommy told him.

"No problem," Johnny answered.

He'd hoped the platoon would spend his remaining time wandering the bush without much contact. Tomorrow they would have to take the lead in rooting out Charlie, second platoon having been inserted first.

Howitz wanted Jungle Boy on point the next day, his best man out front. The platoon dug in carefully for the night, everybody on edge. Nobody slept much.

In the morning, Jungle Boy moved his squad into the lead and took the point position. Not far from the LZ, he discovered three fortified and camouflaged bunkers. Having withstood the barrage of air strikes and artillery, the earth and log structures showed signs of collapse. Charlie had abandoned them during the night.

Jungle Boy found two trip wires that were obvious. He snipped them, releasing the tension and carefully coiled the cords. Thinking they might be decoys because Charlie was rarely that sloppy, he marked each roll and proceeded cautiously.

Cantwell, showing an interest in demolitions, organized the munitions for blowing the bunkers. "Fire in the hole," he shouted before each explosion, which finished the job of destroying the fortifications.

Jungle Boy set out again from the abandoned bunkers. He followed a ridge along a creek bank to where the damage to the trees ended. Entering unscarred jungle, he looked for signs of Charlie's retreat and more bunkers, outer defenses of the well-camouflaged base camp.

An hour later, he picked up a scent, literally. He knew the enemy was nearby. In the same way the Viet Cong smelled their bug juice and sweat, distinct odors emanated from the VC's cooking and the stink of urine and feces lingering in the air. Without being obvious, he slowed the pace. His senses tuned, aware of their presence without seeing them. He signaled Eli behind him, a silent tap on his helmet, a predetermined sign he expected to encounter VC. Jungle Boy scanned to two o'clock and made eye contact.

In that moment, seemingly slowed by an acute and simultaneous mix of instinct and conscious decision-making, and accelerated with the speed of movement necessary for survival, Jungle Boy dove for the cover of a cluster of young palm trees. Firing rounds from his rifle, not expecting to hit any VC from that angle but to alert the platoon to enemy contact, he looked for better cover.

Before he could move, a Chicom grenade was lobbed up and over the fronds on the young trees and detonated near his feet. Shrapnel penetrated Jungle Boy's legs and stunned him, destroying part of the flora that concealed his position. An AK pumped several bullets into an exposed and already damaged foot.

Near the rear of the platoon, Johnny knew the shooting involved Jungle Boy. Rushing forward with his aid bag and rifle, he got close before taking cover when the firefight intensified. From fifteen yards he saw Jungle Boy lying unconscious or dead. Johnny practically dragged the M-60 machine gunner into the position he needed to lay down a protective fire for him to go and get Jungle Boy. He sprinted toward the kid emptying a clip on automatic. Inserting a new magazine into his rifle, he fired more rounds before lifting Jungle Boy over his shoulder and carrying him to a safer spot where he could treat his wounds.

Johnny ignored the cries of "Doc" and "medic" coming from other platoon members. It would be Jungle Boy first. How many times had the kid saved the platoon, walking point more than his share? It had finally caught up to him. Time for the platoon to save him.

From behind a log, Johnny looked at Jungle Boy's foot. Only skin, a thin strip of flesh and a ligament kept it attached to his leg. He cut through the remaining tissue. After applying a tourniquet, he bandaged the stump tightly. Jungle Boy's wounds were on his legs. He would lose a foot but not his life, if Johnny could stem the bleeding and keep him out of shock. The bandaging finished, Johnny injected half a tube of morphine. Coming to, Jungle Boy shivered. His breathing and pulse quickened. Johnny worried he'd lost too much blood, that he'd taken too long to get to him.

He pulled a bottle of IV fluids from his aid bag. Johnny needed to get the intravenous started quickly. He had other casualties to treat, but he was not leaving Jungle Boy until he had done everything he knew as a medic to keep him alive. He hung the bottle above on a branch and wrapped Jungle Boy in a poncho liner after taping the IV securely to his arm.

"Doc, I'm cold," Jungle Boy said, shivering.

"I know," Johnny told him. "Hang in there for just a little while and we'll get you out of here." He'd done everything he could in the field. Now he needed a medevac. "I'll be back as soon as I can."

The firefight continued. Wheels had been hit in the chest. It had missed his heart but collapsed his lung, and he was having trouble breathing. Johnny sealed the entry point with the plastic from the packaging of IV tubing and wrapped a bandage securely over it. He positioned Wheels so any internal bleeding would not accumulate in his lungs.

Johnny, too late to help Cantwell, took no time with his body. Responding to the calls for a medic, he treated two more casualties with minor wounds before rushing back to check on Jungle Boy. With the firefight subsiding, he checked on the status of a dust-off.

"Two serious, LT. We need to get Jungle Boy and Wheels out of here. They'll be okay if we can do that."

"Nothing available yet, Doc. A dust-off was damaged landing in a tight LZ and another is down with a mechanical. Battalion is working on an alternative."

"We need something soon, LT." Johnny no longer had any doubts about Howitz, so he left and returned to Jungle Boy. Anxious about the availability of the medevac, he checked the IV flow into the kid's vein, then looked at his leg to make sure he'd stemmed the bleeding. Wrapping him in another poncho liner, he sent Eli to get an update on the dust-off and check on a new landing zone being cleared near their position. Johnny would need to gather the casualties there.

"Sorry, Doc," Eli said when he returned. "Nothing yet."

"Doc," Jungle Boy said, "I guess this ends my tour. I was hoping to go home together."

"Don't worry about stuff like that right now," Johnny told him. "Let's concentrate on getting you out of here."

"The LZ's ready, Doc," Eli said.

Johnny organized another poncho to carry Jungle Boy to the landing zone. The firefight over, he enlisted the help of the kid's squad. While two of the newer guys each held an end, Johnny carried the IV bottle above Jungle Boy as he walked alongside.

Johnny overheard Howitz on the radio with the captain. "No, Sir, I don't know how many confirmed kills. I don't have the body count yet. I need to get my wounded out."

The captain, concerned about his count, the only measurement in the war now. No ground was ever held. They patrolled the same areas over and over and searched the same villages. Charlie had stayed and fought, giving the VC time to evacuate the camp and take most of their supplies. They were probably already at another one or building something new.

Johnny heard Howitz on the radio again. "What do you mean the LZ's too hot? We just secured a new one. If my guys can be out in the shit, then your guys can come and get them when they're hurt. I've got two WIAs that are serious."

Howitz looked at Johnny briefly while he listened. "Roger that, and thanks. We'll pop smoke as you approach."

Most of the crews were superb, risking their own safety to get the guys out of the field and into the evac hospitals. When Johnny heard the rotors approaching, he had them carry Jungle Boy to the helicopter. He handed the IV to the dust-off medic. He recognized him from a previous rescue. The noise of the rotors drowned out what Johnny said, but he shouted his words anyway. "Make sure you get this kid to the evac hospital alive. If anyone deserves to make it out of the Nam, it's him."

The dust-off medic looked at Johnny and shouted, "We got him, Doc." In case he couldn't hear him, he nodded and gave him a thumbs up.

When Johnny returned from the operation without Jungle Boy, his focus turned inward. It was disorienting not having the kid around. Howitz soon got word that Jungle Boy was alive and in the bowels of the army's evacuation system. He'd lost a foot, but Johnny already knew that.

Eli and Ben Moses attempted to socialize with him when they were off operations, but Johnny was too removed. He functioned by rote now, too drained by the Nam emotionally and physically to respond to anything other than what he needed to do. He remembered Tut and how he'd been at the end of his tour, unable to give anything more.

Johnny was thankful that Jungle Boy had survived the Nam. He'd traded a foot for that certainty. Johnny missed him and realized they had been together for every patrol and ambush since they had arrived in the platoon.

There were more night ambushes, a couple more patrols, new guys arriving in the platoon. And finally, a new medic to replace him, the old man of the platoon now. He'd not wanted to be unfriendly, but there was nothing he could impart to his replacement, a kid from Oklahoma. He told him the basics, what to pack in his aid bag, where to position himself in the platoon. As for surviving the Nam, he would have to figure it out for himself and have luck on his side. There was no magic formula.

In a final mail call, a week before Johnny's departure, he gathered with the platoon. The same mouthy clerk, who liked giving a running commentary as he handed out the mail, had put a letter aside because he didn't recognize the name. It had almost been returned to sender, but he took it with the stack for third platoon because that's where it was addressed.

"Anybody know a Delbert Kincaid?" he asked. At first, everybody thought it must be a new guy, or a mistaken address. But Johnny did know, and he went to get the letter from the clerk.

"Who the fuck is Delbert Kincaid?" the clerk asked.

"That's Jungle Boy," Johnny said. "If it's from Beverley Morrow, I promised him I would make sure he got it. He was hoping to hear from her."

"Jungle Boy has a girl back home?"

"Just shut the fuck up and give me the letter," Johnny said. "It's personal."

"You tell him, Doc," a voice from the back of the room shouted. "Just shut the fuck up and deliver the mail."

Johnny took the letter back to his hooch before opening it. He thought he should respond to Billy's mother and let her know that Jungle Boy had been wounded and was somewhere in the evacuation system.

> *Dear Delbert,*
>
> *I was so pleased to receive your letter. Your kind words have given me the first ray of sunshine since Billy's death. I can see why he valued your friendship and spoke so highly of you. Please forgive me if I am being overly motherly with you (your own mother must be so proud). I hope she doesn't mind sharing you, at least through our correspondence. It has given me great comfort to know Billy had such a friend. I am forever grateful for that. Please write when you get the chance, and maybe we can arrange to meet when you are home.*
>
>

Forever Yours,
Beverley Morrow
>

Before composing a letter in response, Johnny sat and realized how ill at ease he felt not knowing where the kid was and how his wounds were healing. *This must be what having a brother is like,* he thought. Johnny knew the kid would never let him down, and he hadn't. Jungle Boy had prevented many casualties walking point. Johnny felt alone without him.

In his letter, he told Beverley how Delbert lost his foot. He wondered if he would ever be able to call him by his real name, his nickname so fitting for what he meant to the platoon. Johnny explained how it would take a few months to heal, be fitted with a prosthesis and learn to walk with one. Delbert would recuperate in a US facility near his home.

Johnny's final month in-country had been much like his first, night ambushes and patrols through the swamps, villages and jungles of the

Mekong Delta. Lieutenant Howitz kept him in the rear when he could. Johnny had accompanied the new medic on a couple of ambushes and a longer patrol. It would be his platoon to look after now.

Two weeks before his DEROS date, he forced himself to write two letters. He told CC and his father not to worry if they didn't hear from him again before he came home. He was fine and would see them soon. The strain of writing letters, never mentioning the truth about his tour, had taken its toll. The war had seeped deeply into his being, that much he knew. Would it recede? Once so anxious to return home, an apprehension surfaced. His former life seemed so far away he wondered if he would ever reconnect with it. He had missed his girl, maybe too much, and now he wasn't sure about how he had changed. Had CC?

So it was in the Nam. Johnny had survived. When he arrived at Tan Son Nhut Airbase to catch his flight home, he looked for Danny, who would also be rotating out of Vietnam. He searched the extensive complexes full of returning soldiers but couldn't find him.

Men were gathered in boisterous groups drinking cans of beer and smoking the last of their potent stashes. Johnny found it ironic that he used to sell it, had wound up in Vietnam because of it, but had never smoked marijuana in the Nam.

After searching the staging area and not finding Danny, he joined a more solitary group on a knoll overlooking a part of the massive base. Some soldiers squatted Vietnamese style and smoked cigarette after cigarette as he remembered Tut doing. The men nearby were pensive, not wanting conversation, just time to process their thoughts. Twelve months of watching every step, expecting the worst, could not be shaken in a few hours.

The following morning, he stood on the tarmac with 188 other veterans waiting to board their flight. He was not the only soldier that smelled of the jungle and had the blood stains of friends on his fatigues. The mood remained somber and pensive until the plane lifted off the tarmac, and a spontaneous cheer erupted. Men had their lives to return to. They had made it out of the Nam.

PART THREE
WELCOME HOME

CHAPTER TWENTY-NINE

Johnny looked out the tiny window of the Boeing 707. They'd flown for twenty-two hours and were on the tarmac at Travis Air Force Base east of San Francisco Bay. He had his life back. So focused on surviving Vietnam, he'd not thought about the specifics of his future beyond the fantasies of living normally.

With only a few months left on his draft commitment, the army waived the time remaining on Johnny's service. The out-processing took two hours in a small building at the edge of the base, where soldiers from the plane received pay vouchers, leave papers, discharges, and duty assignments. Despite processing out of the army, Johnny was issued a new set of dress greens, fitted and complete with his combat medic's badge and the bronze star for valor that Lieutenant Howitz insisted he receive for the day he rescued Jungle Boy.

Outside the processing center, he flagged a cab and asked to be driven to the nearest Greyhound Depot. In silence, he viewed the streets from inside the taxi as the driver sped through suburban neighborhoods. Tidy and neatly trimmed lawns adorned the prosperous parts of the city. Less manicured and looking worn, poorer sections lacked the same upkeep. Everything looked familiar, but Johnny felt disconnected and ill at ease, unexpectedly a stranger and apprehensive about his return.

He'd made a San Jose connection and waited overnight in the terminal for the first bus to Santa Cruz, which didn't leave until morning. He changed into civilian clothes in the rest room, then smoked and drank coffee until his bus left. He'd slept little in the last forty-eight hours.

What now? he thought. *He'd chosen the army instead of prison, gambling with his life so that he could live normally. Why did he feel even more isolated?*

Nervous, he took a seat near the back of the bus and watched people doing everyday things, visiting, eating packed lunches, checking bus schedules. A red-haired girl sat in the seat in front of him. Her long hair grew below her shoulders and shone from a morning washing, the perfumed scent of shampoo filling his nostrils. How wholesome she looked, unlike the peasant women in the rice paddies and villages. Unlike himself, now thirty pounds lighter with infected pockets of pus all over his body and scars from forgotten thorns and unseen leeches gorging themselves on his blood. CC might be appalled by the sight of him.

He'd always liked the drive through the Santa Cruz Mountains between San Jose and the coast, filled with evergreens, the forest growing thick to the highway. Arriving at the depot on the edge of the downtown area, he exited the bus and stood on the street for a moment, excited to be home yet anxious at what he would find. Their suite only a few blocks from the terminal, Johnny walked west toward the sea. He had little from Vietnam to carry in his duffel bag except for a few civilian clothes and the new set of dress greens rumpled inside. He'd brought the stack of letters from CC, a few photographs the guys with cameras had taken, and the short-timer's calendar with the days meticulously marked off every time he'd returned to Dong Tam after stints in the field.

His apprehension mounted as he walked but was mixed with exhilaration at seeing the ocean, hearing the waves breaking on the shore, and inhaling the salty scent of the sea. Of having his life back and reuniting with CC. It all looked familiar but *felt* different somehow. Johnny's emotions were conflicting and powerful but ill-defined and raw, devoid of conceptualization. Yet, he walked steadily, hoping for the best. Not confident in what he would find, but needing the certainty of his return, and of being with CC again. He thought he would know the moment they were together, for good or ill, whether they had a future now that he was home.

When he entered the apartment she was out, but her presence was everywhere, as was their former life. The record player next to the bed, the coffee pot on the counter, the fading couch across the room from the window with a view of the ocean. They'd had it good for a while.

Johnny set his duffel bag down and sat for a moment. He wanted a smoke but realized he'd finished the pack that morning. Restless, he walked to the liquor store on the corner to buy cigarettes. Smoking, he strolled along the sidewalk listening to the steadiness of the waves and heard the calls of the gulls in the sky and watched the sandpipers hunting for food along the shore.

On his way back, he saw Cecelia running toward him. She had returned and noticed his bag. Frantic he was not in the apartment, she had gone searching for him. Jumping into his arms, CC wrapped herself around Johnny and held him tightly.

Out of breath, she whispered in his ear. "I have worried so much about you, Johnny. Not knowing if you were okay, if I would ever see you again. You must never go away again. Never, never, never." CC squeezed harder and buried her face in his neck and cried.

When she released her hold, she laughed between sobs and said: "Let me look at you." She stepped back. "What have they done?" she exclaimed. "You're so thin. Have you been sick?"

"No," he said. "We all look like this." He stepped toward her and took her in his arms again. "We can talk about it later. Let's go home."

CC nodded and took his arm and squeezed it tightly as they walked. Having her own set of jumbled emotions, elated at having Johnny home yet concerned at the condition he'd returned, knowing how easily she could have lost him. She cried again when they entered the apartment. A year's worth of feelings tumbled out.

"Oh, my," she said, "I must look a fright, crying and carrying on." Pushing her most disturbing emotions aside, she declared: "I have news. Your father and my mother have, sort of, well…," she hesitated, "become a couple. We were afraid to write to you about it." She laughed through her tears but then sobbed. "I never knew what to write to you, what would make you feel better. I just didn't know how to help you."

Johnny took her in his arms and moved them to the couch. He held her tight against him as she cried. "The news was just so bad about the war. Every week there were hundreds of young men dying…and I just didn't know what to do. What I would do if you were one of them."

"It's over," Johnny said, brushing her hair aside to look at her face. "I didn't know what to write either." He left it at that for the moment. "And my father and your mother, that's good news. We can all get back to our lives now."

✦ ✦ ✦

Their first days together were good. More restless than CC remembered, Johnny smoked heavily and never slept through the night. Pretending to sleep, she watched him having a cigarette at the window, gazing at the ocean lit by the moon. One night he had gotten out of bed and put on his coat.

"Johnny," she said.

"Yes."

"Where are you going so late, darling?"

"Just for a walk."

"Let me come with you," she said, hopping out of bed. "I'm starting to worry about you."

"You shouldn't worry," he replied. "But you can come with me. I'm just going down to the ocean. I find it soothing at night, being in the dark and still feeling safe."

CC dressed quickly, put on a light coat and noticed the time, 2:30 in the morning. She put her arm through his as they walked.

"You must tell me if something is bothering you," she said. "I know you are up during the night. What is it?"

"I can't talk about it. Not right now, anyway. I'm not used to sleeping through the night anymore."

"Johnny," she pressed on, "what happened over there? You've changed in some ways. I need to know what's troubling you."

They'd come to the ocean and sat on a large outcrop of rock protecting the shore from the worst of the winter storms that surged at high tide. He couldn't talk to CC about the war yet, not the specifics. He was still piecing things together, but he attempted a start.

"Remember when I went to see my father before I went into the army?

I needed to ask him about his experiences. He'd never talked about it, not once. So I asked him. He told me something I didn't really understand at the time. Now I do."

Johnny looked at CC before continuing. "When he saw what had become of the inmates at Dachau, it changed him. He said that witnessing such cruelty had tainted him, leaving him feeling inadequate as a human being. The fact that we are capable of that kind of barbarity penetrated so deeply that he would never be the same. That's something like what I'm feeling now. No matter how hard I tried to make it better, it was not enough, could never be enough. The war devoured everyone who had anything to do with it."

CC gripped Johnny's arm tighter. "You're home now, darling, please be all right with that. You've said yourself that we just needed to get through Vietnam, and we could have our lives back."

Johnny nodded. "I intend to," he said. "I really want that for us."

"Then what's to stop us?"

"Nothing," he said. His darker mood lifted sometimes, and he felt pieces of himself returning.

"Then let's go home and get back into bed. I need to know you are here and never going away again."

In the morning, Johnny rose and put the coffee on. "I need to talk about something else," he began. "Remember the kid I mentioned in my letters, the one we called Jungle Boy? He'll be in San Francisco at an army hospital. I need to go and see him."

"Of course, darling. Can I come along?" CC felt lighthearted and in a good mood. Part of her man that had been missing had come back to her during the night.

"You can, of course, but it might be a horrible visit for you. He lost a foot a few weeks before we were scheduled to rotate home. He'll be on a ward with a lot of other amputees."

"How come you call him Jungle Boy?"

"It's a nickname the lieutenant gave him. We were on a night ambush early in our tours, and he saw the VC before anyone. Somehow he knew. Somehow he knew a lot of times. He's like a brother to me now."

"Then I will be a sister to him," CC said as Johnny handed her a cup of coffee.

Johnny retrieved his dress greens from the closet and smoothed the wrinkles. "I'm self-conscious wearing the uniform in front of you, but it will open doors at the hospital."

The processing center at Travis had made sure his military achievements were updated in the ribbons above his left shirt pocket. His combat medic's badge stood out above two rows of colored bars. The Ninth Infantry Division insignia, now on his right shoulder, showed he'd experienced combat with the unit. Their significance would be recognized by the military personnel assigned to the army hospital, and any patients they encountered.

"What do all of these mean?" CC asked.

"Mostly for being in Vietnam," he said. He pointed to his CMB. "This one's for being in combat as a medic. This is for going and getting Jungle Boy when he lost his foot." Johnny pointed to the ribbon with the blue stripe centered between the bright red of the decoration for valor.

"Were they shooting at you when you treated his wounds?"

"Yes," he said, leaving it at that.

CC didn't press him, not wanting specifics about the war to intrude on what had been a good night and morning with her man. "Does Jungle Boy have the same ones?" she asked.

"Mostly, with maybe a couple more. The purple heart for his wounds, and the combat infantryman's badge."

Convinced that Jungle Boy would be recuperating in Letterman's Army Hospital at the Presidio of San Francisco, they left in the T-bird the next morning. Johnny had changed the oil on the street and checked the tires when he filled up with gas for the trip. It felt good to fuss over his car and prepare it for the road.

The Santa Cruz Police Department had not forgotten Johnny Ornowoski. Tom Hamilton, the senior detective on the force, had arrested Johnny two years before and had eventually busted Ralph Barnes. He knew about CC's minor dealing and suspected her connection with Barnes might lead them to clues about her boyfriend's relationship with the older drug dealer. The police knew they'd done business together and suspected Johnny would return to his old habits now that he was out of the army.

Hamilton, the lead detective on both cases, thought Johnny had gotten off easy going into the army to avoid prison. Aware of Johnny's return from Vietnam, Hamilton figured he could link Ornowoski to a broader network that included Barnes. Old school, the veteran cop hated the drug culture and everything it stood for. A WWII veteran, he couldn't understand why the current version of the United States Army was having a tough time whipping an underfed yellow man in sandals in the jungles of Vietnam. He often complained about it to his younger partner, Randy Siemans.

"I bet he thinks he's a real war hero now that he's back from Vietnam," said Hamilton. "It's soldiers like him that are the reason we're getting our asses kicked in Vietnam. Today's vets are a bunch of crybabies whining and bitching all the time after smokin' too much dope. How can we win a war doin' that?"

Siemans always nodded at Hamilton's commentary. He'd heard it many times. They'd kept tabs on CC and had not arrested her because they expected to find a bigger connection if they kept an eye out. Barnes had not talked, knowing providing information to the police was far riskier than any punishment the justice system would impose.

On a routine patrol, a squad car had noticed Johnny working on his T-bird.

✳ ✳ ✳

By nine o'clock, Johnny and CC pulled into the parking lot of the hospital complex at the Presidio of San Francisco. With 500 beds and ten stories, Letterman's dominated the tiny base on the bay. Inside, the worst casualties from the Vietnam War--burn patients, amputees and the paralyzed-- filled the wards. When they arrived, the manicured lawns outside the hospital were already filling with wheelchairs and staff taking advantage of a beautiful autumn day between therapy sessions.

They'd taken the scenic Route 1 along the coast, which continued into the city and brought them to the army base. Preoccupied with finding Jungle

Boy, Johnny still experienced flashes of his old life with CC curled up next to him during the two-hour drive.

At the main entrance, a young woman in uniform, a private in the army, greeted them at a reception desk.

"What can I do for you Specialist?" she asked, addressing Johnny with his rank, the equivalent of a corporal.

"We're looking for a Delbert Kincaid," he said. "We were in the same platoon in Vietnam when he was wounded and lost a foot. Since he's from Oakland, I figured he would be here recuperating and being fitted for a prosthesis. I put him on the medevac."

"I see," she said, looking at his uniform. "In that case, I guess he would really like to see you." She smiled and looked at a printed list of patients in alphabetical order. "That is Kincaid with a 'K'?"

"Yes," said Johnny. "He'll be on one of the amputee wards."

The woman scrolled down the list of names with her finger. "I have no record of a Kincaid in the hospital."

He has to be here, thought Johnny. *He couldn't have possibly recovered from surgery, been fitted with a prosthesis, and been discharged already.*

"May I have a look?" Johnny asked. He had to find a way onto the wards to check for himself. He picked a name at random and asked: "How about Murton, Brian Murton? He should be here."

The young private beamed, glad to be helpful. "Brian Murton is here, ward three."

"Thanks," Johnny said, taking CC by the hand and walking away from the reception desk. "He has to be here," he said aloud, but more to himself than CC. "He just lost a foot. Where else could he be?"

"What do we do now?" CC asked.

"We go looking for him on the amputee wards. He couldn't have just vanished. Are you up for this?" he asked. "There will be some pretty bad wounds, but I need to talk to some of the patients, make sure nothing has happened to Jungle Boy. Maybe someone will remember him or know something." Johnny didn't allow his thoughts to consider anything worse than some kind of mix-up, a name being left off a list, some bureaucratic mistake.

On the first amputee ward, Johnny approached a young man sitting in a wheelchair, one of his legs bandaged and amputated above the knee. Given the stage of his recovery, he would have been on the ward for more than two months.

"Hi," Johnny said, putting out his hand, "Doc Woski. I'm looking for a young guy with his foot amputated…"

"Whoa," the man responded before Johnny could finish. "You've come to the right place. Take your pick," he gestured, spreading his arms wide and nodding at the ward full of patients.

"Sorry," Johnny said. "His name's Delbert Kincaid. We called him Jungle Boy. We were in the same platoon. I need to find him."

"I'd like to help you out, Doc, but nobody by those names rings a bell. I been here over three months. When was he hit?"

"About two months ago."

"Yeah, he'd still be here if his foot was amputated. Who were you guys with?"

"The Ninth, down in the Delta. You?"

"Twenty-fifth, around Cu Chi. Three months in when I got hit."

"Thanks for your help," Johnny said. "Good luck, man."

"No problem, Doc. Hope you find your friend."

Several wards were filled with amputees in various stages of recovery. Johnny spoke with at least one patient on each and looked for Jungle Boy. He tried not to bother patients in obvious pain, or who looked depressed, staring at a distant realm only they were aware of. Johnny could not find Jungle Boy. He was not in the hospital at the Presidio.

CHAPTER THIRTY

Agitated about not finding Jungle Boy, Johnny walked with CC through the parking area toward their car. Oblivious to the scenic view of San Francisco Bay on a sunny day, his emotions were a jumbled mix of concern and frustration as he tried to make sense of not finding Delbert Kincaid.

"It's just *like* the kid to do something foolish, but he can't have just vanished. I tried and tried to convince him not to walk point all the time. What does he do? Gets his foot shot off."

"Are you angry with him?" CC asked.

"No, not angry," Johnny said. "It's hard to explain. I just need to find him. We were with each other every step of the way until he was wounded. We looked after each other. It's just strange not knowing where he is, how he's doing."

"Maybe he's at another hospital," CC said feebly. Overwhelmed by all the men on the wards with missing limbs, she was stunned by the number of amputees.

Silent for most of the drive back to Santa Cruz, Johnny remembered writing the letter to Beverley Morrow. *Maybe she would have tried to find Jungle Boy.* If not, Johnny would phone every military hospital in the country. He repressed thoughts that Jungle Boy might have died from his wounds, not likely at this stage of his recovery.

When they arrived in Santa Cruz, a patrol car pulled up behind them. Not overly concerned, Johnny continued driving toward their apartment. When the police flashed their red lights for him to pull over, his old paranoia kicked in, but he knew they had nothing illegal. Two policemen got out of their vehicle.

"Good afternoon, officer," Johnny spoke first, suppressing his frustration. He just wanted to get home and figure out how to find Jungle Boy. "What can I do for you?"

"Just noticing you have a cracked cover on your blinker," he said. "And my partner here," he pointed to a policeman standing at the rear of the T-bird, "noticed one of your tires is low. You have a jack and a spare in the trunk?"

Johnny got out of the car and looked at the rear wheel.

"I see you're in the army," the officer continued. "Just back from Vietnam? Perhaps we can help you with that tire. Anything for our boys in uniform."

"That's really not necessary," Johnny said. "It's been a long day, and we would just as soon be on our way. I think we can make it home. I'll look after everything there."

"Where have you been for the day?"

"At the Presidio looking for a friend in the hospital," Johnny answered. "He was wounded in Vietnam."

"Tough break," the officer said. "What's your friend's name?"

"Delbert Kincaid," Johnny answered, finding it odd that the officer would ask, then write the name in a notepad.

"Let's just make sure you've got everything you need in the trunk to change that tire," the officer feigned concern.

Johnny shrugged and opened the trunk. "Satisfied?" he asked.

"Have a nice day," the policeman replied.

"Nice work," Hamilton complimented the uniformed officer. "We'll check the name out, make sure he really does have a buddy in San Francisco. Want to bet it's of the drug smuggling variety? Better check this out with our counterparts in the army." He handed Siemans the name to trace.

Returning a few minutes later, Randy Siemans shook his head. "Bogus," he said. "The MPs on the base have no record of a Delbert Kincaid ever having been admitted to the hospital."

"Looks like our boy's back in business," Hamilton surmised. "Too smart to be haulin' a shipment back in his fancy T-bird," he continued, "but he'll slip up. They always do."

"Something else," Randy Siemans said, "the MPs say Ornowoski was discharged from the army when he returned from Vietnam. Wonder what he was doing in uniform?"

"These guys would use their own grandmothers to sell an extra pound of dope," Hamilton said, shaking his head.

"Here we go again," Johnny said after the police left. "I might be done with the stuff, but they're not done with me. They think I'm dealing again."

CC had a sick feeling in the pit of her stomach. "It might not be you, Johnny," is how she began. "Remember when I wrote that Ralph had been arrested? The police have questioned me about him. Please don't be angry with me; I can't bear it right now, but I was buying a little marijuana from Ralph and selling it."

"But why, CC? And Ralph was supplying it to you?"

Johnny's old paranoia resurfaced as he realized why the police had pulled them over. He suppressed his anger at CC and waited for his girl's explanation.

"Right after you left for Vietnam, I went through too much of the money you'd left. I started dealing a little to make up for it. I was beside myself with worry. The war kept going on and on, and I knew you were in great danger. The days were so long. I would stay in the apartment and smoke some of it. We have come through so much, Johnny, for so long. Please try and understand."

"But I went to Vietnam to be done with it, to get a fresh start." Exasperated, Johnny realized how naïve he was to think he could just go into the army, and it would all work out. He struggled to make sense of what his girl told him.

"How much were you dealing?"

"Not much, Johnny, a few ounces here and there. I saw Freddy Dempster after Ralph was arrested. He's got his own practice now. He thought it would all blow over because they had Ralph. He couldn't imagine the police making a big deal over the little bit I bought and sold."

"No more dealing, CC, looking over our shoulders. I'm done with it. I never even smoked any in Vietnam. Are you with me on that?"

CC looked at Johnny, tears forming in her eyes. "Totally," she said. "You're home now. That's all that matters."

"Anything left?" he asked.

"Only a little. A customer didn't show, and I hid it in the apartment."

CC removed a loose baseboard when they got home and handed Johnny a small metal box with a few ounces of marijuana.

"Here," Johnny said, "give it to me. I'll flush it down the toilet."

In the bathroom, he emptied part of the contents into the toilet bowl. As he flushed, the can slipped out of his hands, and a sealed packet of marijuana fell into the water. When he flushed again, the drain clogged.

A knock on the door interrupted them. CC froze, looking ashen.

"Who could that be?" Johnny whispered.

"I have no idea," said CC.

"See who it is."

Johnny returned to the bathroom and found the toilet still clogged. Unable to flush any more of the marijuana, he frantically looked for a place to hide the box as he heard CC speaking at the door.

CC returned holding a gift basket of food items. "It was the landlady," she said, "just wanting to welcome you home from Vietnam."

Johnny sat on the sofa still holding the metal box with the remaining marijuana. He trembled slightly. *What if it had been the police?* CC sat down next to him and let out a long breath.

"Here," she said. "I'll get rid of it." She took the box from Johnny's hands. "It was me who got us into this."

Johnny nodded. "That's everything?"

"Yes." She placed the box in a shopping bag and grabbed her purse. "We need some coffee for the morning. I won't be long. Please wait for me if you're going for a walk. I need to be with you tonight."

CC left for the store in a hurry to rid themselves of the final vestige of their marijuana dealing. Arriving at the Safeway, she tossed the package in a large garbage bin before entering the store.

In the morning, a homeless man, wobbly on his feet and reeking of alcohol, was apprehended selling marijuana to some hippies by the pier. The police took him to the station and put him into a holding cell.

"It don't look like he uses the stuff. He says he found it in a dumpster. Maybe we should run some prints on it, find a bigger fish."

Later that day, they had a match on a set of Johnny Ornowoski's.

Johnny calculated the time on the East Coast. Nine o'clock would make it noon in Boston. A woman answered on the third ring.

"Beverley Morrow?" Johnny began.

"Speaking. May I ask who's calling?"

"Beverley, my name is John Ornowoski. I wrote to you from Vietnam about Delbert Kincaid's wounds. Have you been able to locate him?"

"Mr. Ornowoski, it's so good to hear from you. Thank you for your letter. Delbert speaks highly of you."

"You know where he is?"

"Why, yes, he's right here in Boston recuperating at the veterans' hospital."

"What's he doing there?" Johnny shouted into the phone.

Confused, Beverley Morrow elaborated. "They're fitting him with an artificial foot at the VA Hospital."

"Sorry," Johnny said. "I mean, how did he end up in Boston? He's from the West Coast."

"I don't really know," she said. "He just called one day and said he was here in Boston. Here, I'll hand the phone to him, and you can ask Delbert."

"He's there, right now?" Johnny shouted into the phone again.

Jungle Boy came on the line. "Doc, is that you? I can't believe you're phoning all the way from California."

"What are you doing in Boston?" Johnny asked again.

Now Jungle Boy was confused. "I'm getting a new foot, Doc. It's just a fake one, but I'm starting to get the hang of walking on it."

"You're not understanding my question. I just searched the wards at Letterman's. How did you wind up in Boston?"

"When I got back to the States, they asked me where I wanted to be treated, so I told them Boston. I knew you had a couple of months to go in the Nam, so I thought I would look up Beverley before you got back. Is that all right?"

"Of course it's all right," Johnny answered, still a little exasperated, but it was starting to make sense.

The mystery solved, Johnny changed the subject. "How's it going with the foot?"

"It's going good, Doc. Beverley has me over at her place when I can get a day pass off the ward. Like today."

Johnny wondered why he would be surprised at anything the kid did. "I was just worried about you. Glad to hear things are good. Keep me posted."

"Will do, Doc."

"Did you find Jungle Boy?" CC asked.

"He's in Boston."

"How did he get there?"

"It's a long story. You feel like some coffee?"

The homeless man selling drugs was Stewart Brenz, "Stewie" to those who knew him on the street. He drank. That was his drug of choice. He was homeless because he drank. He was unable to work because he drank, and he sold the marijuana he found to keep drinking. The police held him until he sobered up. They did not charge him.

Under the pier at the shoreline, Stewart Brenz sat on the sand with his back against a piling drinking from a cheap jug of wine. That was the last time anybody saw him alive.

His clothes were soaked from the high tide washing over him. His head had a fractured skull, and a tire iron used in the murder was found discarded nearby, a perfect fit with the wound in his head. Whoever had killed the homeless man made no attempt to disguise the murder.

"Think there's any connection to our boy?" Randy Siemans asked his partner.

"I'd be surprised if there wasn't," Hamilton answered. "If Stewart Brenz stole the weed from him, then he's a dead man. Funny how the Polack shows up just back from Vietnam, and there's already a dead body connected with his dealing. Want to bet the only lesson he learned in Vietnam was how to kill?"

"The lab's running the prints on the tire iron as we speak," Siemans responded, smiling.

"Why is Jungle Boy with Billy Warrington's mother in Boston?" CC asked. "Where is his own mother?"

"It's complicated," Johnny said. "He doesn't have much of a relationship with her, doesn't know who his father is and suspects his mother doesn't either. He was the only guy in the platoon who never got any letters, never even showed up for mail call. Then a letter came from Beverley Morrow after Billy died."

"No other family?"

"He talked about a grandfather sometimes. I think he lived with him for a while, but he died. This will sound strange, but everybody hated the cans of ham and lima beans in the C-ration packs. Jungle Boy used to trade for them, says his grandfather loved lima beans and didn't understand why nobody liked them. The smallest things meant a lot to him. I always worried he would get himself killed with his devotion to the platoon. In the end, he lost a foot."

"You're like a brother to him," CC said.

"And I couldn't protect him."

"But you saved his life."

"Maybe. I always felt he saved mine more often." Johnny thought for a moment. "Nothing was ever straightforward in the Nam. Everything felt like it could fall apart at any moment, a disaster waiting to happen."

"I think we have everything we need to put the dumb Polack away for a long time," Hamilton said.

"In a neat package," Siemans added. "Prints, murder weapon and motive all fitting together nicely. Should we pick him up?"

The following morning Johnny sat in the interrogation room, thinking it could only be harassment, a grudge held by the older detective who seemed to have it in for him. His mood darkened when he saw Tom Hamilton holding the metal box in an evidence bag and setting it on the table in front of him.

"Ever see this?" the detective began.

Johnny said nothing, but his mind filled with dread.

"Know a Stewart Brenz, do we?" Hamilton said smugly.

"Who?" Johnny said.

"Don't play dumb with us," Hamilton yelled and pounded his fist on the table. "That's the name of the homeless guy we found selling marijuana to some hippies down by the pier from the same box that has your fingerprints all over it. Funny coincidence, isn't it? Only guess what?"

Hamilton paused and took a step back, glaring at Johnny the whole time.

"Now he's shown up dead. We think you might know something about that. The murder weapon showed up too. And it's a match with your prints."

"You can't be serious," Johnny said. "Why would I kill a homeless man I don't even know."

"For stealing dope from you."

"I just got back from Vietnam for Christ's sakes," Johnny shouted.

"Learn to like the killing over there, did we? From what I hear, a lot of our guys come to like the killing, kind of get hooked on it… like an addiction. That what happened to you, Ornowoski?"

"You don't know shit about Vietnam."

"We know what got you there. Look Ornowoski, even we're surprised at how fast you got back in business. We know about Barnes, and we know about your girl. And now there's a dead guy and a murder weapon with your prints on it. Go figure."

"I'm done with the drugs," Johnny said. "Cecelia is too. We just want to get on with our lives."

"Not a chance, Ornowoski."

CHAPTER THIRTY-ONE

Johnny's arrest had come swiftly and unexpectedly. Cecelia Jones phoned Freddy Dempster in desperation. Thinking her dealing must be at the root of the trouble, she wept as she spoke with the lawyer.

"Johnny is innocent," she sobbed. "I was the one selling drugs. Why have they arrested him? And for murder? I have been with Johnny practically every minute since he got back from Vietnam. I don't understand any of this."

"We'll find out," Freddy assured her. "For now, just make sure you've told me everything. There's more to this than you selling a little marijuana while Johnny was gone."

"I've told you all I can think of," CC insisted. "We haven't used or sold any drugs since Johnny's returned. He's done with it—completely."

"We'll get to the bottom of it, CC. Try not to worry yourself sick, or jump to conclusions. It might take a couple of days, but I'll find out more and be in touch."

Rarely in his years of practicing criminal defense had Freddy seen many of his clients make a clean break from their past. He'd been certain Johnny Ornowoski would be one of them. Perhaps he'd been wrong about the young man. Patterns of behavior were hard to break, but something didn't add up. How could Cecelia, buying and selling a small amount of marijuana while Johnny was in Vietnam, be connected to his arrest for murder? The police had to have some hard evidence beyond speculation.

Johnny didn't even look up when he heard footsteps approaching his cell. Depressed, he figured it must be one of the guards coming to harass him. *Why had he been so foolish to think that going to Vietnam would solve anything? Look at his situation now.*

"Hello, Johnny," Freddy said. "We meet again."

Johnny hopped off his bunk when he realized it was his lawyer.

"I'll get right to the point," Freddy began.

Of course, he would, thought Johnny. Not much had changed in Freddy's approach or appearance in the two years since he had represented him.

"The prosecution has the murder weapon, and your prints on it. Any idea how that could be?"

"I'll get right to the point as well. No. Tell me how that makes any sense?" asked Johnny. "I do a tour in Vietnam to avoid going to prison, come home, and within a few days kill a homeless man with a tire iron. Great start to my future. I thought if I survived Vietnam, I'd have one."

"Your problem right now is not one of logic but of evidence. It's pointing right at you."

"I didn't kill anyone. Probably not even in Vietnam. I was a medic trying to save lives, not take them. I thought I left the drug business by going over there, and the killing when I survived my tour. None of this makes any sense."

"Listen," said Freddy, "I don't think you killed anybody either. The prosecution will have to divulge more as they proceed. In the meantime, I'll see what more I can dig up."

Johnny nodded at his attorney. "I don't suppose there's any point in asking about bail. I may go stir-crazy in here. All I ever thought about in Vietnam was getting back home and starting a normal life with my girl."

Freddy sighed. "I'm on my way to see the prosecutor. In the meantime, try and remember anything that might have implicated you, however tenuous the connection might seem."

Freddy always tried to remain calm and calculating. The law as a framework was constant; the variables were always in the interpretation and strategies, the things a lawyer did best when not overly swayed by emotions. This case bothered him. He entered the office of T. Bradley Smyth for a chat. The two had occasionally been on opposing sides in a courtroom butting heads over minor offenses. Freddy knew Smyth only professionally and hadn't formed a strong opinion of the prosecutor.

"Well, well, well," Smyth remarked when he saw Freddy. "How's life on the outside now that you're making all that money in private practice?"

"Pretty much the same. I just have to collect my own bills now."

"So, what can I do for you?" Smyth asked.

"My client, Johnny Ornowoski, the suspect in the Stewart Brenz case, what have you really got on him?"

"You know I don't have to divulge all of that yet."

"Let's cut the crap, Bradley. There's a young man in jail accused of a murder he supposedly committed a few days after returning from Vietnam. Why? Your motive is weak."

"Why don't you ask your client?" countered Smyth. "Perhaps he should also tell you why the murder weapon was found near the body with his fingerprints on it? Our client, the public, has a right to expect that we lock up the bad guys."

"Your client also expects that you lock up the right guy. Why were the police even interested in Johnny Ornowoski when he returned from Vietnam?"

"Look, his girlfriend was dealing, something he was doing before he was arrested two years ago. We think he never quit his relationship with Ralph Barnes."

"You think he was dealing from Vietnam?" Freddy was incredulous. "Just how was that supposed to work? He was a medic in an infantry platoon."

"That's all I'm going to give you now. But if I were you, preparing a defense, I'd advise you to have your client start levelling with you. I've already got the murder weapon with his prints. It only gets worse from there."

"Come on, Bradley, if your case is such a slam dunk, what does it matter?"

"Why should I tip my hand while we're still developing it? I've already given you more than I have to at this point."

"This is not some game, Bradley. There's something strange going on here."

"Oh, it's strange all right. You'll get more as our case proceeds, but I wouldn't get your client's hopes up."

Freddy saw Johnny the next morning. "They think you were dealing from Vietnam. Is there any way that could have been possible?"

"What? This is just too crazy. I mean, you can ask any grunt in Vietnam about that, but you'd better be prepared for their reaction. Sure, for someone in the rear, a supply sergeant, it might be possible, but not for a grunt."

"So, let's do that," said Freddy, "ask some of your platoon members. Give me some names. Let's get them to testify."

"Bring them here? How do we pay for that?"

"Your first bit of good fortune," Freddy said. "I received a call from your friend, a Cliff Morris, currently on a nationwide tour with his band. As you know, his career really took off while you were in Vietnam. He told me he's always felt guilty about you going to Vietnam while he's been making a 'shitload of money,' as he phrased it. He's offered to bankroll your defense. I think you should take him up on that."

"Cliff has offered to cover the costs of my defense?"

"He has," said Freddy, "and asks only one thing in return. I wasn't even sure what he was talking about, but he insists that you introduce him to Rafe Johnson, one of your platoon members. Says he's the grandson of Robert Johnson. I don't know who that is. I was hoping you could make sense of that request?"

For the first time since he'd been in jail, a faint smile formed on Johnny's mouth. "I think we can make that happen."

"There's something else we need to discuss," said Freddy. "Your future is at stake here, and I've never been involved in a murder trial. I think it would be wise to put your life in the hands of a lawyer with experience in capital murder cases."

"You want to abandon my defense?" Johnny said. "I don't know, Freddy. You got me out of the first big jam I was in." He thought for a moment. "If going to Vietnam could be considered getting out of a jam. If Cliff has so much money, isn't there some way you can stay on the case and assist? What you're saying makes a lot of sense, but I'd feel better having you in my corner."

"I think I know the right lawyer for the job," Freddy said. "We'll make a good team."

⋆ ⋆ ⋆

"Can't look a gift horse in the mouth, now can we?" Tom Hamilton gloated with T. Bradley Smyth. "Thought for sure we'd be able to put him away for dealing someday, but murder?"

"Good work, Tom," said Smyth, his feet on his desk. "The evidence and motives are starting to pile up. The murder case is just icing on the cake. The federal authorities have notified us that they've arrested a Patrick Corker on drug smuggling charges. He was posing as a Sergeant Keenan in Vietnam. The real Keenan was killed in a firefight near Pleiku two years ago. And Corker is linked to a Donald Palino, a drug kingpin operating out of Southeast Asia after deserting the army in Vietnam. And guess what?" Smyth paused for a moment before continuing. "Ornowoski and Palino trained together before deploying to Vietnam."

"Why would Ornowoski let a war stop him," Randy Siemans said sarcastically.

"He didn't," said Smyth. "The feds have connected Corker with enough drugs to put him away for a long time. At his age, he'll die in prison. So he's talking, giving us everything he can think of to reduce his sentence."

"Tell Randy what else you've found," Hamilton said to the prosecutor.

"Our local boy, Ornowoski, showed up in a place called Can Tho while he was in Vietnam, where he approached Corker looking to buy a large quantity of opium and marijuana."

"We've been looking in the wrong place all along," Hamilton added. "A lot of the local dope's not comin' in from Mexico but from Southeast Asia."

"Corker has given us the routes out of Vietnam, which lands in the Port of San Francisco," Smyth continued. "He claims not to know how it's distributed from there. That's where we think Barnes comes in, but he's not talking. The Feds are willing to share what they know as long as it doesn't interfere with nabbing the bigger fish they're looking for."

Smyth got up from his chair and looked at the detectives. "Gentlemen," he said confidently, "I think we've got ourselves an airtight case against Ornowoski and have a real shot at getting a lot of the local drugs off the street—permanently."

✶ ✶ ✶

Freddy Dempster received his degree from the Boalt Hall School of Law at Berkeley. A brilliant classmate from a prominent Bay Area family, intent on making a name for herself, had graduated with him. He remembered the passionate discussions he'd had with Marcella Stearns about the practice of law. Freddy had opted for a quieter life in Santa Cruz, while Marcella had gone on to greater prominence in San Francisco, brilliantly defending two high-profile murder cases. Freddy thought Johnny Ornowoski's case would be just the type that would appeal to his former classmate, making the justice system work for the innocent.

Marcella, who never forgot a name or face, recognized her old friend's voice. "Well, hello, Freddy. Or should I be calling you Frederick now? How is life in Santa Cruz?"

"No, Marcella, it's still Freddy, and life is fine in Santa Cruz. Are you busy? I have a case you might be interested in taking a look at."

"Hell, yes, I'm busy, but you know I always have time for you, especially if you're bringing me something interesting. So, what's up?"

"Two years ago, I represented a young man on a marijuana conviction. In lieu of prison time, the judge gave him the option of volunteering for the draft. He trained as a medic and spent a year in Vietnam with an infantry platoon. He's been accused of killing a homeless man. There's evidence pointing right at him, but I have difficulty believing he committed the murder."

"Why are you convinced of that? What I'm hearing is a lot of guys are going over the edge in Vietnam and are not returning as the same person."

"For starters, the motive is weak. The crazy Vietnam veteran scenario is what the police are figuring, along with some concocted revenge theory about the victim stealing a small amount of dope from the accused.

"According to all of the platoon members I've been able to reach, he spent a year over there being a pretty good medic. Near the end of his tour, he saved the life of a young kid and was awarded the bronze star for valor. He reached the casualty under fire and stopped the bleeding after his platoon member's foot was shot off. I'd like to help him, but I've never been involved in a murder trial. The young man's no killer. Interested?"

"Why are the police so convinced he committed the murder?"

"Because his fingerprints are on the murder weapon."

"That's a good start. Please tell me it's not a gun."

"It's not. My client saw enough of them in Vietnam to last a lifetime. He doesn't own one. I think the police are jumping to conclusions. The victim was killed with a tire iron left at the scene, a stupid thing to do. This young man is very cool under pressure and intelligent. Why don't you come down and meet with him, form your own impressions?"

"You know my feelings on the war, Freddy. I might be inclined to agree with the police. The murder weapon with a suspect's prints on it is not always a good starting point for the defense," she said sarcastically.

"I'm betting your impressions will change after meeting with the accused. How many Vietnam vets do you know?" Freddy asked.

"Not in my circle of friends," Marcella said.

"I've talked with four of his former platoon members. None of them can believe that Johnny Ornowoski would murder somebody. Jim Sanders, his former platoon commander, was particularly eloquent in his comments. He's out of the army now and completing a graduate degree in mechanical engineering. This guy's the son of a doctor and was almost reverent when describing the two medics under his command. He used to write to his father about them. Sanders will make an excellent witness. He's very bright and articulate, and he wants to help."

"What about the others?"

"To a man, they want to do whatever they can for their former medic. Not one of them hesitated in expressing their support. I haven't been able to speak with the young man who lost his foot. He was closest with the defendant."

"Where is he?"

"He was in Boston getting fitted with a prosthetic foot."

"Was in Boston?"

"He's checked himself out of the hospital early and is on his way to California."

CHAPTER THIRTY-TWO

Marcella Stearns studied the documents and case summary sent by Freddy Dempster. After fifteen years of practicing law, and a failed marriage she attributed to the demands of her profession, she chose her cases carefully. Marcella liked matching wits in the courtroom but exhibited her real passion when she believed in a client's innocence. Undecided about taking Johnny Ornowoski's case, she telephoned her old friend in Santa Cruz.

"Frederick," she began, "I still need a little convincing on the Ornowoski file. The case is very circumstantial except for the fingerprints on the murder weapon. How about I meet with the accused, and we can sit down and hash things out in person? If I think he's innocent, I'm in."

"Fair enough, Marcella. I look forward to seeing you and catching up."

"As do I. One other question before I go," she said. "Does your client have a good explanation for being in Can Tho and meeting with Corker and Palino?"

"Even better," said Freddy. "Sanders, his platoon commander, backs him up completely. He authorized Ornowoski's leave to find Palino. And the lieutenant is as straight arrow as you'll find. ROTC in college, volunteers for Vietnam to do his patriotic duty, and resumes his mechanical engineering studies after completing his military obligations. He's adamant about doing whatever he can to help Johnny Ornowoski. In his own words: 'I'm grateful for the job he did as my platoon's medic.'"

* * *

Johnny listened to the footsteps echo off the concrete floor. He could usually tell by the sound and rhythm who'd arrived to see him. Marcella Stearns announced her visit with the quick-paced strides and softer reverberations of a woman's set of shoes tapping the cement floor as she walked toward his cell. Johnny looked up to see her approaching, briefcase in hand, while Freddy Dempster walked briskly behind.

As the lawyers got closer, Johnny got a first impression of the woman Freddy Dempster had recommended defend him. Dressed for serious business in a pants suit, her brown hair pulled tight against her head and tied in back, hazel eyes peered out from behind a set of dark-framed glasses. The feminine slightly repressed in her appearance, Marcella Stearns looked like the professional woman Johnny had pictured in his mind. He'd had several days to think about what Freddy had suggested, a lawyer with experience in murder trials take his case. Like Marcella Stearns, Johnny would base his decision on how this meeting proceeded.

Escorted into a nearby conference room by a guard, Johnny sat across from the two lawyers. After a brief introduction by Freddy, and the good-mannered exchanges that followed, Marcella opened her briefcase and pulled out a file.

"How do you explain the tire iron with your fingerprints on it?" Marcella began. "I'm assuming you owned one, but it's missing."

"Of course," said Johnny. "I had just used it to change a tire."

"And let me guess, you have no idea how it wound up on the beach above the body?"

"That's right, but let me ask you this. How is the prosecution going to explain that? I don't walk around with a tire iron. And then to leave it on the beach after murdering someone? That's pretty stupid. There won't be any witnesses identifying me because I wasn't there."

"Having your fingerprints on it trumps the prosecution having to explain how it got there. The onus is on us to offer a viable alternative. Being with your girlfriend, a known dealer, won't convince anyone. You could have been surprised by someone and just tossed it. You take walks on the beach? During the night?"

"Sometimes. I just don't go around killing people when I do," he said gloomily.

"Well, here's the good news," Marcella said unexpectedly. "That's the only piece of hard evidence the prosecution has. Everything else, from motive to your prior activities, is purely circumstantial. Finding a reason why anyone might want Stewart Brenz dead with a murder weapon that has your fingerprints needs to be addressed. Right now, we have no plausible explanation. So think hard, and let us know anything that might explain it."

"You have no ideas?" Freddy asked Johnny.

Johnny shook his head. "I just got back from Vietnam. None of this makes any sense. I know Hamilton seems to have it in for me."

"Even so, it's a stretch that he would commit murder just to frame you," Freddy said. "He's old school, twenty-five years on the force, not even a rumor of bad behavior."

Johnny shook his head. "I know, it looks bad, but all I've wanted to do is get back from the war and live a normal life. I would never do anything to jeopardize that."

"Okay," said Marcella, "let's leave that for now. Information may come to light. I have a private investigator who can look into it further."

Marcella looked at Johnny. "I need to know more about your meeting with Corker. Why you were looking to buy opium and marijuana from him, and your relationship with Palino. How can you explain being in Can Tho and meeting with both of them? I have to be honest with you. Only Freddy's belief in your innocence has got me even considering this case. In Vietnam, where we have killing and drug use, you actively sought out known dope smugglers. On the surface, it's very damning."

Johnny got out of his chair and turned his back to the lawyers. He placed his hands on the wall before speaking.

"Can I trust you?" he asked before turning around to face them again.

Surprised at the question, Marcella answered. "Everything we discuss is confidential."

"That's not what I mean," Johnny said. "My life is at stake here, and it's been that way for some time. You may not like the war in Vietnam, but I had to survive it. Part of what got me through was the belief that if I did make it home my life could be normal. I was naïve to think that. Let me tell you something about Don Palino.

"We trained together as medics. He was urbane, charming and intelligent. Four of us became good friends. We all got orders for Vietnam right out of training. Nothing unusual about that. After our leave, we met up at Ft. Lewis, Washington, before deploying. It was comforting to be with friends facing the same uncertainties. The rumors about medics were ugly, fifty percent casualty rates. Among the four of us, that proved true. Richie Cordero never made it home, and Don was badly wounded.

"Danny Holt, the fourth friend in our group, ended up working triage at an evac hospital. Palino was also with Ninth Infantry, but in a different battalion. I visited him once when we were both in Dong Tam standing down. I didn't know he was wounded until Danny wrote and told me. Don had a bad concussion caused by his wounds, and he couldn't shake the headaches and dizziness. All the medical tests were coming back negative. Don began self-medicating because his doctor cut back his pain medication. He clashed with the nurses and doctors over it because they suspected he was faking his symptoms to avoid going back to the field. He knew he couldn't pack the gear. He hated his platoon commander. He hated the war. And he deserted."

Johnny sat down again and looked directly at Marcella Stearns. "I've heard the rumors and snide remarks about Don Palino. Do you know what the authorities are calling him? Gash. There's an ugly facial scar from his wounds. You think Palino liked the war? In retrospect, he understood how stupid it was better than the rest of us. He deserted because he knew he wouldn't survive. I was the stupid one, thinking I could go and find him, convince him to return to his unit. It angers me how disposable we were. You think you are against the war, Miss Stearns? Try doing a tour in Vietnam and see how you feel about it. Don Palino was a friend of mine, and I went to find him in Can Tho because I was concerned about him. Lieutenant Sanders will verify that."

Freddy Dempster took a deep breath and exhaled. "Marcella is aware of that, Johnny. Can you tell her why you approached Corker about buying the marijuana?"

"Finding Palino was no easy task, and I only had a three-day window with what's called an in-country R&R. Danny Holt at the 29th Evac near Can Tho knew where to begin looking for him. A brothel named the Garden of Eden was a known hub of black market activity. That's where Corker was posing as Sergeant Keenan. I feigned interest in securing a large buy of marijuana and opium as a possible way of finding Don. I also inquired about ammunition for a zip gun. It was all bogus. My platoon members can verify there was no such weapon used by anyone in the unit, and that I never supplied anyone with drugs. I never used any in Vietnam. Being alert is what got me home."

"I'm beginning to get the picture," Marcella said. "Is there anything else we need to know about your tour in Vietnam? Once we get into the trial phase, we can't be broadsided by unanticipated information."

Johnny shook his head. "Just one other thing," he said. "I need assurances that you both believe in my innocence. I don't want to be represented by someone who thinks I'm guilty of murder. Or that I continued dealing drugs. I quit that before going to Vietnam. I never took one toke of the stuff while I was there. I need for you to know how ludicrous it is to think that I could have been shipping marijuana from Vietnam. That's as crazy as the war."

Johnny sat on the edge of his bunk smoking. Before lighting each cigarette, he tapped the butt end on the steel bars. He remembered King Tut doing the same on the barrel of his rifle. Johnny supposed smoking so much wasn't good for his health, but with the guards constantly reminding him of his likely conviction for murder, he had no incentive to quit.

He heard the doors to the cell block open, and an uneven sound emanated off the concrete, unlike the steady and even strides of the guards. Johnny looked up to see a small figure limping towards him like he had a bad leg.

"Doc, is that you?"

"Jungle Boy? What are you doing out of the hospital?"

"I was going to ask you what you're doing in jail? When I heard, I checked out to come and help." Johnny was glad to see him. The kid always showed a lot of heart.

"It's good to see you, but you shouldn't have left before everything with your treatment was healed and your new foot fitted."

"You mean my fake one?"

"If that's what you're calling it." Johnny put his hands on the bars and looked at Jungle Boy. "How is it going with the prosthesis? I was concerned when we couldn't find you at Letterman's."

"It's going okay, Doc. What's all this about?" He gestured at the cell. "CC phoned Beverley and told her you were arrested for killing somebody. That's crazy."

Johnny just nodded, appreciating Jungle Boy's unconditional support.

"We can find out who did it," Jungle Boy said, as matter-of-factly as he had insisted they'd make it out of Vietnam.

"Who is *we*?" Johnny asked.

"You know, me, and some of the guys CC says are coming to testify at your trial. Your girl is sure nice."

"I'm glad you've met her."

"I talked to her on the phone, and she brought me over here. She said to tell you she would be by to visit after we had a chance to catch up. I told her you saved my life, and she said she already knew that. We're going to get you out of here, Doc."

The kid was showing heart again, but what was he going to do, spring a jailbreak when the rest of the platoon arrived, on one foot, of course?

Even with his missing foot, Jungle Boy wouldn't take the bed to sleep in. CC knows he's up a lot during the night. She notices his wound still causes pain. He's grateful for every small thing she does for him. CC learns more about the war from their conversations.

"Sergeant Morales was the best," Jungle Boy explained. "He helped out everybody in the platoon, showing them stuff they needed to know. Him and the LT worked really well together. I'm glad they're coming."

"They are probably shocked the Doc is in jail. I think we can find who really killed that man. Freddy says they also suspect Doc was smuggling dope out of Vietnam. That's just crazy. Doc shouldn't have to sit in jail for stupid accusations like that. He never even smoked marijuana in base camp like some of the guys.

"Even in Dong Tam he was too busy. Sometimes we'd be out in the boonies for three weeks just looking for Charlie. No dope to smuggle out there. I don't expect those fancy lawyers know about Vietnam. Maybe they'll listen to the LT. He's as smart as them, been to college, too. The Doc got a lot of us out of Vietnam. No way he should be in jail."

Sometimes Jungle Boy talked about Billy Warrington. CC asked about Billy's mother.

"Besides the Doc, he was my best friend. Billy's mom is so sad sometimes she says it's hard to keep going. She jokes that she wants to adopt me. We talk by phone now. It's expensive, but she says it's important to her. You know the Doc wrote her a letter? She was grateful for that. She wants to come and testify at the trial. She told me 'nobody that kind could murder someone.'"

Jungle Boy developed a routine while waiting for Johnny's trial. He reserved the mornings for visiting with CC, Johnny, Gregor, and anyone who would talk to him about the case.

In the afternoon, he would limp to the liquor store on the corner by the pier and buy a pint of whiskey. The proprietor knew he wasn't twenty-one, the legal drinking age, but reasoned if he were old enough to lose a foot in Vietnam, then he had earned the right to drink whiskey.

Jungle Boy didn't consume much, but he tucked the bottle in a pocket and hung around the beach where the homeless gathered and Stewart Brenz had been murdered. Always with whiskey, he feigned swigs from the bottle and shared it with the alcoholics. From a poor neighborhood in Oakland, Jungle Boy was no stranger to the world of down-and-outs and their addiction problems. He knew the street provided a grapevine of information unavailable anywhere else.

Wounds come in many forms, and a limping Jungle Boy's disability helped gain the trust of the men he hung around with in the afternoons. A rainy day had the group huddled under where the pier began at the shoreline.

Jungle Boy leaned against a piling after easing his leg with the prosthetic foot onto the sand.

"This is where that guy was murdered, ain't it?" Jungle Boy said. "Got his head bashed in. You know him?"

"Stewie," a man named Sonny responded. He pointed to a spot close by.

"You saw him get killed?" Jungle Boy asked in surprise.

Sonny put a finger to his lips. "Can't say, can't say." He leaned forward and spoke softly. "Better not talk about it or the man might come and kill you." The rest of the men nodded.

"I thought they had the guy locked up that killed Stewie," Jungle Boy said. Most of the men looked at the ground. Sonny shook his head.

"Then who did?" Jungle Boy pressed.

"Can't say, can't say," Sonny repeated.

Jungle Boy pulled an unopened bottle out of his pocket, undid the cap and took a swig. "Okay, but you can tell me. Do I look like the man? I just ask a simple question and you clam up on me." He took another swallow.

"My mouth's getting dry, is all," said Sonny.

"How about the rest of you?" Jungle Boy feigned irritation. "If somebody's going around killing people, I'd like to know who to watch out for." He passed the bottle to Sonny, who took a long swallow.

"I guess it makes sense," said Sonny, and took another pull. "Some guy in a suit that's been hanging around asking questions."

"Questions? About what?"

"You know, if we saw anything the night Stewie got killed."

"A detective?"

Sonny shrugged. "I guess so, but it was pretty dark." Jungle Boy passed him the bottle for another hit. "I was over by that rock waiting for Stewie to drink enough so he starts sharing. I was just about to go over when the man shows up and looks around. He hit Stewie in the head with something and threw it on the sand. Stewie never woke up."

Freddy stared at Jungle Boy, thinking about what to do with the information. "A homeless alcoholic for the defense; it's not going to fly. We can't use him as a witness."

"Sonny's not going to talk," Jungle Boy said. "He knows if he does, he winds up dead. It gives us a lead."

"What, some guy in a suit? That Sonny thought he saw in the dark? How's that going to help?"

"Do you know all of the detectives on the force?"

"Jungle Boy," Freddy cautioned. "Be careful with any accusations. We still need the police to find the real killer."

"But they won't be looking. The cops think they've already got the killer in jail. And what about that older one, Hamilton, who has it in for Johnny?"

"He's old school," said Freddy. "Stellar record with the department. Don't go poking that bear. He hates hippies and the drugs they're using, something he has in common with more than just his fellow cops."

"Johnny is not a hippie," Jungle Boy reminded Freddy, exasperated by the lawyer's overcautious approach. *How many years of fancy lawyer school did it take to think like that?*

Freddy didn't respond to Jungle Boy's statement. Preoccupied, he tapped a pencil on his yellow legal pad before speaking again. "So where does this get us?" he said, thinking out loud.

Jungle Boy ignored the question. "Have you got Rafe Johnson's phone number?" he asked.

"I've already talked to him about testifying at the trial," Freddy said.

"I was in Vietnam with him, too," Jungle Boy said.

"You're sure that's all your doing, getting back in touch?"

Freddy knew Jungle Boy was up to more, but he didn't want any specifics. He also knew there was a lot more to the young man than he first suspected.

That evening, Jungle Boy dialed Rafe's number. "Is that you, Rafe?" he asked when he picked up.

"Your voice sounds familiar," he said cautiously. "Refresh my memory."

"It's Jungle Boy, Rafe."

"Why didn't you say so? Where in the hell are you?"

"I'm in Santa Cruz, waiting for the Doc's trial. Can you come out early?"

"What's up?"

"I'll fill you in on the details when you get here."

CHAPTER THIRTY-THREE

Freddy Dempster had contacted five of Johnny's former platoon members to testify at his trial. None had balked at coming to Santa Cruz. They would act as character witnesses and verify the absurdity of Johnny smuggling drugs out of Vietnam while doing a tour as a grunt medic.

Jim Sanders, former platoon commander, attended graduate school at the University of Washington in Seattle. Eduardo Morales, still in the army, was based at Ft. Ord, only forty miles away. Rafe Johnson, between gigs in Macon, Georgia, had not been difficult to find. Freddy didn't know he was already on his way to the west coast at Jungle Boy's request. Already in Santa Cruz, Jungle Boy's relationship with Johnny intrigued Freddy Dempster, who had begun addressing him by his nickname.

Russell Tuttley, King Tut in the Nam, had been the most difficult to trace. He'd returned to his native Michigan and lived in a rented room above a Chinese restaurant. Working in the kitchen, he earned enough to cover his twenty-five dollar-a-month rent and support his three-pack-a-day cigarette habit. Not going out much, he viewed the world sitting at a small table from a second-story window above the Dragon Lilly Restaurant. Leftovers from the kitchen kept him fed. Only a brother knew where he lived, who gave Freddy the restaurant's phone number. Kenny, the Chinese proprietor, answered in heavily accented English. Only Freddy's insistence, and Kenny's limited fluency, convinced him to put Russell Tuttley on the line.

"The Doc's in trouble?" Tut repeated to Freddy. "For killing someone?" It sounded impossible. Russell Tuttley agreed to travel to Santa Cruz. Among his developed phobias from the war, flying. He would leave his rented room in Saginaw for California on a Greyhound Bus.

Marcella felt assured by Johnny's platoon members' willingness to testify on his behalf. To a man, they scoffed at the idea he could have murdered anyone, or smuggled drugs out of Vietnam while serving in an infantry unit. As a medic, he saved lives. This gave her confidence in the case and her ability to free an innocent man.

Less convincing was Delbert Kincaid's assertion that the killer might be a detective with the Santa Cruz Police Department. She refused to give credence to the alcoholic musings of the homeless who hung around the beach and drank. She cautioned Freddy Dempster about taking the assertion seriously and chided him for referring to Delbert Kincaid as Jungle Boy.

Her firm used a private investigator, Manny Mancowitz, who she brought in to poke around with the eye of an ex-policeman. He turned up nothing on the murder, but while pursuing a hunch about Ralph Barnes, the convicted drug dealer reached out. He'd sent a message through a visitor that Johnny Ornowoski was telling the truth—about everything. Marcella Stearns dispatched Mancowitz to see Ralph Barnes in prison. Posing as a cousin getting in touch, the meeting never took place. Ralph Barnes died in the exercise yard at San Quentin, a shiv through his neck.

While Johnny's lawyers prepared for the trial, Rafe Johnson arrived in Santa Cruz. Sporting an Afro hairstyle and beard, Jungle Boy greeted him at the door for a planning session at CC's apartment.

"What was you expectin'," Rafe joked when Jungle Boy saw him. "I'm not in the army no more. What are they gonna do, send me to Vietnam?"

They both laughed. CC had no idea what they found so funny. Noticing her puzzled expression, Rafe told her: "A private joke. You woulda had to have been there."

Jungle Boy brought Rafe up to date, while CC busied herself in the apartment.

"It's worth a try," Rafe said. "When do we get started?"

"Right now," Jungle Boy said. He took a black-haired wig out of a bag and went into the bathroom to use a mirror. "You'll have to drive," he said when he emerged. Dark hair hung to his shoulders, and he'd put a wispy fake mustache on his upper lip. A black fedora completed his transformation.

At the curb, they got into the T-bird and drove to the Colonial Bar and Restaurant, a common hangout for off-duty police. Looking out of place, they ordered beers at the bar and attracted the stares of the clientele.

"You sure this Black-guy-as-bait thing is gonna work?" Rafe asked.

"I can't walk point on this one, Rafe."

"You know how much I hated that. By the way, you look ridiculous in that wig."

Jungle Boy smiled. "You can't hurt my feelings, Rafe. Yours don't look that hot neither."

At their customary corner table, Tom Hamilton and Randy Siemans nursed their after-work drinks.

"Who's the scrawny White guy with the bad hair," asked Hamilton, "comin' in here with that Black hippie, like they own the place?"

"Beats me," said Siemans, taking a good look.

"This used to be a good town," Hamilton commented, "before all the riff-raff moved in with their drugs, long hair and communal lifestyles."

Siemans just nodded and took a sip from his drink.

Marcella Stearns watched her counterpart, T. Bradley Smyth, prepare to address the jury. Six men and six women, a cross section of society, looked at the prosecutor as he stood to deliver his opening statement. Confident in manner, and well dressed in a tailored suit that fit his trim frame, he began his rehearsed address.

"Ladies and gentlemen of the jury, I will get right to the point. Seated at the defendant's table is a man who is no stranger to drugs and violence. In fact, Mr. Ornowoski has spent the entirety of his young adulthood in pursuit of those two objectives. Drugs," he paused, "and violence. We will present evidence showing that this young man, even in a war zone, found ways to continue selling drugs, and was ruthless in his illicit pursuit.

"Now, you may hear from the defense that the accused has gone to war in Vietnam, has done his patriotic duty. That is what the defense will have you believe. It is not so straightforward ladies and gentlemen, for we will link Mr. Ornowoski's activities, even in Vietnam, to that of drug smuggling and violence.

"You may ask, is not war violent? Of course it is, but the violence to which I refer is not the sustained violence of our nation at war, but rather of an intentional nature directed at anyone standing in the way of the defendant's drug dealing."

Smyth turned his gaze from the jury a moment to allow his assertions to register. Turning to face them again, he made eye contact with several members before continuing.

"The prosecution will also link the defendant to Donald Palino, a known drug kingpin and friend of John Ornowoski, who continues to ship large quantities of marijuana and opium out of Southeast Asia. Incredibly, Donald Palino deserted from his unit in Vietnam to partake in the lucrative black market and continues to fill the pipeline with drugs from Southeast Asia to the shores of the USA. You will hear from a witness that the defendant approached him in Vietnam looking to secure a large amount of marijuana and opium before meeting with Palino near Can Tho in the Mekong Delta.

"Furthermore, ladies and gentlemen, did the violence in the war zone end with the return of Mr. Ornowoski to his homeland? No, an emphatic, *no*, it did not! We have the murder of a defenseless homeless man, Stewart Brenz, viscously beaten to death with a tire iron, the defendant's fingerprints all over the murder weapon. Mr. Brenz, the victim of a senseless crime of the street, an act of revenge over less than one pound of marijuana. That's right, you've heard me correctly, a homeless man beaten to death for less than a pound of marijuana."

Smyth paused again, pursed his lips while nodding his head. "You are probably starting to get the picture," he stated, "of the common themes in the defendant's life. Drugs…and violence. Drugs…and violence. The prosecution, whose client is the good people of this community, will seek to have the defendant put away for the very length of his life, and have the key thrown away forever. This, the people will prove, without a doubt, to the good members of the jury."

Satisfied, T. Bradley Smyth took a seat at the prosecution's table.

Marcella Stearns rose slowly out of her seat and walked toward the jury. She paced her steps as she approached, then faced the jury directly. She had one shot at changing the narrative established by the prosecution before the evidence would be presented. One early attempt to counter the effective bombast of her opponent and gain the jury's sympathy for her client.

"That was quite a mouthful," she began. "It might make good fiction, but that's all it is. In instance after instance, the defense will show that John Ornowoski is neither a drug dealer nor a killer. You will not have to take my word for it—or Mr. Ornowoski's. You will hear from his Vietnam platoon members that he is not a killer, not even in Vietnam. He was his infantry platoon's medic. You will hear the testimony of a young man who lost his left foot in Vietnam and was saved by his medic, Johnny Ornowoski. Exposing himself to enemy fire, he carried his wounded friend to safety and treated his wounds. Delbert Kincaid is with us today, and not one more name on the tragic list of dead young veterans of the Vietnam War, because of the defendant's bravery and compassion. For his actions that day, the army awarded Mr. Ornowoski the bronze star for valor. These are not the motives of a killer but of a young man whose lifesaving efforts as a medic gained the confidence and respect of his entire platoon.

"We will also learn from his platoon members how utterly absurd it is to propose that he could have been involved in the drug trade from Vietnam. His unit spent weeks at a time in the jungle. They saw heavy combat and took many casualties. Whatever your views on the war, put yourselves in the shoes of these young men. They did not start the Vietnam War. Most of them are too young to vote, yet they were the young men sent to fight in this war on behalf of their country.

"What we have from the prosecution is a case based on much specu-lation and little in the way of hard evidence. You will hear the testimony of an admitted drug dealer, Patrick Corker, stating that he met with the defendant in Vietnam but never actually sold him any drugs. He will testify that *probably* came later. There is simply no proof of this.

"Finally, you will hear that Donald Palino and John Ornowoski were friends. Yes, they trained together as medics at Ft. Sam Houston in Texas. They shipped out together but were in different battalions in Vietnam. There is no law against that. You will hear a different side to what transpired between these friends, and why, and hear it from witness testimony, not something cooked up in the prosecutor's office for the purposes of a conviction.

"And the drugs. Yes, the drugs that are supposedly pouring in from Southeast Asia. Where are they? Why are they nowhere to be found? Because there are none that have ever been linked to the defendant."

Marcella paused from her delivery and allowed herself and the jury a brief interlude before remarking on the murder weapon, the most damaging fact she needed to address.

"Let's turn our attention to the tire iron that killed Stewart Brenz. The tire iron that has the defendant's fingerprints. Partials, I might add. My client is not denying that it's his. What is lacking is a motive for him killing Stewart Brenz. The prosecution is presenting the murder as some brazen form of street justice. But why would the killer leave it near the body to be found? He would if he wanted you to believe it was Johnny Ornowoski who killed Stewart Brenz.

"The defense will provide expert testimony that the trunk of the defendant's car has been tampered with. So, what does that leave, ladies and gentlemen, of the prosecution's case? Pure speculation and nothing more. And speculation is not guilt. Johnny Ornowoski acted out of loyalty to his friends and platoon members. He was never seen or apprehended selling or possessing, or even using, any illicit drugs during his tour in Vietnam. He is not a killer. Finding him innocent is the just and logical conclusion."

The trial progressed to the evidence phase after opening statements. The judge, Warren P. Walker, valued an orderly and quick-paced flow in his courtroom. He would not have been Marcella Stearns' first choice to preside, but he was competent and fair within the context of his stern demeanor. And Freddy had a good working relationship with the middle-aged judge.

No surprises in what the prosecution presented as evidence. The tire iron central to their case, and Patrick Corker on a witness testimony list along with several policemen verifying Johnny's previous brushes with the law for dealing. Corker would establish what the prosecutor saw as the damaging connection to the defendant's continued relationship with drugs while in Vietnam.

T. Bradley Smyth's case against Johnny expanded on the third day of the trial. The name of Sergeant Alden Wesley Magruder appeared on an amended witness list.

Marcella protested to the judge. With the defense listing five witnesses from the defendant's platoon, the prosecution argued that it was not too much to ask the court that one former platoon member offer a different perspective on the defendant's tour in Vietnam. The judge agreed.

Freddy approached the prosecutor during a recess.

"How long have you known about Magruder? We should have been notified sooner."

"We just found him. Can't notify you about something we didn't know about. The defendant is not the choir boy you are trying to make him out to be. Magruder will have some interesting things to say. If you want to compete putting decorated cripples on the stand, then bring it on."

"You have a sick mind, Bradley." Freddy bristled at the smug prosecutor.

Marcella felt ambushed. "Who is he?" she asked at the noon recess. "Why haven't you told us about him?" she demanded of Johnny. "If he's a witness for the prosecution, you can bet it will be damaging. Any idea of what he's going to say?"

Johnny didn't know how to respond. He'd not thought about the possibility of Magruder testifying and hadn't worried about the fragging incident after his tour. He'd not participated, just knew about it. How could he possibly explain the platoon sergeant to his defense lawyers? Should he even try?

"He's going to claim that the platoon intentionally wounded him during a firefight. He may implicate me as being part of it."

Marcella looked at Johnny, and her eyes bored into him. "And…were you? I asked you for your total honesty before taking this case, and now you're telling me about shooting one of your own men? I have to tell you, it's not a good look for you, nor me presenting a defense."

With the futility of Vietnam imploding on him, Johnny felt cornered.

They know nothing about the war. How do I possibly explain Magruder or his role as platoon sergeant?

"And I had asked if you trusted me," Johnny began. "Explaining the situation with Magruder is impossible because none of it makes sense to anyone who wasn't there. The whole platoon hated him, even Jungle Boy."

"Why?" Marcella interjected, still sounding angry.

"Because he was starting to get people killed," Johnny shot back. "Things came to a head when one of the young kids in the platoon had to walk point. He wasn't ready, but Magruder insisted the platoon rotate the point position. As sergeant, he'd already taken unnecessary risks putting the unit in danger. Billy Warrington didn't just die; he was tortured to death after the VC snatched him. The whole platoon blamed Magruder, and rightly so. We found Billy tied to a tree a couple of hours later, his body horribly mutilated. I was not certain that he'd died before the VC had finished with their butchery. Then, another platoon member was killed after cutting the vines that held Billy to the tree. The body was booby trapped. A detonated grenade provided the final indignity to what became of Billy Warrington."

"So, were you involved? You realize that if the jury thinks you might have had anything to do with the intentional wounding of your sergeant in Vietnam, then killing a homeless man over some drugs is not a stretch."

"That's what I mean about trusting me. I don't think you're understanding how crazy the situation was. My platoon didn't go around killing our own men. I was told it was going to happen but wasn't involved. The intent was to wound him bad enough to get rid of him, not kill him. And that's exactly what happened. I treated his wounds right after he was shot. If I wanted him dead, I could have let him bleed to death."

Freddy looked stunned. "What do you want to do?" he asked Marcella. The more he learned about the Vietnam War, the crazier it sounded.

Johnny didn't wait for her to answer. "Magruder is a volcano always about to erupt. Get him angry with your questions, and let him explode. Give him enough rope, and he will hang himself. Ask him why he thinks somebody in the platoon shot him."

"What will he say?"

"Specifically, I have no idea. But I'm willing to bet Magruder damages himself and the prosecution's case. And one other thing," Johnny said.

"His tour with the Ninth Infantry was not his first. He resented not being back with the 101st Airborne. Rumor had it there was an incident with a Vietnamese civilian near the end of his first tour, and he avoided charges because he was re-enlisting. The unit didn't want him back."

"I'll get Manny right on it," she said. Johnny sensed a flickering of understanding behind the stern gaze that had prevailed during her interrogation of him.

CHAPTER THIRTY-FOUR

T. Bradley Smyth put Magruder on the stand. The sergeant would counter the defense's narrative that the entire platoon held Johnny Ornowoski in high esteem. The prosecutor's witness, a highly decorated soldier, would persuasively show a different side of the drug-dealing medic. Smyth would then have Patrick Corker put the final touches on the prosecution's case by testifying Ornowoski sought to buy a large quantity of drugs in Vietnam.

Magruder surfaced when Smyth's legal secretary saw him on television. A newsclip featuring the recovery of wounded soldiers back from the war showed a sergeant working on his physical therapy at Walter Reed Hospital in Bethesda, Maryland. A reporter introduced the soldier.

"We have Sergeant Magruder with us to explain how he was wounded, and why he thinks it may have been intentionally inflicted by his own men. Can you tell us about it, Sergeant?"

The camera showed a close-up of Magruder's face. "I sure can," he began. "When I was assigned to the Ninth Infantry Division in the Mekong Delta, I thought it was to fight the Viet Cong. Instead, several bullets from behind me took out my knee during a firefight. The enemy never got me; riffraff in my own platoon did."

"A remarkable story, Sergeant. Do you know who's responsible for your wounds?"

"I got a good idea. I think the medic was in on it, a Doc Woski. And a rifleman named Johnson, a real slacker."

"Thank you, Sergeant Magruder. There you have it, the unusual story of how one soldier suspects his own men of wounding him."

The name of "Woski" jumped out at Smyth. Could it be our guy? He checked the witness list and found Rafe Johnson listed. It was worth a phone call.

"Sergeant Magruder, this is T. Bradley Smyth from the prosecutor's office in Santa Cruz, California. We're just following up on the interview you gave yesterday. We have a defendant by the name of John Ornowoski under indictment for murder. Can you give us the names of some other platoon members? How about a Rafe Johnson or Delbert Kincaid, known as Jungle Boy?"

"How can I forget," he responded. "We called the Polack medic Doc Woski, but that's the guy. His accomplice was a Negro named Rafe Johnson. Jungle Boy was with the unit. Nothing but a bullshit platoon if you ask me."

"We are asking you, Sergeant. We'll be in touch."

Magruder put down the receiver. Finally, somebody was listening.

The platoon members testifying on Johnny's behalf had arrived by the day of Magruder's testimony. Rafe Johnson, already in town, surfaced with a new look. Gone was the Afro, and in its place was a close-cropped hairstyle that with glasses gave him a scholarly look.

Jim Sanders, still trim, and dressed in a blue blazer with grey dress slacks, could have been mistaken for an attorney on the case. Russell Tuttley, more ruffled, arrived after his long bus ride from Michigan.

Marcella had attempted to get a delay in Magruder's testimony so her team could investigate the details of the sergeant's murky past. Judge Walker denied her request.

"Bring me some facts, and I will reconsider. Sergeant Magruder has interrupted his therapy to appear. I will not have his recovery regimen stalled by rumor."

When called, Magruder limped to the witness stand with the help of a cane. In his dress greens, Johnny noticed a shabbiness in the sergeant's appearance, the coldness in his yellow-tinged hazel eyes unabated.

Prominent on his shoulders were the stripes of a staff sergeant with one rocker below the three bright yellow stripes. The unit insignia of the 101st Airborne stood out above his elbow on the right, and his combat infantryman's badge atop two rows of ribbons on his breast.

"Sergeant Magruder," T. Bradley began, "can you tell us how you know the defendant?"

"We were in the same platoon in Vietnam. I was platoon sergeant, and he was the medic."

"How would you describe your relationship with the defendant."

"It was all right, until I got shot."

"Can you elaborate?"

"The platoon came under fire in the pursuit of the Viet Cong, and I was directing return fire toward the enemy. That was when I got shot from behind."

"Were there any enemy behind you?"

"No. That's why I knew it had to be one of my own men."

"Who did you see first after you were wounded?"

"That man right there." He pointed at Johnny.

"What made you think Mr. Ornowoski had something to do with wounding you?"

"He smirked when I confronted him about knowing it was platoon members who shot me. I told him he would never get away with it. The next thing I know he had me all doped up with morphine. When I came to, I was in the evac hospital getting treated for my wounds."

"How would you describe your platoon members in Vietnam?"

"Some of them were okay. A lot of them were pretty slack, and insubordinate, like the colored boy sitting in the fourth row." Magruder pointed at Rafe Johnson. A murmur went through the courtroom, and Judge Walker banged his gavel.

Marcella chose not to object to the line of questioning, seeing opportunities for her cross. Walker, uncomfortable with what he perceived as racial undertones developing in the testimony, warned the prosecutor: "Move it along Mr. Smyth."

"Yes, Your Honor. Sergeant Magruder, who is the man you have pointed out as being insubordinate?"

"The name's Rafe Johnson. I had lots of trouble with him."

"How so?"

"He didn't like holding up his end, like not wanting to walk point, always figuring he knew better. Told me he was too short."

Confused, T. Bradley had a puzzled look on his face. "Not tall enough?"

"No," Magruder explained. "It's an expression the slackers used to refer to their tours nearing completion. Johnson used it as an excuse for not holding up his end. He and the defendant were tight."

"I see," Smyth said, pausing. "And did you have trouble addressing the situation? You were the ranking enlisted man in the platoon with one combat tour already completed."

"Look what happened to me," he said, pointing to his leg. "A lot of the platoon was too far gone."

"Would that include the defendant, in your opinion?"

"Yes. I can see that very clearly now, him being charged with murder and all. He and that Johnson fellow are under investigation by the army as well."

Marcella objected, demanding proof of the army investigation. The judge instructed the jury to ignore Magruder's last remarks, but she was already plotting her cross-examination.

"Thank you, Sergeant Magruder. We wish you well with your recovery. Your witness." He nodded at Marcella.

Johnny whispered in Marcella's ear before she rose to confront Magruder. Seated in the courtroom, Jim Sanders couldn't believe what he was hearing about the platoon he had commanded only a few weeks prior to the incident the sergeant described. Rafe Johnson, seated next to Tut, feigned a calm exterior but hoped Johnny's lawyer would destroy Magruder on the stand. For Tut, it brought back the despair of the day they'd lost Billy Warrington. Freddy Dempster looked at his watch and wondered if Manny Mancowitz would be able to find any damaging information in time to discredit Magruder.

Marcella began with a simple question. "Sergeant Magruder, how many bullets were fired during the battle in which you were wounded?"

Magruder looked at her like he didn't know how to answer such a dumb question. "A lot," he smirked.

"Can you please quantify that for the court? Was it one hundred, two hundred, or perhaps, thousands?"

"That's right," he said, "it was in the thousands."

"So, it was a lot," she said, agreeing with Magruder's original estimation. "How was it, then, that you could determine so precisely that the bullets that wounded you and did great damage to your knee were actually fired by one of your own men?"

Magruder glared at Marcella Stearns. "I've seen a lot of combat. It was not difficult to know."

"It is safe to assume, Sergeant, that most of the people in this courtroom have not seen a lot of combat. For our clarification, can you elaborate on how you can be so certain it was your own men who wounded you? Has the army done any forensics on the bullets?"

"That's ridiculous, and you know it," he seethed. "Any combat vet could figure it out."

"I see. Let's assume for a moment your wounds were from the rifle of one of your men. Could it not have been an accident? You have clearly stated that thousands of rounds were fired. It is quite a leap to say it was intentional."

"I know what I know," Magruder said defiantly.

"That may be, Sergeant, but has the army charged anyone for shooting you? It is a tragedy, but there are hundreds of our troops being wounded in Vietnam every week."

"Like I said, the army is looking into it."

"Based on your accusations?"

"That's right."

"Let's move on to a different matter," Marcella continued. "You have stated that the defendant, who was your platoon's medic in Vietnam, was the first man you saw after being wounded. He treated your wounds and gave you a shot of morphine."

"That's correct." Magruder shifted in his seat and continued glaring at the lawyer peppering him with stupid questions.

"Wasn't that what your medic was supposed to be doing, treating your wounds? If Mr. Ornowoski were trying to harm you, why would he be treating your wounds? Perhaps that is why the army has not laid any charges in this matter. Your accusations don't make any sense."

"I know what I know," Magruder reiterated.

"Your Honor," T. Bradley interjected, "the witness has answered Miss Stearns' questions. I think his combat experience speaks to his ability to know who shot him."

"Agreed, Mr. Smyth. Move it along, Miss Stearns."

During the cross-examination of Magruder, Manny Mancowitz entered the courtroom and conferred with Freddy.

"Your Honor, may I have a minute to confirm a detail regarding my questioning of the witness?"

"Make it snappy, Miss Stearns," the judge ordered.

"It's pretty straightforward," Freddy explained, handing Marcella the notes from the private investigator. "Magruder left the 101st Airborne abruptly under a cloud of suspicion right before his tour ended. Sources confirm Magruder severely injured a Vietnamese civilian in a village his platoon searched. He was sent home three weeks early."

"Sergeant Magruder," Marcella resumed, "your time with the Ninth Infantry Division was not your first tour in Vietnam."

"That's correct."

"How long did you spend with your first unit, the 101st Airborne?"

"Twelve months. Everybody did a one-year tour unless they were medevaced out or killed."

"Can you explain why you served just eleven months and one week in Vietnam on your first tour?"

Magruder looked uncomfortable, then recovered. "I was re-enlisting, so the army allowed some extra leave before beginning a second tour, which I had requested."

"It had nothing to do with an incident involving a Vietnamese civilian near the end of your tour? I have a copy of a report that states you were investigated for breaking a civilian's jaw in a village. Can you tell us about that?"

Magruder erupted. He'd had enough of the bitch lawyer twisting everything he said into an indictment of him and not Ornowoski, the dumb Polack medic on trial for murder. "The gook was VC," he shouted. "Do you know how many times we'd go into a village and get ambushed coming out the other end? He wasn't talking. It was either him or me. I made god damned sure it was him, for once. The army never charged me."

"I rest my point," Marcella declared. The hushed silence of the courtroom broke into animated conversations. Judge Walker pounded his gavel. "The court will recess for lunch," he stated above the noise of the crowd.

Marcella knew she had to be careful with her continued cross-examination of Magruder. She had damaged his credibility but didn't want to elicit sympathy from the jury by appearing too aggressive in questioning the wounded soldier. She pressed Johnny for more information during the noon recess.

"Why do I have this feeling you've not told us everything?"

"Because I don't have any confidence that anyone who wasn't there will understand."

"Go on," she encouraged.

"The platoon reached a breaking point the day Billy was killed. He had come such a long way since arriving in Vietnam. Billy would not have died that day if it weren't for Magruder's insistence that everybody walk point. He wasn't ready. We all knew that, including Magruder.

"When we returned to base camp, there was a meeting. I won't tell you who was there, but Jungle Boy wasn't. The guys felt, as the medic, I should know what was going down. A vote was taken whether to wound or kill Magruder. I voted to wound him. It was set up so that nobody would know who shot him. I still don't. I guess it would have been better for me if the vote had gone the other way."

Johnny worried he'd said too much, but he sensed a flickering of understanding in the eyes of his lawyer.

"Things did improve in the platoon after Magruder," Johnny continued. "The new lieutenant, Howitz, quickly became an effective combat leader. But we all lost something the day Billy died."

When the afternoon session continued, Magruder remained on the witness stand. Marcella proceeded carefully.

"Sergeant Magruder, you have made a serious accusation that your platoon was responsible for shooting you. Why do you think they would have done that?"

"I've already told you. The platoon was full of slackers more interested in avoiding combat than going after the enemy. When I tried to change things, they were mad. I was disrupting their cozy little situations."

"Like requiring everybody to walk point?"

"Yeah, like walking point."

"And that was good for the platoon?"

"That's right," Magruder said.

"I see. What about Billy Warrington?"

"Who?" he asked.

"Billy Warrington. He was killed walking point. Was that good for the platoon?"

"People get killed in war. Walking point is dangerous. That's why it needed to be spread around. I can't help it if the kid was scared all the time."

"So that was good for the platoon, having someone lead the platoon who was 'scared all the time?'"

"Like I said, it needed to be spread around. I can't help it if the army is going to send weaklings into combat."

"And Billy Warrington was a weakling?"

"Yeah, he was a weakling. The kid walked right into the hands of the VC."

"Because he was walking point?"

"No, because he didn't know what he was doing."

"If he didn't know what he was doing, then wasn't it up to you as platoon sergeant to either train him or not use him to walk point until he did?"

T. Bradley Smyth was on his feet and objecting. "I think the witness has already given us his reasons as to why he thought it was important for everyone to walk point. And I would remind the court that Sergeant Magruder is a highly experienced NCO with two combat tours in Vietnam."

"I will withdraw the question, Your Honor," Marcella said.

"Please move it along, Miss Stearns," Judge Walker ordered.

"What happened to Billy Warrington?" Marcella asked.

"I thought we were done with that," Magruder seethed.

"Please answer the question, Sergeant."

"He got killed."

"The day he was walking point. How was he killed?"

"The Viet Cong nabbed him while we were on patrol, then tortured him to death. It's what happens in a war while you people at home are sleeping in your comfortable beds. It's also what happens when you try and fight a war with a slack outfit like the platoon I was in."

"Third platoon?"

"That's right, and the whole division, if you ask me."

"Okay, let's ask you then. What was it about your unit you thought was 'slack,' as you phrased it?"

"If everybody was going after the Viet Cong like they were supposed to instead of worrying who was walking point, then stuff like that wouldn't be happening."

"I thought you said that's what happens in war?"

Magruder looked at Marcella with contempt. "Sometimes it does. War is not for weaklings."

"Like Billy Warrington?"

"Yeah, like Billy Warrington."

"We will hear from some of your platoon members that Billy Warrington should not have been walking point. He wasn't ready."

"So? It wasn't their call. They were just as bad. Am I the one on trial here? I think you are confused about that."

Jim Sanders squirmed in his seat. To learn that the new platoon sergeant of his former unit could be so insensitive about the death of a soldier was incomprehensible. Rafe Johnson looked at Tut sitting beside him. Not acknowledging his gaze, he stared at Magruder. Transfixed, his mind returned to the day of Billy's disappearance in the bamboo grove. Tut reflexively reached for a cigarette and began tapping the butt against his chair. Jungle Boy was not in the courtroom to witness the cross-examination.

Before Marcella asked another question, a woman who had been silently weeping, stood, and came forward, shouting, "stop it, stop it. You are talking about my son!"

She hurried to the witness stand and confronted Magruder. "Am I hearing my Billy was killed because you insisted on him doing something he wasn't ready for? How can you say those ugly things about him? He's dead! Have you no decency? My son was a human being, and he deserves to be alive and not to have died in some strange jungle all alone while you played God with the lives of everybody in your platoon."

Judge Walker banged his gavel several times and called for order in the court. "Miss, you must sit down," he ordered, "or I will have to find you in contempt and removed from this courtroom."

"I will not sit down," Beverley Morrow shouted through her sobs. "How can the court listen to this man? Will nobody respect that my son is dead and never coming home?"

Magruder, uncomfortable with the outburst, showed it by glaring at the courtroom, then forming an awkward-looking grin that gave the impression of him smirking. T. Bradley noticed the entire jury looking stunned by the scene.

"Will the sergeant of arms please remove this woman from the court," Judge Walker ordered. A uniformed officer came forward and tried to gently usher Beverley Morrow from the courtroom. He reluctantly had to throw his arms around her and physically escort her to a cell.

The judge bellowed: "I will see the councilors in my chambers—now!"

T. Bradley and Marcella followed him as he left the courtroom. "Well… happy now?" he glared at the lawyers.

Furious, Marcella stared back. "You're angry at me? You are the one throwing bereaved mothers in jail."

"You watch your step, councilor," he retorted. "I will find it far easier to find you in contempt than that poor woman who lost her son in Vietnam. The court must be respected."

Walker removed his robe and paced back and forth behind his desk. Agitated by something deeper than the ruckus in his courtroom, he stared at Marcella.

"I take no pleasure in that poor woman's grief. There have been too many sons taken from their families prematurely. I don't often speak of it, but during the Second World War, I was on a troop carrier transporting the many Marines going into the worst battles of the Pacific, Tarawa, Guadalcanal, Bougainville, Iwo Jima. Every time we launched them in their landing craft, I thanked God it wasn't me facing the slaughter on those beaches. Everybody knew that many would not be returning. But they went.

"I will not have my court turned into a circus of grief. Do you understand that Mr. Smyth?" He turned his glare on the prosecutor. "There are so few in this courtroom who have had to bear that kind of tragedy. Both of you keep that in mind when we resume tomorrow."

CHAPTER THIRTY-FIVE

Rafe Johnson related the day in court for Jungle Boy, including Beverley Morrow's arrest for contempt.

"How is that possible, Rafe?" he asked. "What did she do?"

"While Magruder was making an ass of himself on the witness stand, saying some ugly shit about Billy, his mother began crying in one of the back rows. She finally had enough and told him to stop."

"And that's a crime?"

"I don't expect they'll keep her in jail, but it got pretty ugly."

"Why is everything backwards? I mean, Magruder gets Billy killed, and Beverley is in jail. Do you understand how that works, Rafe?"

"Oh yeah," he replied, "been that way for a long time."

From the start, Jungle Boy set out to find the actual killer. He didn't understand why that wasn't everybody's priority. He'd gained the confidence of the homeless who had known Stewart Brenz in a way the authorities never could, but a drunken witness would not prevail in court. In his quest for the truth, Jungle Boy had cajoled and provided enough liquor to the beach alcoholics to glean ample information to form a strong hunch. Now, a simple phone call might reveal the murderer.

"I've got the number we need," Jungle Boy said. "Give him a ring and try and set something up. Ask him to meet us. The sooner the better."

Rafe dialed the number and waited.

"Who's this?" the expected voice answered.

"Let's just say one of your bosses inquiring about why you've got such a clusterfuck going on in Santa Cruz. It's bad for business when you start drawing attention to things while settling personal scores."

"What are you talking about?"

"I've already told you. You better start listening. Eight o'clock at the first bench on the pier. Be there."

"Do you think he bought it?" asked Jungle Boy.

"No question. Tried to bluff his way out, but the man's scared."

Fifty yards onto the pier, a wooden bench overlooked the beach that led to the boardwalk. Rafe Johnson and Jungle Boy found Siemans waiting.

"Right on time," said Rafe. "I guess it would be right over there, under this pier, that you kind of went stupid on us, Mr. Siemans."

"What are you talking about?" Trying to sound gruff, Rafe detected fear in his voice.

"Continue to be stupid, Mr. Siemans, and my friend gets a little crazy." Jungle Boy edged closer to the detective, between them on the bench. They were in their disguises from a few nights before.

"The boss don't like stupid, Mr. Siemans. Just answer the questions."

"All right, what is it you want to know?"

"Why you killed the bum and then pinned it on the dumb Polack just back from Vietnam. He happens to be a friend of the boss."

Siemans looked stunned.

"Kind of incredible, ain't it?" Rafe added with a twisted smile.

"What do you want me to do?"

"We want you to make it right, and pronto. And by the way, no more dead bodies."

"How do I do that?" Siemans asked.

"You'll figure something out, for your sake. Good night, Mr. Siemans."

Judge Walker, true to form, called the court to order at nine o'clock.

"Your next witness, Mr. Smyth."

T. Bradley called Patrick Corker to the stand. Johnny looked at the man he had seen in Can Tho. Mid-fifties and with grayer hair, prison fare had trimmed twenty pounds off his portly frame.

Smyth quickly got the details of Corker's meeting with Johnny at the Garden of Eden into his testimony and then moved to establish Johnny's relationship with Palino.

"Mr. Corker, when the defendant approached you to buy a large quantity of marijuana and opium in Can Tho, did you supply it to Mr. Ornowoski?"

"No."

"Can you tell the court why that transaction never took place?"

"When I inquired about securing the drugs from my supplier, he asked who they were for. I had seen the defendant's name tag on his jungle fatigues and told them they were for a soldier named Ornowoski. My supplier smiled and told me he was a friend and would deal with him directly. He thanked me and gave me one thousand dollars for my trouble."

"Can you tell us the name of your supplier and friend of the defendant?"

"His name is Donald Palino."

Smyth turned from the witness stand and looked directly at the jury. "I would like to inform the court that there is a warrant for the arrest of Donald Palino. He is wanted for shipping large quantities of drugs from Southeast Asia into the US. He is also wanted for desertion by the army."

Smyth turned back to Corker. "Can you elaborate on your relationship with Donald Palino?"

"I met Palino in Can Tho, where we were both involved in the black market. He had established supply routes and markets for drugs from Vietnam into the US."

"Can you quantify the amount of drugs being shipped by Palino from Vietnam?"

"Not an exact amount, but it would be measured in thousands of pounds."

"Thank you, Mr. Corker. Your witness," he said and nodded towards the defense's table.

Marcella rose and quickly moved to establish two facts.

"Mr. Corker, have you struck a deal with the prosecution regarding the testimony you are giving today?"

"I have agreed to cooperate with the federal authorities in the hunt for finding and prosecuting Donald Palino. My testimony today is considered part of that agreement. Certain charges have been reduced in exchange for that cooperation."

"So, you have a vested interest in how these proceedings go?"

"I have given the authorities all the information I have on the shipping methods and routes from Vietnam into the US. I was never privy to who received the shipments in San Francisco, or what the distribution network is once the drugs arrived."

"How was it you came to be arrested?"

"I was on a visit to the US."

"In Vietnam, did you ever sell drugs to the defendant, Johnny Ornowoski?"

"No, not directly."

"So, you never witnessed the defendant actually receive any drugs from either you or Donald Palino, or any other person?"

"No." Corker started to say more, but Marcella cut him off.

"Thank you. No further questions."

Following Corker's testimony, Judge Walker recessed the court before the defense called its first witness.

Jim Sanders, neatly dressed in a suit and tie, looked trim and fit, like he could still command his former unit.

"Mr. Sanders, can you please inform the court where you came to know the defendant, John Ornowoski?"

"Certainly. I was his platoon commander in Vietnam. I had been with third platoon for six months prior to his arrival as the new medic."

"As the medic, was Mr. Ornowoski with the platoon at all times?"

"That is correct."

"And that included the patrols into the jungles and swamps of the Mekong Delta?"

"Yes."

"How long would these patrols last?"

"Anywhere from a few days to several weeks."

"Would it have been possible for the defendant to be dealing drugs while under your command?"

"That would be an absolute impossibility. Even when we were in base camp, Doc Woski would be busy tending to the medical needs of the platoon."

"How so?"

"Spending days and weeks in the field caused many medical issues. Anything from infected leech bites, insect stings, punctures from thorns, and endless foot problems. Called trench foot in other wars, the men called it jungle rot in Vietnam.

"Malaria and dysentery were also problems, and many skin maladies. We all developed boils from eating out of cans for extended periods and rarely having any fresh vegetables. All of these ailments were the Doc's responsibility, besides treating wounds during firefights."

"Just a few more questions, Mr. Sanders."

"Certainly."

"Did you ever witness the defendant use any marijuana or illegal drugs in Vietnam?"

"No. I never did."

"Just prior to your rotation home, the defendant travelled to Can Tho to find a friend, Donald Palino. Were you aware of this, and what can you tell us about how that came about?"

"The Doc confided in me about a friend whose wounds included a concussion, which wasn't healing. Rather than return to his unit, he had gone AWOL in the Can Tho area. Doc Woski was concerned about his condition and that he was AWOL, a serious infraction in Vietnam. He requested an in-country R&R to find him, make sure he was okay and convince him to return to his unit."

"How did you view this attempt by Johnny Ornowoski to find his friend?"

"I thought it admirable that he would want to spend some rare downtime looking for a friend who was in trouble."

"Did you discuss the defendant's trip to Can Tho before you left Vietnam?"

"Yes. Doc told me he had found his friend but couldn't convince him to return to his unit."

"What is your assessment of John Ornowoski?"

"In combat situations, you get to know the true makeup of a man. Doc

Woski was a dedicated medic who had the respect of the entire platoon. I was shocked to hear he'd been charged with murder, something so out of character for the man I knew in Vietnam. I haven't believed the accusations for one moment."

"Thank you, Mr. Sanders." Marcella looked at T. Bradley. "Your witness."

The prosecutor glanced at the jury before asking his first question. He worried the former lieutenant had left a favorable impression.

"Mr. Sanders, did you report the whereabouts of Donald Palino when you learned of his AWOL?"

"No. At the time, Palino was not wanted for smuggling, and the Military Police would already have more information than I could provide."

"You didn't find it strange that your medic would go in search of an AWOL soldier from another unit?"

"No. As I told Ms. Stearns, I admired the defendant's concern for a friend. It was consistent with Doc Woski's character and how he looked after the platoon as their medic."

"I see," said Smyth. "Were you aware of any drug use by the men in your platoon?"

"I knew of some marijuana use when we were standing down. I insisted it not go with us on patrols. In return for that, I turned a blind eye to its use in base camp, as long as it was done discretely."

"You have testified that you never witnessed the defendant using illegal drugs of any kind. Not even discretely?"

"That's right."

"There are reports of widespread drug use by our troops in Vietnam, but you are sure the defendant was not part of that?"

"Quite frankly, Mr. Smyth, I am offended by the reports you are referring to, especially the suggestions that the war is being fought by troops crazy on drugs. The young soldiers under my command performed admirably under extremely difficult circumstances. They looked out for one another as did Doc Woski as their medic."

✷ ✷ ✷

The platoon members who had come to Santa Cruz to testify on Johnny's behalf stayed at a terraced motel along the beachfront near the boardwalk. Built on a gently sloping knoll, patios for the guests presented a view of the beach across the boulevard from where the rooms ascended, each level providing a lovely panorama of the bay. On the right, the pier extended a mile into the sea. Looking to the south, the buildings along the boardwalk stretched to the mouth of the San Lorenzo River, where it emptied into the bay, and a train trestle spanned a ravine.

Bankrolling the entire cost of the defense, Cliff Morris had insisted on providing comfortable accommodations for the witnesses, who gathered as a group for the first time since arriving for the trial.

Jungle Boy had not seen Sergeant Morales or the LT since Vietnam. He limped toward his former platoon leaders smiling.

"Jungle Boy? What happened to your foot?" Morales asked.

"It got shot off," Jungle Boy said, as if reporting an injury as common as a sprained ankle.

"You look good, other than that," Morales said awkwardly. Nobody had told him the kid had lost a foot. "It's good to see you."

Jungle Boy beamed and said hello to the LT, who stood next to Morales and his wife, Rosa. It had been an emotional reunion for the former leaders of third platoon. Sanders felt fortunate to have had a platoon sergeant like Morales, especially after hearing Magruder's testimony.

Nearby, Rafe Johnson and Tut were having a conversation with Marcella Stearns. She'd scheduled the evening meeting because she wanted to address the witnesses as a group and to get a sense of how they interacted together. Before taking Johnny's case, she'd never had a conversation with a Vietnam veteran.

Rafe Johnson had testified after Jim Sanders, and she'd been pleased with the results. He'd appeared every bit the clean-cut Black man and performed superbly, eliciting laughter when asked if he'd ever seen Johnny use any illegal drugs. "No, but I did have the occasional beer with him."

Under cross-examination, he'd failed to be rattled by T. Bradley. When asked how long he'd been in the platoon with Johnny, he'd gotten an inoffensive dig in at the prosecution. "About seven months. I was the colored boy in the fourth row your witness pointed out."

Judge Walker had banged his gavel and looked kindly at Johnson.

Addressing Magruder's thinly veiled racism, he said: "The court apologizes for any inappropriate remarks by the prosecution's witness. Now please continue."

"Yes, Sir," Rafe had said, accommodating the judge's wishes but knowing he'd scored a point for the defense.

Tut would be on the stand the following day, and Rafe was giving him advice. "It'll be easy. Nothin' to it after what you already went through in the Nam. Don't let that shithead T. Bradley mess with you. You been there, brother, he sure as hell ain't."

"Thank you, Rafe," Marcella said, not confident it was helpful. She had difficulty reading Tut's level of anxiety. His sunglasses prevented eye contact, and his chain smoking kept his hands busy. After finishing each cigarette, he would set down the beer he held and light another smoke.

Freddy Dempster sat with a coffee at an outdoor table in the courtyard. When CC arrived with her mother, Benita Diez, and Johnny's father, Gregor, he invited them to sit down. Cecelia had brought her mother so that Rosa Morales, not fluent in English, would feel more comfortable having someone who spoke Spanish.

After finishing her conversation with Tut, Marcella addressed the entire group. Afterwards, she and Freddy would head back to the office for more preparation.

"If I could please have your attention," she began, "I would like to give everybody an update about the trial and put our heads together to make sure we haven't left any stone unturned regarding Johnny's defense. It is very gratifying to him that you've come all this way to testify on his behalf.

"If it weren't for the murder weapon with Johnny's prints, based on your testimony, the prosecution's case would be completely discredited. Jim and Rafe, you were excellent today. Russell is on the stand in the morning. Eduardo will follow, and we will close with Delbert. Is there anything any of you would like to add?"

Jim Sanders spoke. "It was difficult listening to Magruder's testimony. When Eddie testifies, I hope you can somehow contrast his excellent leadership as platoon sergeant with Magruder's dismal performance. Also, how is Billy's mother? I think we should all be willing to help her in any way we can."

"Beverley is with us," CC said, "staying with Gregor and my mother. She wasn't up for coming tonight. The judge went and saw her immediately and apologized for placing her under arrest. He released her at that time. The most devastating thing was learning how her son died. It would mean a great deal to Beverley if you would all see her before going home."

"How are you doing, CC?" Jim Sanders asked.

"I just want our lives back. I was so happy when Johnny made it back from Vietnam. Now his life is in jeopardy again. I don't know what will happen if they find him guilty." She sat down quickly and tried to suppress her sobs.

"The Doc never killed nobody," said Jungle Boy. "Even if they convict him, we will keep working to prove his innocence." The kid had not shared all he'd found with the lawyers, who had their own way of seeing things. He and Rafe had a plan percolating if the trial went awry. Jungle Boy had kept Johnny up to date to ease his anxiety, while Rafe had given some details to Tut, which seemed to calm him on the eve of his testimony.

"Let's remain focused and confident of a not guilty verdict," Marcella said. She said goodbye and left with Freddy.

"It's quite the group," Freddy said on the way back to the office. "The more I learn about the war, the stranger it gets."

"I'm worried about Russell Tuttley's testimony tomorrow," Marcella said. "He spent a lot of time with Rafe tonight, which settled him down, but he doesn't seem quite with it."

"It will go fine," Freddy assured her. "Today, you were worried about Rafe Johnson before he took the stand. Look how well that turned out."

CHAPTER THIRTY-SIX

Tut had not wanted to leave his tiny room above the restaurant and travel across the country. Doc's need propelled the journey. As he walked into the packed courtroom on the morning of his testimony, Tut wished to be back in Saginaw. He was comfortable there, safe, free to smoke, drink a little beer, and watch the world from his second-story window.

Kenny, the Chinese proprietor, hired the reclusive veteran sufficient hours to cover rent and a three-pack-a-day cigarette habit. Kenny joked with Tut in his broken English while also chain-smoking.

"When you stop smoke, Tut? Smoke too much, Tut. Someday, whoosh, big fire, burn place up." Kenny would throw his skinny arms wide and laugh, a cigarette dangling perilously from his own lips.

Tut saw the packed courtroom and worried his frailty would surface. Discharged from the army after returning from Vietnam, he hadn't gone and seen the Cunninghams, the family of the best friend in this world he would ever have. The friend he'd failed to bring out of the Nam. Guilt prevented Tut from contacting RC's family, and the fear they would hate him. And when Billy's mother confronted Magruder in the courtroom, the Nam surfaced. He relived every ugly detail of the day they'd lost Billy, which included Tut's weaknesses and shortcomings. But now, the Doc needed him.

In a daze, he walked to the witness stand when Marcella Stearns called his name. Unable to smoke while testifying, he held an unlit cigarette in his hand. Like out of the fog, Marcella's voice began asking the questions they had rehearsed.

"Can you please tell us, Russell, how long you were in Vietnam with the defendant, Johnny Ornowoski?"

"I think I had been in-country three months when the Doc arrived, so about nine months."

"Did the platoon see a lot of combat during that time?"

"Quite a bit. It all runs together as you try and get through your tour. I think our casualty rate was high. We were always shorthanded and losing people."

"What do you mean by 'losing people?'"

"You know, some guys would get wounded and medevaced out; some guys would get killed. Guys would rotate home, and we wouldn't get a replacement right away."

"You were a squad leader in third platoon?"

"Not at first. When I got to the platoon, I was a grenadier, carrying an M-79 grenade launcher. Usually, as guys gained experience and others were wounded or rotated home, you became a squad leader. When the LT asked me to take over my squad, I didn't want to, but agreed because I was next in line."

"What would you do on your days off?"

Russell Tuttley tapped an unlit cigarette on the seat of the chair. When it disintegrated, he looked down at his hands and got confused. Transported back to the Nam, he reached for another cigarette and looked for his rifle to tap it on.

"Mr. Tuttley, the judge prodded, "Did you hear the question?"

"Sorry," he said, coming out of his daze and trying to focus. "We never really had any days off. Sometimes we would stand down for a day or two in Dong Tam, but we needed some of that time to resupply our field gear. I would usually try and get some sleep if it wasn't too hot, write some letters home or grab a hot meal in the mess hall. That kind of thing."

"It sounds like you didn't have much free time."

"That's correct."

"Did your medic, Doc Ornowoski?"

"It would have been the same for Doc, except busier with guys coming to him about any medical problems from being in the bush."

"So there wouldn't be much opportunity for your medic to be buying and selling drugs while he was with third platoon?"

"I don't see how that would have been possible. You get real tired as well. Everybody's focus was on surviving the Nam."

"Did you ever see your medic, Johnny Ornowoski, use any illegal drugs?"

"No."

"Your witness." Marcella Stearns abruptly ended her questioning.

T. Bradley Smyth rose and slowly approached. Tut tried to focus. He looked straight ahead at nothing in particular while his hand that held the cigarette continued tapping it on the wooden chair.

"Mr. Tuttley, you testified that you were a squad leader for part of your tour in Vietnam."

"Yes."

"Did that include the period when Sergeant Magruder was your platoon sergeant?"

"Yes."

"And Billy Warrington was in your squad?"

"He was before he was killed."

"There was tension in the platoon over walking point?"

"There was after Sergeant Magruder arrived. He began insisting everybody in the platoon share that duty, even the guys who weren't ready."

"There was some anger at him for the death of Billy Warrington?"

"Yes. Billy had come a long way since arriving in the Nam, but most of the platoon felt he wasn't ready to walk point."

"I see," Smyth said, placing his hand beneath his chin like he was thinking. "But Billy was in your squad, was he not? Who actually made the decision that he walk point?"

"Sergeant Magruder spoke with me the night before Billy was killed. We were dug in for the night, and he said our squad would be in the lead so would have to provide the point man."

"So, he left that decision to you, who would actually walk point?"

"Not exactly."

"So who did Sergeant Magruder order to walk point?"

"Someone from our squad."

"Not Billy Warrington, specifically?"

"I guess not."

"So who made the decision to put Billy Warrington on point?"

"The squad. We decided to draw straws."

"But you were the squad leader. Is that how you made decisions, drawing straws?" The prosecutor paused for emphasis, took a step toward the jury box, smug in the realization he had rattled the witness.

"No," stammered Tut, "I had been walking point when it was…"

T. Bradley interrupted. "Mr. Tuttley, please answer the question. Did you often make decisions by drawing straws? Do you consider that good leadership?"

"You don't understand," he said feebly. "None of my guys were comfortable walking point." He wanted to explain how he and Jungle Boy filled that role before Magruder arrived, but the shithead lawyer was interrupting him and twisting his words into other meanings. Tut tapped his unlit cigarette vigorously on the chair. When it disintegrated, he looked down and was confused again. "There are too many new guys. I can't do it anymore."

He drew another cigarette from the package in his shirt pocket and tapped it a few times. Unlike the one that had disintegrated from too many taps, he lit it and inhaled. Suddenly, he was in the Nam again, watching the medevac fly away with his decimated squad. Only he and Eli, the new kid, remained.

"I should have just walked point," he mumbled to himself. *What did his life matter? Look at the grief he'd caused by not walking point. The thought, repeated over and over again, exhausted him, along with the guilt that accompanied it.*

Tut heard the judge's voice asking him to respond to the question, the same question he'd asked himself over and over and was unable to answer. *What was the judge doing in Vietnam? He wasn't part of the platoon saddling up and moving out after the medevac had flown away with his squad, just like it had with RC.*

Now the judge was asking if he was okay. There were other voices crowding around him, taking his arm and leading him away from the bamboo grove where they'd found Billy. *What about Eli?*

"Wait," shouted Tut. "We can't leave Eli."

Johnny had moved from behind the defense table and stood in front of Tut.

"Doc, is that you?" *The Doc would understand they couldn't just leave Eli. He could fix things.*

"Doc, they want to leave Eli. We need to get him out of the Nam, too. He's the last guy in my squad."

Johnny looked into Tut's eyes. They were uncomprehending, far away.

"It's okay, Tut," Johnny said. "We can go now. Eli's fine. He'll be okay."

"You sure, Doc?"

"I'm sure," Johnny said. "You can go home now. It's okay to go home."

✳ ✳ ✳

Furious, Judge Walker had the prosecutor in his chambers.

"So far, this court has managed to jail a bereaved mother and cause the psychological meltdown of a traumatized Vietnam veteran. What's more, while the defendant was up and caring for the witness, you kept haranguing him in the midst of his breakdown. The juror's jaws nearly dropped to the floor. I keep asking myself when your case is going to materialize. The attorney for the defense is not even bothering to object because the prosecution keeps making the defendant look better all the time. Why would they interrupt?"

"Your Honor, if it pleases the court…" Smyth tried to interject.

"It does not please the court, Mr. Smyth. Present some evidence," Walker fumed.

"We still have the murder weapon," protested T. Bradley.

"Until someone discovers it was flown in from Pluto," the judge retorted sarcastically.

At her request, Marcella Stearns also met with Judge Walker.

"I would like to call Beverley Morrow as a witness but am worried the prosecutor will do another kamikaze attack with her on the stand."

"I have addressed the issues with Mr. Smyth," the judge said. "I will accept a written statement by her in lieu of testifying in court. How is she doing?"

"She didn't know her son was tortured, and I didn't know she was in the courtroom when I cross-examined Sergeant Magruder," Marcella said. "It was a big blow to learn the details of her son's death."

Judge Walker nodded. "I think we've all learned a lot about the war during this trial. We need to get this wrapped up before there are any more casualties."

Now Marcella nodded. "The defendant wrote to her from Vietnam. She wants to testify on his behalf to return his kindness. Delbert Kinkaid, the young man who lost a foot in Vietnam, was close to Beverley Morrow's son. I will put him on the stand as my last witness. He visited Beverley while he was recuperating from his amputation."

"I see," said Walker. "Can you have her written statement in my office tomorrow?"

Tut, calm now, had recovered from his courtroom meltdown. The LT and Eddie Morales had brought him back to the motel and stayed for a while. Rafe was there, backing him up all the way. The woman lawyer had wanted to phone a doctor. A nice lady, but stupid about the Nam.

The fancy pants prosecutor had continued asking him in that snotty voice to "please answer the question." He had lost it in the courtroom. It was happening more frequently now, and getting harder to hide, not knowing where he was, or returning to the war. *What good had come of surviving the Nam if it came home with him? He couldn't go back to Vietnam and change things, but he would make sure to do things right this time.*

Finally, alone in the motel room, and at peace with himself, he knew what had to be done.

Tut left his room midafternoon, took the terraced steps to the street and crossed to the beachside. Walking toward the boardwalk, oblivious to the people on the sidewalk, he proceeded south. Just before the trestle, he headed east through a seedy part of town. Passing Ralph Barnes' old place, Tut continued toward the police station located next to the courthouse. He slipped into the back seat of Randy Siemans' car and waited.

The supplies he needed fit easily into a canvas rucksack. He checked the small Weston pistol for six rounds occupying its chambers and laid a grenade on the backseat of the car. A short-bladed knife, sharp and in its sheath, was long enough for his purposes. If the shithead lawyer was going to act smug and think he was crazy, then Tut would give them all crazy. He would free the Doc, make the guilty man pay, and end all of the pussyfooting going on in the trial.

Siemans arrived and slipped into the driver's seat. Sensing another presence, Tut didn't give him time to react. From behind, he stuck the knife into the detective's shoulder, high and right under the joint. Tut placed the barrel of the pistol firmly at the base of Siemans' skull.

"Don't move, or we finish things right here. I'm going to come around to the front seat. You try anything and I start shooting."

Siemans held his right shoulder with his left hand, trying to ease the pain and stop the bleeding. "Are you crazy?" he shouted.

"Bad choice of words, detective. Now shut up while I tell you what we're going to do. If you cooperate, you might get out of this alive. All of my scenarios end with my death, so whether I take you with me is totally up to you.

"We are going to take a drive to a quieter spot where we can begin to set things right. So start the car and head north out of town."

"How am I supposed to drive with my shoulder like this?"

"Stop blubbering and drive," Tut ordered. He shoved the barrel end of the pistol against his temple. Feeling weak from the pain and fear, Siemans managed to pull out of the parking lot.

"Head north on Route 1. It's not far."

Two miles out of town, Tut instructed his captive to turn into the drive of a secluded beach cottage hidden behind a thick row of cypress trees bent from the wind.

"Same rules apply," Tut said. "When I tell you, get out of the car and we'll go inside."

The cottage, small and simply furnished, had a sofa along an inner wall. Tut ordered Siemans to sit and took a seat for himself at a small wooden table by a window.

"What now?" Siemans asked feebly. The sight of him scared and whimpering enraged Tut. He rushed at him and slapped him across the face.

"I do the talking, and you do the listening, unless you're answering my questions. *Wasn't it the way of bullies? Tough guys while they were in control, blubbering babies when they were hurt.*

"The first thing we do is look at that wound. I don't want you dying quite yet, if that's what you've got a mind to do. It's your choice."

Tut placed the pistol on the table and kept the knife in his hand. "I'm going to cut some of your clothes off. No sudden moves and you don't get hurt any further."

He cut the suit coat at the shoulder. Once Tut removed it, he ripped off Siemans' shirt, exposing the knife wound. He doused the shoulder with hydrogen peroxide and watched it fizz. Siemans winced.

"It don't hurt that much," Tut said. "Let's finish this up." He took a tube of antibacterial ointment and smeared it over the wound before taking bandages out of the satchel and taping them over the injury. With Siemans naked to the waist, he removed his shoes and had him finish undressing.

"You can put these on," Tut said, handing him a pair of pajamas. He helped him with the top. "I'm going to give you a glass of water and some aspirin, then we talk. Cooperate and I'll give you something stronger, and you can sleep for a while."

Siemans began to shiver. Tut covered him with a blanket and went to sit at the table. He took out his cigarettes and lit one. When Siemans had stopped shivering, Tut pulled a small recorder out of his rucksack and turned it on.

"Now we talk. Let's start with what you have against the Doc? He was my medic in Vietnam."

Siemans closed his eyes for a moment and began. "Nothing, really. He was a convenient scapegoat to take the heat off. He used to deal marijuana with a larger player, an old hippie named Barnes, who got sent up on a drug conviction. Ornowoski's fingerprints showed up on a box the homeless drunk was peddling marijuana out of to some hippies down by the pier. My partner had it in for Ornowoski, figured he should have gone to prison instead of joining the army."

"We know you killed the homeless guy. The Black guy with the Afro, and the White guy with him? They were in my platoon. In case you didn't notice, the kid was missing a foot. Got it shot off in Vietnam. The Doc saved his life.

But you assholes don't give a shit about any of that, do you? It's making me angry just thinking about it, so keep talking."

"Like I said," Siemans continued, "when your friend returned from Vietnam, my partner already hated him. It was convenient for me to cover my tracks by going along and putting Ornowoski away."

"Your partner, Hamilton, is in on your drug trade?"

"No, just old school. He hates the hippies, their lifestyle, and all of the drugs that go along with it."

"He thinks Vietnam was fun for the Doc, some walk in the park? You bastards don't know shit."

"Hey, I'm just telling you what I know."

"Then keep talking," said Tut, trying to calm down.

"About the time your friend got back from Vietnam, we were privy to the fed's arrest of Patrick Corker, who had a connection with Don Palino, who Ornowoski had trained with. Everything fell into place to blame your friend, a fortunate coincidence that would take the heat off me. My partner and the cocky prosecutor started jumping to conclusions. Prior to Corker's arrest, they assumed the local drugs were coming in from Mexico. By killing the homeless guy and blaming Ornowoski, it would create a diversion and give me time to get a plan together and leave the country. I could still do that, you know. Cut you in for half and go our separate ways."

"Not interested," said Tut. "We have a lot of unfinished business. You're not going anywhere."

"But you said you weren't going to kill me if I cooperated," Siemans said.

"I won't if you keep talking."

"What else do you need to know?"

Tut walked him through confessions on how he knew Johnny had just changed a tire, stole the lug wrench and killed Stewart Brenz.

"That's enough for now," Tut finally said. "I've got some codeine you can take for the pain and sleep for a while. We'll talk more later."

Tut removed the cartridge from the recorder while Siemans dozed. He put a coffee pot on the stove and smoked while he waited for it to percolate. When it was ready, he took a cup to the table and worked on a letter. Finishing well into the night, he put a new tape into the recorder when he sensed Siemans had woken.

"Time to continue," Tut ordered.

Siemans opened his eyes when he heard Tut approach. Pretending to be asleep for the last hour, he'd hatched a plan of his own. Tut didn't give him a chance to organize.

"Let's look at that wound before we get started." It would be sore today, limiting Siemans' movements.

"So, where are the drugs originating from, and how do they get to you in Santa Cruz?"

"It's a fairly contained system. Palino and Corker are involved from Vietnam. The shipments arrive in San Francisco and get picked up by runners within the syndicate. Locally, I partnered with Barnes. I was his ears in the police. It worked for a while. I can't say I wasn't relieved when he died, but I had nothing to do with that. Barnes was upset about Ornowoski's arrest. He seemed to like the kid and wanted to keep him and his girlfriend out of this. Someone higher must have worried he would talk. That's who I thought had contacted me when two of your platoon members showed up."

"Speaking of the money, where is it?"

"Look, what kind of share do you want to drop this whole thing, grab the money and run?"

"Oh, we'll go and get the money." Tut said, rummaging in his rucksack.

"I've got a lot stashed. You can have it all if you want. Just let me out of this."

"So where is it?" Tut had the pistol pointed at Siemans again.

CHAPTER THIRTY-SEVEN

Siemans had a cabin in the Santa Cruz Mountains. "It will take an hour to get there," he told Tut. "The money is buried." Desperate now, he hoped the sight of the cash would convince Tut to grab it and run.

"How do I know you won't just kill me and take the money?" Siemans asked.

"I should," Tut told him, "after what you did to Johnny. Right now your job is to drive."

Tut had him verbally record every road and turn along the route. They came to a bridge and crossed a small stream. Tut smelled the potent scent of the redwoods, musky and of the earth, as the dirt road wound through the forest. Siemans turned into a drive and ascended the side of a mountain. A set of terraced steps led to a redwood-sided cabin. The thick forest blocked the late afternoon sun as dusk fell.

Tut stared into the darkness when they got out of the car. Siemans sensed a change in the way he looked at the forest, crouching and listening for the muffled sounds filtering through the trees.

"Watch for booby traps," Tut instructed. "Charlie's got them everywhere." He pushed Siemans behind the trunk of a redwood and shoved him to the ground.

He really is a sick bastard, thought Siemans, *and who the fuck is Charlie?* With Tut preoccupied with the dangers in the trees, Siemans thought it would be his best chance to escape before the crazed maniac came out of whatever trance possessed him.

When Siemans bolted, Tut had him tackled before he'd taken two steps. He hadn't expected such alertness and strength from someone so deranged.

"Stay down, stay down," Tut whispered in his ear. "I thought I warned you?" he said in a high state of alert. "Charlie's still out there."

Infected now, pain shot through Siemans' shoulder. Still in the pajamas Tut had provided, they were filthy, and he remained barefoot.

"You want to wind up like Billy?" Tut exclaimed. "Have your eyes gouged out, maybe your nuts cut off? I saw the Doc bury one of Billy's ears. Doc didn't know what to do with it. I should never have let Billy walk point. I should have just done it one more time and everything would be okay."

It started to get light when Tut emerged from his altered state. Half-crazed with pain, fear and discomfort, Siemans writhed on the ground shivering. Tut realized he must have returned to Vietnam again. *It's happening all the time now,* he told himself. *Better get on with the plan.*

He pulled Siemans to his feet and the detective shrieked. "It don't hurt that bad so stop the blubbering." He pointed the pistol at him. "You're really starting to piss me off," Tut shouted.

Worried he would shoot him, Siemans stammered: "I haven't shown you where the money is. It's inside."

"Let's get going then. You're starting to remind me of Magruder, and I hated that son of a bitch."

Siemans struggled climbing the steps to the cabin. "Can I have something for the pain?" he asked.

"Later," Tut said. "Let's get this done."

They went inside and Siemans pointed to a floor hatch with a ring sunk in the wood for lifting it. "Down there, in the cellar," Siemans nodded with his head.

Tut had Siemans sit in a chair, took a coil of rope out of his knapsack and wrapped it around him. He opened the hatch to the cellar and climbed down a ladder fastened to a floor beam. At the bottom, he took a shovel and dug a foot into the dirt floor and found a metal box. Inside, a slightly smaller box held the money.

"Count it," Tut ordered after untying Siemans, "and no complaining."

The detective sorted through the bundles and stacked each one according to the denominations, mostly hundreds and fifties.

"How much?"

"Seventy-six thousand," Siemans told him.

"Now put it back."

"In the cellar?"

Tut shoved him towards the hatch and forced him to climb down, throwing the latched box at him after he was off the ladder. "I'm not sure I can climb back up," Siemans complained.

"Then I might have to leave you here," Tut said, weary of his bitching.

Panic seized Siemans and sent another surge of adrenaline through his system. He reburied the box and climbed out of the cellar and collapsed onto a chair.

Two more stashes on the property recovered a total of $212,000. Tut shoved Siemans toward the car.

"I can't drive anymore," Siemans protested.

"If you insist," Tut said. He tied Siemans' hands behind him and wrapped more rope around his torso. The detective cried out in pain and fear, certain that the crazed veteran would kill him now. Tut ignored him and pushed him into the passenger's seat.

"Don't worry," said Tut, "we're just about done."

"Where we going now?" stammered Siemans.

"You're not driving," Tut said. "You don't need to know."

Tut had no problem finding the way back to the beach cottage in the daylight. He would need just a little while longer before he could complete his plan.

Jungle Boy sat with Rafe Johnson in the courtroom. In his dress greens, he was scheduled to be called to testify when the morning session began. He would be the last witness in the trial.

Randy Siemans had disappeared. He'd not reported for work. Rafe and Jungle Boy were nervous.

"Maybe he took the money and ran," Jungle Boy said. "Do you think he's on to us?"

"It's not that easy to just disappear," Rafe said. "Maybe his own guys considered him a liability and did something about it. That's the worst scenario."

Their plan had been to force the detective into anonymously revealing clues that would cast more doubt on Johnny's guilt, if not exonerate him. The police would not accept what Jungle Boy and Rafe had found at this point, so the authorities could deal with Siemans later. The important thing was to avoid a conviction. Maybe their threats were too real, and Siemans thought he had no recourse but to run. Jungle Boy would have to make sure his testimony helped the Doc.

Marcella had coached him the night before. He looked so young it was hard to believe the kid had seen ten months of combat culminating in a lost foot. She hoped the women on the jury would have the same response she did, want to take him home and mother him.

T. Bradley looked glum as he watched Jungle Boy limp to the witness box. Standing erect as he took his oath, a prominent set of ribbons were displayed on his chest. The witnesses for the defense had left positive impressions on the jury, while Magruder had not provided the anticipated counter to their testimonies.

"Mr. Kincaid," Marcella began, "may I call you Delbert?"

"Of course," he responded.

"When did you first meet the defendant, John Ornowoski?"

"At the Can Tho Army Airfield. We were both waiting for a flight to take us to our unit in Dong Tam, headquarters for the Ninth Infantry Division. We were assigned to the same platoon, Doc as the medic, and I as a rifleman."

"So, you arrived in your unit at the same time and were together, for what, ten months, right up until the time you were wounded?"

"Yes."

"I would like to ask you the same question I have of every witness. Did you ever see Johnny Ornowoski use any illegal drugs while you were together in Vietnam?"

"No, not even once."

"Did you ever see or hear of him procuring or selling any illegal drugs?"

"Of course not."

"Thank you. Let's move on to something else. When you were wounded,

Johnny Ornowoski was awarded the bronze star for his actions in treating you. Is that correct?"

"The Doc saved my life."

"At the risk of his own?"

"Yes."

"I don't wish for you to relive the horrible experience of being wounded in Vietnam, but do you mind recounting the details for the court?"

"I can do that, especially if it helps the Doc."

"Thank you. The day you were wounded, and lost your foot, you were walking point?"

"Yes. As I moved through the jungle, I sensed the Viet Cong were near. I had signaled to the platoon to be alert when a grenade came flying over some brush between me and the enemy. I dove for cover behind a small palm tree but was unable to avoid the blast. It rocked me hard, and I was knocked unconscious from the detonation. My left foot remained exposed to enemy fire and took several rounds from an AK-47; basically, my foot was shredded."

"That was when Doc Ornowoski came and got you?"

"Yes. He moved into position as close as possible without exposing himself but had to sprint the final twenty yards under enemy fire. When he got to me, he picked me up and carried me to a safer spot. He stopped the bleeding by applying a tourniquet."

"Not the actions of a selfish man, and not the actions of a cold-blooded killer?"

"The Doc saved lives, including mine."

"Thank you for your testimony today. We wish you well on your further recovery. Your witness," Marcella said for the final time.

T. Bradley Smyth felt he had nothing to lose by attempting to alter the cherubic impressions the jury might have about Delbert Kincaid. The prosecutor was determined to get beneath the surface and provoke the beast that must reside underneath. As a friend of the defendant, Smyth saw him as fair game. The country was growing weary of the Vietnam War, and there were reports in the media of atrocities being committed by US troops. There were a lot of bad apples.

"Mr. Kincaid," he began, "you have testified that while you were in Vietnam you never saw the defendant use any illegal drugs. What about the violence? You must have participated in extreme forms of it. We have heard testimony about Johnny Ornowoski administering aid to numerous casualties under very violent circumstances."

"Objection, Your Honor." Marcella was on her feet. "Is the prosecutor asking a question or giving a speech?"

"How about it Mr. Smyth, is there a question in there? Please proceed," ordered the judge.

"Of course, Your Honor," he continued. "Did you ever witness the defendant use violence towards anyone, sanctioned or not?"

Marcella was on her feet again. "I fail to see the relevance of such questioning. These young men were in a war zone, fighting a war sanctioned by their government. They were sent there by the United States."

"Your point is well taken, Miss Stearns. Where are you going with this line of questioning, Mr. Smyth?"

"I am attempting to establish a link between the defendant, violence and murder. Coming from Vietnam, where the defendant saw and participated in a great deal of violence, is it far-fetched to assume a certain acceptance of it as a way of dealing with situations?"

"Please approach the bench, councilors," Walker instructed.

"This line of questioning is absurd, Your Honor," Marcella stated. "Are we to assume all returning veterans of a war sanctioned and started by their government are murderers?"

"Mr. Smyth?" said Judge Walker.

"I am simply trying to establish a link between violence and the ability to commit murder. The defendant's fingerprints are on the murder weapon."

"Get to the point then, Mr. Smyth," ordered the judge.

"Mr. Kincaid, was the defendant ever violent in Vietnam?"

Marcella threw her hands up in the air in exasperation. Ready to object again, Jungle Boy began answering the question before she spoke.

"There was a lot of violence in Vietnam, if that's what you mean. I wouldn't say the Doc was violent. We were all put in a violent situation. In my view, Sergeant Magruder, your witness, was violent."

"I was asking about the defendant," complained T. Bradley.

"Then, no, the Doc was not violent compared to Sergeant Magruder. After Magruder's first firefight with the platoon, I saw the sergeant kick a dead body. He'd found a photograph of a girl in the pocket of the enemy soldier and began making jokes about how ugly she was."

"Your Honor, will you please instruct the witness to answer the question," T. Bradley complained again.

"Mr. Smyth, are you objecting to your own question, or how the witness is answering it? Since you have opened the door to this line of inquiry, let's hear what Mr. Kincaid has to say."

Marcella relaxed. The prosecutor had underestimated the young man in the witness box.

CHAPTER
THIRTY-EIGHT

His captive still bound, Tut arrived back at the beach cottage mid-morning. He had Siemans sit on the couch and took out his recorder.

"We're going to finish our little chat," Tut said. Slipping in and out of lucidity, Russell Tuttley remained an enigma to Siemans.

The detective waited for the questions, knowing the ordeal was about to end. Neither man could go indefinitely in the shape they were in. Feverish and nauseous, Siemans' body ached as he slumped on the sofa. Tut sat before him wild-eyed and running on adrenaline and whatever crazy energy drove him in his madness.

"Let's start with how you got into the drug business?"

"Right after your medic friend was busted, the first time, before he was even in the army, I came across evidence incriminating Ralph Barnes. I blackmailed him, threatened to reveal it if he didn't cut me in on a percentage of his deals. About that time, a newer and larger source of the drugs opened up from Asia. I faked evidence that kept the authorities looking at Mexico as the source and going after small time players on wild goose chases. My role was to keep the pressure off. It worked well for a while."

Siemans shifted on the couch and looked for signs of exhaustion or collapse in his crazed captor. Tut remained fixated on Siemans. "So what changed?"

"Well, one of the runners got busted and fingered Corker. After his arrest, the bigger picture began to emerge. My partner, Tom Hamilton, assumed all along that Ornowoski had been involved with Barnes. So, when your friend's name came up in relation to Corker, it all sort of fell into our hands."

"And you were willing to have the Doc put away for good by killing a harmless old homeless guy?" Tut waited for a response. Siemans, worried an answer might set him off, remained silent.

"So, two more lives ruined to save your own skin," Tut continued. "You had a plan?"

"It bought me some time. When your friends showed up, I thought the bigger players were watching, and they might kill me. I would have to run a little sooner. Then you showed up."

"What about the Doc's girl?"

"A small player. Barnes never said anything, but I sensed he was trying to keep her out of the drug business. Hamilton hated her because she was Ornowoski's girlfriend. Hamilton's interest in her was always about nailing Ornowoski."

"Okay," said Tut, "I guess we get ready."

Panic seized Siemans. "Ready for what?"

Ignoring the question, Tut motioned for him to sit on a stool he positioned near the couch. Tut took his pistol and checked that it was loaded. After opening the pajama top, he began taping the gun to Siemans' chest.

"What are you doing now?" Siemans protested, his rising exhaustion and anxiety reflected in his voice. "Just take the money, all of it, and go somewhere. You still can, you know."

Tired of his talk, Tut tore a strip of tape off the role and placed it over the detective's mouth, then continued securing the gun to his chest, the barrel just beneath his chin. Siemans began shaking. With the safety in place, Tut tied one end of a length of twine to the trigger. He threaded the rest through a cloth loop on the pajama bottoms and coiled the excess twine, placing it in Siemans' bound hands. Tut released the safety.

"That will do for now. Sit there until I'm done."

Tut went to the table and examined two letters he'd prepared. The longer one detailed what he had coerced from Siemans, a written backup to what the tapes revealed. The second, a short goodbye to the members of the platoon.

Dear Doc, Jungle Boy, Rafe, and the rest of third platoon. I don't know what's happening to me but would like to get some things straight before I go. I am delivering the real killer to the court so the Doc can go free. There is enough evidence to put Siemans away. You guys were the best. Too much of the Nam came back with me.

I'm going to find RC.

Tut

He gathered the tapes and placed them in the knapsack next to the grenade. Certain that he'd thought of everything, he counted on his adrenaline carrying him through another two hours. He would be able to rest then.

The sight of Siemans, panicking in fear, left him cold. RC had been in much worse shape before his death and had to hump with seventy pounds of gear. *If only I'd packed more of his weight,* thought Tut. *How many times had that gone through his mind? Death was so strange and empty in the war. One second a person is there, and in an instant they're gone. Except for the body, so awkward and heavy afterwards. It mattered that nobody got left behind. Everybody had the fear of being left in the jungle, alone, far from home. Where had RC gone? He would know very soon. At the very least he would be at rest, if not in peace, then in oblivion.*

Tut's plan came together quickly now. He pushed Siemans into the passenger's seat and took the wheel. He had the coil of twine in his right hand, the other end attached to the trigger. Siemans, his mouth still taped, breathed heavily and emitted grunting sounds of fear and hysteria. Tut drove towards the courthouse, focused on finishing his task. There was no hope for himself, but maybe the Doc would be okay.

Tut was just so tired, tired of all the killing, the losing friends, the hostility, the fatigue and stress of trying to figure out what was happening to him. With no worthwhile future, why had he ever been concerned about surviving a tour in Vietnam? There was no best friend coming home with him, no pretty sister to meet. It was all a void, a cosmic joke that there was ever any meaning to the life he lived.

Tut drove the detective's Chevrolet Impala right to the steps of the courthouse. In a previous life he would have given anything for a car like that. Too late now. He parked and hopped out, racing to the passenger door. Before hauling Siemans out, he pulled the pin on the grenade and held it in his left hand. Four seconds is all that separated the fragmentation grenade from exploding if Tut failed to keep pressure on the lever, or "spoon" as they had called it in Vietnam. He held the coil of twine in his right hand. "Inside" is all he said to Siemans.

Initially, there was little commotion when they entered the courtroom. Siemans had to keep up with Tut to prevent the pistol from firing. "I have a grenade," Tut shouted, "and no pin to go with it." He held it high above his head. He saw Jungle Boy in the witness box being pestered by the shithead lawyer still asking stupid questions about the Nam.

"If I'm shot or seized before I'm finished, then the grenade will detonate and a lot of you will be hurt. Listen to what I have to say, and nobody dies but me. This is the killer; this is the drug dealer." Tut nodded at Siemans.

"I have three tapes of recorded confessions, and evidence of the drug deals, including where two hundred and twelve thousand in cash is buried at this man's cabin. I have detailed descriptions, and his fingerprints will be on the money. I am delivering this man to the court."

Tut looked at Jungle Boy on the stand. "Can you give this to the judge?" he asked, handing him the knapsack. Tut turned his attention back to Siemans. Confused, he blinked his eyes trying to regain focus.

"What are you doing out here in your dress greens?" he asked Jungle Boy. "Charlie will see you for sure, all that yellow on your uniform. Get Red Robin to take the prisoner. He'll know what to do with him. Charlie was always afraid of Red. I have him tied up, but be careful. I think he's booby trapped. He's got a pistol taped to his chest."

Johnny came around from behind the defense's table and approached Tut. "I can take the prisoner for you, or Jungle Boy."

"I don't know, Doc. You have a lot to do, and Jungle Boy should be on point."

"It's okay, Tut. We can manage. Why have you got the grenade in your hand? Is the pin pulled?"

"It is, Doc. Charlie's out there. Can't you just *feel* him watching us?"

"I gave the judge the information," Jungle Boy said. "He's going to look at it right away. I think it's all clear."

"Are you sure?" Tut asked. "Charlie never just goes away even if we can't see him."

"I think it's okay, Tut," Johnny attempted to assure him. "Can these people go now?"

"Okay, but he stays." Tut pointed at Siemans with the hand that held the grenade.

Johnny looked at the judge. "I think it's okay to clear the court now."

People at the back were already going out the doors. "Please proceed carefully," Judge Walker said. "The jury should exit to the side. Let's clear the court."

Marcella and Freddy backed away slowly from the defense table. T. Bradley exited with the jurors.

"Can you give me the grenade now, Tut?" Johnny asked. "We have the prisoner secured."

"That's good," Tut said. "Make sure the prisoner doesn't get away."

"What are you going to do?" asked Johnny.

"I have to find RC, and Billy, Half Pint, too. They aren't here anymore."

"Can I have the grenade before you go and look for them?" asked Johnny.

"I need the grenade to find them," said Tut.

"You sure?" Johnny had a sick feeling in the pit of his stomach. Before he could think of what to say next, Beverley Morrow came forward.

"I don't think your friends will leave you, Russell," she said.

Tut looked even more confused. "What is Billy's mother doing in the Nam? Mothers aren't allowed over here, are they?"

"Billy's gone, Russell, but your friends are here to help you. I'm here to help you," she said.

"You're not supposed to be here. Did you come to see Billy? We can't find him. Charlie's got him. I'm so very sorry. I should have just walked point and then everybody could have gone home."

"You are home, Russell, and it's okay that you are. Your friends can help you," Beverley Morrow said.

"I need to go and find them," Tut insisted. "Please go. I don't want any more of you getting hurt. Everybody around me gets killed. I need to fix that before anybody else winds up dead."

"We're not going anywhere," Johnny said. "We need to put the grenade away. We don't need them anymore. We have the prisoner, and Charlie's gone."

"You sure? Where are we?"

"We're home now, Tut. All of us. Jungle Boy and Billy's mom. Can you see that now?"

"But I'm still in the Nam. I need to find everybody before I can leave, RC and Billy."

"We can all leave together," Johnny said. "We're not leaving without you. Not this time. No more dead bodies. Are you okay with that?"

"Sure. I guess that would be good," Tut said. "How do I get there?"

"We'll show you, Tut. We don't need the grenade for that. We don't need them anymore."

"If you're sure," Tut said. Johnny reached for the grenade. "Careful, the pin is pulled. Don't release the spoon," Tut said.

"Do you have the pin?" Johnny asked.

Still confused, Tut shook his head. "Must have lost it."

Johnny transferred the grenade into his hands and looked at Jungle Boy. "There's no pin. We need tape to wrap around the grenade."

Two policemen came forward with their guns drawn and pointed at Johnny. He looked at the judge. "This grenade is active," he said. "I need to tape the lever, so it doesn't activate the fuse."

Jungle Boy stepped forward and tore the tape off Siemans' mouth and wrapped it over the spoon. "I need more," he said. "That might not hold it."

"Check Tut's bag," Johnny said. Judge Walker found the roll in the knapsack and handed it to Jungle Boy. Tut stared at Siemans, who started shouting.

"This guy is crazy. He made me say those things on the tapes under threat. It's not true. Not a word of it."

Jungle Boy glared at Siemans. A policeman came forward and took the grenade from Johnny. His partner stepped forward and handcuffed him.

"Careful," said Johnny, "that grenade is live. If the lever is released, you have four seconds until it detonates."

Beverley Morrow came forward and reached for Tut's hands. She took the coil of twine from him and handed it to Jungle Boy, who found the safety on the gun taped to Siemans' chest and began disentangling him. Siemans started to protest his innocence again. Jungle Boy ripped the pistol from his chest, cleared it, and told him to be quiet.

Beverley Morrow held Tut's hands and looked into his eyes. She stood between him and another policeman ready with another set of handcuffs. Noticing, Judge Walker took control of his courtroom. He motioned for the officer to hold off for a moment while Beverley spoke to Tut.

"Russell," she said, "your friends will help you. I will help you. We will not forget to bring you home." She hugged him and Tut sobbed, for the first time beginning to let go of some of the pain and hurt and guilt he had held inside for so long.

"Russell Tuttley will have to be remanded, son," the judge said to Johnny. "I will make sure he gets psychiatric help. For now, I will place you and Russell in the same cell until other arrangements can be made. There's no case left against you. It might take a few days, but your release will be imminent.

"The court would like to thank you for your help today. That goes for you as well, young man," he said to Jungle Boy. "Court dismissed."

EPILOGUE

The crowd in the Catalyst Café on main street buzzed with anticipation. Cliff Morris and Big Rock were back in town after a nationwide tour and booked for a local show. The group enjoyed playing the hometown venue between touring the large cities. They had made the big time, but Cliff liked the intimacy of the smaller clubs where he recognized some of the faces and interacted with the crowd.

Big Rock still opened with "Suzy Q.," and the audience loved it when their own Suzi took the stage with the band's raunchy cover of the rock and roll classic. Her stage presence undiminished, she strutted in her tight leather pants and lowcut blouse. She and Cliff were no longer a couple. The strain of all the adulation heaped on them as big-time rock stars had been too much to keep their relationship intact. They had also lost some of their innocence in the last two years.

Cliff stood at the microphone after the first song. "Ladies and gentlemen, we have a special guest appearing with us this evening. This man can play the blues. Many consider his grandfather the greatest and most influential bluesman of all time. Would you please welcome, all the way from Macon, Georgia, Mr. Rafe Johnson, grandson of the great Robert Johnson."

The band rocked into an electric version of "Dust My Broom," while Rafe hopped onto the stage, picked his guitar off its stand, and joined in. The playing, loud, electric and superb, echoed beyond the walls of the club and drifted down main street.

Cliff Morris had bankrolled the entire cost of defending Johnny Ornowoski. Arriving back in Santa Cruz after the trial, all he asked in return was an introduction to Rafe Johnson. Without the money for a credible defense, the fingerprints on the murder weapon would probably have been enough to send Johnny to prison for the rest of his life.

Simple to arrange, the meeting had taken place before Rafe left to return to Georgia. He'd wanted to stick around anyway and visit with the Doc and Jungle Boy. After the Nam, it was time to take care of business, and his was all about playing the blues. Knowing a famous rock star could only be good for his career.

Johnny and CC did not attend the show at the Catalyst Café. Crowds made Johnny claustrophobic now, and he and Cecelia were spending most of their time readjusting after yet another ordeal that had intruded on their lives.

Freddy had escorted Johnny from jail two days after the trial. Judge Walker sent his regards and reassurances that he would continue making sure Tut received the care he needed.

Johnny's former platoon member had come out of his dissociative state exhausted and confused, and the two had talked for hours. Johnny owed his life to Tut as well, in the Nam and in its aftermath. They had all relied on each other to survive.

Tut had been placed in a psychiatric facility near San Jose, close enough for Johnny to visit. There was research into a post-Vietnam syndrome that afflicted some of the combat vets. Skepticism prevailed in the psychiatric community. A nurse in the facility, whose brother had returned from Vietnam "different," as she expressed it, was sympathetic and promised to keep Johnny informed of any new treatments pertinent to Tut's recovery. She told Johnny about the flashbacks vets were experiencing related to combat traumas and triggered by stressful situations.

Tut felt responsible for the death of his best friend, RC, and the tragic fate of Billy Warrington. Johnny could relate to that. Unable to bring everyone home, surviving the war left a residue of guilt.

Beverley Morrow stayed with Gregor Ornowoski and Benita Diez while she was in Santa Cruz, and they suggested she move to the west coast permanently. Undecided, Beverley would return to Boston, at least temporarily. Jungle Boy would accompany her when she was ready. He would finish his rehab at the VA hospital and would be discharged from the army upon completion of his treatment. Single-footed soldiers had no place in the infantry. Jungle Boy figured it was for the best. The military no longer appealed as it had when he used to stand on the sidewalk outside the recruiting office in Oakland to view the posters of fit and attractive young men and women in uniform.

Jungle Boy had still not heard from his mother. After his rehab, he would return to Santa Cruz to be near the Doc and CC, who joked she would find him a pretty girlfriend. He didn't figure one-footed men would be much of a draw for pretty girls, but he appreciated CC's efforts.

Freddy Dempster had a nagging worry after the trial. Magruder had made serious accusations under oath during his testimony. It took Freddy several phone calls, but he got through to a second lieutenant in the Judge Advocate General's Corps willing to speak about the allegations. Magruder's claims about the fragging incident were stalled and going nowhere. The army could find no one in third platoon to verify his version of events. The sergeant would be discharged soon and on a disability pension. Like Johnny had predicted, Magruder had been his own worst enemy. Not even the army showed any interest, his vitriol destroying the sergeant's credibility.

Freddy felt a twinge of sympathy for Magruder. The Vietnam War was an ongoing tragedy that touched millions of lives across the nation. Freddy had understood little about Vietnam before representing Johnny Ornowoski. He was glad for the young man he'd twice defended. Sometimes, it felt good to be a lawyer.

CC visited Freddy after the trial, to thank him for helping to prove Johnny's innocence and to deliver an invitation. "We're getting married," she exclaimed. "He'll never be out of my sight again," she laughed.

"Congratulations," Freddy said. "I can't tell you how happy I am that you can finally get on with your lives. How is Johnny? I never realized what these young men were going through in Vietnam, or that their experiences would impact their lives so deeply."

"Johnny talks about the war sometimes," she said. "None of them had an inkling of what life would be in the aftermath. Strangely, Tut may have.

"Johnny remembers a conversation he had with him just before Russell rotated home. It was like Tut had a premonition about how things would be after Vietnam. Johnny said they all lived for that one day, thinking everything would be normal, if they could just make it out of Vietnam. Tut seemed to know it wouldn't be that easy. He just had a few days left on his tour when Billy Warrington was killed. Johnny thinks Tut knew he would bring the war home with him. They all blamed Magruder for Billy's death. Tut blamed himself more."

Freddy nodded as she spoke. "I had no idea," he said, "what a hold Vietnam would have on our young men sent over there. I hope to see you guys once in a while. Don't wait until you need my services again," he joked. "And thanks for this." He held up the envelope with the invitation.

Jungle Boy felt good about life now that the Doc was free. Concerned about what would happen to Tut, he and Beverley went to visit. Depressed about being in an institution, there were other veterans with similar stories that helped Tut realize he was not alone in his post-Vietnam life.

Freddy Dempster felt compelled to represent Tut. While the criminal charges were serious, he didn't think the former squad leader would face jail if his treatment went well. Nobody had been hurt except for the minor wounds to Randy Siemans, the man behind the murder of Stewart Brenz and who had been willing to send an innocent man to prison to cover his tracks.

During Jungle Boy's visits with Tut, they sat on a balcony and drank coffee. The institution had cut back on Tut's supply of cigarettes, and it formed the basis of a new habit, coffee consumption. Beverley Morrow visited, and Tut realized if she could forgive him for Billy's death, then maybe someday he could forgive himself.

Beverley did something remarkable when she headed east to Boston. In the same way that getting to know Jungle Boy had helped her cope with the death of Billy, she felt it might help the Cunninghams if they knew about Tut. Beverley found the family in Galena, Illinois. RC had written to his family about King Tut. Turns out, the Cunninghams had been searching for a man named "King" in their son's platoon, which the army had no record of. Tut, certain the family would hate him for being alive and not bringing Richard home with him, began corresponding with the Cunninghams. It helped alleviate a guilt so embedded in his psyche that it had pushed him into bouts of depression and altered states of reality. Slowly, hope for the future replaced some of the guilt that had consumed his life since the war.

That was the way of the Nam, a string of heartache that reached to the other side of the world. All of those dead American boys, and Vietnamese. Not just their soldiers, but civilians caught in the crossfire. Women and children who died ugly and premature deaths, unable to influence outcomes beyond their control, the disabilities, physical and emotional. Much of it could never be repaired.

Johnny and CC had waited over two years to return to some normalcy. They had stuck by each other. That would be the starting point for putting their lives back together.

Jungle Boy returned, and Johnny was glad for that. The kid that had so annoyed him when they'd first met at the army airfield in Can Tho had become the brother he never had. The kid had walked point one too many times, but he was alive.

When Cliff Morris returned from Big Rock's nationwide tour, Johnny's latest ordeal had concluded. With the entourage of a big-time rock star in tow, Cliff confided to Johnny that it was a passion for the music that kept him enthused. After meeting Rafe Johnson, Cliff had invited him to make a guest appearance with the band. A lot more would follow for Rafe's career.

He had completed his epic song, "Mekong Delta Blues." It had dozens of verses, musically and lyrically reflecting the platoon's experiences in Vietnam. The unpopularity of the war prevented the song's release as a commercial venture. Besides, it spoke to the men of third platoon in a private way no one else would fully comprehend. As individuals, the war had impacted them in different ways, but none of them were ever going to lose those Mekong Delta blues.

Glossary

Agent Orange: Slang for the most common of the chemical defoliants used in Vietnam. A 50/50 mixture of the common farm chemical 2-4-D and 2-4-5-T; the latter contained dioxins, one of the most toxic substances created by man. The term originated from an identifying orange stripe around the fifty-five gallon drums it was shipped in.

AK-47: The most common assault rifle used by the Viet Cong and NVA.

Ao baba: A common loose-fitting blouse worn by the Vietnamese, especially prevalent in the Mekong Delta.

Arty: Slang for artillery commonly used by grunts in the field.

ARVN: An acronym for Army Republic of Vietnam, the South Vietnamese Army. Pronounced "Arvin," they were allies of the Americans in fighting the Viet Cong and North Vietnamese Army.

AWOL: Absent without leave.

Base Camp: A permanent base where a division's headquarters are located.

Battalion: Generally, there are four to six companies in a battalion with 300 to 800 troops and commanded by a lieutenant colonel.

Battalion Aid Station: Generally, set up for treating minor ailments in a base camp.

Boonies: The most common slang used by American troops in Vietnam for areas patrolled beyond the relative safety of a base camp.

Brass: Slang for officer corps, usually used in the context of concerns about higher command coming to inspect or require something of troops of a lower rank. "Brass isn't going to be happy with this." Or, "Brass will be all over us for this."

Bronze Star: A US Army award for gallantry on the battlefield, below a Silver Star, the Distinguished Service Cross and the Medal of Honor.

Bug juice: Mosquito repellant.

Buying the farm: Slang for killed in action. The origins of the expression are linked to a $10,000 life insurance policy paid to the family of a deceased soldier. It is often shortened to, "He bought it."

C-4 Explosive: A putty-like substance that is highly explosive when ignited.

C-130: A medium-sized and versatile cargo plane commonly used in Vietnam.

C-Rations: Meals in a can. The most common form of rations for American infantry units in Vietnam.

C-Rats: Slang for C-rations.

Charlie: Slang for the Viet Cong. The term originated from the Military Phonetic System where a "V" was "Victor" and a "C" was "Charles." Hence, Victor Charles for Viet Cong and shortened to "Charlie" by American troops.

Chicom Grenade: A Chinese Communist manufactured grenade commonly used by the Viet Cong and North Vietnamese Army.

Chieu Hoi: Literally translated as "open arms." The *Chieu Hoi* program was designed to entice defectors from the Viet Cong to come over to the South Vietnamese side during the war. Leaflets were often dropped from the air offering rewards for defecting.

Chinook Helicopter: A large cargo helicopter with a tandem set of rotors and a 24,000 pound load capacity.

CIB: Combat Infantryman's Badge.

CIDG: Stands for "Civilian Irregular Defense Group." Basically, CIA developed and financed military units of ethnic minorities, such as the Montagnard units portrayed in *Mekong Delta Blues* and *Poisoned Jungle.*

Claymore Mine: A lightweight mine used by infantry troops to establish a nighttime perimeter in the field. Seven hundred steel balls were embedded in a layer of C-4 explosive. Usually command detonated, it was deadly at close range.

CMB: Combat Medic's Badge.

CO: An abbreviation for commanding officer. It was also used to designate a conscientious objector.

Cobra Gunship: A helicopter designed for combat with a lethal arsenal which included rockets and Gatling guns.

Company: Normally comprised of three to six platoons and commanded by a captain.

Cracker: Slang for "poor white trash," implying the person was racist when used by Black soldiers.

Cutdown: A medical procedure devised to expose a vein in order to get an intravenous started on a casualty whose veins are collapsing from shock.

CWC: A civilian war casualty.

Dear John Letter: A letter from a wife or girlfriend breaking up with a soldier.

DEROS: Date of estimated return from overseas.

Deuce and a half: A two-and-a-half ton military truck common in Vietnam.

DMZ: In Vietnam, a ten kilometer wide demilitarized strip of land separating North and South Vietnam where no military activity was supposed to take place.

Doc: Most medics were called "Doc." The term was so common that medics often used it when addressing each other.

Dog Tags: Metal tags worn around the neck on a chain or tucked into a boot with a soldier's identification and blood type.

Dress Greens: The formal uniform of the US Army.

Dust-off: A term for a helicopter outfitted for medical evacuations of wounded soldiers.

Eleven Bravo (11B): MOS of an infantry soldier.

ER: Emergency room.

ETA: Estimated time of arrival.

F-4: A highly mobile fighter jet also used to drop napalm in Vietnam.

FNG: Fucking new guy.

Foxhole: A two or three-man hole dug in the ground for protection while spending the night in the field, referred to as "digging in for the night."

Fragging: Intentionally wounding or killing one of your own men to get them removed from a unit because they have become a danger to the other men due to incompetence or being overly gung ho.

Gook: A racial slur for Vietnamese common amongst US troops.

Greased: One of the uglier terms for getting killed by enemy fire.

Grunt: Slang most used by infantrymen to refer to themselves as foot soldiers.

Hooch: Slang for living quarters in a base camp.

Huey: A common helicopter used by Americans in Vietnam.

Hump: A term used for being on an infantry patrol. "Humping" through the "boonies" looking for "Charlie" is what the infantry was all about.

IV Corps: Pronounced "four corps," and referring to the southern-most quadrant of military sectors in South Vietnam, which included the Mekong Delta.

Jitterbugging Operation: A Ninth Infantry Division tactic of surrounding an area suspected of harboring Viet Cong and tightening the circle of troops to flush out the enemy.

Jungle Rot: Common body and foot rashes and infections exacerbated by the tropical climate, wet conditions, and unsanitary conditions in the field. The rashes might be fungal or bacterial in nature, or caused by never being able to get one's feet dry. The latter was known as trench foot in previous wars.

KIA: Killed in action.

Kit Carson Scout: Vietnamese nationals attached to American units to act as interpreters of language and customs. They were called "Tiger Scouts" in the Ninth Infantry Division.

Klick: A kilometer.

LBJ: The initials of Lyndon Baines Johnson, President of the United States during the major escalation of American troops in Vietnam. His initials were also used to refer to Long Binh Jail, a notorious prison in Vietnam known for its racial tensions and harsh conditions. It held American Military prisoners facing serious charges.

LP: A listening post. A two or three-man team placed beyond the perimeter at night to monitor for enemy activity.

LT: A lieutenant. Each letter is pronounced and was used to address or refer to a soldier's platoon commander. It denoted respect but also familiarity.

LZ: A landing zone for helicopters.

M-3 Aid Bag: A canvas bag designed for packing a combat medic's field medical supplies. It weighed thirty pounds when fully stocked and contained field dressings, two intravenous bottles and tubing, morphine, and an assortment of first aid supplies, including suture kits and minor surgical supplies.

M-60 Machine Gun: A common and important machine gun used by American infantry troops. The weapon was also mounted and used by door gunners on helicopters and strategically placed to defend the perimeter of a base camp.

MAT Team: A Mobile Advisory Team consisting of a captain, lieutenant, and three NCOs. The five-man teams lived in a Vietnamese village and organized a local militia group of villagers called Popular Forces.

MEDCAP: An acronym for "Medical Civilian Action Program." Medical personnel were dispatched to rural villages for a day to provide medical treatments as a way of fostering goodwill between the Vietnamese civilian population and the Americans.

Medevac: A term for a helicopter extracting casualties from the field.

Million-dollar Wound: A wound severe enough to require medical evacuation out of Vietnam, but not serious enough to cause permanent disability.

Montagnard: An indigenous people of Vietnam mostly living in the Central Highlands of the country.

MOS: Military Occupational Specialty. Each specialty was also designated with a number code. Infantrymen were 11Bs, and medics were 91B20s.

MPC: Military Payment Certificate. American soldiers in Vietnam were paid in MPC to avoid flooding the local Vietnamese economy with American dollars. An MPC dollar was not as valuable on the black market as a regular American greenback, but could be utilized for equal value on American bases.

Napalm: Jellied gasoline dropped from the air in drums that exploded and caught fire when hitting the ground. Flamethrowers use the same basic ingredient.

Night Ambush: A squad-to-platoon-size ambush set in place overnight that attempts to intercept enemy troop movement.

Ninety-day Ribbon: The first and most basic ribbon awarded to a soldier upon completion of his basic and MOS training.

NVA: North Vietnamese Army.

OR: Operating room in a hospital.

PBR: Patrol Boat, River. A US Navy boat, small and lightweight, yet heavily armed, manned by a four-man crew. A double-barreled machine gun was set in a turret in the bow, and an M-60 was mounted in the stern. The craft displaced little water, ideal for patrolling the rivers and canals in the Mekong Delta.

Platoon: Commanded by a lieutenant and usually comprised of twenty to thirty men in Vietnam.

Point Man: Often referred to as "walking point." Somebody had to go first on a patrol. A good point man was important to an infantry platoon to spot any signs of the enemy, including booby traps.

Popular Forces: A village-based indigenous platoon organized by the South Vietnamese Government and US military personnel.

PRC-25 Radio: Pronounced "prick twenty-five," each infantry platoon carried one for communicating in the field; essential for calling for air support, medevacs and artillery.

Psy Ops: An abbreviation for "psychological warfare."

Punji Stake: A sharpened stake, often made from bamboo, placed in a camouflaged pit or attached to a booby trap. Several stakes are normally used in each pit or device.

Purple Heart: Awarded for being wounded or killed by enemy fire.

PX: Post Exchange, an on-base store for soldiers. Prices were often reduced.

REMF: Rear echelon motherfucker. The term was used by grunts in the field to derogatorily refer to troops in the rear. It is pronounced the way it is spelled.

ROTC: Reserve Officer Training Corps. Established on college and university campuses, many assumed their commissions as officers after graduating and became active duty.

RPD: A machine gun used by the Viet Cong.

R&R: Rest and Relaxation. A five-day R&R was given to US soldiers during their tours. Sometimes a shorter in-country R&R would be available, particularly after a long stint in the field.

RTO: The term stood for "radio telephone operator." Every infantry platoon had an RTO responsible for carrying and maintaining the PRC-25 field radio.

Slick: A Huey helicopter without any armaments other than one or two door gunners.

Tet Holiday: A major holiday in Vietnam to celebrate the Lunar New Year.

Tet Offensive: In January of 1968, the communist forces launched a major military offensive during the Tet Holidays. Historians consider it more of a political and propaganda victory than a military success because communist forces experienced high casualties. However, a case can be made that it was a turning point in the war as news of the offensive in the American press tended to view it as an American defeat, as did many citizens.

The Wire: Slang for the perimeter of a base.

Tiger Scout: What the Ninth Infantry called its Kit Carson Scouts. They were usually Viet Cong defectors who acted as interpreters of language and culture for American infantry troops.

Tracer: Bullets that leave a visible path through the air after being fired from an automatic weapon, allowing the shooter to "trace" where his shots are going. At night, these rounds are eerily visible in a firefight.

Triage: A quick sorting of casualties to find the most seriously wounded. In a mass casualty situation, casualties who are not likely to survive are bypassed so that those who are likely to live can be saved. When not overwhelmed with casualties, it also involves treating the most seriously wounded first.

Triage Unit: Where the casualties are initially received in the evacuation system after being wounded. In Vietnam, almost all casualties arrived at evac hospitals by helicopter. A landing pad for medevacs was built just outside of triage. I have used the term interchangeably with emergency room.

Wasted: Slang for "killed in action."

WIA: Wounded in action.

Acknowledgements

So much goes into the writing of a book that it is impossible to thank all of the friends and fellow writers that have supported the effort and made suggestions along the way.

When I first attempted writing about the Vietnam War, I had not yet found what writers refer to as their "voice." Mine arrived and coincided with my looming retirement from beekeeping. Even so, *Mekong* was a long way from being publishable.

The original draft of *Mekong Delta Blues*, a rambling effort filled with too much backstory, and full of mistakes common to first novels, took six more drafts to reach this published version, with many more minor corrections in between.

I wish to thank fellow Edmonton authors, Kimberley Howard and Don Levers, for offering unwavering support. Each has sacrificed many hours to not only this work, but my first published novel, *Poisoned Jungle*. It is gratifying forming friendships while pouring over manuscripts and knowing the suggestions are meant constructively—and accepted as such.

Don and I have developed a method to the madness of publishing our books. I came to enjoy "getting into the weeds" on grammar and style, sometimes spending more time discussing a single phrase than either one of us would be comfortable admitting to. It has only deepened the friendship.

My son, Nathan Ballard, has contributed to not only the novels, but much of the technical support behind them. Besides designing my website, he has found important links and put me in touch with other authors and researchers exploring the seemingly endless ramifications of the Vietnam War.

Finally, not much can be achieved without support on the home front. Lilliane has been there for the writing and the publishing of two books, with more on the way. Sometimes, manuscripts occupy tables and desks for weeks at a time. It's all part of the process weathered without complaint. Her support has meant more to me than I can express.

ABOUT THE AUTHOR

James Ballard's intimate knowledge of Vietnam is explored in his *Mekong River Trilogy*. After graduating from high school in 1967, James came of age as the US escalated its involvement in Vietnam.

Trained as an army medic, by December of 1968 he was in the war zone. Coinciding with the Ninth Infantry's *Operation Speedy Express,* he began his tour while the Mekong Delta remained a bloody battleground for control of Vietnam's major rice-growing region.

The author saw much of the Delta during his tour. As a medic, he not only treated his fellow soldiers, but Vietnamese civilians caught in the crossfire. His experiences altered the course of his life. James has spent a lifetime exploring the pervasive consequences war has on its participants and the innocents ensnared, with effects rippling through societies at large.

After attending the University of Alberta in Edmonton, James immigrated to Canada in 1975. Establishing a commercial beekeeping operation in the Peace River Region of the province, James spent the next forty years on his bee farm. Staying in touch with some of the men from his tour, he continued to follow events in Vietnam and among his fellow veterans.

"If I had to describe my work in one phrase it would be an examination of the 'consequences of war,' which extend far beyond the timelines of the immediate conflict and the individual soldiers on the field of battle."

More about the author and his work can be found at james-ballard.net, where James further explores the subject matter of his novels.